CHUTZPAH!

CHINESE LITERATURE TODAY BOOK SERIES

CHUTZPAH!

New Voices from China

Edited by

Ou Ning and Austin Woerner

UNIVERSITY OF OKLAHOMA PRESS : NORMAN

This book is published with the generous assistance of China's National Office for Teaching Chinese as a Foreign Language, Beijing Normal University's College of Chinese Language and Literature, the University of Oklahoma's College of Arts and Sciences, and *World Literature Today* magazine.

"An Education in Cruelty," translated into English by A. E. Clark, originally published in *Hard Road Home,* copyright 2014 Ragged Banner Press. Used with permission.

Library of Congress Cataloging-in-Publication Data

Chutzpah! : New voices from China / edited by Ou Ning and Austin Woerner.
    pages cm. — (Chinese literature today book series ; volume 4)
    ISBN 978-0-8061-4870-0 (pbk. : alk. paper)
1. Short stories, Chinese—20th century—Translations into English.
2. Short stories, Chinese—21st century—Translations into English.
3. Short stories, Chinese—20th century. 4. Short stories, Chinese—21st century. I. Ning, Ou, editor. II. Woerner, Austin, editor. III. Title: New voices from China.
  PL2653.N49 2015
  895.13'508—dc23

                                2015009883

Chutzpah! New Voices from China is Volume 4 in the Chinese Literature Today Book Series.

Contents

PREFACE

The Story of Chutzpah!

By Ou Ning

TRANSLATED, WITH ADDITIONS, BY AUSTIN WOERNER

When the news that *Chutzpah!* would soon cease publication reached readers in February 2014, the public immediately raised a cry of "There is no market for literature!" and "It's so hard for literature to survive!" If the journal had been shut down for political reasons, I expect the loss would have felt even more tragic. But making the market out to be literature's enemy, or looking to the government to prop up the arts, is the kiss of death as far as literature is concerned, I believe. Only when literature is riding the waves of the market will its true vitality be revealed; our habit of assuming that "there is no market for literature" is a product of deep-seated anti-commercialist prejudices. If there really is no market for literature, then why do we occasionally find the names of authors on top-earners lists? We created *Chutzpah!* with the conviction that there *is* a market for literature, and if we failed to find it, it is because we did not succeed in linking content, distribution, marketing, and ad sales into an effective chain. Our goal was never to reach a mass market, but instead to secure a dedicated niche readership, because we believed that a diverse array of niche markets is the ecosystem in which literature is most likely to thrive. Needless to say, it would be depressing if the only novels available in bookstores were bestsellers. The whole point of niche-market publishing is to provide readers with a variety of choices.

In July 2010, after the first issue of Han Han's literary magazine *Party* sold five hundred thousand copies within twenty-four hours of its release, the Guangzhou publisher Modern Media Group adopted my suggestion to put out a literary bimonthly. Not long afterward, I announced *Chutzpah!*'s launch on Weibo. The magazine's Chinese name—*Tian Nan*, a phrase denoting China's southern region—originally belonged to a journal of folk literature founded in 1982 by the Guangdong Vernacular Artists' Association. In 2005 Modern Media purchased *Tian Nan* with plans to convert it into a book-review magazine. But the magazine never materialized, and the brand name languished unused for five years. After working in music, film, design, and art for much of my career, I wanted to get involved with literature again, which had been the great passion of my youth. During the 2009 Shenzhen and Hong Kong Bi-city Biennale of Urbanism and Architecture, I had dipped my toes into publishing when I edited a book called *Odyssey: Architecture and Literature*, intended to spark dialogue between architects and authors. In the course of that project I had been in touch with a number of writers, and this gave me the idea to start a literary magazine. At the time I had been working for Modern Media Group for close to ten years, and they had immediate confidence in my ability to execute this vision.

Chutzpah!'s inaugural issue was half a year in the planning. First I did some research into the literary periodicals that were already available on the market. In China, *People's Literature* and *Harvest* are the old guard, with long histories and the support of the Chinese Writers' Association. We had no hope of stealing away the authors who contribute to those reviews, but both magazines publish only writing by Chinese authors, and design-wise I found them too old-fashioned. The publications favored by the Post-Eighties Generation have a broad appeal, but I was not so fond of the writing. Taiwan's *INK* magazine has a rich network of contributors, but their attempt to make the magazine seem hip and casual resulted in a somewhat haphazard layout. Hong Kong's *Fleurs de Lettres* employs a democratic editorial system, which means that the style can be rather uneven. Naturally, everyone would like to imitate the *New Yorker*, but marshaling vast resources to support writers through the course of a painstaking long-term editing process would be impossible in a Chinese context. I liked the size and heft of the *Paris Review* and *Granta*, but visually those publications bore the stamp of the narrow and conservative lit-magazine aesthetic. Two new journals out of Brooklyn, *n+1* and *A Public Space*, were serious in topic and refreshing in style, but like other publications of their type, they have extremely small readerships.

I was most taken with Dave Eggers's San Francisco–based quarterly *McSweeney's*. (Later, when Eggers came to Beijing, our editor Yu Bingxia conducted an interview with him for *Chutzpah!*'s website.) Describing the genesis of the first magazine he published, *Might*, Eggers writes in *A Heartbreaking Work of Staggering Genius*: "We [were] sure that we [were] onto something epochal." The original concept for *McSweeney's* was to publish writing that had been rejected by other literary magazines, and each issue had a different paper size and design. Ultimately *McSweeney's* attracted many famous contributors. In the editors' note for issue 37, Eggers uses data from the U.S. publishing industry to poke fun at the notion that "reading is dead." With the literary quarterly as the core product, Eggers spun off a series of other magazines and publications, built a website and developed a social media presence, expanded into apps and e-publishing, and established tutoring centers to teach writing to young people in eight cities across the United States. In this manner, he developed a literary product and a marketing strategy that were entirely novel.

The collective sigh of "There is no market for literature" that the Chinese reading public let out upon hearing of the closure of *Chutzpah!* is a tedious cliché. No one in the media seriously discussed the details of our model for literary production and marketing, instead blaming *Chutzpah!*'s demise on "the brutality of the market." But let's look closer at the specific problems that dog the Chinese publishing industry and make it so hard for good literature to survive. The main avenue for aspiring writers is through the Chinese Writers' Association, which sends the young writers it anoints as promising to the Lu Xun Literary Institute and grants them access to the entrenched hierarchy of literary periodicals under its command. Besides this, there is the "New Concept" writing competition, which offers younger writers a more commercialized route to fame and literary success. Literary education is nonexistent at the middle- and elementary-school level, and few universities offer creative writing classes like those found in Britain and America. Editors at literary reviews rely entirely on personal connections to fill the pages of their magazines, and most simply take orders from authors, having no latitude to propose revisions. Publishers care nothing about literary quality, and sales are the only consideration. No institutions exist to promote avant-garde or experimental literature. There are no critics or book reviews that readers can trust, no incentive mechanism in the form of an independent and authoritative literature prize, and no prominent international literary festival that can foster dialogue with the outside world. Book fairs are merely a platform for ordering goods and transacting copyright deals, and author appearances are rote procedures. The list goes on.

The original proposal for *Chutzpah!* included plans for creative writing classes, a literature prize, a literary festival, a bookstore, and a *Chutzpah!* book series. But all these were distant possibilities; everything had to start with the magazine itself. First, the publication needed an English name, since we planned to engage with the literary world outside of China, and I chose *Chutzpah!*, which I thought perfectly captured the magazine's independent, contrarian spirit. Then I brought on the noted design team Xiao Ma and Chengzi to serve as artistic directors, and asked them to design the font for *Chutzpah!*'s nameplate and the magazine's overall look. In October 2010 I opened a Weibo account for *Chutzpah!* In December I teamed up with the writer A Yi and the scholar Sha Mei to form a three-person editorial board, and we began soliciting manuscripts for the magazine's inaugural issue, entitled "Agrarian Asia." Since the issue would focus on the rise of the rural reconstruction movement among

Asian intellectuals, I commissioned a piece from Liang Hong, who had just published her memoir *China in Liang Village*, and we traveled together through Fujian and Henan interviewing practitioners of rural reconstruction. She did the writing; I shot film footage. This was the only time that *Chutzpah!* had the budget to support in-depth reporting on a particular subject. In addition, while I was on a trip to Thailand to attend an art exhibition, I took the opportunity to visit the Land Project in the countryside near Chiang Mai and interviewed the artists behind this back-to-the-land experiment.

Since *Chutzpah!* had no hope of competing for contributors with magazines like *People's Literature* and *Harvest*, we decided to focus on younger authors born after 1970, and at the same time we broadened our scope to include writing from Taiwan, Hong Kong, Malaysia, Singapore, and elsewhere. In consideration of Chinese literature's low degree of international visibility, we decided to publish a supplement featuring English translations of the magazine's Chinese content. *Paper Republic* founder Eric Abrahamsen chose the name—*Peregrine*, after the peregrine falcon, a bird capable of cross-continental flights—and edited the first few issues. After Eric left the magazine to manage *People's Literature*'s English-language daughter publication, *Pathlight*, I brought on the New York–based translator Austin Woerner as the English editor, and he produced *Peregrine* for the rest of the magazine's lifetime.

Rather than divide *Chutzpah!*'s content into sections based on literary genre, as many magazines do, I opted for a "curated" approach, treating the entire magazine as an exhibition space. "Entrance" and "Exit" contained poetry; "Special Space" featured themed content; and "Regular Space" was given over to unsolicited manuscripts that bore no relation to the issue's theme. *Peregrine*— which we affectionately termed "the parasite"—was a fifty-page mini-journal bound into the center of each issue, with pages 1.5 centimeters shorter than the rest of the magazine. In keeping with *Chutzpah!*'s "curated" style, the table of contents became the "guide," and each issue's contributors, including translators and visual artists, were listed alphabetically on the cover, like participants in an exhibition. Contributor bios were handled the same way, in a section immediately preceding "Exit." In addition to emphasizing our respect for all of our contributors, regardless of the nature of their contribution, this had the added function of hiding our own editorial preferences, so that readers would feel free to read pieces in any order they wished, rather than being swayed by eye-catching cover lines. To reinforce the message that *Chutzpah!* was about the reading experience, pure and simple, each issue contained only eight pages of color photos or illustrations. The rest of the magazine consisted of black-and-white text printed on soft loose-fiber paper, so that the pages would feel substantial but also supple to the touch.

In March 2011, after the first issue had been sent to the printer and our website, also the work of Xiao Ma and Chengzi, went live, we announced the issue's release on Weibo, posting the cover image, the table of contents, and the website's URL. The reaction was immediate and overwhelming. Reporters clamored to interview us, and as soon as the magazine hit newsstands, readers snapped up copies with almost desperate eagerness, leading some to speculate that we had purposefully printed too few copies in order to instigate a buying frenzy. Soon afterward, the editorial team went on a seven-city tour, holding a series of fifteen events in Shenzhen, Guangzhou, Shanghai, Beijing, Chengdu, Hong Kong, and Taipei. The demand for *Chutzpah!*'s first issue was so insatiable that Modern Media's distributor struggled to keep up.

All this buzz put a great deal of pressure on me. Moving forward, we chose our themes carefully, based on the expertise of our editors, the network of writers at our disposal, and our own capability for planning and execution. Keeping the magazine's content new and interesting while ensuring the loyalty of our readership was a tall order for an editorial team of three, so we employed guest editors whenever possible. With *Chutzpah!*'s format already fixed, our job was simply to find good content with which to fill it. Tsao Jerlian, from Taiwan, edited issue 2, "Universal Narratives," our sci-fi issue; Yiyun Li, contributing editor at *A Public Space*, helped put together issue 10, "Worlds Apart"; German author Ingo Niermann edited issue 12, "The Future of Love"; and curators Hans Ulrich Obrist and Simon Castets, from the UK and the U.S. respectively, helped plan issue 16, "The Diamond Generation." Bringing guest editors into the mix broadened our perspective on contemporary literature, drawing on content from different genres and languages and giving our readers an up-to-date view of literary developments abroad.

When President Xi Jinping's anti-corruption campaign triggered a sharp drop in sales of luxury products, companies cut back on their advertising budgets, and by late 2013 the financial situation at Modern Media Group was looking grim. Layoffs ensued, and in early 2014 Modern Media shut down the magazine entirely. And so, after almost four years, *Chutzpah!* ceased publication. In hindsight I wish that I had been more involved in the managerial side of things; at the time, I was focused almost exclusively on editorial work, and only toward the end was I able to take on the role of publisher as well. Expanding our web of contributors and supervising editorial decisions was not something I could very well do while also dashing around the country trying to widen our distribution, drum up advertising, and boost sales by holding literary events. By the same token, Modern Media never assigned *Chutzpah!* a dedicated marketing team, instead entrusting its promotion to the company's marketing department and distributor, who handled promotion for all its other publications. In

Modern Media's product line, *Chutzpah!* fell somewhere between a magazine and a book, and the company never hit upon the right marketing strategy to ensure the magazine's continued development. The marketing department felt that *Chutzpah!* should rely on income from sales, while the distributor believed that it should be funded by ads. Unable to turn a profit for the company, the magazine was forced to cut costs and reduce expenditures. In the end, its closure was no great surprise.

Many hold that the future of literature lies in e-publishing, and from day one *Chutzpah!* was an enthusiastic supporter of this view. Though our website occasionally published selections from the magazine, its main focus was international literary happenings and author interviews; it was a supplement to the print publication, not a substitute. Beginning in June 2012, we began putting out an e-book version of *Chutzpah!*, available through Modern Media's iMagazine app. Modern Media's online retailer, Modern Books, became an important channel for selling print copies. But despite the energy that we put into digital marketing and promotion, *Chutzpah!* was still unable to stay afloat.

Of the sixteen issues we published, the most popular among Chinese readers were issue 1, "Agrarian Asia," and issue 4, "Vision of Eros." Other issues that I thought were particularly successful were issue 3, "Mapping Poetry"; issue 6, "The Revolutions"; issue 9, "Speaking in Tongues"; issue 11, "Xinjiang Time"; issue 14, "Roots"; and issue 16, "The Diamond Generation"—themes that receive relatively little attention in contemporary Chinese society. Some of the authors whose work I was most taken with include A Yi, Arundhati Roy, Liu Zheng, Hu Shuwen, Zhang Chu, Yiyun Li, Li-Young Lee, Li Zishu, Yuk Hui, Sheng Keyi, He Wapi, Chang Hui-Ching, Bao Huiyi, Zhou Kai, Tash Aw, Nam Le, Douglas Coupland, Zhu Yue, Kang He, Alat Asem, Liu Liangcheng, Dong Libo, Dung Kai-Cheung, Na Zhangyuan, Ye Fu, David Meza, Luna Miguel, Zheng Zaihuan, and Ho Rui An. Many of the pieces that these writers published in *Chutzpah!* could not have appeared in other magazines.

With a few exceptions, the pieces included in this anthology all appeared originally in the Chinese section of the magazine, and were translated into English for publication in *Peregrine* either in the same or in subsequent issues. Two pieces—Shen Wei's "A Dictionary of Xinjiang" and Li Juan's "Nine Short Pieces"—are earlier, representative works by *Chutzpah!* contributors that had never before appeared in English. Except for "An Education in Cruelty," all translations were commissioned specifically for publication in *Chutzpah!* In many cases, these authors' publication in *Chutzpah!* was also their English-language debut.

What made *Chutzpah!* special, both to Chinese readers and to Sinophiles abroad, was its focus on younger and lesser-known Chinese writers, its stylistic eclecticism, its broad definition of what constitutes "Chinese writing," and its independent voice—registered in the more liberal Guangdong Province, and beholden to a media conglomerate rather than to a government sponsor, it was able to publish more adventurous work than other publications of its kind in China. (Nevertheless, this is not "dissident" writing; it represents what is possible *within* the limits of Chinese public discourse.) When choosing pieces to include, we considered above all which ones stood up best in translation—the stories that came alive in English are not necessarily the "greatest hits" of the Chinese magazine—while also trying to represent a cross-section of the kind of work that appeared in *Chutzpah!* So within these pages you will find scathing social critique, sensitively drawn domestic realism, and wild Calvinoesque experimentation; Chinese writing from Taiwan, Malaysia, and farther afield, as well from China's far western province of Xinjiang, and by ethnic minority writers; and subjects ranging from village life to the modern city to the immigrant experience, much of it written by authors under the age of forty, and one as young as twenty. You will meet a mermaid-like water spirit who tries to save a small town from disaster, a lesbian housekeeper struggling with her girlfriend's compulsive hoarding, and a teenager plotting revenge against the bureaucrat responsible for the demolition of his home. You will see four decades of recent Chinese history flash before the eyes of a hard-drinking businessman trapped beneath a fallen building after the 2008 Sichuan earthquake, watch family drama unfold during a tomb-weeping ceremony in the suburbs of Nanjing, and ride with jeep-driving samurai warriors through a comic metafictional universe while battling opponents and beefing up on your combat skills by reading Borges and Nabokov. If there is one message we wanted to impart to Western readers, many of whom may open such an anthology hoping for insight into the Riddle of Modern China, it is that contemporary Chinese writing, like China itself, is not a monolith; it is a complex, vibrant polyphony, every bit as diverse as modern Western literature, and every bit as imaginative.

While *Chutzpah!* published a great deal of poetry and nonfiction, *Peregrine*'s focus was always on short fiction, and this anthology reflects that leaning. Nevertheless, the Xinjiang-themed special issue of *Peregrine* included several luminous pieces of lyrical nonfiction that we would be remiss in not including. In addition, Ye Fu's searing essay "An Education in Cruelty," which *Chutzpah!* published in Chinese for the first time in the PRC, deserves a home in this anthology, we feel, not just because it is excellent, but because no other Mainland publication could have printed it.

Special thanks to the University of Oklahoma Press for finding a home for this unusual volume; and especially to the dozen translators whose work appears here—as well as to all the other translators who contributed to the magazine, making *Chutzpah!* groundbreaking not just as a literary journal but as a vehicle for literary cross-pollination, allowing emerging writers and Chinese-English translators to encounter each other's work and forge connections. Without the hard work of our talented translators, this bold experiment in bilingual publishing would have been nothing but a twinkle in our eye, and you would not be holding this book in your hands.

CHUTZPAH!

A Brief History of Time

By Xu Zechen

TRANSLATED BY ERIC ABRAHAMSEN

My friend Qingzhou went to Sichuan on a business trip, and on May 12, 2008, he was buried under a small four-story building. Before he realized he was in an earthquake, he assumed the building was swaying because he'd drunk too much. He'd downed nearly a liter at noon, but it was worth it—he'd closed the deal. He felt himself collapsing drunkenly, his body listing to one side, all his movements in slow motion. It wasn't the way the news described it later, the whole world transformed—*bang!*—in an instant. His last thoughts before he blacked out were: This is some booze. When it puts you down, the whole world comes rattling down with you. I've never had anything like it. Over a decade working in sales, he must have drunk a thousand kinds of alcohol: baijiu, red wine, yellow wine, black rice wine, green fruit liquors, domestic-made, imported, name-brand, handcrafted, and bathtub-brewed. He'd been drunk so often he had early-stage liver disease and a duodenal ulcer; he had experienced light stomach bleeding nearly a dozen times, heavy bleeding four times—they'd had to remove a third of his stomach. Yet none of that could compare to what he'd drunk today. It was an odd brand; he didn't know where the client had gotten it. It was good stuff, mellow in the mouth but with plenty of kick, and what a sense of accomplishment it produced: when you went down, the world went down with you.

He didn't know how much time had passed, but when he awoke he found he had no arms or legs. He couldn't lift anything, couldn't stretch anything, and then he began to feel pain. He opened his eyes and realized with a shock that something rough was pressed up close to his face. If his eyelashes had been any longer, they would have brushed against it. It was covering him from his head to down below his stomach. He couldn't see it, only feel it—when he inhaled, his belly, whose size testified to his prosperity over the past few years, pressed against something flat and solid. Qingzhou was in pain. He smelled dust and concrete, and the world was still rattling, the sounds muted as though they were passing through mountains of stone. Did I drink up an earthquake? he wondered.

   According to video materials from the rescue operation, and to Qingzhou's own memories, he had been trapped under a section of flooring. He owed a lot to that rough chunk of flooring: the whole building had collapsed like kindling, and they only saved five from the wreckage. When the flooring fell, it landed propped up on bricks to either side of him, leaving him a little breathing space, and saving his life.

—Were you afraid?

—I was.

—Of what?

Qingzhou emerged from the hospital three months later, enclosed in plaster and splints. Eventually he regained his old toughness and started answering his friends' questions. His face was blank and his eyes were distant as he described his brush with death. Only someone who'd died and come back again could reach that place.

—What was I frightened of? Sure, I'll tell you everything. There's no reason to stay silent. At first I was frightened of the earthquake itself. No one told me there'd be an earthquake. I was only five when the big Tangshan earthquake happened; all a five-year-old cares about is his dinner. I knew an earthquake was a terrible thing, but I didn't really know what one was like. Now I was in one, and I had no chance to react, I wasn't even sober. Of course I was afraid. After that it was fear of pain, and death. The pain alone was enough to kill you. Look at my hands and feet. There's nothing to see, of course. They were so pulverized that you could have rolled what was left into dumplings. I was afraid of death—scared to death of death. Since then I've thought, if I'm going to die, let me die in an instant, with a whump. Don't tell me first, don't make me wait around. Under that piece of flooring, I felt at first like I was just waiting for death, and I was afraid. Later, though, I stopped being afraid. The world went quiet, like everything would be taken care of. It was all up to fate whether I'd live or die. If it had been you, you'd have accepted it, too. I was afraid of other things: solitude, loneliness, and time—endless time. Before then, I'd never realized how long a minute, or an hour, or a day could be. As long as a lifetime. I was in a hole, in the dark, and though I could strain my eyes until they popped, all I'd see was that dim, rough flooring, nothing but concrete. I was far away from everyone, a world apart from them all, so distant I seemed to be the only person in the whole universe. You remember what that Russian cosmonaut said when he landed on the moon? He called it "bone-deep loneliness." That's a good phrase. All your bones frozen in complete loneliness.

I thought: just let me die. I hoped the flooring wouldn't hold up, that it would come down neat and clean and put an end to time and darkness. To me, death would have been a deliverance from that world of darkness.

—You didn't die.

—I didn't die. Well, I basically died.

—Can you tell us about it?

—Of course. Like I said, as long as you survive, pain, death, loneliness, and time are no longer frightening—of course you can talk about it. I'm saying later on I got hungry and thirsty, mostly thirsty; later the hunger sort of went away. After all that alcohol I'd drunk, water was taking its revenge on me. There was no water to drink, and I had no way of drinking my piss, and after a day . . . maybe less than a day; my only sense of time was of its length, unending and unchanging, nothing else. Day and night no longer existed for me. I'd lost a lot of blood through my hands and feet, and I was utterly exhausted. I slept and woke, woke and slept, my body as stiff as if it were rusted in place. In my dreams I felt like I would catch fire, like my whole body was smoking: the corners of my eyes, my lips, throat, guts, and hair, even my soul. Do you believe in the soul?

—No.

—I do. I saw it with my own eyes, shriveling from thirst, smoking from thirst. The soul itself is like smoke, and half-awake I saw it streaming out from my smoldering hair, coalescing into a second self within the narrow space under the flooring. I watched that self slowly seep out from under the concrete, and re-form again outside the wreckage. I saw him leave the ruins and the earthquake behind, and head for the train station.

—What was he doing?

—Retracing my steps. He was going back by the road I'd come on.

To be honest, I had no idea what he was talking about.

—When your soul leaves your body, that means death. When I thought I was going to die, I immediately relaxed, as if I'd been released, and I lay as languidly as if I were floating on summer waves. Haven't you heard that when a person dies, their soul retraces the entire course of their life? I hadn't heard it before, either. I'll tell you about it.

That day, the soul of my friend Qingzhou passed through the ruins. It knew the way through the ruins. The soul of thirty-seven-year-old Huang Qingzhou arrived at the train station, intending to take the train back to Beijing. When Qingzhou went on these business trips, he always set out from Beijing, flying like a bullet to destinations around the country. The way his job worked, if he wasn't asleep in bed, then he was on a train or a plane, or else he was at the negotiating table or the dinner table—more often the latter, as we Chinese prefer to do our negotiating over drinks. As Huang Qingzhou's soul rode the train, the buildings, the trees, the fields, the wilderness, and the distant horizon all rushed continually backward. The trip was so long that Huang Qingzhou was thirty-five by the time he arrived in Beijing. Little worth mentioning had taken place during those two years, apart from work and travel. But his thirty-fifth year deserved a visit because that was the year he'd gone bankrupt. In 2006, as the wallets of many individual shareholders were swelling, Huang Qingzhou lost his shirt. He himself wasn't sure how it had happened, but several years of savings went up in smoke, just like his soul, and when the wind began to blow, that smoke vanished in wisps, never to coalesce again.

Huang Qingzhou's soul took the subway back to his house in 2006. His wife had had it all figured out and abandoned him the instant disaster loomed. The divorce papers lay on the pale-green glass tea table in the living room. Huang Qingzhou signed them. His wife was eight years his junior, and luckily they hadn't had children yet. He sat on the sofa they'd bought recently—this was before they'd divided the property, and he hadn't known whether it would go to her or him. They'd been happy on the way to buy furniture at Lanjinglijia, an honest-to-goodness pair of newlyweds. Huang Qingzhou's soul smoked a cigarette on the sofa, then left. Unless he was mistaken, he'd bought that pack of cigarettes at the 7-Eleven outside the gate to their compound. He walked out to the road and found it nearly deserted. The few people he met were wearing face masks, hurrying along and avoiding each other as though they were afraid of being robbed. The bus was entirely empty except for the driver and conductor. He slapped his forehead—this was 2003, the year of SARS. He looked down at his belly. In 2003 they'd stayed in their apartment for three months without going out, and besides eating, he'd done nothing but watch movies and play games, as a result of which he'd gained several pounds. He'd found every movie with Chow Yun-fat, Jackie Chan, Jet Li, or Steven Chow in it and watched them all; he'd also mastered Three Kingdoms and Empire in the shortest time possible. Huang Qingzhou began to run toward his office, ran fast enough to outrun SARS. In the lobby of the office building, as he was entering the elevator, he collided with the vice president of his company, spattering his coffee on the man's coffee-colored suit. The vice president's beetle brows drew together.

—Robbing a bank, are we?

—I'm sorry, I'm late for an interview at Baolonghua, I'm very sorry.

He'd seen Baolonghua's job advertisement in the paper. To a twenty-seven-year-old man who had only just thought to seek his fortune in Beijing, the positions and salaries advertised looked pretty good. He'd worked at a different company previously, pulling in clients. Never mind the exhaustion, it paid almost nothing, and what had he come to Beijing for if not to make money? In the interview, he sat across the table from the vice president, whose coffee-colored suit gave off a strong coffee odor. Despite his limited experience, he guessed from the smell that the coffee came from Starbucks. The vice president hired him. Before handing him the contract that detailed his healthy compensation, the vice president asked him a question on behalf of the president:

—In your two years in Beijing, what experiences have you had that are worth relating?

Huang Qingzhou thought for a bit, then answered:

—I had a job I didn't like, and it was running me ragged. People were always scowling at me, and I felt like a sucker for being so enthusiastic. I took part in the anti-U.S. protests after the bombing of the embassy in Belgrade, but before I'd gone two blocks, I met someone from my hometown who'd just arrived in Beijing. He was nearly faint from hunger, and I thought saving him was the more pressing task, so I treated him to donkey-meat sandwiches. You can't let a comrade starve to death, right? Also, one time I went back to my hometown—it was flooding there, and water was everywhere. It was the worst flood in a century, and I nearly drowned working on the dikes.

When he'd finished, the vice president laughed and said, All right, welcome aboard.

In fact he could have said much more. Now, Huang Qingzhou's soul was returning the way it had come. As he passed a bank on Zhongguancun Street, he glanced inside. A group of familiar-looking people were lined up at the counter. He went in to withdraw some money. It was early 1998; he'd just come from a small town and didn't know how to use his bank card yet, so he went to the counter with his bank book each time. There was hardly anything in the account. He got in line behind a young woman, and the two began chatting out of boredom. The line was long, and frustratingly slow.

—What are you here to do? he asked.

—Make a deposit.

—How much?

—A thousand. I just got a bonus.

—What a coincidence, I was going to withdraw a thousand. Look, you're going to deposit, I'm going to withdraw—why don't you just give the money to me? We can cut out the middleman and skip this line.

The woman blinked at him, then actually handed over the money. He took it, thanked her, then headed out the door and started running. He had to admit that the joke had been a half-hopeful con to begin with . . . but he'd succeeded! She hadn't yet learned to think on her feet. He needed that one thousand yuan: he only had eight hundred left in his own account. He ran straight from the bank back to his flophouse, where the three-story, 110-square-meter building was crammed with a total of forty-two beds. He'd rented one of them five days ago. It was near the door, which was usually left ajar, and he liked being able to get a little fresh air. Inside the building, the stench of socks, flatulence, bad breath, and long-unwashed bodies was so dense you could light it with a match. When he'd asked around the area about this building, he'd been advised not to rent there—they'd said that with that many people packed together like swine, the stink could kill you. He'd rented anyway; it was cheap.

The soul of my friend Qingzhou emerged from the flophouse into the night, and went into a pedestrian tunnel. He'd spent his very first night in Beijing in this tunnel. He put his bag down and sat on the ground, then curled up against the ice-cold wall and was just drifting off when a city management officer ran up shouting. Huang Qingzhou knew nothing good would come of this, and he snatched up his bag and fled, the officer in pursuit. After twenty meters, the officer gave up the chase, but Qingzhou kept running, for five kilometers at least. He tasted the pleasure of running as his body warmed. On the very first day of his life in Beijing, Huang Qingzhou felt the pleasure of warmth. Before he knew it, he had run straight out of Beijing.

In a little southern town, a thousand kilometers away, he was a bespectacled middle-school teacher. He'd had a few failed love affairs, and been involved in a few failed business deals. You can't help being unlucky in love: no one wants their heart broken, but who can avoid it? But his business failures, as Qingzhou had seen it back then, were purely due to the dastardliness of his students' parents. Why, while the students were still in his class, were his business deals with their parents so profitable, while the moment the students graduated or transferred, he began to lose money? He promised himself then that if he ever had children and entered into a business relationship with their teachers, he would do what was right and proper, and not inflict losses on the teachers just because his children had moved on. He would never burn his bridges. Huang Qingzhou's soul entered the run-down moon gate of the middle school's employee residential area, and he saw himself sitting idly in his fifteen-square-meter dormitory. A thick journal lay before him, and on it a Hero-brand fountain pen that had drunk its fill of Hero-brand ink. His unexceptional life as a teacher had left him with nothing much to write about.

—You don't believe I kept a journal? Qingzhou said as I helped him lift his plaster-wrapped arm. It was a kind of exercise. I kept a journal before I came to Beijing. Good habit, you say? I was forced. My parents forced me to keep it, starting when I was a child; after a while I got used to it, and then it bothered me *not* to keep it. My parents were hoping I would become a great writer, if not a Dostoevsky then at least a Gorky. I stopped after I got to Beijing. Twenty million people all heaped together like ants—what was so special about me that I needed to keep a journal? I was up to my eyebrows in work, talking my jaw off with clients; why would I go home and continue talking to my journal? But the stuff I wrote while I was still teaching is pretty interesting. I'll show it to you someday. Where was I? Right, my soul. He went into the school campus and looked at the journal I'd opened. He went back through it, step by step, until he knew everything . . .

1997: In accordance with the directives of the Department of Education and my school, I took my students to watch the entire live broadcast of the return of Hong Kong to the Motherland. A student who'd never seen one of the nation's leaders pointed at the TV and said: "Who's that fat guy in the black-framed glasses?"

1995: Thank god I was finally transferred from my township middle school to the county number two middle school. I wasn't vain about the township-to-county promotion, but there was a river in front of the county-level school, and after class I could go swimming. I had a girlfriend who was also a teacher. She taught English, and though her pronunciation was even worse than mine, I decided to be with her for a while. What else did I have to do out there? I played basketball on the school courts every evening—all the younger teachers did; we had energy to spare. Once we were too tired to run anymore and we'd had a rest, our loins were practically on fire. Let's find something else to do, we said. So I did. I agreed to be her boyfriend. Though I was wriggling with excitement down there, I managed to control myself, and after making out, we'd always go back to sleep in our own dormitories. But then one day she said she was pregnant and wanted me to marry her. What the hell? Where was this coming from? I hadn't even used all of my equipment yet. Believe me, I was in a bad state. There wasn't any point in keeping myself pure, so I visited a "henhouse" on a little alleyway at the edge of town. I gave the lady twenty yuan, and she showed me what a woman really was.

—Underneath that piece of flooring, said Qingzhou, before my soul made it out of my body, the faces of both that woman and my English-teacher girlfriend flashed through my mind. I'm not saying I was a saint, Pingyang, but at the time I truly wished I'd married her all those years ago. At least I would have saved her some grief. Later she married a man who beat her when he was happy and beat her when he was angry, all because of "that brat she'd squeezed out." And if I could meet that lady from the henhouse again, I'd give her some extra money so she could go home and take care of herself—though considering her age, I doubt she walks this earth anymore.

1992: I graduated from the Chinese department of the teachers' school, but then ended up teaching politics at the township middle school—they were short on politics teachers. My grandmother passed away the same day I returned home with all my belongings. (Huang Qingzhou's soul heard the earth-shattering wails from the mouth of his alley, and saw the neighbors milling around the door of his house. Qian Dongfang's mother saw him standing there woodenly and snapped at him: "Hurry home now, your grandmother's dead!")

1989: Before the college entrance exams, he played hooky and rode the train to Beijing for free with the older boy next door. It was the first time he'd ever seen a big city. In Beijing everyone thought the two of them were college students, and they were given free food and drink everywhere they went. One evening, sitting on the square with the neighbor boy, he was so exhausted he fell asleep, only to be awakened by a roar like thunder and lightning. Before he had even opened his eyes, the neighbor boy was dragging him up and pushing him along a broad street. He seemed to be in a dream, or thrust into the middle of a war film. They ran, breathless, with the thunder still sounding in their ears. When they reached an intersection, he said to the other boy, This place is terrible. Going home there were no free trains, and they had to hitch rides from one place to another—it took them a full week to get back.

1986: He entered a county-level middle school. Only five people in the township were admitted (three others who had better grades went to a technical school). Wearing leather shoes, a gift from an uncle (they were of very poor quality), he began to play basketball, and he heard tell of chocolate (though it was 1991 before he actually got to taste it, and then he didn't like the bitter flavor), and coffee (the first Sunday after he arrived at college, he finally had the chance to visit the only café in the whole city and buy his first cup). Taking a cue from the oldest student in the dorms, he began a long career of masturbation.

Huang Qingzhou's soul sped up, traveling back against the flow of time. He saw old Qiu the trash collector sitting on some newspaper on the bridge outside the gate of the township middle school, where he liked to exchange a few words with everyone who went by. He saw Teacher Dong, the head teacher for his year, lingering outside the classroom: during study hall, the teacher would sneak over to the door and windows of the classrooms and watch what the students were doing. Huang Qingzhou's soul walked along the dirt track that led back to his village from the school and saw the young Qingzhou trying to borrow a copy of *A Girl's Heart* from a third-grader in his village, and failing. All he'd gotten was a copy of a martial-arts novel called *The Golden Palm and the Day-and-Night Sword*, by whom he couldn't remember. At the entrance to the village, Huang Qingzhou's soul happened upon the tofu maker out for a stroll with his hands behind his back. As he passed the village elementary school, Huang Qingzhou saw himself as a fourth-grade elementary student, in class reciting *Huang Xiguang* for his English teacher. He hadn't been asked to recite; the teacher had only wanted a volunteer to summarize the story, but no one had raised a hand to volunteer, and the teacher, who played both flute and *erhu*, flew into a pique and demanded that all the students recite the text from memory the next day. As a member of the study committee, Qingzhou was naturally obliged to recite first. In another class, he was whipped by the science teacher. The whip, made of indigo-bush switches, broke on his back, and he felt as though a swarm of bees were flying out through his eyes. Past the elementary school was the threshing field. In 1980, following directives from the very top, the local military leaders had announced the end of collectivism and the beginning of a new age of "going it alone." They drew lots to share out the communally owned property, and Qingzhou's father told him to draw for their family, saying that a child's luck would be good. Huang Qingzhou watched himself squeezing in among the legs of the adults and plucking a paper strip, on which was written: One haycutter.

Continuing on. An enormous slogan is painted in red on the wall of the army headquarters: Long Live Chairman Mao! Five-year-old Qingzhou squats on the ground, wide-eyed, and listens to an adult say that a thousand kilometers away, Tangshan has been struck by a 7.8 magnitude earthquake, the whole city reduced to ruins in twenty-three seconds. How many thousands of their class brethren, gone! After delivering the news, the speaker breaks down in tears, and those listening weep as well. Qingzhou thinks he should be crying, too, so he twists up his face and does.

The soul of my friend Huang Qingzhou now walks with a lurching, unsteady gait, his steps smaller and smaller, his body increasingly awkward. He appears ever smaller, and weaker, and finally can't walk at all—he has become an infant. He begins crawling on the ground, bawling and naked, and the farther he crawls, the softer his skin becomes, the more tender his body grows. He sees a warm, damp cave ahead of him, beckoning to him like the Bermuda Triangle, and before he can even consider avoiding it, he's gone in with a plunk. Though incapable of thought, he knows it is his mother's womb, warm and welcoming—the same adjectives used each year by the hosts of the Spring Festival Gala TV program. It's a warm and welcoming world! Then he hears torturous panting, witnesses a battle of the flesh, full of revolutionary spirit and critical will, empty of physical desire. The man who will become his father has just left the stage where he was struggled against, his face bruised and swollen from stones, bricks, and slaps. The woman who will become his mother has just removed a broken pair of shoes, their laces tied together, from around her neck and placed them carefully in a basket behind the door, so she can find them when she needs them. No one has new shoes, and even old ones are hard to come by. Tomorrow, between five o'clock and dinnertime, she must hang them around her neck and parade through the village from east to west, three circuits in all, to give the revolutionary masses an appetite for their dinner.

As the two bodies thrash haphazardly, Huang Qingzhou hears the clamor of the world, sees a great illumination. The illumination of darkness. And then he, my friend Qingzhou, hears a distant voice saying:

—Quick, cover his eyes! He's still alive!

A Village of Cold Hearths

By Sheng Keyi

TRANSLATED BY BRENDAN O'KANE

Dusk spread stickily over the village. Clouds gathered lazily. The sun eased into the Lanxi River, flecking its surface with gold. A swimmer split the surface of the water and paddled deep out into the sunset. Cicadas buzzed languidly on the banks. Locust trees cast their long shadows over the yards, their branches probing into the rear windows of the houses. A cat drowsed on a windowsill. Wicker chairs and benches were set out in the yards for warm days. Blue-gray smoke rose from a heap of grass set alight to drive off mosquitoes, blanketing the yellowy-green weeds that grew here and there on the thatched roofs.

The thin rice gruel sloshed around Liufu's stomach as he left the village canteen and walked through this scene of tranquility toward his own yard. The watery liquid was rinsing his guts clean. He wanted some meat, more than he wanted any woman. He was thinking about catching a few field mice, roasting them over a wood fire until they were tender, and gobbling them down, bones, marrow, and all.

The hills covered up the sun completely and replaced it with their silhouette. Lamps came on, chipping little holes in the twilight. Birds flew wearily back to their nests. The village slipped into another silent night.

Mother was still hungry, but she belched as loudly as if she were full. She was deaf. Mother was like the hands of a clock, moving along in her circles without praising or scorning or passing judgment on anything. After she'd sat there and belched for a while, she went back inside to her bedroom, and the sound of a palm-leaf fan smacking flesh emerged from inside, beating out a rhythm on the night.

The crescent moon slanted like a woman's arched eyebrow. Fireflies flitted back and forth through the melon patch. Bats chirped to one another under the eaves.

The river's waters gave off a dim, dancing light. Hunger swam around in Liufu's belly like a fish. He'd seen how fish would come right up to the edges of the river in spring to mate, without a thought for their own safety. Field mice were too clever, he decided. Maybe fish would be easier to catch. Picking up a meter-long pronged fishing spear, Liufu wended his way through the locust trees to the bank of the river and played the beam of his flashlight over the water. The five tines of the metal spear were sharp and slightly barbed at the ends; once they went into a fish's body, there'd be no escape for the fish.

In the end he caught nothing. As Liufu sat against the rough bark of the locust tree daydreaming, he was startled by a sudden motion in the water, like a huge fish swishing its tail from side to side. He jumped to his feet to look. It was no fish; it was a girl, her head poking above the water as she pushed her wet hair back from her white face. There was nothing strange about people going for nighttime swims in the river, but Liufu had never seen the girl before, and girls from the countryside didn't have skin that pale.

"Turn off that flashlight," the girl said, the beads of water on her body glittering like fish scales. "I can't see you."

Flicking it off meant he wouldn't be able to see her lovely smile. Liufu couldn't bring himself to do it. He told her his name. "Where are you from? I haven't seen you before."

"I'm a fish," the girl said. She ducked her head under the water and kept it there for a few seconds. "You know Weixing Village?"

"Who doesn't? They get three thousand jin of rice per mu from their paddies."

"They may *say* that . . . hey—don't shine that thing in my face." She splashed water up at him.

Liufu turned the flashlight off. He could barely see the girl now.

"You from Weixing?"

"I am and I'm not," she said. "I'm not and I am."

"Sounds like a tongue-twister."

"They're like any model village—anything you can do, they say they can do better."

The girl swam to the bank and sat on a willow branch that poked out into the river, dangling her legs in the water. Her skin and body were snowy white in the moonlight, as if someone had drawn a human form on the night's curtain. The girl smelled faintly of fish grass. She wore a black bathing suit. Liufu had never seen such a bold girl. For a while he had fantasized about Jiazhen back in the village, whose face was always red—sometimes from the sun, sometimes from embarrassment—and who looked like a rain-drenched apple when she was out working in the fields, dripping beads of moisture, steam rising off her, and a sharp, sweet scent of fruit that you could smell from far away.

"What's your name?"

She said to call her "Fish."

Fitting enough, he thought. She swam like one.

"How many jin do you get per mu here?" The girl lifted her legs up onto the branch. Liufu hadn't noticed before, but she had webbed toes like a duck's.

"More than two thousand," he said.

"Stupid, making trouble for yourselves that way," she said. "You'll be the ones starving if you can't produce that much." Fish spoke of death in an innocent tone.

"That's seditious talk and malicious gossip-mongering. Be careful they don't catch you."

"I'm just telling the truth. Two thousand jin a mu—do you really believe that?"

"Believe it or don't," Liufu said. "How old are you?"

"That depends. What year is it?"

"Are you kidding? It's 1959."

She worked it out on her fingers. "Then I'd be seventeen. I'm not like the rest of you—I'm not the sort of person who lets her imagination run away with her. I'm not even a person, I'm a fish. Bye now."

With that, she dived into the water, giggling.

The surface of the river became flat and calm again. The weak light of the flashlight was swallowed up by the darkness after ten meters or so.

People in the village who sold fish they'd caught the night before used to try to sell stories about the strange things they'd seen at night. They said there were spirits in the river. Hardly anyone believed them. Liufu couldn't decide whether he did or not. He didn't see much difference between people and spirits when he read through his old copy of *Strange Tales from Liaozhai Studio*—some of the spirits were better than some of the humans—and he thought a romance with Charm or Tranquilina or Sapientia or one of the other winsome young female ghosts in the book might not be such a bad thing.

He picked up the fishing spear and went home. He knew that a girl who went out swimming at night would be all right in the water.

———

Liufu continued to take his fishing spear down to the river, though most of the time he just sat against a willow tree and waited for Fish. The sight of Fish filled his belly, filled his heart, filled his entire being. He became enchanted with the fish-grass scent that clung to her body like the faint perfume of jasmine.

From time to time Fish would appear, darting and playing in the water. Her body was always dripping, just like her voice. The villagers always spoke in loud, harsh voices, but Fish's voice was as soft as night and as gentle as water. It quenched Liufu's thirst to hear it. One night when the moon was shining brightly and the stifling heat was almost intolerable, Liufu touched Fish's hand.

He'd never touched a woman before, and he was surprised to find her skin as slippery as if it were covered with a layer of soap. Her eyes were small, he thought, but then again there was nothing wrong with small eyes on a small face. Pale skin on a girl made up for everything, and in all his twenty-two years, Liufu had never seen a girl with skin as pale as Fish's. Even the butterfly-shaped freckle on the tip of her nose was enchanting. He began to imagine how even his mother, who never gave an opinion on anything, would praise Fish, how the smile that had died with his father would return to her lips. He told Fish that after the busy harvest season, he would find a go-between to arrange the marriage. His mother could hardly wait.

Fish had taken Jiazhen's place in Liufu's dreams. When he kissed her on a moon-drenched night, her lips moist and cold, her saliva clear and sweet, he tasted the most exquisite thing in the whole world.

The heat persisted, the cruel sun beating down from overhead and cracking the roads. The cicadas grew hoarse; the plants began to wilt. The sky stayed a uniform dull blue.

The nights were electric, and filled Liufu with energy for work in the fields by day. He would run out of the house barefoot, the earth scorching his feet, run excitedly down to the river, his happy secret dancing in his heart like a scampering squirrel. When the harvest came, he scythed his way through the muddy paddies like a machine, faster than all the others. The thresher groaned happily under his pedaling. When it came time to drink, he'd splash water straight onto his face from the spout of the kettle. His hard work inspired the other villagers, and after being roundly commended, he was named team leader—the youngest village cadre, they said.

"If you all don't tell the truth about how much grain you're producing, it'll come to disaster." So Fish was always warning him. She was always making predictions, as if she had second sight. There was something curious about her, some mysterious power that Liufu couldn't help but go along with. Especially the way she would look at her reflection in the river, brushing drops of water from her long hair, like a waving frond of river grass floating just below the surface. He always found himself drawing nearer for a closer look.

The only thing Liufu cared about was getting done with the harvest so he could marry Fish. For everything else, he thought, he couldn't go far wrong by following everyone else's lead.

There were perks to Liufu's new status as team leader, foremost among them the chance to skim. Liufu could stuff a handful or two of freshly harvested rice into his pockets without fear of being caught, and he'd even gotten up the nerve to bring a few whole sacks filled with rice home under cover of night when nobody was around. Mother sewed the rice into old clothes, which she folded and placed at the bottom of their wardrobe or spread on the plank bed. Late at night she would grind small handfuls of rice in the palm of her hand and blow away the husks, humming to herself. Mother was fond of guoba, the crispy rice crust that stuck to the bottom of the cooking pot, and Father had liked to stir flakes of guoba into his rice porridge. Liufu wanted to cook up a pot right then and there, but he followed his mother's lead in chewing a few grains of the freshly husked rice instead, for fear that the cooking smoke from their chimney would give them away.

After the harvest was over and the rice had been stored away in the granary, the atmosphere became tense. The village leaders held secret meetings, and they always looked unhappy. Not until after the meetings expanded to include team leaders did Liufu find out that the rice yield was falling far short of the proud claims they'd made, that the higher-ups suspected the village of holding back, and that the consequences of this would be grave indeed. The village cadres had come in for criticism from the township leaders; the township leaders were getting browbeaten by the county leaders; and the municipality-level leaders had branded them all troublemakers and said that their thinking was insufficiently clear—that they had failed to comprehend the arduous, complex, and long-term nature of the Socialist battle for grain production, to say nothing of the role of grain production as a focal point for the struggle against Capitalism in rural areas; that their mode of thought was paralytic. One of the more honest county-level cadres blurted out that there really was no grain, and was promptly sent for thought reform on suspicion of having a Rightist tendency to oversimplify issues.

Seeing that nothing good could come of telling the truth, the leaders went back to the village to try to think of a plan.

The first village meeting Liufu took part in was held around a square eight-person table in the main room of the village head's home. There was a clay teapot on the table, and a few porcelain teacups, and the village leaders sat around them in rings. In the outer rings, the team leaders and commune representatives squatted, stood, or sat on the ground passing cigarettes around, bumming lights, and chattering. The mood was slightly restless. A get-together like this right after the harvest was unprecedented. Clouds of smoke quickly filled the room. Ten minutes later, by the time the village's Party branch secretary had finished his speech, the mood had turned serious. Even the smoke stopped drifting.

"They could kill us and it still wouldn't make up for a shortfall that big," Poxy Niu said when he heard the requisition figures.

Poxy Niu, the leader of Team Two, was a medium-sized, plainspoken man with pockmarks all over his face. He and his wife had had five daughters in a row. Three of them didn't make it, and when the sixth baby proved to be another girl, Niu delivered her from her mother's womb straight into the river without a word. Niu had been dead set on having a boy, but his wife went barren. People said you could hear a baby crying from the river at night, and some people said they'd seen a little girl swim past them, quick as a fish. More and more strange things had been happening these past few summers. A fisherman said he'd seen ripples on the river one time when there wasn't any wind, and a chill had come over him. Sometimes, he said, he could just make out something that sounded like a young woman singing, and—most vividly—he said he'd stopped to squat down by the riverbank for a smoke one night when a dripping-wet creature leapt into the river using his shoulder as a springboard and stained his shirt with muck. Not that anyone really believed the story. Some people said he was making up spooky stories to scare off anybody else who might be thinking about fishing there, because the river was getting fished out.

"What gives you the right to speak, Poxy? Or did you forget about the life you threw into the river years ago?" The doughy-faced village chairwoman had a knack for touching on people's sore spots that way. It may have been how she rose to her position.

This knocked Poxy Niu off balance. He looked as if he wanted to reply, but he just sat there, red-faced and thick-necked, looking like a toad that had just swallowed a fly, holding in whatever he had been about to say.

But it was too late for Niu to take back what he had already said, and he was immediately relieved of his responsibilities, stripped of his title as team leader, and docked two days' worth of meals.

No one spoke up. No one knew what kind of dirt the chairwoman had on them. People made sure to act meek and mild in front of the village-level cadres, and in the presence of cadres from the township or the county they were as uneasy as slaves facing their masters.

———

As a member of the Anti-Hoarding Squad, Liufu wore an olive-green uniform with a Chairman Mao badge on the breast. After a half-day of training at the civilian militia base, they began storming people's homes and searching their chests and wardrobes for hidden rice. They conducted surprise nighttime raids that left the whole village wondering who would be next. He could sense his power in their flinching gazes. Glory! It was like getting away with a prank: he could slap people and they wouldn't hit back, kick them and they wouldn't cry out. It was as if they submitted to the uniformed squaddies out of some instinct that told them they deserved it.

Thoughts of Fish made Liufu one of the more tenderhearted squaddies. He even encouraged the others to stick to searching for grain instead of beating people. Someone reported him for Rightism, siding with commune members against the squad, and not showing enough initiative in anti-hoarding actions. The team had a talk with Liufu, and—understanding that someone had it in for him—he kept his mouth shut when the beatings started, and got in a kick or two of his own when the opportunity presented itself, just to show where he stood. Soon enough his fists and feet grew restless, like hungry beasts looking for an opportunity to pounce on their prey. He couldn't say himself when it was that he got into the habit of beating people.

One afternoon the squad found a half-cup of peas at the old herdsman Li's home, and they dragged him to the drying ground to make him hand over the rest. A scorching sun hung overhead, and soon Li's legs were shaking and he was covered in sweat. "Those peas were from last year's harvest," he said. "I kept them for planting this year. Take them if you have to take them, but even if you beat me to death, I won't have another kernel of grain for you."

A kick landed in his upper thigh before he finished speaking, and he fell to his knees. Like wild beasts swarming upon fallen prey, they punched him in the nose, slapped his face, pulled his hair, kicked him in the stomach, and tore at his clothes. In the blink of an eye, old Li lay flat on his back, blood streaming from every orifice. Liufu got in another kick for good measure.

They sloshed a pan of cold water on him, and it dripped down from his white hair. He came to.

"Th— there's . . ."—the words came out faintly—"there's really not . . . any more . . . grain . . ."

The word "grain" set the wild beasts to ravening again. They hauled the old man to his feet, yanked down his trousers, stuffed the peas up his asshole, and rammed them home with a stick. "We've planted them for you, you old wretch. You just wait for the harvest."

The old herdsman died late that night.

People said it had been a stroke.

———

They splashed around all summer, harvesting mussels, catching fish, chasing and racing one another, playing hide and seek. The lotus ponds, the lakes, the irrigation canals—all were their playgrounds. They picked lotus roots and water chestnuts in moonlit ponds, leaving Liufu's body covered with bloody scratches that made him look like a whipped criminal. Fish was playful, even flirtatious, in the water, dancing lightly around any obstacles and giggling as she showed off her aquatic agility. Sometimes she'd hold a lotus leaf and dive underwater so that the only sign of her was the leaf drifting along on the surface.

On land Fish was as quiet as a virgin. She would get a faraway look in her eyes and begin to talk about the future. She said people were going to die, more than Liufu could even imagine. She described a village where death filled the air, where lives ended one after another like dead leaves falling to the ground. She said the people would become locusts, woodworms, aphids, ants, weevils, horseflies, fleas, overrunning the crops and trees, destroying every living creature in their path. They would kill everything they could eat, and then everything they couldn't eat, and then they would turn on each other, and underwater would be the only safe place.

And then Fish talked about the world beneath the waves. Liufu listened attentively, playing along. Fish's fantasies were his favorite, like something out of *Strange Tales from Liaozhai Studio*, a whole other world—a whole other life— that he had never imagined.

"When the time comes, I'll let you eat me." Fish didn't sound like she was joking.

"No," Liufu said, "I won't eat you. I'll kill myself while there's still some flesh on my bones, and you can eat me and go on living."

The atmosphere grew serious. A chill came over Liufu when he thought about it afterward. He didn't believe that people would eat people, let alone the people they loved. Not unless they were monsters.

———

A cold autumn wind blew. Liufu stood on the bank of the Yangtze; behind him was a village of cold hearths where no cooking smoke rose. The crops were withered and brown. People's voices were weak and faint.

It had been Fish's dream to swim in the Yangtze. She'd never seen such a vast expanse of water—many times broader than the Lanxi. Fog curled over the surface of the river, and the buildings on the opposite bank were only faintly visible. Birds passed through the mist and flew into the distance. Every now and then a massive craft would clumsily and arrogantly make its way down the center of the river, white smoke rising into the sky. The river churned behind the boats.

As he walked from the yellowing grass down into the river, the surface of the water suddenly looked oily. Squat black willow trees lined the banks, and birds chirped amid the leaves that remained on the branches. Liufu had hung his clothes on a branch and was clad only in his underwear. The water was even chillier than the wind, and he shivered for a moment. When he was waist-deep, he paused and splashed some water up onto his chest. A few dozen meters ahead of him, Fish had already dived beneath the surface of the water. Embarrassed, he plunged resolutely forward.

Fish swam toward him, circling her body around his waist and spinning around behind him, her buttocks brushing against him. She stuck her head around over his shoulder and kissed him from behind. Then she was gone. Another somersault and she was in front of him, and he thought about how fish looked when they were mating, their mouths round Os, their fins spread open, their bodies taut and quivering. Nearing each other, opening up, darting away, butting heads, tails lightly slapping . . . Fish was like a dancer caught up in her dance, her eyes filled with passion.

Try as he might, Liufu could not hold on to her. She kept slipping through his hands, just like a fish.

He lifted his head up out of the water and caught his breath.

The mist had dispersed; the night was a clear, tranquil indigo; the distant scenery, visible in outline, looked like a woodcut. Liufu gulped mouthfuls of air. Fish grabbed the lower half of his body tightly, tracing the lines of his body with her head. He held her close, and the temperature of the water rose suddenly. "Ah—I've got to get onto the bank." His legs had cramped up at the crucial moment.

Liufu lay on the grassy bank. The night was a light gray. Scattered stars shone overhead.

"That's better." He kissed Fish, his vigor returning. "Are you ready?" Fish's eyes sparkled, maybe from nervousness, like stars that had fallen into wells.

"I've waited so long for this," she said. "To be with someone who loves me—to have a whole new life."

Love flooded over him. He didn't see the guarded look in her eyes.

"Mm—a new life. Me too. So what if we don't have anything to eat?"

Members of the anti-stockpiling squad were treated well: two bowls of cabbage-leaf porridge a day, with at least a few grains of rice in it. "We might not have any grain now, but we'll get through it like we always do. We'll have a proper wedding feast—fish, meat, and a big bowl of rice."

"There you go, dreaming again."

"I'll marry you if it's the last thing I do," Liufu said heatedly, rolling over on top of Fish. "Promise me?"

The beam of a flashlight picked them out.

It was Poxy Niu. He dropped his fishing net on the grass, the weights of the net clicking like pebbles.

"What's gotten into you, Liufu? Talking to yourself out here?" Poxy walked over, flashlight in hand.

Startled, Liufu glanced down at Fish, then jolted into a sitting position. Where Fish had been, there was now only a puddle. The river water rippled faintly, dimly reflecting the light.

"I don't know how long I'm going to last, boy," Poxy Niu sighed, sitting beside him. "Heaven's going to starve me for the wrong I done."

Liufu sat there dumbly, feeling an icy chill in the pit of his stomach. "You believe what they say about there being spirits in the water?" he asked.

"Why not? I'd believe just about anything these days. You could tell me the daughter I threw away seventeen years ago was still living, and I'd believe it. I wish she were. Maybe then I could tell her I was wrong. It was a terrible thing I done. I looked for her body in the river, you know, but I never found it. Learned to cast fishing nets just so I could find her and bury her right." Poxy Niu croaked out his words like a dying bird.

There was a sudden noise from the river, like a big fish leaping.

"Even if she were still alive, I don't expect she'd live through this. They won't let us cook at home, won't let us go out looking for vegetables, won't let us leave the village . . . three more people died today, and I expect I'll be joining them soon." Poxy waved his flashlight beam back and forth over the river. "Not a single fish. And me not even able to cast the nets . . . tell me, boy, are we really just going to wait to die?"

"Of course not, Uncle Niu—how could anyone starve with these bumper harvests?" Liufu answered easily, his heart beating with excitement over Fish.

Poxy Niu got half a liter of soybeans from Liufu's home that night, and from then on Liufu took special care of the man.

———

"Grain" was like a magic word that held everyone in its sway. The higher-ups came for an inspection, and the starving villagers roused themselves and affected expressions that they hoped would show the perseverance and correctness of Socialism. The yards were piled high with grain: a thin layer of rice at the top of the baskets and heaps of chaff and weeds beneath. Having placated the higher-ups, the village leaders were awarded Major Commendations, and promptly went back to searching for stockpiled grain, beating and interrogating the villagers ever more harshly.

No wedding banquets. No gatherings. No celebrations. No farewells. No cooking smoke. The village canteen closed down. Some people lay down and never got back up; some people swelled up; some people suddenly fell down; some people got locked up; some people got put on trial. It was all very quiet. The village was as quiet as a grave.

Sentries patrolled at the village gate, their guns fully loaded. Vultures circled. A rising wind scoured the land.

The bark was gone from all the trees, and the white wood underneath had gone brown and then black. The earth was scored and lined where it had been clawed at, the mud churned up like the ground around a mouse's nest.

Liufu's mother racked her brains to find ways to fill her stomach. When the weeds, rats, roots, and bark were all gone, she took to chopping up rice straw and corncobs, which she would cook and crush and mash into a paste late at night. She would go out and collect egret shit by the paths to wash and steam. The secret was to imagine that they were your favorite foods when you ate them. That the egret shit was egg custard.

Mother and son didn't look like they were starving. That must have been why Jiazhen came to beg for rice.

"My father will die if he doesn't eat something." Jiazhen stood in the doorway, her hair disheveled, her lips pale. She swayed back and forth like a piece of paper in the wind.

Jiazhen had gone to high school. Mother liked her, thought of her almost as a daughter-in-law. She pulled Jiazhen inside and sat down next to her, speaking loudly, as if to a deaf woman.

"Look how thin you are, my dear! Are you ill? Aiya—wait here and I'll find you something to eat."

Mother turned around and walked into the kitchen.

Indeed, the once healthily glowing, faintly apple-scented young woman now looked like a gourd that had withered on the vine. Every drop of moisture was gone from her body. Liufu was rather startled not to smell her clear apple fragrance. He had never spoken to Jiazhen much to begin with, and had even less idea of what to say now. Mother emerged and broke the silence with a bowl of "egg custard."

Jiazhen couldn't thank her enough. She hesitated a moment on her way to the door, then steeled herself: "Liufu, you know the villagers haven't been hoarding grain . . . you have to tell the higher-ups the truth . . . someone has to tell them the truth. Maybe the truth is the only thing that can help us."

Her eyes were clear and bright, as if all the moisture in her body were concentrated there.

"Who's to say what's the truth and what isn't?" Liufu said. "You want me to go against the government? To say we didn't make any progress?" He began to grow agitated. "I'd be getting myself killed—and they'd never believe anything I said, anyway."

"Starving will kill you just the same . . ." Jiazhen turned to face Liufu. "Better to die telling the truth. Why not try it?"

Liufu pushed the door shut hastily. "You can't go around saying things like that—it'll only make things worse."

"Worse than starving to death? You've changed, Liufu. You've become one of them. You hurt innocent people, just like them."

Jiazhen's cold tone struck a nerve. He knew that his position had kept his family's house safe from searches, had meant they'd always have something to keep them from starving—and that the villagers had not looked at him the same way for quite some time.

"I . . . I'm just doing what I have to," he mumbled. Jiazhen looked silently at the half-bowl of "egg custard," then slowly set it down on the table, unbolted the door, and left.

Mother had watched all of this knowingly. She patted her son on the shoulder to comfort him, then walked into her room and pulled something from the pillow: a lumpy black sock filled with snowy white rice.

"This is the last of our rice." She poured out half the rice, then tied the sock tightly shut and handed it to Liufu. "Go give this to her. And don't forget to tell her you're sorry."

Liufu stared at her.

———

The sky was a flat gray. All around were death rattles and ghosts. The silence was filled with a silent howling. The earth had become a black-and-white photograph. Lonely stragglers picked over the roads between villages, bent over in search of anything that could satisfy their hunger. The struggle against hoarding went on unabated. Beatings and gunshots kept the people as quiet as cicadas in winter.

Fish had vanished after their swim in the Yangtze. Liufu waited for her on the banks of the Lanxi every night. These past few days he'd been carefully rereading *Strange Tales from Liaozhai Studio* to see if he could learn more about water spirits. It was a shame so many of the love stories in the book were tragedies, he thought. The water spirits, too, were tragic figures, unable to choose their own fates. Their interactions with mortals were motivated by love, or gratitude, or sheer jealousy of the humans—though there was nothing to envy in the humans around him, all of whom were simply waiting for hunger to kill them. If he could have become one of the spirits or otherworldly creatures that filled the books, for the sake of Fish, he would have.

The autumn moon was moored in the middle of the river, casting its cold silver light over willow branches that hung down as fine and close as raindrops.

He stood there in the water waiting for her, not caring whether Fish's love for him was pure or not, and finally she appeared at his side.

"I told you before, I'm not a person." Her body glittered. "I've just had enough of cold and loneliness in the water. I like the sun, I like flowers and grass, I like fruits and melons and human laughter. I always knew you'd realize that I was just a mermaid someday . . ."

"I'd be happy with you even if you were a mermaid, Fish. And I know that you're the baby Uncle Niu threw away seventeen years ago. No matter what you are, I want you to be my wife." Liufu reached out his arms to embrace her.

"Let me finish." She ducked away from him. "I've always tried to understand why people act the way they do, but I've never found an answer. I'm only a fish. My world is a simple one. All I know is swimming. The elders told me I would only understand what it is to be human if I were born again as a human . . . and then, at just the right time, I met you."

"It's not easy here, Fish. There are struggles every day . . ."

"The water is a cold prison. I can't just float up to the surface whenever I want."

"There are sentry posts everywhere here on land—and jails, and red-letter notices from the government. One wrong word and they'll have your head. It's not as wonderful as you think it is, not by a long shot."

"The human world is the way it is because you made it that way. None of you would speak the truth, and now disaster is upon you."

"Tell me how I can become a fish like you. "

"You can't become anything else, not while you're still alive. You can only be a man. And I won't be able to be reborn until I mate with the person I love . . . and then my body will become nothing more than a bubble on the water that will soon disappear."

"No, you mustn't disappear. I want to have a simple life with you, to go swimming every day."

"Forget your own problems, Liufu, and think about what's happening to your village." Fish dropped below the surface of the water for a moment, then stuck her head back out. "Have you never thought about how you might save other people, and also save yourself?"

"Me? Save them?" Liufu snorted. "I'm unarmed and powerless, and they have guns pointing at you wherever you go. What could I possibly do?"

"Where there's a will, there's a way. When I heard my father's confession that night . . . I stopped hating him. He was right—you can't all just wait around to die."

"But then how—unless you use your . . . magic?" Liufu said, grasping at straws.

"I'm a cast-off body. The arts you speak of are forbidden to me."

"But you know how to disappear."

"I can't live out of water for more than an hour."

"We'll find a way," Liufu said, not believing his own words. "We'll get by."

"You can't just lie down and accept your fate."

"What should I do, then?"

"Staying silent means death. Speaking out means death. Both mean death—but they're not the same thing at all." Fish drew close and kissed him. "Go on, Liufu. You know what you have to do."

She slipped from his arms back into the water.

————

Staying silent means death. Speaking out means death. Dead meat either way, Liufu thought. What was the difference? But then, Jiazhen had said almost the same thing.

Jiazhen lived at the end of the village. It was a five-minute walk around two lotus ponds and straight down along the redwood-lined irrigation canals to the grain-drying ground outside their door.

There was a crowd in front—a festive one, it seemed. As Liufu drew nearer, pushing his way through the throng, he saw someone from the anti-hoarding squad grabbing at Jiazhen's chest and shouting that the lumps there must be where she stored her illegal grain. Jiazhen was doing her best to cover her chest, biting her lip, biting back the shame and the humiliation. Everyone knew that talking back or resisting would get them locked up on charges of opposing the Party. Several times Liufu wanted to rush forward, but his feet were nailed to the ground, as if he were held in thrall by what was happening before him. He hardly dared breathe, until one of the squaddies ripped a white brassiere out from under her shirt and Jiazhen fell to the ground, crying piteously. But an even better show was soon to follow: Jiazhen's father, the soft-spoken old village schoolmaster, was stripped naked and trussed up like a hog, the nylon rope cutting into his rather ill-developed muscles. His face was covered with blood and dirt, and Liufu had only to look at his vacant eyes to know he had been subjected to the entire roster of techniques: being doused with ice water; having his hair pulled out, his ears cut off, bamboo splints driven through his palms, his teeth "brushed" with pine needles; as well as what they called "lighting heavenly lanterns," when oil was splashed on someone's body and set aflame, and "stir-frying beans," when a person was surrounded by squaddies and then jostled back and forth violently, like a soybean being stir-fried in a wok, until they were shaken half to death.

Liufu was perversely impressed that the reedy old village schoolmaster had managed to survive it all. He remembered literature classes with the old man, who had worn a long, old-fashioned robe and a bookish pair of glasses, and was always soft-spoken and even-tempered. Even now he was calm, fixing his gaze on the ground as if death held no fear for him.

"Where? Where did you get the rice?" The brigade leader threw the loose end of the rope over the branch of a locust tree. It dropped down on the other side, slicing the mild blue sky behind it in half.

Liufu's heart stopped. *I'm done for!*

The old schoolmaster slowly raised his eyelids, blood beading on his eyelashes. He was smiling, almost apologetically. "S . . . saved it from last year. I kn . . . know it's a crime . . . I accept the p—"

"Pull!" At the brigade leader's order, the schoolmaster and his "—*unishment*" were yanked up off the ground.

People craned their necks to look up at him hanging there like an oversized rice dumpling, to watch how his face would go from white to red, from red to purple; how beads of sweat the size of soybeans would slowly form and roll down and drop onto the ground; how fine threads of fresh blood would unravel from the wounds; how the threads would suddenly be snipped.

If he died, it would be like a lunar eclipse. Nobody wanted to miss the chance to see it.

Liufu watched more closely than anyone—as if, if the secret fell from the old schoolmaster's lips, he might be able to catch it in time.

But in less time than it takes to smoke a pipe, a cry from above dashed his hopes.

"I'll talk! Let me down, please, let me down and I'll tell you everything!"

The secret squeezed past the old schoolmaster's lips and fell to the ground with a clatter.

The village canteen was used for the interrogation and imprisonment of "criminals," as overseen by the anti-hoarding squad. Inmates had arrived on a number of charges: attempting to flee the village, or hoarding grain, or speaking snidely about the Three Red Banners, or claiming that the harvest had been anything but bountiful, or abandoning their children, a crime called "attacking the government with hand grenades of human flesh." They were locked in the pigpen behind the canteen. The pen had been cleared of everything except pig excrement, which covered the ground in pools; Liufu could smell the pig shit through two walls. The schoolmaster had landed him here: to save himself, he had coughed out Liufu's name with the very last of his strength. The crowd had surged toward its new target. Not ten minutes later, the squad had turned Liufu's home inside out like a pants pocket without finding a single grain of rice. This was taken as a grave insult by the squaddies, who exacted their revenge by beating Liufu to a pulp and locking him in the canteen without another word.

You get rice from harvesting paddies, not searching houses. The squad seemed to have understood this, at least to some degree, or perhaps they had simply lost heart. The way they treated Liufu was almost kind: a halfhearted interrogation, after which they shaved him bald and threw him in the old canteen bursar's office with nothing but a threadbare old quilt. Length of sentence was determined by how long a prisoner could go without food or drink—a day if it was a day, a month if it was a month. Once the door had locked behind you, no one was going to come knocking.

The small window in the cell faced directly onto the Lanxi River. It was sealed off with wooden bars that gave off a scent of pine, drawing and quartering the cold-colored sky and the water. The opposite bank was completely empty. Liufu's longing for Fish was not diminished in the slightest by the damage done to his body. He leaned over by the window, staring out at the river, until his legs went limp. The temperature fell precipitously overnight, so he wrapped the quilt around himself as he stood by the window. Everything was unnaturally still, as if the entire world had stopped breathing, and for an instant Liufu had the terrifying sense that he was the last living thing on earth.

After two days of loneliness and boredom, of not eating or drinking, of a cold that became a fever, Liufu's mind began to slip, and he began to experience a sensation of giddy lightness.

One hazy night he dreamed that Fish came and kissed him. Afterward he felt the coolness and the moisture of the kiss continue down and throughout his body. A chill spread through him, his organs turned to ice, and he realized that this was death, that death was like a massive hand wiping every last trace of heat from his body. He tossed and turned, trying to escape, and began to scream. He awoke covered in sweat. It had only been a nightmare.

In the pale, cold moonlight, everything had an otherworldly glow. The air carried a faint scent of jasmine, and he sensed that Fish was near him.

The smell of roasting fish startled Liufu into sudden alertness, as if hauling him to his feet. Life flooded back into his limp body with startling speed, and he sat up.

In the dim moonlight, Fish had appeared as if out of nowhere, holding a large porcelain bowl in her hands. Her face was whiter than the moon, and her hair spilled down over her shoulders. Her lips were slightly open, as if gasping for air.

Liufu didn't rush for the food, or for the woman. He hesitated slightly. Fish uncovered the bowl, and the smell of roasting fish grew richer.

"I found this in the river. You're in luck . . ."

Abandoning all pretense of manners, Liufu snatched the bowl and buried his face in it.

"I don't know what you're waiting for," Fish began, watching him eat. "You've got to think of a way out of here. Those bars on the window wouldn't be hard to get through—they're only from a sheep pen."

"I was waiting for you," Liufu replied. "I knew you'd come."

"No, you were waiting for death. You could have . . ." She softened her tone. "I thought you'd break the bars on the window and come rushing out like a hero."

"They'd only drag me back here and put iron bars on the window."

This silenced Fish for a moment. "Your mother—"

"What is it?"

"Hunger."

"She won't go hungry. She always finds a way to get her hands on something."

"She fell into a pond. Only a shallow pond, but she didn't have the strength to crawl out."

"You mean my mother's . . . dead?" Liufu looked as if he were about to laugh.

"Nobody came to bury her. They cut all the flesh from her legs . . ." Fish seemed worried that her voice would bother people. "And . . . the schoolmaster drowned himself in the river an hour ago. People are dying one by one, falling like leaves."

Liufu found himself imagining falling leaves. He realized he'd never paid attention to how leaves fell from trees, just as he'd never imagined that death would have anything to do with him. It was as if he had only just realized that people could die, that simple, happy lives could suddenly end. He looked up at Fish uncertainly, as if she were the only person he could believe.

"It's the same in the water as in the mortal world. Big fish eat small fish, small fish eat shrimp. The powerful set the rules of the game, and the fish follow them. If I were as cowardly and compliant as you, I'd have died long ago." Fish spoke with a wisdom beyond her years. Nobody could know what trials she had endured in the world beneath the waves, what hardships and sorrows had befallen her as she grew from abandoned baby to mermaid.

It was remarkable that she should have such a kind and generous heart. When in thought, she looked like an old witch-woman; when excited, she looked like a tender young girl; happy, she was innocent and free of guile.

She sat down, a tender young girl again, and leaned against Liufu's shoulder. "Everyone knows the story of the emperor's new clothes, Liufu. You have to be the child who tells the truth."

———

The village looked as if it had been sketched roughly in pencil, spidery lines in slate and charcoal. There were no birds in the sky, no fowl on the ground.

Belly distended, pale, dazed, Poxy Niu wriggled on the ground like some ancient, inhuman creature. At the sight of Liufu, he forced himself to open his vacant eyes, open his mouth, and make an indistinct croak, like the bats under the eaves. His hair had gone hoarfrost gray, and he was monstrously bloated. He seemed to have been beaten senseless with something. Liufu could barely recognize the man.

"Y'eat yet?" had been their usual cheerful greeting; deprived of this opening line, they could only size each other up awkwardly.

That afternoon, Liufu had made his first attempts to escape the village. He drew near the exit several times, but shrank back, seeing guards at their posts. His heart beat out an irregular rhythm, pattering against the letter folded in his shirt pocket. The letter gave him a sense of calm but also of danger, as if it were part tranquilizer, part time bomb. He wished he could tell Poxy that he was doing something important.

"Y'eat?" Poxy settled on this after a long hesitation, and followed it with "I've got food at home, good food."

Poxy Niu having food at home was doubtful enough, but "good food" was still more startling. Liufu decided he would go there to lie low for a while before trying again to find a way out of the village after dark.

The two men walked quickly. The only sights along the way were the dry irrigation canals and the muddy ponds. The farmhouses were tightly boarded up for the most part. The open ones were deserted ruins without a sign of life.

Poxy Niu's home was another scene entirely: dim and gloomy, and surprisingly chilly. He was the only person living there; his wife and daughters had starved, one after another, leaving Poxy Niu to haunt his own house.

Closing the windows and doors tightly, Poxy Niu said he was all alone in the world now, with nobody to bury him when he died. He'd been a bad man and done bad things in the past, but he remembered his friends and he paid his debts.

There was no sign that he was grieving for his wife and daughters. He grew animated, in fact, making no attempt to cover his excitement at having someone to share his food with.

"Heard they locked you up. Went to the canteen to look for you, but you weren't there. I thought you were dead." Poxy Niu's love of chatter, at least, was undiminished. "You escape or something?"

"Jiazhen's father left a note saying he'd lied, that I was innocent . . . so they let me go."

"Long as you're alive. Won't have to worry about nobody burying me when I die." Poxy Niu smiled slyly. "Not that I'll ever die, mind you."

They walked into the cluttered kitchen. A brick stove took up two-thirds of the room. There were two burners on the stove: one was an empty hole; the other supported a lopsided, cracked wok. Poxy crouched down by the stove and shoved straw and kindling into it. Liufu caught a faint whiff of decay, and as he remembered what Fish had said, he was suddenly convinced that the man had stored his wife and daughters away and was eating them piece by piece.

His blood froze, and he kept his gaze tightly focused on Poxy's hands as he plotted his escape. There was a sudden flash of white flesh as Poxy dragged out a leg, straining against its weight, and the stench of rotting flesh became more pronounced.

Pale with fright, Liufu prepared to make his escape—only to see that the body Poxy Niu was hauling out had four legs. A dead pig.

"Found this lying around. Ought to last a while." Panting, Poxy produced a sharp knife. "It's your lucky day, boy."

Poxy drew his knife over the pig's belly, and a clutch of piglets tumbled out—an unexpected bonus, at the sight of which the speed of his butchering picked up happily. He counted: eight of them. He even laughed. Liufu's eyes lit up and his mouth watered, and he no longer even noticed the stench as he and Poxy Niu carved up the animals, slicing meat into the wok. A foul smell filled the room like fog, but neither man paid any attention to it.

"Can't light the fire until it's dark out. Hang on a little longer, boy." Poxy flopped down on the ground, exhausted. "If we had some wine, we'd be set for a New Year's feast."

The light outside the window was already growing dusky. The prospect of a feast of pork drove away the darkness of hunger, like the light of a full moon. A great sense of contentment came over Liufu, and he prayed that it would soon be too dark to see his hands in front of his face, so that they could safely light the cooking fire.

The night was as black as ink, and it flooded over everything like water. Wordlessly, nervously, excitedly, the two men stoked the fire and boiled the meat. The firelight danced, and the aroma of cooking meat rose with the clouds of steam that came from the wok. They couldn't help but taste it as it cooked, and by the time the pork was done, they were already full.

Several times, Liufu brushed against the letter in his chest pocket and thought how wrong Poxy Niu had been to abandon his daughter all those years ago. Fish was the perfect woman—or the perfect mermaid! If he were to tell Poxy, who didn't believe in spirits, that Fish existed, the man would only take it as more crazy talk in a world that had gone crazy. Liufu would only tell Poxy about the letter, he decided. But first—an idea came to him, and he filled a bowl with boiled pork and hurried to Jiazhen's house under cover of darkness.

———

He could just make out the chalky gray path under his feet. The darkness was like a wall. From time to time he saw pricks of lamplight like distant will-o'-

the-wisps. Liufu felt as if he were walking in a gigantic cemetery. He thought back to the village as it had been in summer, the paddies swollen with rice, how he had sweated in the paddies so that he would be able to marry Fish. The harvest had been far beyond anything he could have imagined, and the villagers had suffered more than in any lean year ever before. He had never stopped to think about it before; it had all been simply too much for him to comprehend. It was Fish who had prompted him. Not to follow her plan, not to clutch at any chance of survival, was no different from awaiting execution in a time when people were falling like leaves in autumn. And if he were to die like that, what would Fish think of him? He didn't want that. The letter in his shirt pocket warmed him now. It was a seed of hope, one that he would soon plant.

Liufu thought of the old schoolmaster's suicide note as he walked, and he began to worry about Jiazhen. Her house was dark now, and he assumed she must be sleeping to distract herself from the hunger. He hesitated a while before knocking on the door, which opened to reveal Jiazhen holding a kerosene lamp that gave off a faint, flickering light that made her features glow. She moved as unsteadily as the shadows it cast, but her sense of smell was as sharp as ever, and she instantly understood why Liufu had come. She opened the door to let him in, then closed and barred it behind him before eating the finest meal of her life.

"You were right, Jiazhen. Someone has to tell the truth. I'll risk it—I have to try." Liufu withdrew a thick envelope from his shirt pocket. "I'm going to slip out of the village tonight while it's dark and mail this from the township post office."

It might have been the dim light, but he had a hard time understanding the mix of emotions that played over Jiazhen's face. The thrill of having her hunger satisfied remained, however, and she hastily wiped the grease from her lips and drew closer to read the letter.

"You're writing to the *governor*?" she asked, startled.

Liufu nodded solemnly. "You sign at the bottom, too. A joint letter."

"Who'd have thought it, Liufu!" Jiazhen laughed.

Liufu wanted to say that it had been Fish's idea, but he stopped, keeping the sweet thought of his mermaid to himself.

"Staying silent means death," he said. "Speaking out means death. Both mean death—but they're not the same thing at all." Fish's words.

"When you send this, we'll have something to hope for. The sentries at the village gate are armed—be careful."

Liufu tucked the letter back into his shirt pocket and was preparing to leave when he saw torches burning in the distance, at Poxy Niu's house. He and Jiazhen ran, but by the time they arrived, it was almost over. The men from the anti-hoarding squad had carried the rotting sow out of the house. Poxy

Niu had been beaten for "theft of public property," and he lay there, his face covered in blood, his body shaking, the ground around him covered with the vomit of his last meal.

They carried him inside, but Liufu saw a red bubble emerge from the corner of his mouth and heard him draw his last breath.

"He really *must* have been worried there'd be nobody to bury him," Liufu said. "Had to make sure he died before I left."

"Give me the letter," said Jiazhen. "I'll send it."

———

Death could be no darker than that night was. The kerosene lamp dispelled the gloom, casting a bright world of its own. As Liufu cleaned up Poxy Niu's body, he imagined the man's ghost meeting Fish, at last having a chance to be a father to his daughter, his sins forgiven, in that other world. Liufu didn't know how things worked in that world, or how many other worlds there might be besides this mortal one, but he hoped that death might be the beginning of happier things. For his mother, too.

He dozed after the sky grew light, and dreamed that he saw Fish in a gown of white lace, her black hair dripping past her shoulders, painting her lips with the water for a mirror. She said she'd seen her father, that he was preparing for her wedding. She said he had slaughtered pigs and sheep for a huge three-day wedding feast, to which all the villagers were invited.

He woke up happy. The dream had kindled his appetite. He went to look for something to eat, but the kitchen had been picked clean, and the bowls shattered on the floor for good measure. A faint whiff of cooked pork seemed to linger in the air. Holding his hunger in check, Liufu took up an iron spade and went to dig a hole in the back yard. A wind whistled down from the north, sweeping up fallen leaves and dust.

By noon he had laid Poxy Niu in the ground and heaped fresh earth over him.

Death hadn't been such a lonely thing before. In his mind, Liufu lit firecrackers and boiled rich porridge, watched scraps of red paper fly through clouds of blue smoke, a raucous, busy banquet. But before him there were only withered trees and dry earth, and Liufu suddenly felt lonelier even than the dead man. Tired and hungry after his half-day of labor, he thought about lying down next to the grave and keeping Poxy Niu company for a while, until he realized that there had still been no sign of Jiazhen. He rose slowly, propping himself up on the spade. He went to Jiazhen's house first, but there was nobody there; then to the entrance of the village, where he gazed beyond the security line, down toward the township as far as his eyes could see. He almost asked the sentries if they had seen her. He tried to walk out, but the sentries shouted for him to turn back.

Jiazhen had not returned. For the next three days, there was no trace of her.

At a loss, Liufu spent his days pacing up and down the bank of the river, his eyes shut against the cold wind.

Fish had vanished. When he thought back to the nights he had spent with her, Liufu couldn't be sure that she had ever been there at all, and he began to wonder if he had simply imagined it after reading *Strange Tales* too many times. But he remembered icy kisses, slippery skin, and a voice like water.

Liufu was dizzy and blurry-eyed with hunger. There was a ringing in his ears, and he could no longer be sure what was real and what was hallucination. The world in which he lived became ever more insubstantial.

At night he played the beam of his flashlight over the water listlessly, unsure whether he was looking for Fish or only for fish. He thought he might fall to the ground and give up at any moment from the hunger and the cold. At a sudden glimpse of a pale fish back in the water, his stomach reflexively ordered his body to hurl his fishing spear with every ounce of strength it had. He reached out, grabbed the spear tightly, and pulled it from the water to reveal a fish the size of a human infant. Blood dripped from it. It was stiff with cold, barely moving. Its tail was curled like a person bent over with an aching stomach, and its body trembled.

"Keep . . . sending out letters . . ." The fish's mouth opened and closed, and Liufu heard Fish's voice, faint and wet.

The Balcony

By Ren Xiaowen

TRANSLATED BY ELEANOR GOODMAN

The air smelled of trash. A dead rat lay pasted to the middle of the road, flattened by car wheels. The rain washed garbage from the nooks and crannies, and it collected on the sewer grates—plastic bags, wrapping paper, wutong leaves, disposable containers—their wet surfaces reflecting the dawn.

A pair of flip-flops squeaked. With every step Zhang Yingxiong took, the bottoms of his feet slipped a bit against the plastic soles. He turned and caught sight of Lu Shanshan. She was near the frybread vendor's cart, holding a transparent plastic pouch stuffed with what looked like hundred-yuan bills. Zhang put his hand in his pocket and fingered his switchblade. He walked half a meter behind Lu Shanshan, pretending to watch as the vendor sprinkled on sesame seeds, shaking the jar like dice so they scattered over the half-burnt, scallion-dotted frybread.

Lu Shanshan leaned her head forward to bite into the fry bread. It shattered, and crumbs tumbled down her front. She repeatedly brushed off her mouth and clothing. Zhang followed right behind as she crossed the street and stopped in front of an iron gate to an alley. She pushed at the gate but it didn't open. She stood there and focused on eating her frybread. Zhang pretended to swat at a fly, grabbing at the air with his left hand and flicking with his right, while he made sure there was no one else around. He held the switchblade in his pocket, feeling its shape, rubbing it against his pant leg, as he walked toward her.

Everyone said that Zhang Yingxiong had grown into an elegant young man. His father, Zhang Suqing, would retort: "Elegant my ass. He's like an embroidered pillowcase over a bag of straw." Zhang Suqing liked to set up a small table by the door with a pot of braised pork and three bottles of erguotou, and he would make his son sit there with him.

Zhang Yingxiong gulped down a shot of liquor, and his face turned red.

"You worthless shit." Zhang Suqing made a fist and thrust out his arm. "Here, get a load of this."

Zhang poked at the arm with his finger.

"What do you think?"

"Hard as a rock."

"With muscles like these, nobody's going to try anything with me."

After they'd had quite a bit to drink, Zhang Suqing would grab his son from behind by the armpits, trying to swing him as though he were still a child. Sometimes, still unhappy despite all his drinking, he would slap Zhang Yingxiong on the side of his head—*wham wham wham*—until his glasses flew off. Zhang Yingxiong would run away and squat down to look for his glasses, pretending that he couldn't find them. Zhang Suqing would soon forget that he was angry and propose a loud toast: "Son, come have some meat!"

Zhang Yingxiong's mother, Feng Xiujuan, urged him to not to eat too much meat, but Zhang Suqing told her: "Who says eating meat isn't healthy? Chairman Mao ate meat his whole life, and he lived to be more than eighty years old. I won't last that long, but I'll at least make it to seventy."

The pork was greasy, covered in soy sauce and stewed until the flavor was overwhelming. There was also a plate of sweet-and-sour fish. A stray cat caught scent of it, and it started to meow frantically and jumped up onto the windowsill, scratching at the window railings. Zhang Suqing stuck his chopsticks into the fish and teased the cat, jabbing the fishy tips of the chopsticks at its eyes. "Worthless shit, he won't even catch rats for me." He spoke as though he were lecturing another son.

The old Zhang residence went back to Zhang Suqing's grandfather's generation. The rats that lived in the sewers were fine specimens, indolent and completely unafraid of people. One of them ran along the foot of the wall, starting and stopping, at first glance looking like a windblown ball of fuzz. Ants had colonized the ground, the concrete was sticky, and a bluish mildew grew all over the backs of the furniture. Zhang Yingxiong was often startled awake by rainstorms, as the rain would seep through the roof to drip onto his face and *ting* into the dishes left on the table from the night before.

Zhang Suqing would say: "Zhang Yingxiong, that worthless shit—he can't even buy his old man a new place."

The neighborhood's few dozen two-story buildings formed a little valley surrounded on all sides by high-rises. Zhang Yingxiong often went up to the top of one of the high-rises to look down at his home. It was a mess of tiled roofs, and underwear, strips of meat, and rags were hung out to dry on the electrical wires. The cheap green corrugated PVC roof panels were scratched and faded gray from being exposed to the elements. Under the awnings were the backsides of air conditioners and little ads for ID cards written in red paint. The white sign with black lettering, "Old Yu's Barbershop," belonged to the Zhangs' next-door neighbor. Old Yu would cut Zhang Yingxiong's hair and hack at his sideburns, and as he helped him up from the stool, he would say with a laugh, "Kid, I really shouldn't take your money." Zhang would pull a ten-yuan bill from his pocket. Old Yu would resist for a moment, then take it.

Old Yu's younger daughter's husband was the head of the neighborhood tourism bureau. Zhang Suqing said to him: "Old Yu, when are you going to help us out? I'd like to take a trip or two, see America."

Old Yu said with a smile: "He doesn't do America, just this neighborhood."

"What's there to see in our neighborhood—a bunch of old hovels?"

Old Yu laughed and brushed a towel across his leg. It was the towel he used for washing feet and shaving heads.

Last December there'd been a rumor that they all might have to move. At first only a few people were talking about it, then everyone was. Men and women, wringing their hands, hunching their shoulders, gossiping under the eaves. Word was that a Hong Kong businessman had bought their land for three hundred million yuan, and then it was said that it wasn't three hundred million, it was one billion.

Zhang Suqing had grown hoarse from talking so much, so he'd gone to bed and only talked to Feng Xiujuan. He wanted to buy a new place in Baoshan, ideally right on the subway line. Feng Xiujuan said: "You were laid off, I'm retired, why do we need the subway? I just work temporary jobs now, and I can get everywhere by bicycle."

Zhang Suqing said: "Hey, son, what kind of place would you get?"

After he'd been asked twice, Zhang answered with an irritating sluggishness, "Doesn't matter so long as it has a toilet."

Zhang Suqing said: "That's all you can hope for, you worthless shit."

He started chattering at his wife again, and the more he talked, the more worked up he got. He called his sister Zhang Sujie. She said: "The first thing you need to think about is getting a decent relocation compensation fee. If money's tight, you won't be able to buy any kind of apartment at all." Zhang Suqing hung up on her and waited until she called back. Then they continued to discuss the matter for more than an hour.

The next morning at dawn, Zhang Suqing hurried to the police station. At 8:30, the officer working the window at the Residence Permit Bureau sauntered in. She'd gone to the bathroom, made some tea, and straightened up her desk, and now she squinted at him and asked, "What do you want?" As soon as she heard he wanted to change his residence permit, she said: "That service is frozen for this area."

"There's no way to do it? No way at all?" Zhang Suqing pestered her fruitlessly for a while, then stalked to the corner, scratching his scalp ferociously until it hurt. He left to find a convenience store, and he had to go to seven or eight in order to buy three packs of Zhonghua cigarettes. He went back to the police station to find that the officer had gone out to lunch. When she finally came back at 2:30, Zhang Suqing pressed against her window and passed the cigarettes through.

"What's this for?" the officer said, looking nervously at her coworkers to either side. "Take them back, take them back!"

"Help me out, comrade!"

The officer pushed the cigarettes back out, then stared at her computer screen, refusing to look at him. Zhang Suqing sat dejectedly on a bench by the door, watching the people coming in and out. Then his eyes caught on a silk banner hanging on the opposite wall. It said in gold characters: "Our gratitude to comrade Zhang Yingxiong for his great public service." Zhang Suqing's heart skipped a beat, but when he looked at it again, he saw that it said "Zhang Yinghao" and not "Zhang Yingxiong." He slumped back in disappointment, resting the boxes of cigarettes on his thigh, twisting his white gloves between his fingers.

When three o'clock rolled around, he was so hungry he went out for a bowl of noodle soup, then slowly made his way home. At the entrance to the alley, he bumped into Zhang Yugen. "Have you applied for a new residence permit?" he asked her.

"There's no time to do it now. We're planning to clean up the old pigeon coop and put a bed in it."

"That's illegal."

"We've made good with the right people, and calculated the living space. You can come over and have some pigeon with us."

"No thanks."

"Pigeon is very nutritious. Besides, we can't eat a whole pigeon coop's worth of meat—it'll go to waste."

"Nutritious my ass."

"Hey, why are you pissed at me? Do you know how many new residence permits Old Yu got? Eight."

Zhang Suqing turned and headed to Old Yu's house. He banged on the door. Someone called from inside: "Who is it?"

"Me."

"What is it?"

"You didn't bother to fucking tell me? What kind of man are you?"

"Tell you what?"

"That you got so many new residence permits—why didn't you tell me?"

"I didn't get any permits."

"You get yourself eight permits and you still say you didn't get any! Why didn't you tell me?"

"Residence permits are a matter of timing. If you wait until you've heard something, it's already too late. You shouldn't blame other people just because you didn't plan ahead."

"Am I blaming you? I'm just mad at you for not telling me what you knew."

"I told you, I don't know anything."

"If you didn't know anything, why did you apply for new residence permits?"

"Everyone has to figure this stuff out for himself."

"If you don't know anything, how can you figure it out?"

There was only silence from within the Yu house, cutting off the argument. Zhang Suqing beat at the door: "Come out here and talk to me face to face."

"It's chilly out. I have a cold."

Zhang Suqing grabbed the "Old Yu's Barbershop" sign and furiously ripped a hole in it before he went home. He couldn't eat a thing, and instead opened a pack of Zhonghua cigarettes and lit one up. "Damn it, that convenience store sold me fakes." He smoked one after another.

Feng Xiujuan said: "Fake or not, you spent real money on it. How can you stand to smoke such expensive stuff?"

Zhang Suqing said: "A new residence permit costs a few hundred thousand kuai. That would buy a truckload of Zhonghua cigarettes."

"What are we going to do?"

"If you have to ask that, what is there to do?"

When he was done smoking, he lay down in bed depressed, his head pounding. When he got back up, his fingers were numb. After a while he couldn't stand it anymore, and he went to the local emergency room, where they found that his blood pressure was up to 160. He was prescribed an imported medication for hypertension that cost more than three hundred yuan. He crumpled up the prescription. "This poor life isn't worth that much."

After the Spring Festival, the neighborhood Razing and Relocation Subcommittee sent someone door to door to talk to the residents. Her name was Qian Li, and she wore a black-and-white acrylic cap that revealed her stiff reddened earlobes. Every night at seven, she came and knocked on the door. There was a rumor that after the houses were torn down, a public park was to be built in their place. "As for you," she said, rifling through her papers, "you'll receive three hundred and fifty thousand yuan!"

"Highway robbery!" Zhang Suqing pounded the table. Qian Li flinched back and unconsciously raised her arm in defense. Feng Xiujuan pressed Zhang Suqing's hand.

"Think about it. I'll be back tomorrow."

The next night at seven o'clock, she returned and knocked on the door. Zhang Suqing didn't let Zhang Yingxiong answer. Qian Li called out crisply: "Sir, open the door. I'm begging you, help me do my job." Feng Xiujuan sighed and stood up. Zhang Suqing said: "What are you doing?" She sat back down. No sound came from outside the door. Zhang Suqing said: "It has to be this way."

By spring they had all moved out, one by one, leaving behind empty rooms and a pile of rumors. It was said that Old Yu had received eight million yuan, had bought himself a place with three bedrooms and two living rooms in the center of the city, and was living a high-class life. It was said that Zhang Yugen had secretly slipped the surveyor five thousand yuan, and the pigeon coop had been measured three square meters larger than it really was.

"Did you have some of their pigeons?"

"Who wants to eat their pigeons?"

"Exactly. They were all droopy-headed and sickly anyway."

"One time I got a new shirt, and the first time I washed it and hung it out to dry, it got covered in pigeon shit. I told him he should compensate me for it, and he refused. We should've told him to leave before; raising pigeons in that nasty shed, it's all illegal. The people who suffer are always the good law-abiding folks like us."

Zhang Suqing couldn't resist listening to every last rumor. Afterward, he couldn't eat a thing and instead drank himself to within an inch of his life. He called his relatives, friends, old classmates, and one after another they told him: "It's over. We're just ordinary folks, too, there's nothing we can do." Zhang Suqing said: "Goddamn it, if I had a section chief for a son-in-law, I'd be sitting pretty, too." Sometimes he hit Zhang Yingxiong, saying: "You worthless shit, at your age you still eat your parents' food, still depend on us for everything. If you had any prospects at all, we wouldn't be in this mess."

One night, Zhang Suqing was awakened from his drunken stupor by the sound of knocking at the door. "Don't open it," he ordered his wife. The knocking continued for more than twenty minutes, fast and slow, loud and soft, without stopping. Zhang Suqing tossed and turned, then rose with a groan.

Outside the door was a skinny middle-aged man. "I'm Mr. Lu, head of the Razing and Relocation Subcommittee for parcel 52-3." He waved an ID.

Zhang Suqing steadied himself with both hands, filling the entire doorway. "What do you want?"

"I've come to talk with you."

"It's the middle of the night, can't you let a man sleep?"

"Miss Qian comes every day, but you won't open the door. It hasn't been easy for her."

"There's no one here during the day."

"Which is why I've come. Someone's home at night."

His name was Lu Zhiqiang, Zhang Suqing saw as he carefully examined the ID card. He said a few times: "I'm not going to forget you." But no matter how much Zhang Suqing blustered, Lu Zhiqiang spoke slowly and softly. He spread his papers over the table, pulled out a calculator, and tapped in some numbers. "Four hundred fifty thousand. That's my best offer."

"What can anybody do with that? You can't even buy a bathroom for that much."

"We're just following regulations. Whatever amount comes out, that's the amount."

"So how come my neighbor Mr. Yu got so much money?"

"How do you know how much he got? You shouldn't listen to gossip."

Zhang Suqing lowered his voice and said: "Cut me a little slack, okay? I'm asking nicely. You can't live on that amount of money."

"What do you mean, you can't live on it? You have a Shanghai residence permit, you have a house, a pension, a wife and child. You can just sit around drinking all day. Think of the recent grads who weren't born in Shanghai, like Qian Li. Her parents are farmers in the countryside. She doesn't have any relatives here, and she makes about a thousand kuai a month. You don't even know how much better off you are."

"I have a family, of course I have to have a house. And if I lose my house, I'll make a complaint. I'm warning you."

"There are 1.3 billion people in this country. If people file complaints about every little thing, how can the country possibly keep up? We have legal policies, we have to do things by the law, that's the basis for administering a country."

Lu Zhiqiang pulled out a stack of pamphlets titled *Foundations for Administering a Country* and handed Zhang Suqing the one called "Rules and Regulations for the Compensation for Razing and Relocation." Zhang Suqing flipped through a few pages, then tossed it aside. He continued to argue, sometimes pounding on the table and sometimes passing over water and cigarettes. Lu Zhiqiang pulled out his calculator again, punching in numbers as he explained his methods of calculation. The final number came to 42.742.

"Qian Li said three hundred fifty thousand, which is in strict accordance with the regulations. I'm giving you a break and counting that big sink outside the door as part of your living area, and then I'm rounding up. Is four hundred and fifty thousand yuan a small number? Your pension can't be that much."

Zhang Suqing lifted the calculator up in the air and stared at him fiercely. Lu Zhiqiang held his hands out, fearing he might suddenly smash it on the ground. Zhang Suqing put the calculator down and went back to bed. Feng Xiujuan followed him. Zhang Yingxiong turned his head under the covers to spy on Lu Zhiqiang. From that vantage point, he looked like a teacher correcting papers, with his brow furrowed and pen in hand, deciding whether to pass or fail a student. Finally, he drew a thick line across the paper, collected his things, and left.

The next day, Zhang Suqing woke up early and sat on the edge of the bed in a daze. "Feng Xiujuan, get me a hot water bottle, my stomach hurts."

"You drink and drink and then your stomach hurts. What are we going to do?" She filled a hot water bottle and sealed the top.

After a while, Zhang Suqing said: "I feel awful. I'm going to sleep a little longer."

He slept until five in the afternoon. Feng Xiujuan was cooking dinner when she heard him suddenly cry out: "I'm dying! I'm dying!" She dropped her spatula to go look and found him tearing at his collar and gasping loudly. She rubbed his chest and said: "I'll call an ambulance." As they were waiting, she massaged and comforted him, and finally cradled his head against her body. She thought of when her water had broken twenty-two years ago, how as they were going to the hospital in the back of a pedicab, he had held her the same way. She caressed his face, the soft flesh and rough stubble. She caressed his hair, that white hair that bent under her hand like grass rippling in the wind. And against her chest, Zhang Suqing suddenly went quiet.

————

After Zhang Suqing died from a heart attack, Feng Xiujuan signed the agreement to have their house torn down, and they moved in temporarily with her brother Feng Baogang. She told Zhang Yingxiong: "Don't ever forget that bastard, Lu Zhiqiang."

Zhang Yingxiong couldn't sleep. He kept picturing Lu Zhiqiang. One of Lu's eyelids had a single fold, the other a double fold. When he spoke, the eye with the single fold kept wandering. He wore a blue-and-gray checkered sweater, and the hand that hung from the sleeve was small and white like a woman's.

Feng Xiujuan told Zhang Yingxiong to go look for work. He said: "Mom, you don't understand how it is. There are college graduates everywhere, and even the ones from famous universities can't find a job, let alone someone like me from a technical school."

Feng Xiujuan said: "Didn't you go to night school to study English? It shouldn't have anything to do with education; hard work is what matters."

"Mom, no one cares about hard work anymore. You can give it your all and still not be able to buy a house, and then no woman will want you."

"Why would you say such things? Are you trying to hurt me?"

Zhang Yingxiong couldn't stand to see his mother cry, so he turned his head and grunted, "Huh." The next morning at seven o'clock, his mother woke him up. He ate some rice porridge, put on a white shirt and imitation-leather shoes, and went out to look for a job. The clear sunlight was scattered by the morning breezes and settled on the pedestrians. They were all carrying bags and chewing their breakfasts with furrowed brows as they hurried forward, unaware of their own glimmering beauty.

Zhang wasted the morning in an Internet café, ate lunch at a little noodle shop, then decided to go see the old house. The temporary office for the Razing and Relocation Subcommittee that had been set up at the alleyway entrance had already disappeared. A red banner with white letters still hung between electrical poles: "To show good sense is honorable; to complain is shameful." Tall buildings silently encircled the pile of ruins: hemp ropes, cloth, cotton batting, crushed bricks, broken concrete flooring, national flags. Weeds sprouted from crevices, withered and yellow from lack of nourishment. Someone had set up a bamboo frame and was airing out clothes over the bricks and tiles. A man with long hair was kneeling in front of a broken window frame, taking pictures with an enormous camera.

Zhang wiped away a few tears and went back to the Internet café to play "League of Legends." He'd killed a lot of monsters, but was still progressing slowly. Someone who had no money to buy pearls of knowledge or diamonds of protection was destined to be insignificant even in the virtual world. Zhang "died" again. He rubbed his shoulders, rolled his neck, and went off to find something to eat. It was already dark outside. As he walked, he lost his appetite and slowed to a stop, not knowing where to go. On the roof of the market across the street was a large advertisement showing a family of three. They were close together, their mouths open with laughter, and their teeth looked like rows of corn. The young mother was holding a tube of toothpaste, and next to her was written "Family Love Toothpaste: Your whole family will love it."

Zhang stared at those enormous teeth, feeling like nothing was real. A fat little man hurrying past bumped into him and scolded: "Idiot, standing in the middle of the road!" Then a girl brushed past him: "I'll be there in a minute. You all start without me." Hanging from her ear was the thin cord of a cell phone earpiece, but it seemed at first like she was talking to herself.

Zhang thought to send his mother a message, but as he felt in his pocket, he realized he had forgotten his cell phone. He walked into a convenience store and saw a public telephone by the cash register. But he didn't want to call anymore, and instead asked for a pack of cigarettes. At that moment, a voice behind him said: "A bottle of yogurt. Ring it up for me." Zhang's heart jumped. He stepped aside, pretending to look for money in his pocket. Lu Zhiqiang glanced at him, lifted the dripping bottle of yogurt, and left.

"Forget the cigarettes," Zhang said to the cashier. He ran out, searched left and right, and fixed his eyes on that gray-and-white checkered jacket. He crossed two streets, turned left, turned left again, and walked into an old state-owned building complex. He stared at the windows in the hallway as they gradually lit up, and a tendon in his knee started to pulse. A guard with a truncheon at his waist appeared from somewhere. Zhang met his eye, then left.

It was already eleven when he got back to his uncle's house. His cousin was still out on the balcony studying. His aunt came out of the bathroom, twisting her wet hair between her hands: "We've been waiting for you." His uncle Feng Baogang said, "It's late. Do you have anything to say for yourself?" Zhang muttered something. Feng Baogang's house had one bedroom and a living room. Zhang's cousin slept on the balcony, his aunt and uncle slept in the bedroom, Feng Xiujuan slept on the sofa in the living room, and Zhang Yingxiong made a bed on the floor next to her.

Everyone said Zhang was like his uncle. Feng Baogang had a long, thin face and wore gold-plated glasses. He was a middle-school politics teacher. "No, he isn't. How is he like me?" Feng Baogang responded the first time he heard someone say they looked alike. After a while, he just pretended not to hear, and would turn away so as not to look at his nephew.

Feng Xiujuan lowered her voice and said: "Forget about what the others will say. Really, where did you go?" She dug her nails into Zhang's arm, and although it didn't hurt, he began to cry.

She whispered to him: "Have a little pride. Your father never cried. Now, where did you really go?"

"I went to look for work."

"You're lying. How could you be out looking this late?" She raised a hand to slap him, then hesitated, and laid her hand lightly on his cheek. "There's no news from the Home Management Office, either. If things keep going like this, we won't have the money to pay your uncle rent."

Zhang opened his eyes wide and tried to speak.

She called: "Brother, tomorrow we'll figure out how much we owe you. I'm the type of person who always makes good."

There were a few coughs from the bedroom, from either his uncle or his aunt. Feng Xiujuan stopped talking and pulled her son into her arms, stroking his hair and rubbing his ears. Then she pointed to the floor, and Zhang Yingxiong obediently lay down.

The next morning, Feng Xiujuan woke her son. Breakfast was fried pork buns, and she had bought nearly a pound of them. Feng Baogang said: "Did you buy them at the place downstairs? Those traveling vendors all use that recycled gutter oil. You watch the news, right? You know about gutter oil, right?" His uncle's family all ate wheat rolls that came wrapped in plastic. He offered some to Feng Xiujuan, but she said: "We're having pork buns."

Zhang finished breakfast and was pushed out the door. He wandered along the street for a while, then took the bus to Lu Zhiqiang's building. He sat in the last row, taking up a lot of space with his legs spread and his hands clasped over his belly. The bus was oddly empty. Was it the weekend? He wanted to take out his cell phone to look at the date, but his eyelids were too heavy to open. The bus jolted and bumped along, and with each bump, the taste of pork buns returned to the back of his mouth: oil, onions, gravy. He felt quite content and drowsy, and for a while he forgot what he was about to do.

When he got off at the Fazhan Street stop, half of his rear end and a leg were asleep. Twenty meters north of the bus stop and through an iron gate was his old home. The iron gate had been put up two weeks before the buildings were knocked down: an unturnable turnstile. Zhang had once seen a middle-aged man get his bicycle stuck in the gate. People passing by cursed and competed to help him, but they just managed to force the bicycle further between the iron bars.

Zhang hesitated, not sure he wanted to see that pile of ruins again. He stopped in front of the iron gate for a moment, then turned around and went back the way he had come. He walked for ten minutes, his back starting to sweat, and then saw Lu Zhiqiang's building. It was an old six-story state-owned apartment block built like an army barracks, two solitary rows stuck between Fu'an Street and Funing Street where the two roads intersected at an angle. From the time he was a kid, Zhang had passed it too many times to count. Then he remembered that he was exhausted, and he began walking slowly along Fu'an Street. The cars honked their horns, spitting out exhaust from their tailpipes, passing him one after another. He and Lu Zhiqiang had probably crossed paths at just such a moment. But who would've noticed? Ahead was the vegetable market, where Feng Xiujuan often asked him to get onions and eggs. Sometimes he remembered and sometimes he forgot. On one side of the street was a row of vendors selling snacks, and the scent of the hot frying pans stopped pedestrians in their tracks. Zhang liked the rice-flour pancakes and fritters wrapped in fry-cakes. He carried his lunch across the street to the "Ottoman Internet Café." When it got dark, his cell phone began vibrating nonstop at his waist. It was Feng Xiujuan urging him to come home for dinner. He closed his phone, paid his bill, and started for home.

Only once had Zhang Yingxiong noticed those two rows of apartments through the dense scaffolding. The wall of the apartment block facing the street had just been painted pink. Why hadn't the other three sides been painted? He was curious, but too lazy to think about it.

This time, Zhang stopped in front of the building. The pink side had gotten dirty and turned gray. A banner hung halfway up the building: "The city makes life even better!" A new two-meter-tall Haibao cartoon figure stood next to the building. Something that looked a lot like a dishrag was hung out to dry on his outstretched arm, making him look like a big blue waiter.

Fu'an Street was paved with asphalt and stone. A yellow-and-black-striped construction barricade was blocking the sidewalk, forcing bicycles to go around. No one had thought to move it aside. The fast lane had been separated off by a new silver-colored iron guardrail. Periwinkle flowers, lily turf, and tawny daylily were growing in the divider; their leaves and branches had gotten covered with silver paint, which in the mornings sparkled in the sunlight.

Zhang went around to the back of the building. Every entrance was protected by a security grate. The night before, Lu Zhiqiang had entered the door marked 12. Below the number hung two metal signs: "No Parking" and "No Peddlers or Scavengers Allowed." Zhang retreated a few steps and leaned against a car. It was a black Citroën, with a rounded front and top. He wanted to scratch it, or mess with it somehow. But he only thought about it. An older woman wearing a silky turquoise sweat suit, two red dance fans stuck under her armpits, came out of number 12. He scurried forward and stopped the door from closing.

In the building, there were two apartments on each level, and each door had an iron grille. The corridors were littered with brooms, mops, bicycles, and open trash bags. Zhang guessed that Lu Zhiqiang probably lived on the top floor, though he had no reason to think that. He climbed up five flights of stairs, panting a bit. He stopped and pressed himself against the wall. Thinking of how close Lu Zhiqiang was, he heard his own bones clacking against each other. On the sixth floor, the two apartments obviously belonged to the same family, since it was the stairway exit that was blocked off by an iron grille. The corridor was painted a honeycombed red-and-white mosaic pattern, and a heavy walnut armoire stood on the side. One of the armoire doors was inlaid with a full-length mirror, and in it, Zhang Yingxiong saw an image of his own reckless self. A woman wearing fleece pajamas opened the door marked 601 and crossed over to 602. She caught sight of Zhang and thrust out her awl-shaped chin at him: "Who are you looking for?"

"Lu . . . Zhiqiang. Is Lu Zhiqiang at home?"

"Who's Lu Zhiqiang?"

"Your neighbor?"

"I don't know any Lu Zhiqiang. Now get out of here, or I'll yell for help." She banged on the iron grille.

Zhang Yingxiong flew back down the stairs, stumbling several times. That damn Lu Zhiqiang had hidden himself behind some peephole. Zhang hurried outside and heaved a breath. The round-headed Citroën squinted at him with one headlight. He kicked it angrily, then took off running.

Funing Street had just been designated a commercial entertainment street. A big plastic arch stood at the entrance, adorned with multicolored light bulbs. One side of the arch sported a neon coffee cup, the other a high-heeled shoe. At nightfall, the steam rising from the cup and the butterfly bow on the shoe began to glow. Some of the storefronts were still being renovated, and the cloth that was spread out to catch stray paint and debris said in English: "New World Entertainment Street: Opening Soon."

Construction had begun on the entertainment street before Zhang Ying-xiong had moved. That sort of place is a rip-off, Feng Xiujuan had told him. They'll sell you a slice of bread for more than ten kuai, and it doesn't even taste as good as a steamed bun you can get for a kuai and a half. Zhang went into a bakery and saw that they sold a little round loaf for four and a half kuai. He bought one and took a small bite. But he wasn't really hungry, just a bit thirsty.

For every shop selling clothes or accessories, there were two selling food and drink. The restaurants all had "Help Wanted" signs on their doors, looking for wait staff, dishwashers, cooks, hostesses. Zhang went into a fast-food place called "Good 'n Fast." The renovation odor was strong, and he coughed a few times before he got used to it. He ordered a cup of soymilk and sat down by the windows. He suddenly realized that just across the way was an old state-owned building. He leaned out the window and saw to his surprise that the number on the door was 12. He hurried out, his head pounding and hot. It was only ten meters away—if he threw a stone, he could break the glass or even hit someone inside. A waiter came over and said, "Hey." Zhang sat back down, holding his cup with both hands, breathing hard. The soymilk had cooled, and it felt astringent against his tongue.

That night at ten, Zhang left the Internet café, went over to the building marked 12, and pressed the door buzzers one after another. "Is Lu Zhiqiang there?"

One answered, "Who?" One said, "Hello? Hello?" One said, "Wrong house." One didn't answer, and one just hung up. When he pressed the buzzer marked 302, it was silent for a few seconds, then a girl's voice delicately called: "Dad."

Building 12, apartment 302. Zhang Yingxiong lay in bed trying to think back, but he couldn't think of anything distinctive about that apartment. Some of the doors had upside-down "Wealth" signs, some had "Cultured Family" signs, and one door had two cat eyes that stared at him balefully. None of those were 302. He decided not to think about it, since anyway Lu Zhiqiang couldn't escape. He would hide in the corner, and when Lu came out, he would deal him a deathblow. And as Lu's blood spurted out, the heavens would turn red. He would stand amid fountains of pouring blood, heroic and exalted. No, that was too easy. He should torture Lu first, just like in the movies, the way the arrested underground Communist Party members were tortured. Do you know what it means to cry? How did they treat you at first? Have you thought about what it's like for us? . . . Zhang tossed in bed, his mouth dry. Only when he heard his aunt get up to go to the bathroom did he return to reality, as though awakening from a dream. Daybreak came quickly, and he was awakened by Feng Xiujuan. He ate some rice porridge and left.

Zhang sat in the Good 'n Fast. The apartment facing the window, was it 301 or 302? He thought back to the arrangement of the building floors, and concluded that it was indeed Lu Zhiqiang's apartment. The balcony had concrete walls and composite aluminum windows hung with red and yellow curtains. A girl came out onto the balcony, opened the washing machine, and started to hang clothing up to dry on a line outside the window. Lu Zhiqiang's gray-and-white checkered jacket flapped between a bra and some underwear. Zhang fixed it with a marksman's gaze. The girl closed the window, sat down at a table, and began to embroider. She had inherited Lu's round face, and her hair was pulled back with a plastic clip.

Zhang went to the restaurant office to find the manager and told him he wanted to work as a server.

The manager's name was Mr. Luo. "We don't hire Shanghainese."

"I'm not asking for benefits. I used to work at a convenience store, and they didn't give benefits."

"Well, you'd have to write it into the contract that you don't want benefits."

Manager Luo interrogated him about his work experience, home address, and schooling, and said: "We pay eight hundred a month during the probation period, then regular wages are a thousand. That includes food and lodging, but since you're Shanghainese, it won't include lodging."

The next afternoon at four o'clock, Zhang Yingxiong went to the restaurant, filled out the forms, and gave them his ID. Then he followed Shen Zhong around. Shen was from Fujian and had lived in Shanghai for three years. His hair was dyed a yellowish red, and his fingernails were each a centimeter long. He had worked at Good 'n Fast for a year, and a month before had been transferred to the new branch.

Shen taught him how to promote their new value meal: "The profits are good, but it won't sell if you don't push it. Thirty percent of people will think about it, ten percent will buy it . . ." Then a customer came in, and he left Zhang on his own.

Zhang watched Shen take the customer's money. He watched a waitress named Yan put the meal together. In her haste, she spilled some soup. Zhang went to help her, and she said in alarm: "Don't mess with anything. I'll do it."

By eight that night, there were no more customers.

Shen said: "You, Zhang, mop the floor."

Little Yan said: "The short mop and the long mop both need to be washed. They haven't been washed in a long time."

Shen said: "Just don't use too much water."

The mop had hardened into a slab. The window by the janitor's sink in the men's room faced building 12 at an angle. On the balcony of apartment 302, the round-faced girl was still doing her embroidery. The furniture was all from the eighties. A man was leaning over a desk, his white hair swirled around a bald spot. Zhang stared intently at him, ruthlessly plunging the mop into the sink. The wood handle stabbed his chest painfully.

Cleaning was finished at nine. Little Yan leaned idly against the wall, examining her fingernails. Shen played with his cell phone. Zhang saw his reflection in the window and started. His cheeks had sunk in, like caves.

Shen said: "Hey, got a cigarette?"

"No."

"What are you waiting for? Go get some."

Zhang went out to buy a pack of Double Pleasure. Shen said: "Fuck. These are peasant smokes." Zhang opened the window. The embroidery girl was nowhere to be seen.

He got off work at eleven, and by then the last bus had already left. He waited by the side of the road. A motorbike came by.

"Where do you live?" The voice was muffled by a helmet. It was Shen Zhong.

Shen rented a place with a few other people, about a twenty-minute walk from work. He'd bought a Suzuki motorbike with a borrowed rural residence permit and gotten a yellow C license plate. With that kind of license, he wasn't allowed to drive in the city, so he only drove at night.

"You must have a lot of money, to buy a motorbike," Zhang said. He got off the back of the bike and found that his knees wouldn't straighten.

"Coward. You practically broke my back, clinging to me like that." Shen's voice was hoarse. He'd been drag racing, and he'd taken off his helmet and howled like a wild man. In the light of the streetlamps, his hair looked like a twisting red snake. "I only ride at night. *Wawawawa*—it's like flying." He ran a hand over the bike. "I ride every single night. It's the only happiness I have."

"Gaming is fun, too. I like to game."

"Fucking little kids play games." Shen made as if to hold a cigarette. "Want one?"

Zhang shook his head.

Shen took out a cigarette and felt in his pocket. "Shit. I don't have a lighter." He straddled his bike. "Just remember, I like to smoke Zhongnanhai."

On the third day, Zhang Yingxiong began to do real work. Putting together a meal looked simple, but it involved a lot. Soymilk to be drunk in the restaurant had a lid fastened only on two sides, while soymilk ordered to go had to be capped tightly. Each time he made a mistake, Shen Zhong yelled at him and Manager Luo wrinkled his brows over his acne-scarred face.

Zhang finished work, grabbed his copy of *Legend of the Condor Heroes*, and hid himself in the "little banquet room." That's what they called the interior section closest to the window, where one table was set off from the others by an aluminum railing.

"Zhang Yingxiong, what the hell are you doing?"

"Reading."

"Pretending to be some fucking intellectual." Shen went back to flirting with Little Yan.

It was a pirated version of the book, which Zhang had stolen from his local library as a kid. The spine was broken, and the cover picture of Huang Rong had been scribbled on with a ballpoint pen to add long pointy teeth, curly hair, and a pair of large breasts. Zhang stroked the breasts and stared at the building across from him.

Sometime after five o'clock, Lu Zhiqiang finally appeared. He was wearing gray pajama bottoms with light-green stripes, and he stood in his kitchen window chopping vegetables. The thin rusted red bars of the railing made him look like a convict. He and his daughter silently ate dinner. He ate quickly, washed his bowl, and then sat in his easy chair to watch the news. When the news was over, he read the newspaper. When he was tired of that, he got up to peel an apple for his daughter. His daughter stared dumbly at it. He grabbed her hand and pressed the apple into it. At some point before he went to bed, he hid in the kitchen to smoke, flicking the ash into the sink. With his round face, drooping features, and receding hairline, he looked like a political leader feeling deep concern for the nation.

At six in the morning, his daughter would go out to buy breakfast. At eight, Lu Zhiqiang would leave for work. The daughter stayed at home all day, doing her embroidery and taking care of the house. Sometimes she would get bored and play with her hair. Her hair was shiny and thick, and she would braid it, put it up in a twist, pull it into a ponytail, then twist it up again. As she pulled at her hair, she would reach out to touch her reflection in the mirror. Zhang

laughed at that. He liked to look at himself in the mirror, and he often practiced smoothing his bangs, or casually swinging his jacket over his shoulder. He
could never make it seem natural—he was the nervous type. Security guards
always gave him a second look.

Every weekend, a young man came to visit. Lu's daughter would wear a
dress, and her hair would be slicked back into a bun. When she moved her
neck, it made Zhang Yingxiong think of swans.

The young man would sit down on the balcony and take out his cell phone
or laptop, dropping a bulging plastic bag by his feet. Lu's daughter would hand
him tea, cookies, fruit, and roasted melon seeds. The man pushed them back
like they were in his way. Lu's daughter would pick up the plastic bag and pull
out underwear, shirts, and socks. When she was done washing them and hanging them up to dry, she would rub her moist hands and walk back and forth to
get his attention. He wouldn't move. She'd bend over the computer. He'd wave
her off. She'd go over to his side. He'd close the computer and glare at her.
She'd leave and sit on a stool by the door.

After a month, Zhang Yingxiong was formally hired. His pay was docked
three hundred yuan for a uniform and one hundred yuan in training fees, so
he was left with four hundred yuan for his whole training period. Zhang spent
two hundred and fifty yuan on a pair of pocket-sized binoculars. Through the
lens, Lu's daughter's cheeks were covered in moles and her nose was small and
pointed. He could even see the books on the shelves clearly. The first two were
Theories of Civil Law and *China Is Not Amused*.

"What are you looking at?" Shen Zhong snatched away the binoculars.
"Some pretty girl in the shower?" He peered through them, then said dryly,
"What are you up to? You've been holding out on me."

By the time their shift ended, Zhang Yingxiong couldn't hold it in any longer
and told him.

Shen exclaimed: "So it isn't a girl. You're watching a cop."

"He isn't a cop. He does razing and relocations."

"They're practically the same, or just as bad, anyway. I once beat a cop half
to death. He searched me. Like he could just search anyone he wants. He didn't
even look at who I was. Pfffh—"

Zhang wiped spit off his face.

"Take it from me, you've got to get mean." Shen threaded his fingers together
and stretched his palms. Zhang took out a pack of cigarettes, saw it was Double
Happiness, and put it back. He pulled out a pack of Zhongnanhais and gave one
to Shen.

"So what should I do?"

"Beat him up."

"That's too good for him. My dad's dead because of him."

"What do you want to do? Kill him?"

"It's not impossible."

Shen bared his teeth, and a burst of cigarette smoke hit Zhang in the face. "You? You've got the guts of a chicken, and you still talk like that!"

Zhang Yingxiong's expression turned solemn. He hesitated, then put the pack of Zhongnanhais into Shen's hand.

———

Shen Zhong tried to convince Zhang Yingxiong to move into his apartment. "Two bedrooms, one living room, facing south. It has an air-conditioner, a shower, even a DVD player. There are five people including me. The others are pretty boring. So are you, but at least you're not a jerk."

Zhang Yingxiong told Feng Xiujuan that he wanted to cut down on his commuting expenses and move closer to work. The rent was three hundred kuai, which was the same as what his uncle asked.

"Who's going to cook for you?"

Zhang looked at the mole on his mother's chin and said in a low voice, "Don't worry about it."

The other four roommates were all white-collar workers, and they resisted the idea of Zhang moving in. Shen said: "Their bark is worse than their bite. Don't pay attention to them." The bedroom was packed with three bunk beds. Zhang slept above Shen. Every morning he was awakened by a smell like mustard, which came from the German hair gel the other roommates used. When he heard Zhang complaining, Shen threw the hair gel out the window. "Still not satisfied? You complain like a little girl. Like you Shanghainese say, you're just a moocher. You go out and act like you're really somebody, but when you come in and take off your shoes, your socks are full of holes."

Shen and Zhang were on the same schedule, one week on morning shift, the next week on evening shift. Their white-collar roommates complained constantly: "You come back late at night and make so much noise it drives us crazy." Shen said: "Don't blame me if you can't sleep because you're thinking about some girl!" He threw open the bathroom door and peed in a resonant stream.

When they had morning shift, around five or six A.M. there was a battle for the bathroom, and someone would manage to lock everyone else out. Shen would curse whoever it was, and then would go out to piss in the hallway. The white-collar roommates debated behind his back: "How can he be so uncultured—even a dog won't shit and piss just anywhere." They worried when he came home late that he would go up to some other floor and piss where no one would see him.

Shen said: "Yingxiong is a good name. It means 'hero,' but you're an insult to the word. You ought to be named 'coward.'" He made Zhang Yingxiong examine his tattoos. On his bicep was the word "fist," faded to bluish-black. On his inner arm was a tattoo of an animal, and judging by the word "king" on its forehead, it was supposed to be a tiger. Zhang poked at the "tiger's head," and the flesh was soft and flabby. He thought of his father Zhang Suqing's muscles, firm and striated like chestnuts.

Shen said he had a lot of friends, some of whom had made a ton of money, and others of whom were gang leaders. But popular Shen Zhong stuck with Zhang all day long—eating out, cruising the supermarket, looking at girls on the street. Shen's wallet was sometimes fat and sometimes thin, but he was never broke. One time Zhang saw him playing with an iPhone, and he went over to watch for a while. The phone had a lot of photos on it, all of a young girl. The girl puffing out her cheeks and making a V sign with two fingers. The girl with another girl, leaning their heads together and seeming to compete to see who could open her eyes the widest. The girl carrying a Louis Vuitton bag and standing in the entrance of the Henglong Shopping Mall. The girl sitting with her legs crossed in a sushi restaurant, leaning forward slightly. The girl stretching out her arm as though waiting for someone to kiss her hand, with a Cartier ring on her middle finger.

Shen quickly flicked to another photo. "Goddamn. There are so many nice things out there."

"Is she your girlfriend?"

"Don't know her." He paused, then added, "I found the phone on the street."

After a few days, the iPhone disappeared, and Shen invited Zhang to a sushi dinner and a movie after.

Most of the time, they just watched videos at home. Shen made Zhang watch the same Hong Kong gangster movie over and over again. The disc was all scratched up, and it often pixelated and froze, and the actors' mouths would get stuck. Shen would do voice-over for them. The line he liked best was: "I'll tell you three things I want to get. The first is money, the second is money, and the third is money!"

"A lot of people say I look like Zheng Yijian." Shen put on the sunglasses he'd bought from a vendor for ten kuai and smoothed his T-shirt. "My old girlfriend was even prettier than Li Zi."

"Why aren't you with her anymore?"

"I got tired of her, so I dumped her." He gave Zhang a few whacks. "Next time I'll pass the girl on to you."

One night at work, Zhang went to buy Shen some cigarettes. He was five minutes late getting back, and when he came through the door, he saw a bunch of people waiting at the counter. Little Yan's voice carried ten meters: "Someone was murdered last night." Everyone began to stir, and the customers forgot what they wanted to buy, pushing and shoving, perking up their ears, afraid to miss something wonderful. Little Yan kept coming in and out, gathering information: "Julia from the coffee shop said that the guy who was killed was a city official." "Ah Fen from the nail salon says he worked in razing and relocations." "Xiaobing says that last night a group of people beat someone up, and she heard the sound of bones breaking, *crack snap*—it was terrifying." "Kevin says he didn't die, but he was taken to the hospital with serious injuries. His cousin works at the police station."

Manager Luo said: "Okay, okay. Let's focus on work."

"Aiya, Manager Luo, I've never seen a dead body in my life. Have you?"

"No, I haven't." Manager Luo stared at her fiercely, then gave up and laughed. "Why would you want to see a dead body?"

Shen and Zhang sneaked away. Sure enough, beside the newspaper stand on the street were traces of blood, which at first glance looked like a dirty water stain. Shen squatted down and swatted away a fly. "Smell it, it reeks even worse than dog's blood."

Zhang took a step back, pretending to check out a girl passing by.

Shen said: "Was it your nemesis?"

"I'm not that lucky."

"Yeah, you're not. So you still have a chance. You've seen that gangster movie so many times now, did you learn anything from it?"

The whole day, Zhang couldn't stop thinking about the blood, and the flies landing on it. He felt a bit sick, like he'd been forced to take a bite of raw fatty meat, and it had gotten stuck in his throat and wouldn't go down. He hid himself in the "little banquet room," lost in thought. Lu Zhiqiang hadn't returned home on time. His daughter was standing on the balcony with a tin of cookies. She slowly stopped chewing, although her cheeks were still bulging. Through the binoculars, she seemed so close that if he stretched out his hand he could touch her.

After eight, Lu Zhiqiang came home. Carrying a cookie tin, he put a dried pork roll on the table, and, leaning on the door to the balcony, he took a bite of his own roll. His daughter didn't look at the food. Lu came back over and put the dried pork roll in her hand. She still didn't look. Lu put down his roll and stroked her hair, lock by lock, stopping at the nape of her neck. His daughter continued gazing forward, but her hand nimbly grabbed hold of the roll. With each bite, her head rocked back, as though eating was hard work for her. Lu held her in his arms. His face was completely gray, while hers was white with a hint of a flush. Tears dripped slowly down her flushed white cheeks.

Zhang put away his binoculars. The whole night, he kept seeing her chewing the roll as she cried. For some reason, it made him think of Feng Xiujuan, and he called her but her phone was off. The curtains on Lu's balcony windows were drawn, though the lights were still on. Shen told him to rinse out the cleaning rags, and he said angrily: "Wait a minute, can't you see I'm mopping?" His own vehemence startled him.

Shen laughed and said: "Maybe you've grown a pair, talking back to me like that."

When they got off work, Zhang said to Shen: "You go ride your motorbike, I have to go see my mom."

"You're so full of shit, you're about to explode."

"I'm going home to see my mom."

Shen Zhong stared at him. After a moment, he said: "Okay. I'll give you a ride."

His aunt opened the door, fluffed up her hair, glared at Zhang Yingxiong without saying hello, then turned around and went back inside.

Feng Xiujuan came out and asked worriedly: "What happened?"

"Nothing. I just wanted to come see you."

"At this time of night?" She looked at him, her eyes shining.

Zhang took her hand and put it against his head. She stroked his hair. There were footsteps inside, and she pulled back.

"Sweetie, are you sleeping here tonight?"

"No, my friend's waiting downstairs."

"Are you used to living on your own now?"

"Mm."

"Are you eating okay?"

"Mm."

His uncle came over: "Don't stand in the doorway. The neighbors will think something's wrong."

"I'm going."

"You're really not staying? Okay, then . . . say goodbye to your uncle."

"Bye, uncle."

His uncle didn't answer, just kept his hand on the door, ready to close it. Zhang waved to them. Feng Xiujuan and Feng Baogang stood side by side, with their matching long faces and wrinkled foreheads. Feng Baogang closed the door, and Feng Xiujuan's face disappeared behind it.

Zhang hid in the stairwell until he'd stopped crying. His phone rang. He rubbed his eyes, then slowly went down.

Shen was leaning on his motorbike, his T-shirt rolled up to his chest. He held his phone against his sagging belly. "That took forever. What'd you do, die up there? And why were you crying?"

Zhang sniffled: "My mom . . ."

"Don't give me that mom shit. It's like you want to be breastfed again or something."

"You don't miss your mother?"

"My mother's dead. I didn't even have time to be happy about it," he said angrily.

"My dad's dead, too."

"You idiot, my mother isn't really dead. I just treat her like she is."

"Why?"

"That fucking bitch, if she'd ever acted like a mother, I wouldn't be this way. You really think I was born to be an asshole, a fuck-up, a scumbag? Who doesn't want to be a good person?"

Zhang touched his face. His tears had stopped and his skin was tight under the tearstains.

"I'm a scumbag." Shen paused. "A scumbag, admit it."

Zhang hesitated: "Mm." He shook his head.

Shen raised his eyebrows and slipped his phone back in his pocket. He started punching his motorbike.

Zhang said quickly: "I mean, actually, you're great."

"Oh? How am I so great?"

"You're generous. And loyal . . . and . . . um . . ."

"Okay, okay." Shen waved his hand, then gestured for a cigarette.

Zhang pulled out one Zhongnanhai and one Double Happiness.

Shen said: "Get real, do you really care that much?"

Zhang switched to Zhongnanhais, a cigarette for each of them, and started to smoke with Shen.

The wisps of smoke intertwined in the moonlight. In the breezeless air, they looked motionless, neither falling nor rising. Shen Zhong and Zhang Ying-xiong stared silently at the smoke the other expelled.

"Nothing's wrong, is there? . . . Brother?" Zhang said.

"What could be wrong?" Shen threw away his cigarette and straddled his motorbike. "You're being a complete dumbass today."

Zhang threw away his cigarette, too, and silently got on the back of the motorbike. Halfway home, he took off his helmet. The night air blew against his ears, stuffed up his nostrils, even blew his eyelashes back up against his eyelids. Shen howled as though he were crying or singing. They were on a wide-open road, and they passed a truck carrying wastewater, passed a dump truck, passed all the shady-looking people out at night. The streetlights stretched out the distances between objects. Zhang closed his eyes. He felt like his spirit had left his body.

"Do I really need revenge?" he asked Shen. "My dad's dead, what good can revenge do?"

"I knew if you delayed long enough, you'd back out. Just quit talking and practice on the weekends."

"Practice" meant stealing things.

Zhang asked: "How do I practice? Snag coins out of boiling water?"

Shen said: "You've watched that movie too many times. Forget that, just go out and give it a try. I taught myself how to do it. First you have to know how to look at people—who has money, who doesn't. And where they keep their money. The first time, don't go after someone with money. Find somebody totally ordinary, someone who looks stupid, preferably someone from out of town. That way if you get caught, there won't be too much trouble." Shen didn't like to use a knife. "Crowded places always have a few 'freebies.' We're just small fry; don't think too big."

Shen helped Zhang pick his first mark: a woman who looked to be about forty with a nylon bag slung over her shoulder, carrying a little boy. The boy's nose dripped snot, and he kept wriggling like he didn't want to be held. The woman stopped in front of a window display. The manikin was wearing silk, and its wig was askew. Its face had no features, and it was tilted slightly toward the window. Shen pushed Zhang forward: "Go."

Zhang said: "Are you sure she keeps her money in her purse?"

"You idiot, look, does she have any pockets?"

The woman started to walk again, and stopped in front of another display with her nose pressed against the glass. Her son saw Zhang over his mother's shoulder, and Zhang stared back without blinking. The boy turned his face away. Shen dug his nails into Zhang's arm. Zhang crept up behind the woman; he could smell the rusty odor of her sweat. He took hold of the zipper on her nylon bag and pretended to look up at the display. The zipper was tight, and the bag swayed a bit. Zhang heard Shen singing quietly: "Sweetheart, fly slowly, be careful of that rose's thorns . . ." The song seemed to get louder and louder, rising above the hubbub, booming in Zhang's head. The woman bounced her son and switched her weight to her other foot. Shen pushed Zhang again. Zhang wiped his sweaty hand on his pants, held his breath, and pulled the zipper open.

Suddenly the woman started walking again. Zhang slipped his hand out of the bag and said to Shen: "Let's just forget it." Shen slapped his hand on his forehead. Zhang followed him silently. The woman passed by a food stand, and her son started to cry. She hushed him, then pretended to be angry. The boy refused to calm down, so she went back to the store and got in line to buy a meat pastry. The boy immediately stopped crying. Zhang and Shen stood behind her. Shen made a signal with his eyes, and Zhang fished around in the woman's bag. A bottle of moisturizer, a sticky handkerchief, a folded newspaper. There was something about the size of a hand, something not too hard that felt like a wallet. The newspaper chafed Zhang's hand. Suddenly, the woman turned her head and glared at Zhang. She started to look down at her bag, but Shen pushed his way forward, shouting: "What's taking so long? How long are we going to have to wait?" The woman looked confused and said angrily: "What are you doing? Be civilized, would you? Stupid hick!" Shen pulled Zhang away, and they quickly left.

They went to McDonald's and ordered two meals. Zhang drank half of his Coke in one gulp. The square plastic wallet held an ID card, one hundred fifty-four yuan and eighty cents, and three tickets for a train from Shanghai to Anzhuang, Anhui Province, which would be leaving in four hours. The photo on the ID made her look older than she was in person, her hair oily and plastered to her scalp. One eye was opened wider than the other, as though she had just asked a question that hadn't yet been answered. Her address was in Yuexi, Anhui, and her name was nearly the same as Feng Xiujuan's—Wang Xiujuan.

"If these tickets were for tomorrow or the next day, we could sell them on the Internet." Shen tore them into strips.

Zhang picked up one of the strips and twisted it between his fingers. "Why did we pick her to steal from?"

"She was a good one to practice on."

"Stealing from her has nothing to do with getting revenge on Lu Zhiqiang . . ."

"Stealing takes guts, and beating someone up takes guts. Being evil just takes some guts and two hands." Shen started to laugh. "Teaching someone to be evil is pretty fucking awesome."

Zhang looked over the ID card. "I still think stealing from her wasn't such a good idea."

"God, are you still on this? It's not a lot of money, but it's still money. This McDonald's meal was more than sixty kuai; you go ahead and pay for it!"

Zhang fiddled with his straw, and the ice in the paper cup clinked. Shen grabbed the ID back and put it in his pocket. "This'll pay for a few more meals at McDonald's."

It was dinnertime and every seat was taken. A plump server stood to one side holding a tray. Shen chewed slowly and deliberately. The french fries had gone cold and limp. A man called to his daughter: "Come here, this table will be free soon." He lowered his head and asked Shen: "Are you guys done eating?"

Shen licked the salt off his fingers. Zhang continued to suck through his straw, making an empty slurping sound. The man sized them up, then went off to find another table.

Shen started to laugh: "Hey, Coward Zhang, did you know, I screwed Little Yan."

Little Yan was small and slight, but she had a big head. When she got off work, she would put on a tight T-shirt and jeans, and from a distance she looked just like a lollipop. She called herself Lily, and made all of her coworkers call her that, too, even telling Manager Luo: "I think everyone should pick an English name. Our corporate culture would improve if we did." Manager Luo coldly answered: "We sell soymilk, not coffee."

"Lily is the name of a flower." The background image on her phone was a lily, and the case was covered with stickers of pretty young girls and some rhinestones, a few of which had fallen off. She'd made Zhang look everywhere for them.

"Look at her, all phony-pure, like she's still a virgin," Shen said. "Nowadays, they've done it before they even get to kindergarten."

Little Yan liked it from behind, Shen said, and there were little moles between her butt cheeks. That kind of woman was hot for it all the time. Zhang stopped playing with his straw and listened.

Shen saw his expression and laughed nastily: "What's the matter with you?"

Zhang tried to relax and said: "Nothing."

"Let's talk about you for a minute. One time in the middle of the night when you were sleeping, you suddenly started moaning like a woman."

"Me? No way."

"Hell yes. It was a week ago. You must've come in your sleep, but when you woke up you didn't remember it. What a waste."

Zhang shook his head.

"Have you ever fucked a woman?"

Zhang continued to shake his head.

"Shit, you can't still be a virgin, are you?" Shen poked Zhang painfully between the ribs.

"Do it while you're young, cause you won't be able to get it up when you're old . . . Hey, why don't you go screw Lu's daughter? If you're afraid you'll get hurt if you beat him up, you can screw his daughter, and that'll make you feel better."

Zhang had once seen Lu's daughter naked. It had been raining and sticky that day. She'd taken off her nightgown and walked to the edge of the bed to put on some clothes. It was like it was happening in slow motion, and Zhang's brain had tick-tick-ticked incessantly, like raindrops falling on his body. Her waist was long, her rear end flat, and her panties were caught on her hipbones. Whenever he thought of her breasts, the ticking started up again. Her breasts were nothing like the ones in porn. Perky but delicate and small, they quivered slightly with her every movement. After she'd changed clothes, she realized it was raining. She'd stood out on the balcony, her hands pressed against the glass. For a moment, Zhang thought she had seen him watching. But she turned her head away and stared at something in the air. Her body was hidden inside her floral dress, and her neck jutted out from the tight lace collar as she turned away silently. The rain grew heavier, hitting the glass and dripping off. She seemed not quite there, like a character in a romantic film.

One weekend, Shen Zhong disappeared. Zheng Yingxiong went by himself to the New World Entertainment Street and bought a pair of counterfeit Nike socks. He went into the store just to look, but the large-eyed salesman said: "This kind is very athletic. Your calves are so good-looking, it would be a shame not to buy them." He also said: "They'll be on your feet, who can tell if they're real or fake?" Zhang looked down at his calves, hesitated for a minute, then bought the socks.

He tore open the package and was stuffing the socks into his pockets and thinking about going to the Internet café when he caught sight of Lu's daughter. She had just crossed in front of a group of gaudily dressed girls. They could have been models or cheerleaders. A few of them turned their heads to look at her. She was wearing an old-fashioned yellow checkered blouse and straight black pants that came down over the tops of her shoes, making her trip with each step. She went into a clothing store. Two salesgirls in tiny miniskirts were standing between the clothing racks chatting. Lu's daughter picked up a T-shirt. A salesgirl came over to her and said: "That one's three hundred kuai." She held up another shirt. Everyone had stopped talking and watched her. The salesgirl snatched the shirt back and said: "Are you here to buy?" Lu's daughter still had her arms out. After a moment, her hands dropped, and she ducked her head and stumbled out of the store. "I could tell she was crazy the instant I saw her," the salesgirl said. Then she asked Zhang, "Can I help you find something?" Zhang said: "You're the one who's crazy."

Lu's daughter walked to the next store and stood hesitantly in the doorway. She went down the whole row that way. When she got to the end of the street, she went into a convenience store and bought a lollipop. Ten kuai minus two-eighty—is that eight-twenty or seven-twenty? The old man behind the counter pointed to the total on his cash register. She stared at it, seeming not quite to understand. Her body smelled of mothballs. "He's right, it's seven-twenty," Zhang broke in. Lu's daughter shot a glance at him, then she picked up her change. Zhang bought a pack of cigarettes and left after her. "Hey," he called. Lu's daughter just kept walking. Zhang tapped her shoulder, and she turned her head.

"Is your . . . is your dad Lu Zhiqiang?"

She thought for a moment, and then, as though in the midst of a sudden realization, she nodded vigorously.

"I'm Lu Zhiqiang's friend. What's your name?"

"Lu Shanshan."

"So . . . what's your boyfriend's name?"

Lu Shanshan sucked on her lollipop, running her tongue around it.

"You know, your boyfriend. The one who comes around on Sundays."

She hunched her shoulders and giggled, looking uncomfortable.

Zhang wanted to say: "Come hang out with me," or "I'll take you somewhere fun." But he couldn't manage to get any words out. He watched Lu Shanshan turn around and walk away. The last button on her shirt had come undone, and the hem flapped and flapped.

———

The whole next week, the weather fluctuated wildly. It rained steadily, then turned bright and sunny, then rained again, then turned hazy. Shen Zhong said: "Is God going through menopause or something? That guy Luo sure is." Manager Luo's face had grown hard, and he paced around the store with his hands clasped behind his back. If he suddenly spotted a corner that wasn't clean, he would pick up a dust bunny, march over to the nearest worker, poke a finger in his face, and say: "Look, there's ten years of dust over there."

All the workers had to line up by the entrance and listen to his scolding: "How many times have I told you, you have to be responsible workers. You have to pay attention to the details. You're all a bunch of lazy good-for-nothings."

Shen said quietly: "With so few customers, why bother to clean? Who does he think he is, anyway? He's just a part-timer, too."

Manager Luo was a little afraid of Shen, and so he scolded Zhang the most. When he yelled, he would get excited and wave his arms around. Shen had somehow drifted apart from Zhang. One morning, Zhang had seen him with Little Yan, holding hands as they came out of a movie theater. Little Yan put on the helmet and sat on the motorbike, holding on to Shen so firmly that it seemed she'd grown out of his back. They hadn't noticed him there.

The apartment that Zhang rented with the others was also across from an old state-owned building. In that building, apartment 302 belonged to a young married couple, and on their balcony they were raising a little gray dog. The dog would stick its head between the balcony railings and stare out in a daze. When the couple were at home, they would eat dried sweet potato and play computer games. Zhang quickly grew bored and put away his binoculars, hiding them under his bed. He couldn't stop thinking about Lu Shanshan's body. He felt like he'd known her for a long time. If he revealed his frustration to her, she'd probably smile and stroke his hair.

One Saturday, a dozen customers finally came in for lunch. Manager Luo kept yelling at Zhang. The tables hadn't been set up properly, and the rags they used to wipe them down were dirty.

Shen interrupted: "The rags are always dirty."

Manager Luo said: "Can a dirty rag get a table clean?"

"If you wipe it enough, it will."

"Shen Zhong, Shen Zhong, I see you think you're really clever. What's headquarters going to think of you?"

Shen was about to answer back, but a man had just come in with a freckle-faced woman. Zhang recognized him. The two of them went into the "little banquet room." The woman dropped her bag and sat down angrily.

"What the hell are you up to, Song Fang?" she said.

"Quiet down," Song Fang said.

"I don't care. No one's in here. Tell me, what are you really up to?"

"I already explained it to you . . ."

Little Yan came by and tossed a menu down on the table. She asked lazily: "What do you want?"

Song Fang ordered a cup of milk, and the woman ordered lemon tea and vanilla ice cream. Shen sat nearby, playing with his cell phone. Zhang noticed that he turned the ringer off.

"I just don't get it," the woman said. "You're really going to marry that dimwit?"

"It's only a fake marriage."

"A fake marriage is still a marriage."

"Old Lu just bought two old apartments. He's getting insider information, and he's just waiting for them to be knocked down. When they are, he's going to make a lot of money."

"Maybe so, but it's not your money."

"If I'm married to his daughter, isn't it my money? She'll be easy to deal with."

"So you're saying you're selling yourself."

"To whom? I came to Shanghai without a cent. Only you wanted me."

"I'm not even better than that dimwit."

"Yaoyao, are you for real? I have no house and no car; are you really going to marry me?"

She said nothing.

"So," Song Fang snorted, "don't say I don't want you. You've got somebody, too, the one who buys you Gucci."

She put her bag on her lap and leaned forward to protect it: "I bought this myself. It's the real deal."

"Don't try to fool me, you—" He stopped short and changed his tone: "What I mean is, whether it's real or fake, it sure looks good on you."

Shen suddenly coughed. The couple in the "little banquet room" fell silent.

"It's called 'working with what you've got.'" Song Fang lowered his voice. "After we have a house, we can really be together."

"But she's a dimwit. A dimwit, a simpleton!"

Zhang rubbed his hand on a rag, stopped Little Yan, and dipped all five fingers into the two cups on her tray. Little Yan and Shen sniggered silently.

The couple drank their dirty milk and lemon tea, and talked a little while longer. She asked him where he was going, and he said: "Back to the dimwit's place." They started to leave. Song Fang took her hand. She pulled it away. He took her hand again and wouldn't let it go.

Shen said: "Shit, what a pair of idiots. They act like they're on a TV show."

Zhang hurried into the "little banquet room." The balcony across the way was empty. Where had Lu Shanshan gone? For some reason, he thought about the way she ate, nibbling at her food with her sharp teeth and her little mole-like mouth.

Zhang asked Manager Luo if he could get off early because he wasn't feeling well. He really did feel some pressure in his chest. "Feeling lazy again?" Manager Luo looked at his face, then said, "Okay, if you're sick, go lie down and drink some water."

Zhang went to the convenience store and bought a switchblade. He squatted by the entrance to building 12. The knife was twenty centimeters long and had a dark red case. He poked the tip into the bottom of his foot and felt a dull pain in his toes. He turned the knife, wanting to really experience that kind of pain. His stomach had twisted into a knot, as though the cigarette smoke he'd breathed in had coiled in his abdomen and refused to disperse.

Sometime after eight, Song Fang came out of the building. With his khakis, leather shoes, briefcase, and slicked-back shiny hair, he looked like a broker who'd just failed to make a sale. Zhang followed him, stepping on his shadow. The shadow kept lengthening and shrinking back down. Between streetlamps, he had one shadow in front and one behind. He stopped at a bus stop. The back of his head was flat, and his hair covered his collar. Motherfucking white-collar worker, Zhang secretly cursed, just as he'd learned from Shen Zhong. The bus came too quickly. Zhang grasped his switchblade tightly, and just as Song Fang was getting on the bus, he poked him in the back with the closed knife. The bus doors closed, and Song Fang looked back at him. Zhang couldn't see his expression clearly, but his eyes were yellow like a wolf's.

Zhang hung out in the Internet café until three in the afternoon. He'd just gotten home when Feng Xiujuan called: "When they tore our house down, they said they wanted to put up a park. Now they're putting up a building. The compensation is different if they put up a building. We would've been able to buy an apartment . . ." Zhang heard his mother breathing heavily, and he realized she was crying. He felt dizzy and hung up the phone. He slept until six-thirty, when he was roused by one of his housemates gargling. He thought of what his mother had said and gradually came wide awake. He tried to call her back, but his phone kept saying "outside the coverage area." He rubbed his face and went out.

On the ruins of their old house stood a new building, surrounded by scaffolding and green safety netting. It was taller than the other buildings, with a bright red mosque-like dome on top. The dome seemed to expand. Zhang stared at it. It really was expanding. What's going on? Where am I? He thought of Zhang Suqing, and suddenly he couldn't remember what his father looked like. He thought of Lu Shanshan. God, he hadn't realized she was slow. He came to his senses, and saw that he was standing in front of a print shop. Next to the door was a life-sized cardboard woman in a blue uniform and red silk scarf, holding an ink cartridge. Her face was wide and her hair was pulled back in a bun, which made Zhang think of Lu Shanshan. In reality, they looked nothing alike. Zhang took out his switchblade and thrust it at her a few times. The cardboard woman was light and swayed away from him. Zhang thrust at it again. Someone came out of the store. Zhang turned around to leave, and realized that the passersby were looking at him strangely. He lowered his head and saw that he was still holding the knife.

He sat down on the sidewalk in a shady spot, and a short time later, his phone rang.

"Your mom is sick."

"Who is this?" Zhang asked weakly.

"Feng Baogang."

He thought for a moment. His uncle.

"We're busy working double shifts. Your little cousin is taking his college exams soon. There's no one there to look after your mother."

"I know."

"What do you mean, I know?"

"I know means I know."

"You can only help somebody for so long, you know. We can't just let her stay here forever. We have to look after our own . . ."

Zhang took the phone from his ear, brought it to his mouth, and started to blow on it. He heard "Hello? Hello?" and then several beeps. He wiped a few fingerprints from the screen. He suddenly remembered how his father had looked, lying in his coffin, his face so pale, with lipstick on his mouth, his throat a grayish yellow. He had shrunken a size, and seemed like a stranger.

Shen Zhong said: "What's the matter with you, have you been shooting up or something? You look like you're turning into a skeleton."

Zhang said: "I'd shoot up if I had the money." He couldn't eat. Sometimes he felt desperately hungry, but no food enticed him. He couldn't sleep, either. His housemates ground their teeth, farted, talked in their sleep. The stray cats outside cried like infants; little creatures chirped. Someone pedaled by on a bicycle with flat tires, *kacha kacha*, as though riding out into the void.

Endless days followed endless nights. As soon as Zhang got off work, he would stroll over to building 12. One time a middle-aged woman asked him: "I've seen you here a lot lately. Your girlfriend leave you?"

Each morning at eight, Lu Zhiqiang went to work. It took him about half an hour to get to his office. Once someone was biking on the sidewalk, and he jumped aside as the bike sped past, as though he had eyes in the back of his head. Once he stepped in dog shit, rubbed his shoe against a tree, and kept walking. Aside from that, his movements never varied. His head tilted forward, his shoulders were slightly raised, one hand carried a briefcase, and the other swung back and forth like a pendulum. After swinging for a while, he would switch hands. He switched more often the farther he went, as if walking were some horrible duty he had been assigned.

A bit earlier, around six in the morning, Lu Shanshan would come out to buy breakfast, wearing her pajamas, her face slightly swollen and her hair messy. She would stroll around, eating her breakfast right there. She liked to buy frycakes, crullers, fried wontons. She took large oily bites, and then would start to sing, crooning like a little animal. She would reach out and pick a few weeds and stick them in her hair so they looked like sales labels. Once she choked on her breakfast and squatted down, curling up into a little ball. A fat guy carefully picked his way around her.

Serves you right, you dimwit, you idiot, you mental case. Zhang silently cursed her, but it didn't make him feel any better.

That Sunday, it rained for half the night and then cleared up. After Zhang got home from work, he couldn't sleep. He tossed and turned until five in the morning, until he finally got up and went out. His flip-flops quickly got wet, and his feet felt a little chilled. The faint gray light started to brighten, and after another hour turned golden. A taxi was stopped by the side of the road, its windows washed clean by the rain. The driver was lying on the lowered front seat, his mouth half open, his eyes showing a bit of their whites. Zhang took out his switchblade and scratched a line down the side of the car. He suddenly felt amazing, and he looked around hoping someone had seen him.

After a few minutes, he closed the switchblade and kept walking. Past the next bend in the road, he saw Lu Shanshan standing in front of a frycake cart. She was out early today.

She was eating the frycake as she crossed the street toward the alley. The alley gate was locked, and she stopped in front of it, concentrating on her breakfast. Zhang touched the switchblade in his pocket and walked over. "Hey," he said.

She continued to eat her breakfast.

"Hey, Lu Shanshan."

She turned her head. She had crumbs on her chin and kept right on chewing. Zhang walked up to her. "How are you?

She didn't recognize him. Her pupils were big, one eyelid open wider than the other, as though they wanted to pull him in.

Zhang put his arms around her. She started to cry and pulled her hand away, holding up the frycake so she wouldn't drop it. He pressed her against the iron gate and kissed her one time on the forehead. Her hair smelled of honey shampoo. He used the same kind. She was short and thin, and her breasts felt cool, like two drops of jelly. Zhang lifted her shirt and took one in his hand. He felt something like an electrical shock and was overwhelmed with shame. Lu Shanshan hadn't moved. Her head was bent over his arm, the nape of her neck burning hot. Her back was stained in strips by the rust from the gate. Zhang hugged her tightly, then let her go. He recalled a few happy moments in his life. She still hadn't moved. He straightened her body as if she were a doll. Hating to let go of her, he held on to her arm. She picked up her frycake and brushed off the dirt. He took out some money and held it in front of her face. "For your breakfast." She clutched the frycake to her chest and avoided his hand. She held it so tightly it might have been her child. At that moment, the dawn suddenly turned warm. Zhang blinked his eyes. Lu Shanshan was walking away. She went around a bend and disappeared into the golden light.

Retracing Your Steps

By Zhu Yue

TRANSLATED BY NICK ADMUSSEN

So you find yourself in a world like this: There is only one kind of plant—the cactus, in all its different varieties; and there are only two kinds of animals—grizzly bears and rabbits. The rabbits are all brown and they're enormous, as big as the grizzlies. The bears eat the rabbits and the rabbits eat the cactus. The rabbits don't worry about getting pricked in the mouth; their mouths don't have any nerve endings.

This world has only one road, a downhill asphalt switchback that's in pretty good shape. There is endless scrubland on each side of the road, and one side is always a little bit lower than the other. In that wilderness grows a scatter of cactus, hiding the bears and the rabbits. As you walk along the road, you might be tricked into thinking that it is the axis of the whole earth, but viewed from the open space along each side of the highway, it always represents a boundary, a border.

This winding highway is extremely long, frighteningly long. It eventually leads somewhere, although it's hard to say what that place is. There's no way to prove who has really arrived there. But there are a lot of rumors about the place, the most common being that it is a light blue freshwater lake. Some say that the road ends at a transparent public phone booth, and inside it is a telephone, and whoever can reach the place can make phone calls for free. The most trustworthy version is that at the end of the road there is an oval ice-skating rink, with a withered old man serving as the gatekeeper. Regardless, you can only follow this road as it spirals downward, because you are a wandering swordsman, and as long as you are a wandering swordsman you can't stop, you can't live on the side of the road. Wandering swordsmen must stay on the road and pursue other wandering swordsmen, which inevitably ends in a fight to the death.

As a wandering swordsman, you have two simple pieces of equipment: one light truck and one Nepalese scimitar, curved like a dog's leg. The provisions for all wandering swordsmen are identical. In this you have no advantage over the others; you can't hope to suddenly obtain an XM806 machine gun. In this world, the only way you can become stronger is by reading literary texts, specifically novels, essays, and poetry. The more literary works you read, the better: your strength to fight will grow, and your odds of victory will increase. This law, or perhaps we should call it a principle, is something you should remember.

So, okay. That's enough about the macroscopic situation; let's get back to practicalities. Right now you are faced with a corpse, the corpse of a wandering swordsman. He was plenty valiant, had certainly read a fair amount of literature, but he died, got exterminated, was turned into an angry ghost. You know exactly who killed him; the person who did it is the target of your pursuit. Wandering swordsmen don't always have fixed targets; most of the time their battles are chance encounters. Your goal is clear, though, and his name is "the Moldovan."

You take a closer look at the corpse and find only one wound, albeit a fatal one: his heart has been skewered. You examine the wound quietly and carefully, but you can't figure out how this happened. You must find a magician and ask him to help. Magicians have also read great quantities of literary work: they are rich in experience, vicious in vision. From the wounds on a corpse—their position, shape, size, and depth—they can discern the killer's sword technique, and tell which literary works the killer has most likely read. But magicians do not join in the hunting or fighting, and no wandering swordsman will provoke them. That's against the rules. Magicians serve only as advisors. They live in tents scattered throughout the wilderness on either side of the road, having lost interest in the end of this murderously swift journey. Magicians were once wandering swordsmen themselves, but eventually they took wives. They lost—gave away—their identity as swordsmen, and they'll spend the rest of their lives on the side of the road. Magicians have women and they have large numbers of books, but nobody but the magician himself can find those women or those books. The women bring the books out into the deepest, most secluded places in the wilderness and hide them, and those are the true homes of the magicians. Their tents are just offices where they can receive passing swordsmen.

You heave and haul, wasting a huge amount of energy, before you get the corpse lifted into the back of your little truck: this guy sure was chunky. After this bout of hard labor, you brush the dirt off of yourself, hock a wad out onto the highway, and squeeze back into the driver's compartment. You've got to get back on the road. You want to bring this corpse to show the closest magician, unless, of course, you run into the Moldovan before you get there. As you tear down the road, you mull it all over: in most situations, of course, swordsmen hide the corpses of their slaughtered adversaries. It's not very hard, as the wilderness is dotted with cracks and crevices like wounds in the earth, and when a corpse is thrown into those cracks, it's very hard to find. Leaving an enemy dead on the road is a kind of arrogance, a provocation. Men who do this aren't worried that their pursuers will use the corpse to figure out their fighting style. This means that they've read an incredible amount of literature, and trying to make guesses about them could lead to a fatal error in judgment. The Moldovan is just this kind of guy: frustrating. Perhaps he is already aware of your existence and knows you're chasing him. Perhaps he has left you the corpse as a signal. Or perhaps it's a trap, and he is misleading you. This is what you think about as you drive. You think about it a lot.

While you're driving, the scenery on both sides of the road repeats without variation. Cactus, cactus, and more cactus, with an occasional glimpse of a grizzly bear chasing a cottontail and the trail of dust they kick up as they run. You pay no attention to them, because you have plenty of food. In the same way, you are too busy to pay attention to the metal mailboxes standing by the roadside, corroded and pitted by the rain and wind. These mailboxes aren't ever used to circulate letters; the wandering swordsmen use them instead to exchange books. If you want to obtain a book you've never read before, you get out of the truck, open the mailbox, and take the books you need from it. Then you have to put a corresponding number of books into the mailbox. The owner of the book you've taken hides nearby, watching your every move. If the trade is more or less fair, you'll likely escape notice, but exchanging a piece of trash for a classic is a test of vision and luck. Sometimes, if you're feeling sure of yourself, you can elect not to trade, simply taking the other person's book for yourself. Then there will be a fight to the death: the owner of the book will rush out to cross swords with you, until one of you falls. You might get a good book for nothing, or you might lose your life and all your property. Sometimes, even though you've put in a book of your own, the owner will still charge out to kill you. This means that there was never any transaction offered, that the book in the mailbox was nothing but bait, and so you're stuck in a duel to the death anyway. No matter how you act, getting out of your truck and walking up to a mailbox is a gamble. But today you are not in the mood for gambling; you've owned enough books, you've gone mad reading them over and over. At this moment, you have no desire but your goal—the Moldovan.

At nightfall, as the temperature drops, you turn on the truck's radio to dispel the boredom of the road. A song plays: "This wicked city . . . this wicked city . . . this wicked city . . ." The song goes on like that without changing, accompanied by heavy static. Every truck in this world has a radio, but there's only one broadcaster, one station, and one song, a nameless song with just one lyric—"This wicked city." Nobody understands this lyric. This world not only has no cities, it has no wickedness. The rumor is that the singer is a wizened, one-eyed old man. Through the long night, you hear this song many times.

When a wedge of light appears on the horizon, you see a small truck parked on the roadside, and then a corpse laid out horizontally across the road. Next to it stands a dark shadow. You stomp on the brake, throw the truck door open, and leap out with your curved Nepalese sword in hand. With the cold morning wind on your face, rattling you to your very soul, you lift your sword and stride forward. Soon, though, it's clear to you that the shadow standing next to the corpse is a scrawny girl, facing away from you and trembling uncontrollably. She can't be the Moldovan. Your attitude softening, you lean down to examine the corpse. This body was also left—given to you—by the Moldovan. You recognize his technique, even though it is completely different from the first: this corpse is covered with wounds, each one sufficient to take a life.

When you raise your head, looking into the just-risen sun, you can see the girl's face clearly for the first time. Her eyes have been gouged out, and their sockets brim with blood.

"What happened to your eyes?" you ask.

"They're gone."

"Where did they go?"

"I was walking alone on the road, and I saw two swordsmen fighting up ahead of me. One killed the other—I was petrified. The killer came toward me, saying I had seen something I shouldn't have. I said I didn't want to see it, but he didn't listen. He used his scimitar to cut my eyes out. I passed out from the pain. It feels like it happened a long time ago . . ."

"What was he like?"

"Give me a ride and I'll tell you. I don't want to die on the road."

"Fine, I'll take you a ways." You turn and heft the corpse onto your shoulder. It's a slim corpse, and you don't need to exert yourself to transfer it into the back of the truck. You lay it alongside the corpse of the other swordsman, the chunky one. You take a pen from your pocket and write "1" on the forehead of the first corpse, then "2" on the forehead of the second corpse. You get in the truck, reach over to open the opposite door, and call for the girl to get in. She gropes her way over by following your voice, then clumsily hauls herself up into the passenger's seat.

As you drive, you size up the girl beside you. If she still had eyes, she would be pretty. Her skin is fair, her clothes are simple, and her hair is in a long, long braid. She carries a white satchel.

"So tell me now: What is he like?"

"Once I tell you, you'll throw me out and kill me." The girl speaks with great calm.

"That won't happen."

"Fine, then. If it won't happen, then I'll tell you. He's tall and sturdily built, and he has a square chin that sticks out. He's thirty or so, but his hair is already white. He has green eyes, and when you see them you feel sick to your stomach. He seems calm and collected, like he doesn't care about anything, but he's just pretending; he's going mad . . . yes, and his truck is covered in rust, it's iron-red."

While you listen, you take a box of matches from your pocket, pull one out, light it, and stick the stem between your lips. In this world, nobody smokes cigarettes. They smoke matches. There are two kinds, long-stemmed with red tips and short-stemmed with green tips. You are partial to the long-stemmed ones with red tips. The match stems are made from a blend of several different types of cactus hearts, and each match factory has its own recipe. You hold it between your lips, your nose tickled by the white smoke, your eyes blinded by it, and you imagine the Moldovan's face.

"Do you want one?" you ask the woman.

"No, thank you, smoking matches makes me dizzy," she replies with a small shake of the head.

"You saw him in such careful detail, no wonder he wanted to carve out your eyes."

"Yes . . . Perhaps it's an occupational hazard."

You restrain your curiosity enough to avoid asking her occupation: you know not to talk too much to a girl. But now the floodgates have opened, and she tells you her whole life story—she is an orphan, raised by the proprietors of a motel. She's been a motel maid since the age of five, working her fingers to the bone day and night without any reward. All she could do was hide the tips a few customers gave her, and in this way she accumulated a small sum. Later she fell in love with a man, a swordsman recuperating from his wounds at the motel. Although she never revealed her feelings to him, she felt that he loved her, too. She was very pleased by this silent love, until one day the swordsman was caught on the road outside the motel and hacked to pieces. So she left the motel and wandered along the road, only to meet the Moldovan and have her eyes gouged out.

You ask: "So you still have a bit of money set aside?"

"Yes." She speaks softly and clutches her bag with both hands.

"Can I see it?"

"You'll steal it."

"That won't happen."

"Fine, then I'll show it to you." She takes a sheaf of book pages out of her bag and passes it to you.

In this world, people use the separated pages of literary volumes as a kind of currency. Reading these scattered pages can provide a certain level of improvement in one's ability to fight. You manage the wheel with one hand and leaf through the girl's pages with the other.

"These are comics. Look, this is the comic *Superman*, this one is *The Adventures of Tintin*; they're not literature, they're counterfeit. You've been tricked."

The girl reaches out, fumbling for her pages. "How is that possible?"

"Oh, wait, there are a few pages from a poetry collection mixed in here. These are worth a little, but they're only fit to use as postage stamps. Cut four lines out and that's one stamp, do you understand? You can write a lot of letters, there are quite a few poems here."

"But who would I write letters to? God, I don't understand anything about literature," she mutters.

You turn the radio on, and the cab fills again with that song, the singer's voice thin and hoarse. "This wicked city . . . this wicked city . . . this wicked city . . ."

Suddenly she says, "You haven't asked my name yet."

"What's your name?"

"Isaura. What's yours?"

You have no reply.

At noon, you stop the truck on the shoulder. You light a bonfire on the roadside using sun-dried bear scat as fuel. You bring out fresh water, a few pieces of pickled bear paw, rabbit meat, and slices of cactus with their spines removed. You skewer them and roast them over the fire. You and Isaura split the meal. Isaura eats very little; her dejection is written on her face. After lunch, she uses some of the fresh water to wash the bloodstains from her face. Stumbling over to a cactus, she feels out two white flowers, which she picks and places in her eye sockets.

She says, "This feels much better."

You look at the two white blossoms of her new eyes. They're very pretty.

After that you get on the road again, still listening to that monotonous song. Isaura's head tips and she falls asleep. It's not until dusk that she wakes again.

As soon as she does, she asks, "Where am I, and why is it so dark?"

"You're in my truck. You've gone blind."

"Oh, yes, I remember." She covers her face with her hand. "I was dreaming . . ."

"Stop right there. Saying any more is against the rules." In this world, a wandering swordsman who listens to the dreams of others is considered a sort of plagiarist.

She doesn't listen to you, though, and selfishly begins to tell you about her dream: "In my dream I saw our days divided into two types, bear days and rabbit days. On bear days, only bears can speak, and on rabbit days, only rabbits can speak. But there are no human days, so people can't speak, they can only listen to the animals. On a bear day, I heard a blind mother bear tell me, 'The only road is the struggle to live.'"

"That's a line from Valéry's 'The Graveyard by the Sea.' Somebody must have read that poem to you." You really have read a lot of literature. You think that perhaps the poem was read to her by the swordsman she once secretly loved, and the line drifted into the deep places of her memory.

"No, it wasn't Valéry, it was a mother bear, it was she who said it." She sighs heavily and stops talking.

After dark, you decide to stop driving. You give Isaura a blanket and let her sleep in the truck cab. You bring a lantern around to the back of the truck and sit on the edge of the bed. You study the two corpses, number 1 and number 2, and you're so transfixed that you don't sleep a wink.

When you set out again, you have a premonition that soon you'll encounter a third swordsman lying in the road, and your expectation is correct. It is not yet noon when you discover him, but this time the situation is different. You cannot find any wounds on the body. You crouch down and pry his mouth open with your sword, but all you can see is a mouthful of rotted teeth.

Isaura pokes her head out of the truck window. "What's going on?" she shouts.

"Nothing, stay in the truck!"

As she speaks, a light truck speeds up from behind you; it careens to a halt right next to yours. The door opens, and out jumps a guy in a broad-brimmed felt hat, thin and tall, red-faced with acne. In his right hand he holds a Nepalese scimitar.

"Gotcha." His voice is strong and resonant. He moves toward you.

You stand unhurriedly, running the edge of your sword back and forth along your pant leg.

"Guess what? I've been following you for a long time. Learned all about your blade work. I even asked a magician, but later I thought I was making a big deal out of nothing. Basically, you read Poe and Borges. Am I right?"

You make a soft dismissive grunt, scrutinizing the kid's every move.

"Borges is just an essayist, and Poe is too crude, isn't he. Poe's best works are nothing more than freakish Gothic myths. They're not even novels, and that's to say nothing of his lousy verse. You've got to admit that neither of them has any real power, and so your swordplay is fated to be mediocre . . ." Lifting his scimitar, he begins to circle slowly around you while continuing to talk shit.

He finally finishes pontificating and makes his move, one maneuver flowing into another. You're immediately surrounded by a silver blur—but his gambit is a hollow one, and none of his thrusts are sufficient to send you to your death.

Suddenly your truck door opens and Isaura tumbles out, frantic to escape, running toward you. The white flowers fall out of her eye sockets onto the pitch-black asphalt.

"Nothing but trouble," you say, irritated.

Your opponent is also startled, but he understands immediately, his face cracking into a contemptuous smile. This is the precise moment that your blade edge slices open his turkey neck, severing his windpipe. He covers the wound with his left hand, staring at you, looking like he still wants to launch some kind of epic critical tirade. But he says nothing, simply falls to the ground and dies.

Later, under the midday sun, you've done a couple of things. First, you've yelled for Isaura to get back in the truck. Second, you've taken out your matchbox, removed a long-stemmed red-tipped match, lit it, put it in your mouth, and peacefully smoked it all the way down. The matches here burn very slowly because their stems have been specially treated. When it was about to burn your lips, you spat it on the ground. Third, you've dragged the swordsman you defeated into the wilderness and thrown him into a deep crevasse, because you didn't want to leave behind a corpse that might cause you trouble. Fourth, you've lifted the corpse whose wounds you couldn't find into your truck bed along with the other two. On its forehead, you've written "3." Fifth, you've taken a look around the dead swordsman's truck, but found just two decent novels, *Lolita* and *The Razor's Edge*. You've flipped through them; the handwriting on the pages is a bit unclear, but they're real. (If you do away with an adversary, you can get in his truck and take his books. This is not against the rules.) Sixth, you've gone back to your own truck, bundled *Lolita* up with your other two books, then carefully cut loose each page of *The Razor's Edge* with your sword. The individual pages will be spent as money.

When all this is finished, you say to Isaura: "Okay, let's get going."

After another grueling drive, you see a magician's tent in the endless scrubland. You drive the truck off the road and right up to the tent, crushing a few cacti in the process.

"Wait for me in the truck."

She responds firmly: "I want to go with you."

"Fine, suit yourself."

You carry the three bundled books with you when you get out. Isaura follows carefully behind you. The tent flap is open, and you enter the dim, half-sunlit room. The magician watches you quietly from behind a long official-looking table, elbows propped up, fingers intertwined. He is a skinny, wizened old man with waxy skin; he wears an exquisite black wool fedora, with a pair of gold wire-framed eyeglasses perched on his nose. From his mouth hangs an extinguished match.

"Good afternoon, sir." You smile unnaturally.

"Hello, young man!" The magician motions for you to sit on the long sofa across from him. You sit, but Isaura continues to stand quietly where she is, her arms crossed in front of her.

The magician asks, "Are you a wandering swordsman?"

"Of course."

"Then how is it that you have brought . . . a woman?"

"She's a hitchhiker."

"Do you want my help?"

"Yes, sir, I want to ask you to take a look at three corpses."

"So many . . ."

You set the books you've brought on his table. "This should be adequate compensation."

The magician deftly unwinds the twine and spreads the books out in front of him. They are Nabokov's *Lolita*, Cather's *A Lost Lady*, and J. G. Farrell's *A Girl in the Head*.

"Not bad." The magician nods almost imperceptibly. "Considering that nobody's going to bring me their best," he adds, then puts the three books into a small safe that sits next to the table.

"Well, then. Where are the corpses?" The magician stands and threads his way out from behind the table.

"In the truck outside." You show the way. Isaura is still standing there numbly, but you don't pay any attention to her. You drag the three corpses down from the truck bed, arranging them in numerical order from left to right. The magician bends over corpse number 1 and starts to examine him meticulously and with relish.

"This man you're chasing, at the very least he's read the first ten chapters of *Ulysses*, and he's familiar with the Homerian epics, Tolstoy, Dostoevsky, Kafka, Robert Musil, Thomas Mann, Teffi, Petrushevskaya, as well as Shikibu's works, which is a strange addition. He is a strong opponent. Extremely strong."

Then he kneels beside corpse number 2. "Ah . . . this is *Finnegans Wake*, the book of legend. It takes a thousand hours to read from start to finish; the magicians worked for three hundred years before we decoded it in its entirety. Look at this—he's used his sword to write his understanding of the masterpiece into his enemy's body." The magician indicates the crisscrossing wounds, and then turns his head to address you, raising his voice: "Unless you know *Remembrance of Things Past* like the palm of your hand, you'll never be his equal!"

You point to corpse number 3. "Then what's with this one? He doesn't seem to have a scratch on him."

"Let me see!" The magician seems almost overstimulated: for a long time, he examines the body with what looks like physical longing, but he says nothing.

You feel impatient. "How did he die?"

The old magician now speaks in a low voice, with a blank expression. "It's hard to say. Perhaps the only explanation is that this man died of hopelessness. His opponent demonstrated such incredible swordsmanship that he died of despair. In situations of extreme hopelessness, human beings can die suddenly. It looks a lot like this."

"This technique, the one that can make a man die of despair—what book does it come from?"

"I don't know . . . I'm sorry, I've never heard anything about such a book. I daresay you've never encountered such a thing, even in your dreams."

At some point, Isaura has come up silently behind you. She grasps your arm tightly with both hands and asks the magician, "Are you saying the Moldovan will kill him, too?"

The magician gets to his feet with great difficulty and looks at you. "That's right. You might not even present a challenge."

"I see. I should go." You shake off Isaura's hand and take a deep breath.

The old magician can't restrain himself. "Why in the world would you keep going? Why not stay here and become a magician?"

"Impossible."

"Why is it impossible?"

"I have to go to the end of the highway."

"Do you know what's there?"

"Do you?"

"It's hell," he says, "where the souls of all the dead swordsmen go. The living swordsmen follow this road, rushing toward the end. The most fortunate outcome for the wandering swordsman is nothing more than reaching hell alive."

"I have a rare edition," you blurt out, moving toward the truck. "Would you please allow the girl to stay?"

The magician smiles. "That I cannot do. My wife would never agree."

"I understand. Would it be possible, then, for you to help me by taking care of these corpses?" You get into the truck, and Isaura finds her place as well, visibly angry.

"Of course. I can bury them in my cactus garden; they'll make excellent fertilizer." The old magician waves goodbye to you both.

On the road, you and Isaura sit in complete silence. The wind picks up, blowing in from the deep parts of the wilderness, sobbing, carrying a fetid stink. The sky is a solid chunk of gray. You know that it will storm soon. Out here, storms last several days, and each time a great number of cacti soak up so much rain that they rot and fall to the ground.

Isaura eventually breaks the silence. "Would you make me your wife?"

You remain silent, watching the road ahead, as if you haven't heard.

"It can't be every day that you meet a woman."

She's right, women aren't common in this place. It's possible to drive several thousand miles without seeing a single one. But you still don't say anything.

"You can make me your wife, then you can put up a tent on the roadside and become a magician. I'll help you hide your books. After you finish working, you can come back to our house out in the field. I'll roast bear paws for you, rabbit meat, and thick slices of cactus. Doesn't it sound good?"

You force out a sentence between clenched teeth. "That's not going to happen."

"Please kiss me." She tilts her face, pointing her nostrils toward you. In this world, lovers kiss with their nostrils, and when they kiss they exchange breath. But you do not meet her nostrils with yours; you have refused her kiss. Disappointed, she slowly curls into a ball in the seat.

"You know what happens when a woman is refused? She fades into an unreal thing, into a dream." She asks directly: "Are you refusing me?"

"I am," you say softly, and then turn on the radio. The cab fills again with that song—"This wicked city . . ."

You ask Isaura, "Have you closed the window? It's raining." She closes the window obediently. She is very calm.

The sky seems determined to drown the overgrown scrubland. The rain sheets down, and the scenery outside the window blurs. You turn on the wipers, lean toward the windshield, and peer through the rain and fog. This weather is impenetrable; you have to find a motel alongside the road. Though the magicians appear and disappear like spirits, their offices are often near motels so that they can send their children there for apprenticeships. Some of them work in the motels all their lives; the others become wandering swordsmen.

Before long, you've found one, a two-story building roughly constructed of chalk-white stone. This is the moment when you see a rust-red truck parked in front of the motel. Washed clean by the torrential rain, its mottled color is even more striking.

You can't help but murmur, "It's the Moldovan . . ." You feel Isaura shiver next to you, but you don't look at her. You kill the engine while your truck is still a good distance from the motel. Then you raise your sword and charge into the falling rain.

You reach the front side of the motel only to discover that its door has somehow been torn off the hinges, making it seem even more like the mouth of a stone cave. You enter: your adrenaline ensures that your eyes immediately adjust to the dark room. Everything inside is out of place, as if a twister has just blown through the room, and in the midst of all this chaos stand three people wrapped from head to toe in bandages, like three mummies.

"What's happened?"

One of the mummies responds. "A swordsman has gone insane, we're terrified!"

"What's his name?"

"Moldovan. At least that's what he wrote in the guest register."

"Where is he?"

"In the hospital. He went crazy and destroyed our motel; we tried to hold him down, but this is how we ended up. Later, though, he just fainted on his own . . . we run a motel, we don't have the power to hurt anyone. All we could do is take him to the hospital nearby."

"Thank you." You leave the motel and run back to your truck. Your two trips to and from the door have left you soaked to the skin.

Just as she said, Isaura is gone, faded into a dream, the kind of dream from which you awake feeling choked. On her seat there are only a few scattered pages of books, her whole life's savings. Some comics, some poems, most of them counterfeit. You start the truck, roll down the windows, and throw the pages out into the rain.

You drive fast even though the rain is fierce. Your plans have been ruined, and that makes you angry. You find the hospital easily, right next to the road. The hospital is a three-story rectangular building, much more imposing than the motel. You get out of your truck, wipe the rain from your face, and stride toward the structure.

The hospital is so empty that you hear nothing but your own footsteps. After circling the place a few times, you find a doctor smoking matches on the second floor. He's got ten or more of them hanging from his mouth, long and short, and a cloud of white smoke floats in front of his face. He has to spit out the whole mouthful before he can talk to you. He's a fat guy, with a fierce face like a butcher's, and his full beard is curled and yellowed as if singed. If he weren't wearing a white coat, you'd never think he was a doctor.

"Who are you looking for?"

"I'm looking for the swordsman who's gone insane."

"Ah, I understand. You're chasing him. I'm sorry, but he's our patient now, and you can't assault patients."

"I don't want to assault him, I just want to see him. I've got no weapons."

"Really?"

"Honestly."

"Then come with me." The fat doctor leads the way. You stop in front of a room at the end of a hallway on the third floor. The fat man pushes the door open, indicating that you should both go in together.

It's a single-occupancy room, and the Moldovan is lying in his sickbed. He is just as Isaura described. He's still unconscious, but he doesn't seem weak in the least. A lock of snow-white hair tumbles down over his closed left eyelid.

"I'm the only doctor in this hospital," the fat man says, looking down at the Moldovan, "and I've got my hands full. I know a procedure that will wake him, but I've got no time to perform it."

"What procedure?"

"Read this to him." As he speaks, as if performing a feat of prestidigitation, he produces a book from his large white coat. You take it and flip through it. The title is *Differential Forms in Mathematical Physics*, which you suppose is not a work of literature.

"If you want your target to wake up as fast as possible, read him this. Okay?" Without waiting for an answer, the doctor pulls the door open and leaves.

The room is completely quiet, and the gales of rain outside only intensify that quiet. You pull a chair over, sit next to the sickbed, and try to slow your racing heart as you begin reading *Differential Forms in Mathematical Physics*. You don't understand anything about its content, and there are some symbols you can't read. You have to skip so much that you start to feel a little embarrassed, but you slowly become accustomed to it, reading softly, clearly, and without stopping. You think this must be some sort of incantation. Medicine is so mysterious.

You lose track of time, and then the Moldovan suddenly begins to speak. Your heart leaps; you're convinced he's awake, but he isn't; he's speaking strange words in his sleep. "I'm up, I'm up here, I'm standing up, I see, I don't believe, but I see, I see how it'll be, so I'm up here seeing, don't you see what will be? I see how it will be up here, I'm up here, you see how I'll be up here, so I'm stand-ing, seeing how my standing will be, so I stand like this, so I see like this, and I don't believe. I see, I'm up here seeing, this I see, so I'm standing up here . . ." But really he is lying in bed with his eyes closed. All you can do is read your incantation more loudly, drowning out his somniloquy.

His mumblings continue, stopping and starting. You feel tired. You lay the book down and move to the front of the sickbed. Balanced on the window-sill is a potted cactus, which has opened two small white flowers. Outside the window the rain is still a violent torrent, a heavy curtain. You look out at the indistinct silhouette of an animal moving across the scrubland with small steps. Because the two sides of the highway are of different heights, the rainwater from the wilderness on one side is slowly flowing down into the other, scrubbing the black road clean. You think: this water will eventually flow all the way to the end of the highway. It seems impossible that there would be no flooding there. Then you realize: the Moldovan is waking up. Soon you and he will be two tiny shadows, locked in combat on an asphalt road between these open fields . . . perhaps underneath this very rain.

Paradise Temple

By Lu Min

TRANSLATED BY BRENDAN O'KANE

I

Paradise Temple had none of the tranquility a graveyard ought to have in the early morning light. Two monstrous engines were roaring on a construction site just a few steps away, and the clanking, hammering construction workers had already gotten hot enough to strip down to their red cotton undershirts. Fu Ma, meanwhile, was hunched against the cold. Da Guma, his father's sister, had wrapped a snake-print scarf around her neck. "These places are always colder than the city," she muttered. Her husband was looking around in search of a toilet. Fu Ma fished out a pack of cigarettes, and Xiao Shushu, his father's younger brother, took one sleepily and leaned over to get a light from Fu Ma.

Grandmother—his father's mother—was the last one to get out of the car, supported by Xiao Guma, his father's other sister. A massive, old-fashioned gold ring glinted on Grandmother's hand, and she looked around appraisingly at the assembled family members before stepping out. All of them were wearing something gold—to "weigh them down" in the graveyard—except for Xiao Shushu, who had forgotten and was left with no choice but to put on a woman's braided gold necklace. Grandmother usually knew enough, as an older person, to consult with the younger people in the family before going ahead with things, and to play dumb when necessary. When it came to visiting the graveyard, though, she was very particular. She would begin consulting the traditional calendar at the start of the lunar new year, selecting an auspicious day and insisting that everyone—except for the children who were still in school—take a half-day off, the proceedings scarcely less lavish than a New Year's celebration.

Not that it ever worked out exactly the way she wanted—people were busy. This time, for instance, Fu Ma's father was out of the country, and Da Guma's daughter said she had an important job interview.

Grandmother looked around, wrinkling her brow. "What's this? Construction, even here?"

Her daughter-in-law—Fu Ma's mother—was talking into her phone about bed linens in careful newscaster Mandarin, haggling back and forth with the customer over some minor issue of price. The others listened, eyelids drooping, and Fu Ma lit his cigarette. Finally his mother laughed, curling her tongue. "We'll talk again, Manager Zhang—do keep me in mind the next time there's an opportunity."

Snapping her phone shut, she reverted to Nanjing dialect: "You haven't heard? It was in the papers—they're moving the old Shizigang crematorium to Paradise Temple. That's where the new building's going to go. How do you like that—graves here are bound to get more expensive." In any situation that came up, her mind would go to what it would cost.

"It's just as well," Grandmother said. "The old man always liked making friends. It'll be nice and lively here." She looked at the building site. The others looked, too, their gazes hovering in midair as if the smokestack were already sticking up into the sky, with slow puffs of pale smoke rising from it.

By now the group was surrounded by vendors proffering chrysanthemums, firecrackers, sticky cudweed cakes, paper mansions, cardboard sedans, and the like. The family members knew enough to ignore them and walk straight ahead. Grandmother had already taken care of planning the grave offerings. She had set aside stacks of gold and silver grave money at home a month in advance, and phoned everyone to tell them what to bring: red silk ribbons, bananas (she specified Chinese-grown plantains), red Fuji apples, Nanking cigarettes (the ones in the gold box), Yanghe liquor, candlesticks, incense—sounding a little like a public service worker as she reminded them that everyone would have to do their part and bring something small, even if it was just a lighter.

Fu Ma's uncle on his mother's side, Xiao Jiu, lingered behind the group. Unable to resist the vendors, he bought a willow twig, then ran forward, his shoulders slumping, to join the others. He had been taking part in more and more family events since the divorce. The previous year, he'd brought along a big-breasted girl he was dating to the Mid-Autumn dinner, but for the grave visit he was alone again.

The path into the graveyard took them past a long flight of steps. Da Guma and her younger sister, who were usually arguing about something, walked hand in hand, looking around and quietly discussing the gravestones along the way. *This* was a new grave, from a burial just before the New Year; *that* one had three people in it. Would you look at that picture, how bright that young man looks. Such a pity.

As they approached Grandfather's grave, Grandmother was drawn first to the two young cypress trees that flanked it, just like every other year, and she clasped her hands in front of her as she addressed her descendants: "See? Still growing—and so green! The old man down there is looking after you all."

Her sons and daughters nodded hurriedly, as if receiving signals from Grandfather via the trees, and their responses were more or less the same as they were every year: "Yes, yes, Dad is looking after us."

Two shabbily dressed strangers approached, a man and a woman, and Fu Ma was startled to see the man begin clicking a pair of wooden clappers he held in his hand. "Wealth and riches, sir! Wealth and riches, ma'am! Wealth and riches, mister! Wealth and riches, miss! Wealth and riches for the whole family, for many generations to come!" At every pause, the woman beside him barked out a rhythmic "Yes!" The two drew closer, chanting their rough benediction. Xiao Guma's husband reached into his pocket for money, but Da Guma's husband raised a hand to stop him. "Let them keep going a little longer. Very good."

The noise from the construction site quieted suddenly, and the surrounding gravestones pricked up their ears and held their breath, listening to the man and woman chanting in their Huaibei accents: "Wealth and riches, sir! Yes! Wealth and riches, ma'am! Yes! Wealth and riches, mister! Yes! Wealth and riches, miss! Yes! Wealth and riches for the whole family! Yes! Wealth and riches, for many generations to come! Yes!"

Fu Ma patted his cigarettes but stifled the urge to take one. He normally had no patience for superstition, but he always found himself going along with things once he got here, proceeding dumbly but respectfully through every step of the whole complicated process: brushing away the dust from the grave and tying the red ribbons around it, then offering incense, lighting cigarettes and placing them on end like joss sticks, raising toasts of liquor in thimble-sized cups, kneeling and touching their foreheads to the ground before the grave, setting the paper money alight and calling out for Grandfather to accept it, and so on and so forth. Including listening to the chant now.

Contentedly, almost greedily, Fu Ma took in the sight of his assembled relatives. None of them looked anything like their usual card-playing, eating-and-drinking, squabbling, familiar selves. Including him. Every year, Fu Ma took his time when he knelt before the grave, as if savoring the rare ritual: how his knees bent, how his buttocks lifted, how his head inclined deeply toward the concrete, his eyes taking in the shoes next to him and the rough earth as it approached. It seemed as if his forehead would hit the ground in an instant, and also as if it would never hit the ground.

And now—there was another important matter to be discussed. The writing on the tombstone.

It had been eight years, after all, and the characters on Grandfather's tombstone had faded: the black characters to gray, the red characters to white. It didn't look good. Next to some of the new tombstones nearby, or the tombstones whose characters had been redone, Grandfather's tombstone looked neglected, as if it had been abandoned to the elements.

Redoing the characters would be easy enough: the graveyard would take care of it for them, for a fee. The problem was . . . there had been changes in the family over the past eight years, and one or two of those changes involved family members whose names were inscribed in red on the tombstone. Next to Xiao Shushu's name, for instance, was the name of the wife he had divorced. Xiao Guma's son had changed his name the previous year, after a fortuneteller told him he needed more of the "water" element to balance out his luck.

"And then there's Fu Ma," Xiao Guma's husband murmured to Fu Ma's mother. "You say he'll be getting married at the end of the year? If we're going to redo the tombstone, we'll want to add the name of the old man's granddaughter-in-law."

Fu Ma had been distracted, but at the mention of his name he quickly waved a hand in an attempt to decline, as if he were turning down a drink at a banquet or yielding the floor in a meeting, then thought better of it. His throat tightened with a sudden fear: Married? Really? And then stuck together for the rest of their lives—it was hard for him to imagine. And anyway, he was pretty sure she wouldn't like the idea of having her name carved onto a tombstone in Paradise Temple that belonged to an old soldier from Shandong whom she'd never met; who had crossed the Yangtze and liberated Nanjing and with whom she would have had nothing at all to talk about. She barely even spoke to Fu Ma these days. The inexplicable chill had begun right about the moment they had set the wedding date . . .

Fu Ma's mother, pulling rank as the wife of the eldest son, observed the angle of Grandmother's raised eyebrows for a few seconds before saying: "If that's how we're going to do things, who knows how many times we'll have to change the tombstone? What if Xiao Shushu remarries? Or if Fu Ma and the other children have children of their own?"

Grandmother shook her head at the tombstone as if Grandfather were sitting there. "You see how it's been," she sighed. "So many problems in the family that you haven't even heard about."

Fu Ma had a guilty sense that she was talking about him. He hadn't done a damn thing with himself these past years, other than to fall in and out of love with a succession of questionable girlfriends who had been judged by his family and found wanting. The oldest had been twelve years his senior; two were girls from other cities he'd met online. One had burst into his house holding a sonogram and tried to slit her wrists; another had actually started flirting outright with Xiao Shushu . . . he looked up, guiltily, and was startled to see that everyone present wore an embarrassed expression. True enough, they had all had their share of problems. Da Guma's husband, who worked as an overseer of construction projects, had narrowly escaped a corruption probe, and Xiao Guma had embarked upon a series of ill-advised extramarital relationships. Mother had been tricked into investing everything in a pyramid scheme, even Grandmother's retirement money.

Da Guma's husband shifted his weight back and forth—he had to pee again. Xiao Guma rubbed her nose red with a tissue before piping up: "If you ask me, I think we should go by what was on the tombstone to begin with. That was what Dad knew about, and we should stick to that."

It was a reasonable thing to say. Faces relaxed, and everyone looked over at the tombstone, as if the dates carved into it eight years earlier had taken on a new meaning. The pale gray incised characters were written in a stiff, thick Wei-style script, and the family members' gazes played over them unhappily. Eight years was a long way to look, too long by far to make out clearly.

———

They all bade farewell to Grandfather before leaving the graveyard. This was Grandmother's rule, too: they only came once a year, so why not say something to the old man?

The sun rose through the somewhat grimy fog, shining down on the vast, crowded graveyard, down on the tomb slabs that lay flat on the ground, down on the tombstones covered with names of ancestors, deceased, and descendants, down on the old green cypress trees that stood between the tombs and the gravestones. And on their little group. Fu Ma's mother and aunts had applied their makeup carefully and dressed for the occasion, Fu Ma noticed, but they and the men looked old, saggy, weak, and powerless in the sunlight.

Mom closed her eyes, her unevenly mascaraed eyelashes fluttering. "Your oldest son is out of the country again, Dad. You know I don't like it when he flies, so make sure you take good care of him and see that he gets there safely. And look after all the rest of us. And look after my business—you know how it is. I still have to pay back Mother's money . . ." She nattered on and on, as if she were chatting at the family dinner table. Fu Ma poked her.

Da Guma cleared her throat. "Yingying, who you always liked so much—she's going to be starting work this year, so you don't have to worry about her." She stepped forward and added quietly: "I know you'll look after Yingying, Dad. Her interview today is really important. A foreign company, so it's all in English."

"I've been in good health, and that's what matters most," Xiao Guma said, pressing her palms together. "Your grandson's a bright boy, so when he takes his exams to go study overseas next year, just make sure he can perform like he always does." She spoke as if emphasizing the simplicity of her desires, as if she didn't dare trouble the old man by asking for too much.

"I went around to a lot of different stalls today, Dad, but they only had imported bananas," Mom said. "I don't know why, but I had to look all over to find plantains for you, and when I finally found a place that had them, the seller called me 'ma'am,' like I was an old woman . . ." Fu Ma nearly laughed at this, but noticed suddenly that Xiao Guma was crying. Her husband's face was blank and unmoving. The two had been living apart for some time now, since she'd started having affairs. Fu Ma remembered when the two of them were still in love. They'd take him to the zoo, then leave him to fend for himself while they sneaked off behind the giraffe pens to kiss each other. He could almost see it now.

Xiao Shushu dragged his feet. He asked Fu Ma for a cigarette and took a few drags before setting it upright on the gravestone. His lips moved faintly, as if he were whispering to Grandfather, but nobody could hear what he was saying, including Grandfather, who had been so deaf the two years before his passing that lightning could have struck right next to him and he wouldn't have noticed.

Now it was his turn, and as in previous years Fu Ma found himself at a loss for words. He had never gotten used to the ceremony—as if Grandfather had stopped being Grandfather after he died and become a bodhisattva to whom they could entrust their health, professional careers, and grades at school. Fu Ma's mother, standing off to one side, finally lost patience and spoke up to offer a prayer on his behalf: "You see? Hopeless. Take care of his wedding, please, for our sakes."

Grandmother lingered behind to stand on her own at the grave for a few minutes. As she got back in the car, her expression was unreadable, but peaceful.

———

It was only 11:00, but they went out for lunch together at the usual restaurant—Da Guma's husband could pick up the check there, and the state would foot the bill.

Yingying joined them, fresh from her interview. Despite the cold, she was wearing only a cream-colored suit, her waist almost invisibly narrow, and a pair of stilt-like leather shoes. The others looked like squat, bloated hens in comparison as they surrounded her and pressed her for details about the interview, and she answered easily, occasionally sprinkling her responses with English. As a member of the third generation, Yingying was always the center of attention at family gatherings. One of the viaduct projects her father oversaw had covered three years at an Australian college that Fu Ma could never remember the name of, rendering the "Education" section of her CV instantly a million times prettier than his own, and now it looked as if the "Previous Employment" section would follow suit. What was Fu Ma, anyway—never mind Yingying; pick any ten people off the street, and eight of them would be better than him, or so his mother said, and so he agreed . . . Yingying greeted him warmly and complimented him on his "stylish shirt." He looked down and saw that he was still wearing his jacket, with only a little bit of his shirt peeking out.

Xiao Guma had gone to pick up her son Doudou from school. "The food at that school is no better than pig swill," she said. Fu Ma barely recognized the little butterball, who panted as he called out, "Hi, big brother!"—when had Doudou put on the extra weight? He looked like one of those fat kids in American movies who are always getting pushed around. Doudou carried a little book with him, and at his mother's prompting he sat down in a corner to study, his lips moving silently as he read. Fu Ma went over to another corner to get a cigarette, not wanting to bother him. After five or six minutes, he realized Doudou wasn't turning the pages of his book at all; aside from his lips, which moved almost imperceptibly, the boy looked just like a statue. Ma Fu thought back sadly to a memory of Doudou from a meal like this one a few years before. The boy had been as chirpy as a magpie, with an enviable memory that let him rattle off pitch-perfect imitations of TV commercials word for word: *"Grandma's cooking is blah. Mooooooom! Use Taitaile bullion cubes! Tasty and fresh, just like it should be!" "Time just keeps ticking away. There are twenty-four hours in a day—how many do you save for yourself? Stop, treat yourself, and baby your beauty with Jimei facial masks." "The all-new Chery Cowin. Save money. Save gas. Sturdy safety with style."*

The family members pulled out each other's chairs, all of them insisting on being the last to sit down. Grandmother took the seat of honor and directed Yingying and Doudou to sit on either side of her, as if in recognition of their roles as future captains of industry. Fu Ma's mother shot him a furtive look, a complicated expression flashing across her face despite her best efforts to hide it. Fu Ma hated that about her. So they were successful, he thought—so what? Next to him sat the perpetually morose Xiao Jiu, who patted his shoulder sympathetically in a way he probably thought was comforting. Grandmother was still talking to Da Guma: "Yingying should have called and told us so we could tell the old man the good news back at Paradise Temple! Hired on the spot—amazing!"

Fu Ma picked up his chopsticks. He was hungry, not having had time for breakfast, but didn't know where to begin. Grandmother had picked the dishes: braised tofu with greens, sweet potato noodles, ribbonfish, bean sprouts. All of these were mandatory after a visit to Grandfather's grave. The others were things Grandfather had always liked—red-braised eel, sweet steamed pork with brined cabbage, salt fish, dried bitter gourd, stinky tofu, scallion buns. The family members spun the Lazy Susan that held the dishes, turning their attention to the task of eating for Grandfather.

Once they had picked up their chopsticks, nobody said another word about Grandfather. They reverted to their usual topics of conversation, just like at New Year's and Mid-Autumn, playing the same old assigned roles, spouting the same old moldy lines.

Da Guma's husband was unabashed in discussing the source of his pain: his swollen prostate. "It just keeps getting worse," he said, looking around the table at the others as he ate. "I had to go four times at the graveyard just now. I don't know how they haven't come up with a cure yet; it only affects half the people in the whole damned world."

Xiao Guma's husband was talking to Xiao Shushu about cars. "Most things you can't trade up on," he guffawed. "People, say. May as well trade up on cars." He glanced at Xiao Guma as he spoke. Xiao Shushu responded with an analysis of different cars' fuel usage, and the two men were transported back in time by memories of the oil prices of three years, four years, even five years earlier, figures so low as to be almost meaningless.

Xiao Guma discussed a writing assignment with Doudou, carefully picking bones out of his fish as if the boy were a three-year-old.

Da Guma and Fu Ma's mother were discussing the endocrine system and liver spots, rejuvenating poultices, uterine tumors, and the timing of menopause, their voices sharp as only middle-aged women's could be. Yingying sipped her soup daintily as she listened, occasionally chiming in to offer the latest international findings, such as that the best way to ensure ovarian health was to lead a regular lifestyle, especially after menopause. Turning his attention to a crumbling piece of tofu, Ma Fu thought about the times his girlfriend had argued with him about contraception over the phone, wondering to himself if this was what all women were like now. But he remembered the girls he'd seen when he was younger, their clean, shy beauty, and how he had fallen in love with them.

Ah, the girls of yesteryear. There were no real girls in the world anymore, he thought. There was nothing left, nothing but boredom, sky-darkening, suffocating boredom.

With nothing else to do, Fu Ma lowered his head and began playing with his phone. His mother glared at him from across the table, and he was sure she would have kicked him if her legs were long enough. *You think I want to be playing with my phone, Mom? You think all those people playing with their phones while they cross the street or sit on the toilet want to be playing with their phones? What else am I supposed to do, when everything is pointless and boring?*

He had only recently switched to a new phone, and he tapped his way aimlessly through its menus until he found a World Clock. Global Weather Forecast. Pedometer. Calorie Counter. Flashlight. Bar Dice. Kingsoft PowerWord (English *and* Japanese). Panorama Editor. He tried each of them out. It passed the time, anyway. Especially "Stopwatch." He watched the numbers flipping past on the screen—10, 50, 80, so fast he couldn't keep track, 100, and *there*, one second had passed. The numbers blurred together again: another second . . . He watched, genuinely rapt.

Xiao Shushu nudged him, and Fu Ma looked up to see Grandmother conveying a chopstick-load of sweet-braised pork toward his plate, as if to console him for having been left on his own. He quickly rose and held his bowl out to receive it. "Eat well while you're still young," she mumbled. "The more, the better." Her face had lost its expression of authority, Fu Ma noticed. Now that the visit to Grandfather's tomb was finished, she had reverted to being an afterthought, a bystander. She sat down unsteadily, two bean sprouts stuck to the front of her shirt, working half a scallion bun with her remaining teeth. Fu Ma watched her for a moment with a faint newfound sense of respect. He suddenly felt very full.

Da Guma's husband's phone rang, and he answered in a tone that made it clear this was an important call. The others fell silent, remembering that he was the one paying for the meal. Da Guma waved over a waitress with an exaggerated gesture. Xiao Guma quietly asked Doudou if he'd like one more piece of pork. Yingying took out a compact and freshened up her lipstick. Xiao Shushu stuck a hand into Fu Ma's coat, fishing for cigarettes, and as if in thanks leaned forward and whispered clearly, suddenly emotional: "A word of advice—you're better off not getting married. Really. I've spent a lot of time thinking about it, and—well, you've seen it, too. There's not much point, really." Fu Ma looked up sharply, but Xiao Shushu closed his eyes and exhaled a big puff of smoke into the air above the table.

Chairs scraped against the floor, squealing unpleasantly, making their movements as they stood, donned coats, and tied scarves even more reminiscent of animals scattering. Grandmother leaned against the table as she rose to her feet, looking wistfully at the remaining food as she grumbled about the waste— nobody taking a doggy bag, not even to feed the neighborhood strays. No one paid any attention. The waitress returned with the check, but Da Guma's husband had run off to the bathroom again, and so they all stood there patiently, no one even making the pretense of trying to pay.

Something occurred to Grandmother as she looked around, and she pulled Da Guma toward her solemnly, then—after thinking a moment—did the same with Fu Ma's mother. ". . . after I'm gone, it'll be up to the two of you to take care of all this. Plan it in advance, and don't forget to check the old calendar to find an auspicious day!"

"What are you talking like that for?" Da Guma asked, shaking her head. "You're still in fine shape." She pursed her lips as she tied her scarf in a bow. Fu Ma's mother made a fuss over Da Guma's new scarf, but quieted after she found out what it had cost, her interest considerably lessened. She turned toward Grandmother, repeating Da Guma's words: "You're in fine shape."

Grandmother carried on briskly while she still had their attention. "You two remember what foods I like, don't you? Besides the old man's favorites, you'll have to remember to order rice porridge, soup dumplings, snails stir-fried with chives, and osmanthus pudding with red beans." Dishes from Changzhou, where she came from.

Fu Ma grabbed his phone as he got up. The stopwatch was still running, and he hit the "Stop" button: 00:21:37:95. He stared for a moment before realizing that this was the 21 minutes and 37.95 seconds that had passed just now, right here, in this room. He snickered.

Xiao Shushu stubbed out his cigarette. "What are you sneering at?" he asked, a little touchily.

II

Fu Ma stood at the side of the road, his arm raised. A taxi pulled up, but the driver got out and vaguely flipped a hand in Fu Ma's direction before walking to a newspaper kiosk to buy two packs of yellow paper and a few bundles of ghost money. He lit a cigarette as he got back in the car, and began talking away at Fu Ma as if he'd known him for years. "Lookit, the money's got pictures of white people all over it. Is that Washington or Clinton? Bet my grandma never imagined I'd be burning American dollars for her."

Fu Ma nodded in response, thinking meanwhile that it would be a waste to go back to the office so early. He didn't have to clock in until 2:30, and even a little later would be fine, since everyone knew he had been to visit his grandfather's grave. Might as well . . . do something. Though he'd have to arrange it first.

Fortunately, "The Girl" was logged into QQ Chat day and night. That was her screen name, "The Girl." Fu Ma had met her through QQ's "message in a bottle" feature, which let you send messages to random users nearby. Some of the ways people used the feature were indecent, but honest in their indecency, and you could quickly look through the crowd to find people who were looking for the same thing. "The Girl" was two years older than Fu Ma, and he thought she had marriage plans of her own. They didn't do much talking when they met—there was no pretense of romance or tenderness. It sounded cold when you put it that way, but whatever—you couldn't be too picky with this sort of thing. The weirder the better, in some ways.

"The Girl" cheerfully accepted his suggestion. She said she'd just been sitting around anyway.

By then the cab was nearly at Fu Ma's office, and he had to tell the driver to turn around and head for the other side of town. The cabbie chuckled knowingly upon hearing that the destination was the Hanting Express Motel, and made a big show of sighing and furrowing his brow. "Oooh, that's a ways away. Might take a while, so cool your jets." He turned on the radio and sat back in his seat as if preparing for a long haul. After the grating stock reports and grating commercials, a grating announcer came on and launched into a seasonal report about natural burials, tree burials, burials at sea, flower-bed burials, all in the same tone of voice you'd use to talk about regional cuisines, then attempted to be clever by asking his listeners whether they'd rather be buried under a bed of peonies or a clutch of rosebushes, and whether they'd prefer a burial at sea in the Pacific Ocean, the Arctic Ocean, or Mochou Lake downtown. He even started talking about how some small city overseas had come up with an environmentally friendly design that had the city's crematorium providing free heat for the city's bakeries. Fu Ma nearly choked at the thought of bread baked using human bodies for fuel.

The traffic grew heavier, and soon the taxi was locked in bumper-to-bumper traffic in an underground tunnel. A line of sickly pale fluorescent lights hung overhead like a paper necklace, making it feel like the depth of night. The cab driver flicked irritably through the channels, but got nothing but static. His breathing grew labored, as if there were floodwaters rising to his neck. "I hate tunnels," he said. "All of them—the Xuanwu Lake Tunnel, the Jiuhua Shan, the Fugui Shan, the Yangtze River Tunnel, all of them. Now they're saying they're going to tear down the Hexi Overpass and put in a tunnel there, too. I won't be able to work if they keep doing it, I'm telling you."

Fu Ma passed him a cigarette, which he took reluctantly, rolling his eyes. "I didn't use to be like this, but after the Wenchuan quake I just lost my nerve. I can't even ride the subway anymore; you couldn't get me on there for anything. How about you? You don't worry there'll be an earthquake or something?"

Fu Ma nearly laughed at the brusque tone the driver had affected while saying these things, but he was too busy calming down "The Girl" on QQ, explaining to her that he'd be late.

"It's something about Nanjing, don't you think?" The cabbie was still going. "Whenever people from out of town get into my car, they always want to go to the same places—the Xiaoling Mausoleum, or Sun Yat-sen's Mausoleum, or Yuhuatai Memorial Park, or the Nanking Massacre Museum, or the Taiping Rebellion Museum, or the Southern Tang Tombs. Or the old Presidential Palace or the Qinhuai River; it's the same thing, isn't it? 'Ancient city' this and 'capital of six dynasties' that, just layer after layer of dead people, stacked on top of one another."

Fu Ma nodded absentmindedly. He was absorbed in planning the afternoon's positions with "The Girl." The plans would change once they actually got down to it, but you could call it a kind of foreplay. Time was tight, after all.

The cars ahead finally began to move, and the cab driver instantly started twiddling the radio dial again, flooding the car with noise. He seemed a little bit annoyed at Fu Ma's indifference. "Aw, look at you. Like you're really that busy." After a moment, he continued, to himself: "Nothing wrong with that. Get it while the getting's good." Fu Ma glanced up at the driver. Sometimes he just wasn't in the mood to talk. He might have chatted if the driver had been on QQ, too.

Finally they rose above the ground, and Fu Ma turned his gaze to the bleak streets outside. He tried framing the view with four fingers, as if that would make it more pleasant. As he looked through the little rectangle, he noticed for the first time that many of the cigarette shops, convenience stores, and newspaper kiosks were displaying paper grave money and tinfoil gold bricks alongside the newspapers, chewing gum, and bottled water, like a special hand signal, a patiently repeated code sign flashing at the pedestrians hurrying past. Fu Ma was startled. The cab driver sensed an opportunity to regale him: "They sell that stuff all the time—the Ghost Festival, the winter solstice, New Year's Eve, the Grave-Sweeping Festival, it's all over the place. You see people burning it, too, if their birthday falls on an unlucky day or that sort of thing. You young people, just thinking about your own happiness—you might have forgotten, but everyone dies sooner or later."

Fu Ma parted his lips, lowered his phone, and turned back to stare through the window at the paper money as it fluttered in the breeze, fell into the distance behind them, reappeared, and then vanished again. Fragments of the cabbie's chatter played intermittently in his brain, as if on a tape delay. Grabbing the seat to keep from swaying as the car turned, he was struck by a sudden sense that this car was the very last one in the city; that it was rushing toward an apocalyptic date through a crowded yet desolate land where the bodies of the dead, the ruined splendors of the past, were lurching back to life from where they lay, one on top of another, sighing deafeningly.

———

After showering, they always liked to lie in bed and talk. "The Girl" complained that her new pair of Belles was hurting her feet, then got onto the subject of a body composition analysis she'd had done at the gym recently: her PBF, her SMM, her WHR. Her body was something she cared deeply about, and left to her own devices she might have been able to talk about the topic for hours, even if Fu Ma never said a single word. One time she discussed the history of her hair, starting four years earlier: hair extensions one Valentine's Day, a bob cut one birthday, this color that summer vacation, that relaxing product the one other weekend, all recounted in meticulous detail. It made Fu Ma feel sad, the utter solidity of her loneliness.

As she continued her constant autobiography, Fu Ma turned on the television and flipped through the channels until he found Animal Planet. It was the same thing as always—scenes of stalking and strategizing, leopards and hyenas and their long-running disputes about the allocation of fresh and old meat—but Fu Ma thought it would work well enough as background noise. He watched the screen out of the corner of one eye as he began to caress "The Girl" and her PBF, her SMM, her WHR. "The Girl" squirmed and began to complain about her migraines, how her head had been hurting for almost a *week* now, not badly, she guessed, but constantly; not enough to affect anything, but certainly not comfortable at any rate, sometimes on the left, but then the next day it'd be the back of her head . . .

Fu Ma kept busy, hoping to improve her mood, and hoping to improve his own. For a few moments then he felt as if time had slowed down, softly congealing like candle wax, and a feeling of despondency wrapped itself tightly around him. He could hardly recognize himself at that instant—an instant too tedious to remember, spent on a bed he would never use again, with a girl who talked absentmindedly the whole time. He looked almost pleadingly at the television, where a hyena, his moment having arrived, was now tearing greedy mouthfuls from a putrid gazelle carcass against a tangerine sunset, his muzzle flecked with bloody spatters of meat.

Turning the other direction, Fu Ma looked at his phone next to the pillow—a small, finely made square of metal for which, in this helpless moment, he felt a sudden teary warmth welling up in him like a geyser. If nothing else, it was the one thing in the world with which he was truly intimate, the only thing that retained his body temperature and his scent. It was like an all-purpose shim that could fill in every ugly, impassable gap in his life. Like this one, for instance. An idea came to him: he could use the Timer function to see how long the encounter would take. Might be fun, anyway! But he just couldn't work up any enthusiasm, no matter how he tried, and he felt his hands growing sweaty on the girl's body. Perhaps he had been too hasty today—especially after the meal, with all those depressing little details piling up and all his relatives and himself even more disappointing than usual. It was like reminding him of every unhappy aspect of his life at once. And then there was that chicken-shit cab driver and all his talking . . .

"The Girl" jerked and clapped a hand to her mouth. "Oh, I know! The migraine—it must be my dad thinking of me. I was thinking, it's almost time for the Grave-Sweeping Festival, and every year at this time there's always *something* uncomfortable happening—a fever, or problems with my stomach, or my skin starts itching, and medicine and drips won't take care of it . . . but as soon as I go visit my father and burn some paper for him, everything clears right up. Really, for the past few years—it's amazing! Tomorrow, tomorrow I'll go . . ." Fu Ma was startled, not at what she was saying but at how his body reacted—it was as if a violent rush of hormones took over and forced him to jump on top of her, like a robot whose "on" button had been pushed. "The Girl" grunted, then began to emit long, thin moans of pleasure.

Fu Ma hadn't forgotten to press the "Start" button on his phone, and he watched out of the corner of his eye as the numbers on the timer began to roll by. Frozen time, slapped back to life, began churning in his body and hers, rushing, zooming faster and faster. He held his breath, as if he were riding a dangerous horse, and as his nerve endings grew engorged, he smelled the gamy reek of decay and corruption, and imagined himself as the hyena wolfing down his dinner in the weeds . . . But another program had come on the television, an "Unsolved Mysteries" sort of thing. The host was staring out at Fu Ma's contorted posture with an inscrutable expression. Scowling at the announcer, Fu Ma pointed at the timer on his phone, at the churning numbers, in hopes of distracting himself and prolonging this instant that seemed the only remaining proof of his ability to feel. The wind whistled in his ears; a bestial panting came from beneath him. He clenched his teeth and prepared to fight, to shake off, break away from, the figure that forever dogged his footsteps, face half-concealed, black robe fluttering, casting the long, thin shadow of Death . . .

There was a sudden loud sob from "The Girl," and tears began running down her face and onto the pillow. She dug her fingers into Fu Ma's back and said, falteringly, "You—my—my headache's gone."

———

Everything around him was as dark and calm as the depths of the ocean. He could almost see the undulating fronds of seaweed and the deep blue light shining down from above. He had become a single transparent cell, expanding constantly in all directions . . . Fu Ma opened his eyes slowly, saw the crappy light fixture hanging from the ceiling, the art print on the wall, the lifeless, limp window drapes, and the dim light beyond them that signaled the onset of dusk. It had been a long, deep sleep, as if he had been transported to another world. If only he could have stayed there.

Fu Ma wriggled his legs and arms. No wonder he was tired, given how early he'd had to wake up that morning to go to Paradise Temple. He glanced at the time: too late now even to clock out of work. Not a problem; he could try asking a coworker to run the fake rubber fingerprint he'd bought online over the scanner.

He blearily tapped out a text message, dreading the sensation of warmth returning to his body as if from some distant plane, and with it the capacity to perceive grief and happiness. Despair—at having nothing to his name, nowhere to turn—came rumbling back, like a freight train right on schedule, soon to crush him beneath its wheels. This was no surprise. It happened every time after sex; it was his brain's revenge on his lower body for leaving it alone with its own wretchedness, a complication no medicine could treat.

He showered and dressed, gazing at his slightly distorted reflection in the mirror and noting that his stubble had darkened. His mother had remarked on this at Paradise Temple this morning, though it sounded like she was complaining about the price of electric razors: at 680 kuai a pop, you had to shave every day for it to be worth it. But stubble was one of the body's crops; why shave it all off? Embarrassment? So what if he didn't want to shave? Would his coworkers or his bosses be looking at him closely enough to notice? He didn't look at them closely, either. Fair was fair.

The clerk downstairs looked preoccupied as Fu Ma paid, as though she too had her fair share of worries, and she regarded him with a sympathetic expression. Or maybe he was looking at himself through her eyes. Annoyed, Fu Ma looked straight at her, rudely, until she lowered her gaze. He looked around. Seeing a "No Smoking" sign, he took out a cigarette and lit it, feeling a little more cheerful now.

At that instant, Fu Ma thought of Grandfather. At that instant, an instant he'd been planning to forget, to squander—the instant he accepted his wrinkled change from the clerk—he remembered his dead grandfather.

There was a time, early on weekend mornings, as early as he'd left for Paradise Temple this morning, when Grandfather would take young Fu Ma, not yet a teenager, to the outskirts of the city to climb Purple Mountain. They'd start from White Horse Park, on a path that began on a gentle grade before growing steeper, passing pack after pack of panting hikers, sometimes with white puppies or big golden dogs, and people listening to rousing old songs on hand-held radios. On the right-hand side of the path walked people who were focused on climbing the mountain; on the left-hand side, more relaxed crowds descended contentedly, the two sides complementing each other like a self-contained circulatory system. There was a pleasantness about the mountain path that seemed completely independent from the world below. Sometimes Grandfather would pause for a moment at a kiosk, counting out his wrinkled small change to buy a cucumber and a tea egg for Fu Ma. A moment later, he would take Fu Ma's hand, and they would slip back into the crowd, tiredly but assuredly continuing their slow climb toward the observation deck at the mountain's verdant summit.

Fu Ma's legs trembled, as if that vanished, impossible happiness were slapping against his calves.

He glanced up at the clerk one last time, embarrassed at the tears in his eyes, and saw no surprise in her expression.

———

Twenty-five minutes later, Fu Ma stood at the foot of Purple Mountain, on the path that started from White Horse Park. The place had changed, but he still felt a vague sense of familiarity. He was surprised at the number of people walking on the path in couples and groups, some of them talking and laughing, a vision of everyday life. Who'd have thought there'd be so many people climbing Purple Mountain at night? He couldn't make out any of their faces, though these weren't the same people as before, that was for sure.

The night was like a thick, heavy gown. Fu Ma hesitated a few moments before joining the dark crowd making its way toward the top of the mountain. There were no lights by the path, and car headlights swept by every now and then from the mountain road, passing through the silhouetted trees and casting a shadow like moving bars, which made Fu Ma feel like he and the people around him were marching arduously, unknowingly, in an abstract prison. What a beautiful, sympathy-inspiring image, he thought.

He tried to remember Grandfather again, but found that his brain was now dulled, that the flash of pure emotion for his childhood years had lasted only an instant before vanishing again. Bullshit sentimentality—Fu Ma had never had time for it anyway. Better just to keep walking, vacant and emotionless, up the mountain.

When he was halfway up the mountain, parts of the city became visible. The lights of the buildings and the flowing lines of traffic lay spread out in a classic, predictable pattern, like a minor work by an amateur photographer. Fu Ma shut his eyes, opened them again, looked as far into the distance as he could, seeing at the edge of his vision a ragged, teeming blackness—mountains, rivers, fields, trees, insects, graveyards, roads, windows, doors, faces, things gone forever, things yet to come. The darkness encompassed all these things, and all these things were swallowed by the darkness.

After gazing at this sight for several minutes, Fu Ma slowed his pace, feeling as if a fine rain were falling on him, or as if a cobweb had fallen on his head. He didn't know what it was. He brushed at it futilely. He stopped in his tracks, his desire to climb the mountain gone.

It was awful. Even Fu Ma couldn't understand why everything eventually ended the same way: in boredom. A boredom as vast as the sky, as hard as an old tree root, ineluctable. If the spirit of his dead grandfather really could look after him the way it looked after others, he hoped it would protect him from boredom, would see to it that he could be like the others, could always appear full of energy.

Fu Ma felt in his pocket, but he'd smoked all of his cigarettes. There was only his phone. He took it out, unhappily, and flicked back to the Timer function, hit the "Start" button. He turned around listlessly and walked back through the crowd, against the flow of the half-lit rising and falling silhouettes, back down the mountain. He put the phone back in his pants pocket, letting the numbers flip past like ants, second after biting second.

INTERLUDE

Excerpt from

A Dictionary of Xinjiang

By Shen Wei

TRANSLATED BY ELEANOR GOODMAN

Study, Wilderness

For a time I loved to travel: the lakes region, Tibet, the Tianshan mountains that run north to south. Road of rising dust. Sweat-stink of the long-distance bus, coughing, the smell of cigarettes. Dialects and pop songs. The retreating scenery like a black-and-white movie from the last century, gradually growing dark and blurred . . . Traveling means drifting from one recipe to another, from flatbread from a backpack and a few bits of dried fruit to a bottle of liquor at a roadside stand—the high point is the songs of drunkards; from one bed to another, undressing and lying down until the next morning, and only your own breath can disperse the loneliness, the lingering warmth left behind by strangers.

On the road I remember a smile, a complication, a fixation . . . the evasive dusty fragrance of a sumptuous, unobtainable face. In it, I preserve an early afternoon: the tranquil vision of a white-bearded man wandering a luminous vineyard in Hetian; a little town called Chen's Grave in the Sunan lakes region, where an unnamed imperial concubine has slept at the bottom of a lake for three hundred years. Even now, I still harbor a surrealistic sort of love for her . . .

Sometimes I get tired of traveling. No, traveling gets tired of me; the wilderness is sick of me, all the toing and froing is sick of me. I flee, escaping from the infinite distance into my study: The final spiritual lodging? Or a paper tomb? Now the breath of the wilderness paces with me in my room as I flip through this book, flip through that book. Five thousand books collect five thousand kinds of dust, old and new; five thousand kinds of breath envelop me. Five thousand bricks are enough to build a secluded tomb. I feel the penetrating gaze of the books, of the dead; the roads through time and space over which ghosts travel are longer and more arduous than mine. They mutter and titter, whisper to each other; clearly they know exactly where my soul is going . . . I sit there, bored. I smoke. Shower. Listen to music. Kill a cockroach. Answer a phone call: wrong number. Then I go to the kitchen and make a bowl of noodles. The scene through the window is too vast; it can only be peeked at, never stared at.

Enough. No use looking at this world anymore.

"When you're writing, you're just like a tiger, and when you're not, you're depressed," a woman once said to me. I don't know if it was meant as praise or an insult. Could it be that I was born to write? But writing doesn't necessarily love those who only love it; what writing loves is the infinite. Similarly, I'd say that the wilderness is outdoor reading, and the study is indoor traveling. Yet I always feel that I understate things.

There's a type of person who's divided between his study and the wilderness, like a silent, damaged ball unable to control its own rolling or aim. Such a person becomes the Other, an onlooker, watching himself get kicked rudely back and forth. In this struggle, there is no ultimate winner. He isn't even there.

Where is he? Where am I?

Tianshan

If the Tianshan mountains were the spine of a book, Xinjiang would be an opened dictionary. Southern Xinjiang and northern Xinjiang extend out into vast page numbers, an extraordinary hybrid landscape. The Tarim Basin and Zungarian Basin rest on either side, two bowls filled with the sands of time, two pages scribbled with fragments of memory. The chaos of the silent desert contrasts with the clear blue of the Tianshan. Tianshan, meaning mountains in the sky. An enormous feat of engineering, given to the earth by the sky. A sacred dispatch, a spectacular banishment, running from east to west, from dawn to dusk, like a line of poetry winding across inextinguishable perfection. Let the spirits recite this line in reverence, let the earth listen and from its throat let roll a trembling, scorching voice choked with tears. Birds wing, steeds thunder, snow leopards blossom, cool breezes and springs stir dombura strings, Akun chants offer unceasing praises. These snowy peaks are the imperial crown of Central Asia; these glaciers are the many thousand meters of a great man's white hair. The rocks and cliffs are his gown, the pine forests and clouds his winter blankets, the prairies and valleys his cashmere cushions. And the treasured lakes in their midst: exquisite chunks of jadeite.

Tianshan, mountains of the nomads. Yurts dot the plains, smoke tangles with the clouds, sheep seek fresh water and grass, children grow up on horseback, honeybees and dragonflies fly over inexhaustible seas of flowers. Home of wild poppies and snow lotuses, domain of black grouse and red deer, mountainside homeland of flowing milk and honey . . . These are the rewards of the herders' toil, the treasures of Asia.

Tianshan, radiant mountains. The backbone of Asia, an upswell of inspiration, the landscape collects here, blends here, calls out to all. Oh, chariot sun, oil-lamp moon, cherish them, draw them in, ignite them—these chaste, glorious mountains proclaim the beginning of a lyric blue epoch . . .

White Poplar Village

From a speck of dust to a note of birdsong, White Poplar Village shrinks to a button forgotten by the world, a shiver on the tip of a stalk of withered midautumn grass. No, it isn't that the village is too small, it's that the wind is too big, the wilderness too wide, bleak and desolate and limitless. It grows in the midst of forgetfulness, and like an almond enclosed in a gray husk, it has no chance to sprout in that secret corner.

Marked by white poplars, oases unfold into villages, tilled fields, and the distance. The dawn slants down over low mud huts. Rusted mattocks lean in corners. Cabbages quietly rot in cellars. An old donkey bears welts on its back and rump. Throats destroyed by drink burst into raucous song . . . White Poplar Village displays its quietude and petty smugness, and its other particulars scatter in the wind, and in the midst of vanishing continue to vanish.

Before the village's breath, heartbeat, and shape are reclaimed by dust and distant horizons, the uneven mud buildings under the white poplars produce an earthen pot resting on the slight shoulders of a girl drawing water. The girl treasures this pot with her whole being, as though it were her future child—she will not let it break. And so her delicate face shows a faint blush of maternal love, and a hint of worldly care. Thus, in the girl's swaying shoulders and timid gait, White Poplar Village becomes whole, and lingers unforgotten in our eyes and hearts: a beautiful vanishing, a beautiful decline.

Turpan

There have always been two Turpans, dead Turpan and living Turpan. Traveling on this flaming continent means crossing through these two worlds. The things that constitute dead Turpan: the famous Jiaohe City Ruins, old Gaocheng City, the Astana Tombs, the Thousand-Buddha Caves with their wall murals depicting fragmented memories, the damaged Manichaean texts written on mulberry-bark paper, Flame Mountain red as an ember, the Aidingkol Lake at the second-lowest point on this savage earth, mummies and the fossil remains of huge rhinoceroses in museums . . . These are the generous gifts of time, redolent of years and dust. They are a great withering-away, yet are well within reach and can be touched by the hand. Dead Turpan is an omnipresent nowhereland.

And living Turpan? It lives in the form of grapes, and only in the form of grapes. On this arid, rainless "continent of flames," aside from the underground Karez irrigation system, water can survive only in the form of grapes. Grapes are the jadeite lamps of Turpan, and under the grape trellises one finds beautifully dressed girls, lively nazirkom dances, muqam concerts, all-night feasts . . . With a stubborn hedonism they resist the forceful violations of another world. Listening from a distance, one sometimes can't tell which world the faint drumbeats come from—this Turpan, or that Turpan?

The two depend on one another for existence, and appear to blend seamlessly. But if one looks closely, this fiery chunk of jadeite shows cracks, and no human hand can sew together the lines that divide it. Dead Turpan has a self-satisfied loneliness. It is the other world's mirror, illuminating life's unreality and equivocality. It moves ruins, tombs, and ashes into the sky, pulls death inch by inch toward dizzying heights. The living Turpan, then, is like a solicitous footman, ceaselessly offering the world its enthusiasm, water, soil, nourishment. It turns dead Turpan into a sturdy grapevine, growing in the vast wasteland of death, with flourishing roots and luxuriant leaves. A savage grapevine!

Dead Turpan wants to be bigger than living Turpan. Here, in "the world's largest outdoor archaeological museum" (Gunnar Jarring), the dead world is magnificent, overbearing, blocking the living Turpan from view. It returns girls to silk paintings, to their mothers' bodies; sends ripe grapes back to their shy sprouts and tiny flower buds; weakens grapevines so they cannot reproduce, withering, struggling in useless labor in the dust and scorching sun. Can it be that living Turpan is only a stand-in for dead Turpan, a last testament?

In Turpan, therefore, death is real, and extraordinarily palpable. It hangs everywhere in the air you breathe. It is an indestructible fossil.

The life that the heavens entrusted to her had its limit, just as the passage of time could not be delayed. Like a bolt of lightning, it was ephemeral. When time comes to its end, life will also be exhausted. The jade tree has withered. She has left this age forever, having broken through this world's web of suffering.

—Epitaph on the grave of a woman from Turpan excavated
at Astana, 667 A.D.

Dead Turpan is as heavy as an enormous millstone, pressing down from the sky on the endlessly moving, living Turpan, making it groan and sing, pressing out grape juice and liquor from some hidden place . . .

Merceles

It has been made for two thousand years, for as long as grapes have been grown in western China. In Tang poetry, the lines "Fine grape liquor in a white jade cup / I want to drink, but the pipa sends us to our horses" refer to merceles. Merceles and wine are a bit different. Merceles is a natural, slightly alcoholic drink that falls somewhere between wine and grape juice.

The process of fermentation goes like this: Wash ripe grapes well, extract their juice, then add the juice and two parts water to a large pot. Heat to boiling over a high flame, then lower to a simmer. Let it boil down to the original volume of juice, then pour it into a large vat or earthen jar. Seal the jar and place it in the sun where it will ferment, and in forty days it will be ready. As the merceles ferments, it may make a burbling sound like boiling water or the grunting of cows or sheep, or it may explode with a *bang!* The best winemakers can tell from these sounds how good the merceles will be.

Merceles is different from modern artisanal wine in that its color is a little weak and cloudy. It seems rustic, or as though a sandstorm got into it and stirred it up. This most ancient, most primitive of wines is unique in its simplicity, naturalness, and mellowness, and drinking it makes one feel as if one has returned to nature and the countryside.

Uighurs like to add things to their merceles: pigeon blood, or most often wolfberry, saffron, cistanche, and other medicinal herbs. People from Hetian like to add rose petals so they can get drunk on the fragrance. People from

Awat will add an entire roasted lamb, and when the meat has completely melted and the bones have been fished out, the wine is ready. This kind of merceles is very nutritious, and also the cloudiest—some simply call it "meat wine."

According to a folktale from Yarkand, merceles was invented by a man named Mailiwuni. In order to raise the drink's alcohol level, he added tiger, fox, and rooster blood, so after drinking it, a man would be as fierce as a tiger, as cunning as a fox, and as lascivious as a rooster.

The Uighurs in southern Xinjiang villages all seem to make merceles. It's as common for them to do so as for Han Chinese in Jiangnan to make rice wine at New Year's. Every household's wine has a different flavor. In one village there might be a hundred households, and no two merceles will be the same. It depends on the age, gender, mood, and so on of the winemaker. He puts his temperament and personality into the wine. An old man will make a subdued brew, but one worth delicately savoring. A young man's wine will be full of vigor and make the blood run hot. The wine of a bad-tempered man will go straight to the head and burn the throat. A mild man's wine will be smooth and soothing, and hard to get drunk on. Wine made by someone in love will taste like roses and honey, and those who drink it will grin in elation and need to sing out loud. The jilted and divorced make bitter wine, and those who drink it will think of their own heartbreak and cry.

During the village merceles festivals—now a lost tradition—each villager would offer a jar of his best wine, which was poured into a big vat with the others, mixing together into a communal merceles that all the villagers drank from. It was a symbol of unity. Everyone was born from the same roots, like the wine in the vat; the same blood ran in their veins. Every villager, without exception, drank this "hundred-family wine," using wooden and ceramic bowls. Even toddlers who had just begun to walk would join in the fun and have a taste. For food, they would boil an ox head in a hot steel wok. For three days and three nights, they would drink and sing and dance. On the third day, the most revered elder would speak. In a low and unsteady voice, with everyone gathered around him to listen, the elder would explain that merceles represents forgetfulness. When people drink it, they forget all the misunderstandings and grudges and slights that arise between neighbors. The sad cheer up, and the poor pray to heaven that tomorrow will be happier. Merceles can even cleanse the souls of sinners, he would say; from that moment, they can start again.

Saksaul Tree

The saksaul is so dense it sinks in water. It puts out as much energy as coal when burned, so it could be considered the living coal of the desert. Both varieties of saksaul, black saksaul and white saksaul, go dormant twice a year, sleeping all through summer and autumn. As a friend of mine once said, "Despair makes it impossible to do anything but sleep." But I don't think this "desert slumberer" sleeps because it's hopeless and worn out. Its dormancy comes from a need to build up energy. Its dormant period is more like a monk sitting in a trance. It has its flowering season, though brief, as a night-bloomer. Careless people never see those humble, unassuming night blooms, so unlike the gaudy tamarisk blossoms.

Like the poplar and the tamarisk, it is one of the desert's most tenacious plants, a hero of the vegetal world. It takes to the extreme environment of hot sun, sandstorms, salinity, and aridity like a fish to water. Its requirements are minuscule: a little moisture, a negligible amount of nourishment. It seems not to rely on the outside world at all, and its leaves curl down so they look like little scales lining the branches. If it didn't have to photosynthesize, it would simply drop all those leaves. It is economical in every way, coveting nothing, hoping for nothing.

Its slow growth takes great patience; it is the embodiment of forbearance. A two- or three-year-old saksaul is only as thick as a man's arm, so it must possess iron strength and a grain as fine as jade's. It flowers briefly, sheds unnecessary twigs and leaves, draws in the desert's last drop of water . . . Using every last bit of its patience, it turns a curse into quiet growth, into a ceremony of life.

It is accustomed to a deathly desert, and immersed in the joy of increase. Its disheveled shape is like that of a man on a long trek, travel-worn, weary, his hair matted and uncombed. It trudges on through the loneliness of time, transplanted from the far side of death, traveling miles without moving. So it is for the saksaul: it feasts on aridity like a sumptuous banquet, takes root in desolation as in rich soil.

If the desert were a prison, the saksaul would be serving a life sentence.

Under its own weight it will sink deep into the earth, into darkness, and become a piece of coal.

Snow Leopard

The snow leopard is a totem of the border regions. It roams the high mountain peaks like a rebel soldier, exiling itself to the remote, the lonely, the hard. Its value is revealed in its spiritual and ecological symbolism; it is a divine creation bodied forth into the world. Yes, those dazzling patterns were painted on by the gods.

The snow leopard is a cat writ large or a tiger writ small. It synthesizes the roles of soldier and sage, living high up and hunting down low. It is a sprightly beast of roots and wings combined: exquisite, nimble, eyes like torches, master of an arrogant brutality. According to Kazakh herders, the snow leopard preys on sheep, deer, musk deer, snow hares, and birds; when it rushes into a herd of sheep, it attacks the weakest member and will not harm the others, nor will it make a mess of its prey like a wolf will. Its natural instincts keep its cruelty in check. Most days, it lives only on melted snow, and in that way it passes the endless winter. But the moment its appetite has been sated, its gaze turns mild and its gait elegant, like a cultivated and amiable prince, and it returns to the snowy peaks to meditate in silence, the thoughts of a philosopher turning slowly in its head.

When a person says the words "snow leopard," he has made a choice, just as in the thirteenth century God chose the leopard to be part of Dante's *Divine Comedy*. All rare animals, all great creations, were handpicked by God. It isn't too late for Man to have the courage to be chosen, like the leopard.

The snow leopard lives side by side with Man, and this means Man can still be saved. Look, above the snowline the snow leopard moves like a flame, flaring amid the desolate cold, offering us a point of reference, spurring us on to greater efforts.

Old City

The old city—a dead city, its ruin and collapse hiding its erstwhile prosperity from view: mixed-blood residents, beautiful perfumed women, spice dealers, warriors and bandits, drunkards' songs, temple bells, tavern lamps, traffic, the fragrance of roasting meat, figs hanging from branches, the silvery glint of the oleander trees . . . the dead city is time's masterpiece. Wind, drought, war, and plague have all left their handwriting upon it, a record of disasters and amazements. Men were buried in the sand, written scripts died away, details were lost in the wind, and the dead city stood deserted. A ghost town, a huge ruined cemetery. The living saw the dead city as an asset, a rich vein of memory, and tried by every means possible to enter it, searching madly for a desiccated corpse, a Buddha's head, a piece of pottery, a wooden tablet, a document, anything that might be used as an "open sesame" key to decode the silent, splendid past. But all the reports and exploration led to nothing of interest, lacked vivid detail, and all this suggested that the knowledge of the wise included vast amounts of ignorance. Man's life is limited; his imagination can't shore up a rotted pillar, or repair even the smallest breach in a fallen wall. Although dead cities are riddled with holes, although they are open to the air, they are still tightly closed. People may learn to appreciate the beauty of a ruin, but they will never be able to enter a dead city. It isn't that people abandon cities, but that cities, in dying, make people orphans. Just as before their own deaths, people are the orphans of the dead.

Rocks, the Gobi

Three men are walking in the Gobi. Rocks are strewn into the distance.

The first man says, "Look, what an ugly rock!"

The second man squats on his heels, picks up a piece of gravel, and puts it in his pocket: "To me, every rock is precious. The entire Gobi Desert is my home."

The third man looks at the other two, then says with a sigh: "The Kazakh proverb has it right—since you can't chew on a rock, you might as well kiss it."

The three men start walking again. The first man is prejudice, the second sentimentality, and the third wisdom.

The Failure

By Aydos Amantay

TRANSLATED BY CANAAN MORSE

I

I am a Kazakh who grew up in Beijing, far away from my own people. It wasn't until April of last year that a stroke of good fortune allowed me to travel to a county town in Xinjiang Province to teach Chinese to Kazakh middle-school students.

I had to fly to Urumqi, then spend many hours on a long-distance bus to get there. The bus sped across the grasslands, a bright-green expanse dotted infrequently with snow-white yurts that flicked past the eye.

I knew the people living in the yurts were Kazakhs, but I would never know what kind of life it was they led there. Who was I? A Kazakh who had grown up in Beijing. I had never experienced the grasslands, never kissed that soil. Even when I was there, it was only as a traveler, and like any other tourist, all I could do was take a couple of meaningless pictures as evidence of my presence.

I harbor deep-seated feelings of failure and self-contempt.

There's nothing I can do about it.

Even if I were to abandon Beijing and move to the grasslands to herd sheep, would I have found the Kazakhs? Would I have found myself?

Even in Xinjiang, I was still the same boy with a Beijing accent who loved reading Kafka and going to coffee shops on weekends with his girlfriend. No one who wasn't born on the grasslands can have the spirit of the grasslands within him. The bus wasn't crowded at all; more than half the seats were empty. I smelled an overpowering stench. It may have only been the smell of mud, and I was simply unaccustomed to it. Thinking of this, I sighed and looked out the window.

Sunset burned over the grasslands. It was indescribably beautiful.

We got into town. To me, these county-level towns were just short of being nowhere, but to young kids from the grasslands, this was already "the outside world." I didn't have time to take in the local scenery because I had to report to the school. When I arrived at the front gate, I hesitated for a long time before creeping forward like a thief and peering inside.

The first thing that caught my eye was not the children, but the children's smiles.

———

Immediately I was surrounded and hustled into a dilapidated old classroom. As the former secretary general of my high school's student council, I didn't fear public speaking—yet I was deeply nervous now, as I faced these students for the first time. I wasn't just facing children; I was facing their eyes. Never had I been examined with such intensity. I couldn't tell whether there was special meaning in it, but it made me feel happy. I introduced myself in broken Beijing-flavored Kazakh: "Um, so . . . Uhh . . . I—um—I—ahh—am your new teacher." Before I had even finished, the room erupted in laughter. I scratched my head and stuck out my tongue in embarrassment.

The room laughed harder. I laughed, too.

———

Minutes later, the Head of School got up and gave me a very earnest introduction. He said I was the pride of the Kazakh people, and that I had come from Beijing, our country's capital. That it was such a fortunate surprise that a young man from Beijing would actually agree to come all the way to a backward place like this one to dispense knowledge to all of you. We should all heed his example, he said. He is the true pride of the Kazakh people. The students paid no attention to him. Their little black eyes were too busy running up and down my body. A few of the more impudent boys even made faces at me.

I stood enveloped in the children's collective gaze and listened to the Head of School's embarrassingly exaggerated praise of me. I had intended to deflect his compliments with an apologetic reply, but in the end I let it go.

First of all, my Kazakh was so bad I wouldn't be able to make myself understood.

Second, when I looked into the kids' eyes, I realized it would be utterly meaningless to try.

I was only five years older than they were, but I still like to call them "kids."

The kids in my section liked to go around boasting to the other sections, "We have a teacher from Beijing." They were passionately curious about Beijing. Their questions were all very simple: "Are the buildings tall? Are there a lot of cars?" And I replied in my limping Kazakh, "So tall, so many."

My every answer was followed by an awed "Ohhhh!" from the whole class.

I'm not sure what that exclamation was supposed to imply. I don't think they knew, either.

In fact, life in Beijing was fairly boring. On the weekends, my girlfriend and I went either to the bar and café street, Nanluoguxiang, or to the 798 Art District. Or we went out for coffee. Life was so bland that we had to replace one kind of boredom with another.

Of course, the kids would never have understood that, and I would never have told them.

And yet I couldn't figure it out: these children all came from the grasslands. Growing up in such a vast landscape, how could they think the city was big? Perhaps their definition of big was different from ours, a definition only they could understand.

Conditions in our classroom were as poor as one could imagine. The blackboard was only a section of wall painted black by the students. Even the whitewash on the walls had been done by them. It was a boarding school, and the students all slept there at night. An on-duty teacher, who was responsible for room check-in and security, slept in a small reception office. The administration had wanted to find me an apartment in town, but I refused, offering to live in the reception room full-time. That way, the other teachers wouldn't have to do night duty. Everyone was pleased with this.

The kids were happy about it, too. At first I assumed that this was because they figured their "child teacher" would be easier to negotiate with; but during my time on duty, they seemed even more respectful of the rules than they ordinarily were.

This was a Kazakh school. I was responsible for the students' Chinese language classes. To them, Chinese was a foreign language. Their Chinese was bad, but they liked to speak it. They would tell me in faltering Mandarin, "Teacher, we . . . we really . . . really . . . we really like you."

Naturally, it warmed my heart to hear such things. Their Chinese and my Kazakh were equally bad. Yet we communicated more fluently with each other, using childlike gestures and baby talk, than we did with fellow speakers of our own languages.

They made many moving declarations, though there was one that was particularly unforgettable. It came from Aygelin, a young girl in my class. One day, she rushed excitedly up to me, a wide grin on her face. With determined effort she managed to say, "Teacher is from Beijing. We are Kazakhs. We love our teacher." She was wearing a skirt with a floral print that was too loud for its own good and a shirt that was somewhere between pink and purple. Two glowing cheeks in a baby-fresh face. As soon as she finished, she turned and ran off, giggling.

She believed she had said something that would really please me.

They were fascinated by Beijing. Even though they would probably never learn what Beijing was really like. They each had their own imaginary Beijing. They loved hearing me talk about it. I would say to them in my execrable Kazakh, "Beijing real, real big. Wangfujing Street real, real pretty. The girls real pretty, too!" There would be a roar as the room exploded with cheers and laughter.

These were the only Beijing stories my Kazakh would allow me to tell.

There was one class in which everyone was surprisingly energetic—because, it turned out, they wanted to hear me talk about Beijing. I asked them what they wanted to hear, but the class went quiet in response.

A boy piped up, "We want to hear the last one you told."

So I repeated the story about the buildings being tall and the girls being pretty.

They laughed just as happily as they had before, as if they were hearing it for the first time.

II

The class had one female student who was older than I. Her name was Aydana. She had worked as a waitress for several years in Urumqi. She had settled down, made a little money, made a life for herself. But when the hotel manager wanted to promote her to head waitress, she responded, "Ma'am, I'm leaving." The manager, a middle-aged woman of almost fifty, asked, "Are you unsatisfied with your compensation here? Or have you found a new job?"

"I want to go to school," Aydana stammered.

"You're such a focused worker, and you don't even talk much. You know, you're the only Kazakh worker in this entire hotel, and yet I'm asking you to be the head waitress. It has nothing at all to do with 'ethnic unity.' You're dependable, and I think you have a fighting spirit. I look on you like my own daughter. Think about it."

Aydana replied, "Ma'am, do you know why I don't talk much?"

"No, I don't."

"It's because I don't know any Chinese."

The manager gave her some money. She told Aydana that when she graduated, if she wanted to come back to the hotel, the head waitress position would be waiting for her.

After Aydana finished her story, she kept looking at me silently, as if there were something still unfinished.

The town may have been utterly unremarkable, yet to a Beijing boy like me it seemed full of wonder.

The first contrast that comes to mind was the restaurants.

————

There was one restaurant right near the school entrance called "Yellow Flour Steamed Buns." You walked in and the owner hollered at you, "You want dumplings or noodles?" You chose one of the two. For a kid like me, who was used to picking his way through heavy menus with lots of options to choose from, this was something novel. It gets better. There was another place simply called "Pilaf," with a big Uighur man at the door who asked you, "Big bowl or small bowl?" Then he gave you your bowl of pilaf, and you walked inside to find a seat. Food so fast, it left even KFC in the dust.

At first blush, places like these may have seemed too dirty to me. Yet once I'd taken the time to experience them for what they were, I found their method easier and more sensible than restaurants in Beijing.

I was most impressed by a restaurant called "Mr. Hai's Place." It had no servers, just an old man named Mr. Hai. He sat in his restaurant reading the paper and pondering the great problems facing the nation. There weren't many guests. One day I brought one of the students there. There was a menu, and with no shortage of dishes listed on it. But when we finished ordering, the old man closed the menu, turned, and trotted out the front door, even calling back to us, "Watch the place for me," as my classmate and I looked at each other in disbelief. Five minutes later he came loping back, breathless, a plastic bag of groceries in his hand. Apparently, the food there was all made to order. Prices were astonishingly low; you could have fed five people on twenty yuan. The dishes were good, too. While we ate, the owner sat next to us with his newspaper, occasionally inquiring, "How do you like the beef dish? Does it taste good? Not too much salt in it?"

Beijing has nothing like Mr. Hai's Place.

III

To the students, though, I was still a Beijinger. Whenever I joined their company, they turned reticent. Aygelin was the only exception. She came to my office every day at noon to get help with her Chinese.

She was my favorite student. Her Chinese was nothing special, yet she always fixed her gaze tightly on me during class, and her laugh was so easy and amiable.

Her declaration "Teacher is from Beijing. We are Kazakhs" also gave me reason to like her. Slowly she began to treat me like one of her own. There was a sense of having conquered or proved something—and regardless of which it was, it was expressed with great delight, the kind of delight that's impossible to mute or conceal. She could see it and feel it, though I doubt she knew what it was.

I often took her to the only passable bookstore in town to read during the free time before evening study period. On the way, I would do my best to talk to her in my broken Kazakh. "Kafka . . . Kafka—ahh—umm—he is an author, an outstanding author, he wrote a lot of things Kazakhs don't have. If you can, you—you should learn Chinese. Learn it well. And read him."

She had no idea who Kafka was, so she could only smile and nod. In reality, though I was supposedly the city boy from Beijing who had read books, I didn't really have much to teach her. All I could do was explain to her what I believed to be true using my thoroughly awful Kazakh.

I can no longer remember what exactly we talked about. Most of it had to do with universal equality, democracy, liberty, that sort of thing.

Maybe I didn't express myself clearly; at any rate, she still didn't understand.

That evening, as I returned to the dark reception room, I chided myself for introducing such messed-up ideas to a girl like her. What could a girl from the grasslands possibly want with Kafka? Walking to the window, I looked into a night far blacker than Beijing's. I wanted to smoke a cigarette, then discovered I was terrible at it.

In that moment, that little provincial town seemed like a better place than Beijing.

Though I may have had more knowledge than the people here, that knowledge made me shallower than they.

Restless and unable to sleep, I left the reception room. The sports field was all sand, but I didn't care, and I lay right down on my back. As I stretched out, I inadvertently heaved a long sigh. Lying on the sand, I felt as if Mother Nature were holding on to me. My field of vision was filled with stars. I thought of my first girlfriend. She loved stars. Her greatest dream even now was to look at a sky full of stars.

There I was doing just that, and she was thousands of miles away.

She moved to Beijing from a small city when she was eight. While we were dating, she frequently told me how their house used to face a mountain that was blasted to rubble by miners. They also used to have a huge tree right in their front yard, which she would play under when she was little. Later, she watched as the tree was cut down by men with chainsaws.

She was only a child then, and she thought she was losing her home, though the reality was that people were building. One time, several years after moving to Beijing, she went back home to see relatives. She discovered that everything about the city had improved, and the quality of life had risen. But that evoked a feeling of pain and fear from the very bottom of her heart, worse than when she saw her tree being felled by a chainsaw.

We were sixteen when we dated. I didn't understand her at all. All I knew how to do was constantly promise her that I would become a successful, reliable man. I told her I'd buy her a forest, and build a little house for her in the middle of it. This always made her laugh. Back then, I thought she was laughing because I had made her happy, but now I realize she was simply laughing at me. I admit I never really listened to her. Perhaps because I was only her boyfriend then, not her friend. All I wanted was to make her laugh. I didn't know that smiling and laughing weren't all that happy, or all that important.

I never could understand why, when she spoke of the destruction of her hometown, she never showed any anger. She just repeated the story over and over with no trace of emotion. Sounding utterly unmoved, she'd say, "It's all very hard to accept."

But from the tone of her voice, I could tell that she had already accepted it.

———

We ended things with an inexplicable breakup, just like all other couples that age. Afterward I realized that the reason she'd talked to me about her hometown was not because I was her boyfriend. It was because I was Kazakh. Even though I had grown up in Beijing, the Kazakhs are from Xinjiang, so I had the air of a wanderer, like she did. It may even have been the reason we dated in the first place. We remain good friends to this day, supporting and encouraging each other.

She's currently studying mechanical engineering at a very good university here in China. This girl who always hated machines, who watched machines bulldoze her childhood memories flat, decided when she was nineteen to learn how to build them.

This apparently contradictory situation somehow makes perfect sense to me.

Only I don't know why it should make sense, just as she didn't know why she accepted it.

———

Becoming friends with Aygelin brought me closer to the other female students in the class. Sometimes in the evenings they would invite me to their dormitory to drink milk tea. When the girls from the adjacent dorms heard I was there, they would come by, too. Everyone would squeeze together in one little room. It was a warm scene.

The surface of the narrow table in the middle of the room would be jampacked with cups of all different kinds. Some had cracked lips, while some of the ceramic ones looked like they'd seen a century of use. They were nestled together on the table, their colors mismatched and garish. When each one had been filled with steaming hot milk tea, no one immediately reached for her own, but sat there, watching.

Perhaps drinking milk tea is a happiness only a Kazakh can know.

———

I imagine my ancestors. On bitter cold winter days and nights they crouched together inside a yurt, a pot of milk tea between them. Anyone traveling across the vast plains could step into any yurt and receive the host's attention. That same pot of milk tea would be placed in front of them.

Several people have said to me that the Kazakhs never produced any heroes. To me, this seems no great cause for anxiety. I am moved by the fact that, no matter how much hardship these people have had to face, even in their darkest hours they have held fast to a bowl of milk tea. They understand the happiness it holds. They understand the happiness of a group of living, breathing people, dark-eyed and red-faced, gathered around a bowl of milk tea. Everyone around me reached for their own cups, and they sat looking at each other, giggling and sipping.

Aydana pulled out some rounds of nang flatbread and quickly tore them into manageable pieces. Several people reached out to take some. It was the first time I'd observed the hands of Kazakh girls. They were larger and stronger than mine. The skin above their knuckles was thick and creased. Aygelin's hands were no exception.

When I extended my hand for a piece of nang, Aygelin cried out, "Look! Teacher's hands are so soft! Just like a girl's!" I immediately yanked my hand back while the girls laughed heartily. Beijing girls are all very polite when they laugh, and hold their small hands lightly over their mouths. The girls in front of me guffawed loudly, like the hard-drinking bandits of legend.

They ate their nang by spreading it with a thick layer of butter before dunking it in their tea. They said this was the Kazakh way of eating it. I followed their example and crammed two big pieces of nang into my stomach. There were cheers and applause. Aygelin was watching me eat and smiling, as if to say, "Teacher, now you are a real Kazakh." She tore a piece from the half-moon she held and stuffed it into my hand. "Here! One more piece!" I ate it using the "hundred-percent Kazakh method." More applause and acclaim.

I didn't tell any of them that I didn't like to eat nang this way. I wanted them to call me a Kazakh, Aygelin especially. I don't know why.

Finally, we sat on the beds and sang Kazakh songs. The nights in Xinjiang are cold. Yet we were all together in one room, drinking tea, eating nang, and singing. All feelings of cold—those blown in from the window as well as those risen within the heart—were banished without a trace. They sang:

> I love the one I hold, may all things rest
> Do not believe the world   has only beauty
> When you believe everyone   in the world is lovely
> Don't forget that earthly beauty   is only in the mold
>
> Galloping toward the mountain pass
> The pass is right before your eyes
> Sitting at table with family and friends
> Happiness is right before your eyes
>
> A star on my steed's brow, I've come to see you
> I built a railing around the well, afraid you'd fall
> I come purposefully to your door, O my girl
> Don't pretend not to know me, and turn on your heel
>
> Galloping toward the mountain pass
> The pass is right before your eyes
> Sitting at table with family and friends
> Happiness is right before your eyes

Such a lovely song. Whenever I hear it, I wonder if the Kazakhs really are a race free from care and anxiety. But not all things are as beautiful as songs.
Life is still life.

———

There were two problem children in my class. They were bad students. One was called Kaysa, the other Kaylat. They went out drinking every night. I frequently invited Aygelin and her roommate out to dinner, and we would invariably find those two drinking in the restaurant. "They aren't good students. We don't like them," Aygelin would whisper to me. I could only smile weakly in response. Whether or not they were good students was not a crucial issue.

Yet their way of drinking confused me. They would face each other across the table without saying a word. They'd simply pop the caps off their bottles of beer and drink in total silence. Neither would utter a single syllable to the other the entire time. To me, it seemed boring in the extreme. But they did it every night.

They just stared at each other and drained the bottles in front of them. Restaurants in small cities are always loud. Most of the guests at even the halal restaurants were Han people from the city, and there was a constant squawking in Mandarin Chinese. I watched the two of them drink quietly, their fingers wrapped tightly around their beer bottles.

If you're a Kazakh, you know that many of our people are alcoholics. That such people drink doesn't concern me, but I am interested to know how they get drunk. Is it at the dinner table, singing with friends and family, or are they like these two boys, drinking alone in some loud or quiet but nevertheless lonely corner of the city?

———

IV

Aygelin and I had a lot of good times together.

One night, as she and I were coming back from the bookstore, she fell silent for a moment, then asked, "Um, you know what?"

"What?"

Before she even responded, she burst out laughing. "You look like a little bear! You look like a bear when you talk to me."

I smiled and shook my head. Whether they're from the grasslands or from Beijing, girls say some nonsensical things.

———

Still, this nonsensical little girl had some brawn to her. One day when we were out on the sports field, she said, "Teacher, let's see who's stronger!" "Um, maybe that's not a good idea," I replied, but she had already sat down in the grass and assumed the position. So with a laugh, I sat down as well to arm-wrestle a fourteen-year-old girl. Now, I'm no weakling, but as soon as my hand gripped hers, I regretted my decision. I couldn't put her down. Nor was she impatient to beat me; she merely looked at me with those impish, twinkling eyes. My ego had been wounded. I relaxed my wrist, and the conflict ended quickly.

She grinned in exultation. I felt a momentary disgust for her. "The weaker one has to do what the stronger one says," she mandated. I grunted in assent. "You have to do what I say," she continued. I grunted again.

Moments later, she declared that I needed to be punished by receiving a hard flick on the forehead. I closed my eyes and awaited the impact. But I felt a soft tickle next to my nose instead. Opening my eyes, I found Aygelin holding the stalk of some plant, which she was twiddling over my face.

I may be wrong, but at that moment she seemed almost bashful.

"Zhysang," she told me.

I stared blankly.

She pointed to the herb, and repeated, "Zhysang."

———

She gave me the plant. Its odor wasn't sweet like a flower's perfume; it was the pure scent of grass. Later in life, whenever I smelled that odor, I thought of Kazakh girls. The dictionary revealed that "zhysang" was actually just the Kazakh word for mugwort, a common enough plant.

I don't know whether this plant holds any special significance in Kazakh culture, but frankly, I would prefer that it didn't. I would prefer that its background were as clean and uncomplicated as its aroma.

I gave Aygelin a Chinese nickname, "Miss Nonsense." This Miss Nonsense frequently made me nonsensically annoyed, as if she were making fun of me for being from the city. At other times her nonsense would move me in ways Beijing never could.

Happiness is extended in time spent simply. The days kept repeating themselves, yet without becoming monotonous. Everything was so simple, until the day when little Miss Nonsense fell nonsensically in love with me.

———

It was in the wee hours of the morning. I was sleeping soundly in the reception room. There was a knock on the door. I sat up and turned on the light. It was 2 A.M. Beijing time.

Who could it be?

My clothing in complete disarray, I went to the door and opened it to find Aygelin standing in front of me. She was wearing a pink skirt and, incredibly, had even put on makeup. Seeing the bright red of her lips through the half-light, I felt that something bad was about to happen, though I couldn't imagine what.

"Aygelin, is something wrong? It's so late." She didn't reply; she said nothing. It was the first time I had ever seen her serious.

———

I had just woken up, and my mind was a jumble. It was the first time I'd ever seen her with her face so clean and made up. My heart quivered, and I realized she was actually quite pretty. But I quieted my emotions, smiled, and asked, "Aygelin, is there anything I can do for you?"

Tears welled up in her eyes. Her face was contorted. She started babbling in Kazakh, speaking much too fast for me to understand. Then she pulled out a few notecards and read me Kazakh poems. I stared at her in complete confusion. She spoke to me some more. I merely looked at her through a sleep-drunk haze, as if she were a dream. The only thing I understood was the final question: ". . . will you?"

I shook my head. "I didn't understand you."

Her head was down, but she raised it now and gazed at me with glistening eyes.

There was a long silence. The only sound was her heavy breathing.

Then, in broken Mandarin, she said, "Teacher, I . . . I have fallen—fallen in love with you."

———

My only thought was that this couldn't be real, that I must be dreaming. Without thinking, I replied, "I don't know. I need to sleep," and shut the door heavily. I shouldn't have said that, but I had no choice.

But when I lay back down in bed, I was as awake as I'd ever been. I stared at the cracks in the ceiling. I should have been thinking of ways to deal with this girl, yet my mind was drawn uncontrollably back to Beijing.

Beijing, land of my childhood. Beijing: Tian'anmen, the Forbidden City, the Great Wall, Beihai . . .

Walking hand in hand with my girlfriend through the crowds at Shichahai, I felt like I had found my lost self. I would take her to the Museum of Art, not to look at the paintings, but to look at her. On summer nights we'd sit on the rooftop terrace of some restaurant in Nanluoguxiang, and I would watch her drink beer. Winters in the Temple of the Earth Park. The roots of the ancient trees curled and twisted, the setting sun so beautiful it stopped the breath, sparrows dancing in the air around us.

These times weren't entirely without their uncomfortable moments, of course. That discomfort was caused by one particular difference. Whenever I walked alone down the streets or narrow alleys of Beijing, old women would often smile at me and say, "Welcome to China!"

When I told the most recent "Welcome to China" story to my girlfriend, she merely giggled. I laughed with her, though I knew it wasn't something to laugh about.

Ever since I was small, I have hoped to make my differences invisible. Those differences are often very hard to bear.

————

My thoughts were in chaos.

I was only a guest; in two weeks I would be leaving this small town, never to return. In the end, I thought, I am still different. More importantly, Beijing represented development, modernity, opportunity . . . Those were all things this little town would never have. Only, in Beijing, I often felt like a wanderer. As if I didn't belong to that land, but couldn't find my own home. I had never slept with my girlfriend. But tonight, after Aygelin's confession, I felt a burning desire for my girlfriend to be with me. I could smell my own weakness. It had settled into the deepest pocket of my life and put down roots.

I lay in bed, unable to sleep and feeling like I was quietly breaking down. The next day, I would have to see Aygelin's naturally beautiful face. I would catch her by the hand and say to her, "Aygelin, we can't be together. We're just too different." Once I said those words, I would lose the most precious hope and emotion I had felt to date. I couldn't give myself resolve, nor come up with a reason to have it.

The sun rose. The day had started too quickly, I thought.

————

V

Before class that morning, I screwed up my courage and explained myself to Aygelin. "I'm only here for two months in all, and I only have two weeks left. For the two of us to be together just isn't realistic. You're a good person."

I figured that once I told her, everything would be fine.

————

Yet I had no sooner stepped into the classroom than Aygelin started to cry. It appeared that everyone knew her problem already. No one spoke. My own mind was awash in delirium. Feelings of shame mixed with a sensation like moving through a dream with no way to escape. I couldn't help missing Beijing and my girlfriend. I hoped she would come and rescue me, though I couldn't say exactly why I needed to be saved.

So I stood awkwardly at the blackboard and taught my lesson. Today's example was "Excuse me, how do I get to Wangfujing Street?" Everyone did their best to listen and pronounce it correctly. I was kicking myself, wishing I hadn't picked this kind of example.

As the entire class repeated it in unison, it set off the noise of Aygelin's sobbing, which echoed throughout the classroom. I finally lost control of my emotions and yelled, "Aygelin! Go stand in the corner!" Only when she stood up did I realize she was still wearing the pink skirt from the night before. She wiped her cheeks as she walked to the far corner.

During that class, Aygelin cried from the starting bell all the way to the end.

When the period was over, I put on my teacher's face and scolded her: "Pay attention to your work and stop crying! Do you hear me?" She just wiped her eyes and said between sobs, "You're leaving soon, anyway—."

Every day she came back to tell me she loved me. When she made me genuinely angry, I asked, "What is it you really want?" She realized I was mad and got scared. She apparently hadn't expected that I would ask her such a question, or that such a question might even be raised. She stared at me and replied, "I just . . . love you."

Perhaps I did injure her pure heart.

"Aygelin can't see! Teacher! Aygelin's eyes hurt!" Aydana ran over to me, breathing hard. I ran out of the office to find Aygelin covering her eyes with her hands. I pulled her hands away and saw that both of her eyes were bright red. I put her on my back and set off for the town's health clinic, my mind a total blank.

The smell of cleaning fluid pervaded the clinic. I carried Aygelin all the way to the doctor's office. The doctor unhurriedly went on about his business for a while before finally putting on his stethoscope and cursorily examining her eyes. Then, still unfazed, he said, "Oh, this is nothing. Just an infection."

"Doctor, how could it be nothing?" I exclaimed. "Her eyes really hurt, and they're all red."

The doctor replied, "There is a medicine for it, but I'd recommend she just use a normal eyewash instead."

"How come?"

"For her benefit. The medicine isn't for her."

"How is it not for her?"

The doctor got annoyed and looked up at me. "Ninety yuan a bottle! I'm saying this for her own good. Have her use a normal eyewash and she'll be fine; it'll just take a little longer."

I looked at Aygelin. Her face had turned red, and she lowered her head.

Glaring at the doctor, I pulled a hundred-yuan note from my wallet, slammed it on the table, and growled, "Keep the change."

———

She rode on my back the whole way home.

On the road she remarked, "I thought you wouldn't even care if something happened to me."

———

Even today, as I am writing this story, I doubt she fully understands how important she was to me. She was the first Kazakh to smile at me that way. I've had a lot of Kazakhs tell me I'm a fine young man.

Yet none of them had ever smiled at me the way she did.

———

Aygelin was recuperating in her dormitory. That day the students all had gym class, so I took the time to go to Aygelin's room to see her and administer her medicine.

As I was dripping it in her eyes, she asked, "Why don't you like me?"

I sighed and replied, "You know I have a girlfriend back in Beijing."

"A Han girl?"

I gave a half-smile and nodded.

Our race usually doesn't allow intermarriage with Han people. I hadn't planned on telling her any of this. Still, after I'd said it, I felt it wasn't the reason she and I would never be together.

She paused for a moment, then asked, "Is she pretty?"

"Uh-huh, she is."

"Probably better-looking than I am?"

I didn't reply. She sighed, then said, "Well, I wish you both happiness!"

Then she snatched the bottle from my hands and applied her medicine herself.

"It's really not because there's anything wrong with you," I continued. "Ten more days and I'm gone. And I won't be coming back."

She pulled herself close to me, and in a soft voice asked, "Why won't you come back? We're all Kazakhs. We're your people, we love you. There are none of your people in Beijing."

I inhaled reflexively the moment she came near. Her body had a strange perfume to it, entirely different from the way Han women smelled.

It was the smell of fresh milk. She had been milking cows her whole life.

I like that smell.

Yet I said resolutely, "I can't live in the grasslands. We'll never be together."

I didn't know how things were going for my girlfriend in Beijing.

At the end of 2008, I tested into a good university in Beijing. Unable to adapt to the university method of education, however, I chose to drop out. While I was there, I studied in the Chinese department. But I decided to take control of my own life and work as a freelance writer. Quite a romantic ideal, but it put a lot of pressure on me and my family. I loved my girlfriend, even hoped to start a family and spend the rest of my life with her. But I didn't know what to do. I knew the racial issue would mean that we wouldn't have many well-wishers.

And what about me? Never went to college, spending all my time writing stuff nobody reads—even if we did end up together, how would I support her?

She was the calm, collected type, with a very unexcitable personality. She always found my love to be a little too intense. She preferred slower, more stable men. Being with her gave me a feeling like I couldn't stretch my arms. If only she could love me the way Aygelin loved me, I thought. But if she did, that wouldn't be her.

Yet if I loved her dispassionately and soberly, would that be me?

VI

There was an open interview at school. A company came to interview Kazakh high school seniors for positions as tour guides. Aygelin, Aydana, and I went to listen in.

The interviewer was a Han. Dressed in a suit but with the air of a provincial buffoon, he sat grandiosely on the stage.

"Any special abilities?"

"Singing, dancing, playing the dombra."

". . . Any special abilities?"

"Singing, dancing, playing the dombra."

The interviewer shook his head pretentiously. "How is it that none of you can do anything but sing, dance, and play the dombra?"

The audience went dead quiet.

The interviewer made a stupid joke to cover the silence. "This isn't good at all, ha ha; all your race can do is sing and dance, nothing else? This won't work."

The Head of School, who sat next to him, laughed, too, almost more heartily than he did.

The students seethed with dissent. Everyone began talking and arguing together. Aygelin touched me on the shoulder and said, "What he's saying is, he thinks we're all dumb, like we don't know anything."

Aydana chimed in, "Right. Teacher, you're the only one of us who speaks Chinese. You can't let him talk like that."

Every single student there possessed a sensitive mind and a pure spirit. These are the fundamental qualities of being human. It was only the difference of language that kept them from displaying their talent. It might be easy for a stranger to mistakenly believe that all they did was dance and sing all day. But how could they make this man in front of them understand otherwise?

I stood up. I had no idea what to say . . .

––––––––

The eyes of the "boss" doing the interviews and of all the other teachers turned to me. They knew this was a Kazakh who could speak flawless Mandarin. They were waiting for me to stand up for them. My mind replayed scenes of the students tearing off pieces of nang for me. We had sung, danced, and spent carefree days together.

Glancing to one side, I noticed Aygelin staring fixedly at me.

My race can do more than just dance and sing. We understand the very nature of man's relationship to man. From one perspective, even that is enough. The boss was looking at me with a smirk on his face. "Do you have something to say?" "I . . ." I lowered my head and looked back at Aygelin.

I don't know why I was shaking with excitement and anger. I slowly lifted a finger and pointed at the "boss."

Nor do I know why I suddenly shouted:

"Fuck you! You're the one who doesn't fucking know anything!"

Every kid in the room seemed to understand the meaning of what I said. Their soft black eyes were all trained on me.

Aygelin gazed at me with an expression overflowing with love and excitement.

I nodded and swallowed. Then I said:

"Hell, you can't even sing or dance!"

Dead silence, then enthusiastic applause, followed by boos and catcalls directed at the "boss." Aygelin hadn't laughed so heartily in a long time.

I had never done anything so crazy before. When I realized what had happened, I grabbed Aydana and Aygelin by the hand and hightailed it out of the room.

From a moral standpoint, I shouldn't have done it. He wasn't a bad person, he just didn't know enough about my people. I understand him. My protestation was really more of a vent for my own emotions. I was filled with a nameless anguish. It was because of the good times I had had with the Kazakhs, as well as the pure spirits of my students, who had been so hardworking and persistent in their studies. They shouldn't be judged so hastily, especially not as a group.

At that moment I realized it would be impossible to explain myself to someone I didn't know.

I only had five days left at the school, so the administration didn't punish me for what I had done. They appeased the visitor by saying I was a child who didn't understand the world, and I would soon be leaving the school anyway. By the second day, everyone in my class knew. When I walked into the room, they all applauded. Called me a Kazakh hero.

Yet I was strongly conflicted. Not because the man had said what he'd said, but because I knew that on some level he was right. The Kazakhs are a great race. Yet if the outside world can't see our true spirit, how will they ever understand us? So they don't; they think Kazakhs are all singers and dancers. Some of this is our responsibility.

First we need to understand our own most valuable character, then transform it into a motivating force. We have to make ourselves known to others and, as we do so, look to create value. If we don't, but instead abandon or reject society and the times, the day will come when not only will others be unable to recognize our quality, but we will hardly be persuaded by it, either.

I addressed my students intently. "It's nothing. You are the ones who need to prove yourselves! You see, they don't know anything about us. Why? Because we haven't shown them who we are." I paused, then continued: "If someone praises you for being able to sing and dance, then you've really failed, because every one of you is intelligent and talented. You have to strive for success, to keep them from misunderstanding us like he did."

By the time I finished, the children were quiet. Even though there had been silence before, only then, as I looked in their eyes, did I feel they were quiet.

No one spoke.

I went on: "What I want to say is that he doesn't represent Han people, either. For instance—Aydana, your manager is a good person. I grew up in Beijing. My friends are all Hans, and they're good to me. Everything I know, I learned from them. I'm sure you all have met Hans who are good people, haven't you?

I looked over the entire class. The majority of the students nodded, while a few simply stared at me, their faces expressionless.

Kaysa and Kaylat were among the expressionless ones.

VII

Still, I was disappointed. The students worked their hardest to imitate my line "Fuck you! You're the one who doesn't fucking know anything!" I regretted ever saying it. They described how heroic I had been, how I had humiliated the bad guy. Some of the tales were embellished even further. Something about the bad guy sweating bullets, his legs shaking uncontrollably.

The most ridiculous version included a whispered final line: "I'll never go up against the Kazakhs again!"

I mean, come on. It was totally faked!

Even so, the students were still climbing over each other to tell and retell the "never go up against the Kazakhs again" version. They'd huddle up in a group, repeating it over and over to one another.

One day I overheard Aygelin's version. It never even mentioned the interviewer. It was all about how handsome and courageous I had been. How my beard quivered once my blood was up.

After hearing that, I couldn't help but laugh long and hard.

Aygelin's version of the story reminded me: even though the Kazakh people do have their shortcomings, we still possess our own inimitable charm.

I was afraid the incident would spark some kind of racial tension among the students, but they were kids, after all, and within a few days they had forgotten all about it. Two days before I left, the administration suddenly announced an all-school assembly, in order to implement thought education.

All classes were canceled for the sake of thought education.

During the assembly, the school leaders called out "two students" for special criticism. Said they had shirked their responsibilities, and even attempted to encourage the backward practice of young love outside of school. One of the students was Kaysa from my section. He and a girl from another section were made to stand in the center of the assembly hall, surrounded by watching eyes. The Head of School made a vigorous proclamation: "The Kazakhs must not be a race of failures!"

Some of the students bowed their heads, while others looked on impassively.

The Head of School went on. "There are those among you who resent your parents, resent them because they didn't have much to give you. But there is only one way you can change that, and that is persistent study! Your parents give you money to study here, and you spend your time on romance? What would you say to them?"

I was a little put off. What he said was basically correct: students ought to spend their time studying. But I always felt that the Kazakhs were a free and open people, and shouldn't be worrying about this set of ethical baggage.

Just as I thought this, I discovered Aygelin looking directly at me.

The Head of School repeated his question: "Are there any others involved in romantic relationships? Honesty will be met with leniency!"

Aygelin was looking at me with an impassioned eye and an inexplicable smile.

I frowned and shook my head. I even put a finger to my lips to encourage her to keep quiet.

She saw my fear and sighed, then laughed out loud.

———

Later I asked her what she had been thinking. She said she wanted to confess, to say, "Sir, I am in love with our teacher from Beijing." Though she didn't love me.

I asked her why.

She said that way we could be together, standing in front of the entire school, with everyone looking at us. That would make her happy.

I was leaving in two days.

Looking at this lovelorn girl whom I'd never see again, I found it hard to let her go. But when I smelled that sweet tang of milk on her body, I understood that she belonged here.

Curious, I asked her: "Aygelin, tell me, why did you fall in love with me?"

"Because you look like a baby bear."

"Tell the truth."

"Because of Cofka."

"Cofka? You mean Kafka? Why because of him? You don't even know who he is."

"You told me about him. Just like you told me about democracy and liberty."

"Do you understand democracy?"

"No."

"Why would you fall in love with me because I told you about that crazy stuff?"

"Because no one told me about these things before. I don't know what kind of crazy thing Kafka is. But I know no one ever told me about him before."

I gently stroked her hair.

She said, "I promise I will study hard, read a lot of books, and learn who Cofka is."

I felt like crying. I held her like I was holding my entire people.

I whispered in her ear, "One day you'll know who Cofka is. One day you'll know everything."

And on the day you know who Kafka is, you'll realize he's utterly meaningless.

Aygelin leaned softly against me as I held her, without saying a word. She started singing that old song:

> A star on my steed's brow, I've come to see you
> I built a railing around the well, afraid you'd fall
> I come purposefully to your door, O my girl
> Don't pretend not to know me, and turn on your heel
>
> Galloping toward the mountain pass
> The pass is right before your eyes
> Sitting at table with family and friends
> Happiness is right before your eyes

On the eve of my parting, the song seemed deeply meaningful.

————

Aygelin left. I passed the night alone on my bed, staring at the ceiling. I remembered when I was her age, fourteen or so, and I fell in love with a girl. She liked to write poems in the Song dynasty classical style, and her beauty was as graceful and moving as her poetry, echoing strongly the old classical ideals of the female figure. We got along very well; I gradually fell in love with her, and eventually confessed it. I was still a child back then, and everything I said was childish. I told her that I loved her, I wanted her to be my girlfriend, and maybe someday I'd marry her.

Of course, my unexpected zeal frightened her. I believe she actually liked me and thought I was a nice boy. Yet in the end she rejected me. My love was too fierce for her, too much like a ball of flame, which made her afraid.

I was severely disappointed.

Thinking carefully about it now, I see that the way I chose to love back then was the same way Aygelin chose to love me. I had always thought my way of loving was unique to my personality; after Aygelin, I wondered if it might be related to my ethnicity.

Yet there I was only five years later, at nineteen, looking at her the same way my first love had looked at me, afraid of her love because it was too intense, too headlong, too difficult to defend against.

Wouldn't denying that love mean denying myself?

————

My friends' influence made me more realistic. But what is reality? They told me, "Nobody loves the way you do, like a volcano ready to erupt."

But maybe I love this way because I'm Kazakh?

————

While the Kazakhs are not the most successful race, never invented airplanes or cannons, they hold a certain truth in their bones. A certain sentiment. It isn't very noble, nor is it complex. But if you give a Kazakh a handful of earth, he will know how to hold on tight to it, and teach you what a handful of earth feels like.

This is a kind of genuine truth.

————

I once believed that all other reality disappeared in the face of this truth.

I still believe that.

VIII

In the midst of my all-night meditations, I fell ill. The thermometer measured my temperature at 39.5 Celsius. I repeatedly whispered Aygelin's name. To this day I'm still not sure what kind of illness it was. Not only did it come with a fever, it made my fingers ache.

Through my delirium, I saw the outline of Aygelin approach my bed. I caught the scent of milk, and some empty space inside me was temporarily filled. Her face seemed far from me, and only her bright pink dress fluttered before my eyes.

In my exhaustion I seemed to find a measure of satisfaction, which only led to deeper exhaustion. My eyelids drooped. Aygelin might have been crying; I couldn't hear clearly.

"Teacher, teacher, what hurts?"

"My—a fever, and . . . and my—my fingers hurt."

———

She fell quiet for half a minute, then I heard the sound of running footsteps leaving the room.

It was a full five or six minutes before she came back.

Aygelin sat by the edge of the bed and said to me, "Teacher, this disease is common on the grasslands. Kazakhs have the best medicine for it. I have some with me. I'll put it on you. Just lie here a while; the pain will go away and the fever will break." My world was fading in and out, and I could only nod my head.

———

I felt her take hold of my hand. I touched the abrasive calluses on hers, and they instantly made me feel safe. With her other hand she painted the medicine on my fingers. "Good, don't be afraid, you'll be fine soon," she comforted me gently. "Don't be afraid, don't worry, go to sleep and it will all be better."

She was the very model of a mother comforting a sick child.

The tears came unbidden from my eyes. I felt I had been wrong—that I had been making the same mistake over and over again for so many years, without ever knowing why. I grasped her hands tightly, as if she were the one leaving, not I. While I held one hand, I played my thumb across the thick, lined skin on the back of her palm, and over the calluses that had risen there who knows how long ago, as if I were looking for something.

She started to sob. In my half-conscious state I asked, "Is this your hand?" She didn't reply, nor did she need to.

As I held those hands, I thought about how different we were.

I understood that my mistake was not recognizing or admitting this difference before.

I hadn't admitted the difference, but after admitting it, I realized that nothing was significantly different.

I am and will always be a Chinese-speaking Kazakh.

My hands will forever be like a woman's, soft and smooth and unlike the hands of a Kazakh.

I am different from the Kazakhs of the grassland. I know I have a home there, but I can never go back. This often made me feel inferior. I felt like I'd been abandoned. Yet on that day, I finally understood. Difference and similarity don't show in the hands. And the degree of difference between my hands and Aygelin's has nothing to do with whether mine have calluses.

It is whether or not we hold on to each other.

———

This is a fairly superficial truth, but I couldn't have learned it from a book. One can only know what a Kazakh is, what one's own race, one's family, is, by holding a Kazakh's hand.

The two of us cried for a long time, yet neither could guess why the other was crying.

I recalled that I never cried in the city. Not when I broke up with a girlfriend, failed at something, felt lonely or in pain. As if I were stronger there. Or had tears and emotion already become discourtesies in the city? Everyone must do their best to restrain tears and emotion, love and hate. Sit on the subway and look serious as you play games on your hand-helds. Then, only when the recorded voice reminds you to "Please get ready for your arrival," you should stand up and force yourself unwillingly toward the door. Then get off and disappear into the endless crowd . . .

———

Exhaustion carried me off to sleep again. When I awoke, Aygelin was sitting beside me, a smile on her face. Sure enough, my fingers didn't hurt and my forehead was cooler. But when I looked down at my fingers, I broke into a sweat anyway. My fingernails were painted with a light-pink nail polish, and they glittered in the light.

Having just woken up, my face wore an expression of surprise and dull confusion. Aygelin couldn't help but laugh.

"So your special Kazakh medicine is really nail polish?" I asked in astonishment.

"I bought it for a lot of money. And look, your fingers don't hurt anymore, right?"

It was weird, but she was right—they didn't.

"As I put it on," she continued, "I thought, Teacher will get better, he has to get better. And you're better."

I stared at her and nodded.

IX

It was almost time to go. I spent hours on my own wandering through the city. Everything was beautiful under the setting sun. I thought several times about writing a detailed record of this town, afraid that it would lose its present face, as the great tree in my first girlfriend's front yard was eventually cut down. Yet even after long deliberation, I didn't do it.

Before I left, Aydana and I went out to Mr. Hai's Place. I asked Aydana if she would go back to the same restaurant where she'd worked before. She said she didn't know. I told her she'd certainly end up successful. She said again that she didn't know. I realized that she still wasn't talking much. I worried that her reticence at work was not due to her limited Chinese. Maybe if she graduated and went back, life would still be difficult. But I didn't say that.

We were all in or near our twenties. No matter what we faced today, we would get through it.

Everyone should face their own future in the manner of Kazakh songs.

I bade goodbye to Mr. Hai. Surprised, he asked me where I was going. I told him my home was in Beijing.

With sincere gravity, the old man put down his newspaper, stood up, and shook my hand, saying, "Child, no matter where you are, always study hard. I wish you the best of luck on your journey. Make our country stronger and more glorious."

Had someone in Beijing said that to me, it would have sounded insincere. Yet this white-haired old Mr. Hai, I thought, must have been one of those first Party cadres who were sent over to help with Xinjiang's restoration all those years ago. Every sentence was as earnest and as genuine as his restaurant.

That evening, I broke bread with the students one last time. They sang for me again:

> I love the one I hold, may all things rest
> Do not believe the world   has only beauty
> When you believe everyone   in the world is lovely
> Don't forget that earthly beauty   is only in the mold

> Galloping toward the mountain pass
> The pass is right before your eyes
> Sitting at table with family and friends
> Happiness is right before your eyes

The day of my departure was almost here. Both narrative and story continue in the form of a farewell.

———

An uncomfortable Aygelin walked into my room. It was my last night.

We looked at each other, neither of us knowing quite what to say.

I asked her, "Where will you be in the future?"

"On the grasslands, of course."

"It's nice there," I replied, as if talking to myself. No one spoke again for a long while.

———

She asked, "Was it because I was bad that you got sick?"

"Silly girl. I got sick because I was stupid."

I looked at that face. She was actually quite beautiful, just hardened by wind and rain. I imagined her milking cows, and the image touched me.

With a sudden passion, I said, "Aygelin, will you hold me? I'm sorry—even though I don't love you, and I'm leaving tomorrow, will you hold me for a while?"

Perhaps I shouldn't have asked, but she wrapped her arms around me anyway.

I had long ago forgotten that I was her teacher, even forgotten that this was a girl who loved me. I curled myself into her embrace, and deeply inhaled that scent of milk. Only then was I fully conscious of how much I cherished that smell. Beijing may have towering skyscrapers and all kinds of luxurious, beautiful things, but it will never have that faint smell of fresh milk.

———

I said to Aygelin, "You know, there's something else I'd like to do."

"What?"

"To write something, once I have the opportunity. I want to write about you. And about the happiness of Kazakhs eating nang and drinking milk tea together. About our people's simple, profound love for the world. So they will really understand us."

She nodded vigorously. I never thought I'd be confessing my dreams and ambitions in the arms of a fourteen-year-old girl. But there's nothing you can't say to a friend like that.

"You're going back to Beijing soon, you'll get to see your girlfriend. Are you happy?"

I nodded, then shook my head. And then I said something strange: "You know, when I'm in Beijing, I really don't like the sun."

"Why? Why don't you like the sun?"

"The sun rising means another day of work and problems. Sometimes I just wish it would never come up."

"Don't say that. The Kazakh people love the sun. We Kazakhs must love the sun."

The hands that held me squeezed. There was a childlike earnestness in what she said. Perhaps childlike earnestness is the way in which Kazakhs regard the sun.

"One day, when our Han friends read the things I've written, they will truly understand our race. Now they only come to the grasslands to breathe the fresh air and take a few quick pictures." I looked into her eyes and said softly, "They will come to the grassland and love the sun like we do."

After saying that, I was overtaken by incredible fatigue, and drifted to sleep within the smell of milk and her embrace. She continued to hold me, not daring to move. This man she loved had been a bit brutish with her, not intimate at all. Only on this final night could she hold him like a baby. He lay quietly and obediently in her arms, as if he weren't going anywhere, as if he would sleep there forever.

I smacked my lips and fell dead to the world. She kept gazing at me. She knew that this man, this man who was sleeping in her arms like a child, would be leaving her the very next day. She held her man, her prince who belonged to her alone.

Even at the end, I felt like I never saw her as the callow love-struck fourteen-year-old she was. I looked at her almost as if she were my entire people.

Perhaps this is a tragedy.

———

This boy of hers was a bit of a bookworm. Sometimes I wonder, why was his fear so great? Could this embrace truly change or comfort him? Why did it all happen?

We won't worry about all this. It was the last embrace of his last night in town. Holding on to the man she loved, our Aygelin fell asleep, too. They were lovable people; whether or not their lives go smoothly, lovable people will always find happiness . . .

———

X

———

The hour of my departure finally came. The whole class went with me to the bus station to see me off. Before the bus had even arrived, the girls started crying, sobbing together with Aygelin.

Aydana grabbed me and said, "Teacher, no one ever taught me as much as you did."

I looked at them all in confusion. Isn't that what teachers are supposed to do? Although, to that day I still wasn't sure what, if anything, I had taught them.

————

I had worn cheap clothing during my time in town in order to avoid attention. Only that day did I take the name-brand clothes back out of my suitcase and put them on. I looked at myself in my nice clothes. Clothes that pulled me so far away from all of them.

The bus arrived. I bought a ticket and got on. The other passengers saw the crying children and gave me strange looks. They leaned close to the window and gossiped in dialect, "What d'you think, why are all these kids crying? What're they crying about—what happened?"

When I wore my old clothes, I didn't really care how people looked at me. Now the entire bus was looking at me and talking, making idle conjectures. I timidly replied, "I'm a teacher from the city. The children don't understand politeness; please don't be angry."

Everyone else on the bus was looking at the kids, yet I turned my head away.

"Goodbye, teacher! Think of us," all the students yelled in unison. Everyone was crying. I couldn't help but look back at them. Even Kaysa and Kaylat, the two boys I had never really liked, were crying. They all waved to me in farewell.

I turned my head away again and yelled out, "Driver, let's go!" The driver, who had probably never seen such a scene before, sat dumbstruck in his seat, looking at the children. I yelled again, "Driver! Let's GO!"

The driver roused himself, and the bus backed slowly out.

I stuck my head out the window. The children were running behind the bus, calling out in their tender young voices, "Teacher! You have to come back someday!"

Aygelin was not among them. She was there, with her face made up and wearing her best pink skirt. She was covering her face and crying. She did not chase the bus.

I knew her voice well; she definitely didn't yell "goodbye."

She just cried, helpless and alone.

Her normal cry was a voluble howl, but this time, as I left, she wept silently.

————

The moment her pink skirt disappeared from my field of vision, I wanted to sob violently, as violently as they had done.

But everyone on the bus was looking at me—me with my Italian clothing and my Beijing accent.

So I merely remarked overly loudly to myself, "Poor little kids don't know how to behave."

My original plan was to bring home a few stalks of the mugwort zhysang, but I had forgotten.

The bus sped across the grasslands, a bright-green expanse dotted infrequently with snow-white yurts that flicked past the eye.

XI

Back in Beijing, I represented my nationality at a meeting for minority writers. People discussed techniques for depicting minority life more vividly. It was a good class, but it left me with a strange sadness. How should I write you, Aygelin? I felt silly just thinking about the question.

I finally met up with my girlfriend. I gave her a cashmere stuffed camel I'd picked out especially for her in Urumqi. She didn't seem to like it, though I couldn't tell why. It's hard to know what people in cities will like.

"Were the children there cute?" she asked me.

"Not bad. Aren't I one of those children?"

She asked me if the girls there were exceptionally pretty. I mentioned you, Aygelin. Though she listened attentively, I could tell she really didn't care.

I took her hand. "That's right, there's something I wanted to ask you. What do you know about Xinjiang?"

"Uhhh, singing, dancing, and dombra music . . ."

"And that's it?"

"Well, then there's you," she laughed.

She sensed my slight unhappiness and followed up with a concerned question: "What's wrong? Has something happened?" I should have taken the opportunity to talk to her about my people, but instead I just put on a surprised face and said, "Something wrong? No, I'm fine."

"Oh!" She suddenly remembered something. "You also have a dance where girls wave their necks."

I had to think for a minute before replying, "That's not our dance, that's the Uighurs'."

But she gave me a strange look and said, "Uighurs, Kazakhs, what's the difference? It's one of your dances out there." I nodded silently.

It wasn't her mistake. The problem was that urban people live lives unconnected to race.

She wore expensive makeup, and her dresses were prettier than Aygelin's. Thinking of Aygelin and the Kazakhs made me hesitate even more. I hugged my girlfriend tighter, kissed her harder. When I was close to her, her body did not have the familiar smell of milk I loved so much.

She smelled of French perfume.

———

I loved her. She was a successful, thoughtful girl. But she made me tired. One of our dreams was to open our own café.

Yet I was only nineteen, with no college education, getting by by writing unremarkable stories and poems.

We'd often sit in the lawn chairs in a midstreet park on the boulevard and dream of our ideal café. Then both of us would feel depressed. Perhaps young people love to dream. But life without dreams is utterly bland. One goes to different places to eat, drink, and have fun, but it's nothing more than a zombie happiness.

I kept thinking about Aygelin. Why had being with her been so simple?

My girlfriend was taking enrichment courses during her vacation, so I frequently found myself alone on the streets of Beijing. I discovered that nothing was as nice as I'd remembered it. The 798 Art District was filled with affectation and art that was either arrogant or designed to trick teenage girls. The souvenirs sold in the shops on Nanluoguxiang were merely cheap notions and entertainment, products of an industrial assembly line.

———

I did manage to see my first girlfriend.

As soon as we got together, I told her about the stars in Xinjiang. All she could do was listen politely. A starry night is a thing you have to be there for.

Though only a rising sophomore, she was already considering learning English and studying abroad in America.

It felt to me like she had once been herself, but had gradually transformed into an action item in society's larger plan. Everyone was fighting tooth and nail to move upward, as if their lives had already been scheduled for them. If they ever got lazy, some quota wouldn't be met. Even love and marriage were part of the plan. She told me she never thought about love. She just hoped that once she hit twenty-eight, her parents would help her land some reliable, unexcitable guy and she would get it over with. I wanted to say something then. Though in this society, that was exactly how it should go.

I looked her over once, this girl I had at one time held close to me, who was now telling me, "Love and marriage are part of the plan, they aren't my problem."

There wasn't anything abnormal about her, but the impression she left me with was indescribably weird.

―――――――

I asked her if she believed in love.

She said basically, yeah.

An understandable thing to say in this city.

She still couldn't accept the fact of that tree having been cut down.

That happened more than ten years ago, and the entire world had been turned inside out since then. How could she still not accept it?

Because it was that one tree.

I said I basically understood.

―――――――

There followed a long interval in which nobody spoke.

―――――――

I described Aygelin to her.

She said that Aygelin and my people were my tree.

I didn't get it, but I didn't ask about it.

She asked me what I wanted.

I told her that in the city, it wasn't a good idea to borrow trouble by thinking about that question too much.

She said she thought everyone should have a goal of some kind. When you reached it, then *swoosh*, you'd discover yourself.

"Swoosh?"

"Oh," she said, "that's just a description. Anyway, you'd discover yourself."

―――――――

This has nothing to do with ethnicity. People like you and me live in this city. We don't have ethnicities. We've all turned into beetles, just like in Kafka's story. One day we finally have an epiphany, and then we turn back into people. Right now we're still young, but one day we'll *swoosh* discover ourselves, and transform back into human beings.

As if the reason we worked so hard in this life is only to become what we are.

She said: "That's basically how it is."

She was right, yet I couldn't figure out why she would say what she did about not caring about love and getting marriage over with. The tree was not what she cared about. The tree was merely a symbol of loss. We are constantly losing ourselves, right from birth.

The situation is now clearer to me. But in the city, clarity only means the beginning of confusion.

I feel longing for that girl who kept talking about her tree being cut down, not this sanctimonious young woman. If it were possible to *swoosh* discover oneself, why did it seem that she was moving farther and farther away from that?

XII

The narrative moves to the city, and its style comes unglued. Aygelin becomes a symbol. This is all inevitable. If Aygelin was a symbol, then what did she represent? My girlfriend and I underwent a totally suspenseless breakup. I knew it would happen, but I was hurt anyway.

She said: "The idea of the café is too much, it would only be a burden on you."

She said: "You're a very nice guy, but I'm not what you want."

She said: "I'll remember you, you're a good person."

My only thought while she was saying all this was to grab her and keep her from leaving. If she left, I'd be on my own. Yet the truth was that even if she didn't leave, I'd still be on my own. Holding on to her, I could have proof of my own existence. Her leaving was losing a part of myself.

Everything she said was true. Yet there was one more true thing she didn't say, which was that she didn't love me anymore. She was smiling at me the same way she always had. I didn't know when she'd stopped loving me. Perhaps she never had?

I wanted to hold her and make her stay. Instead, I just smiled and said, "Goodbye."

She flashed an enchanting smile. "You're already more mature, just like a real man."

But I doubted this maturity would allow me to *swoosh* discover myself.

My first girlfriend was too busy studying for graduate exams to be bothered. So were my other friends. I discovered that I had become friendless in my own city, with no one to help me.

Having broken up with my girlfriend, and thinking constantly of Aygelin, I bought a subway ticket. I got on at one end of Line 13 and rode the loop all the way to the other end. I sat on the plastic bench seat and stared with stupid intensity at the passengers getting on and off. I was like an item in a lost-and-found, but no one came to claim me. I rode back and forth, from one end to the other.

––––––––

At 1 A.M. on a Beijing summer night, I left my apartment and went out into the street. I bought two rice balls wrapped in seaweed from the 7-Eleven and ate as I walked. The street was totally empty, yet I wolfed down my food as if someone were rushing me.

I wanted to lose myself in the depths of night, yet I didn't want to fall. I wanted to love myself, but also thoroughly humiliate myself. But in the end I had nothing, and I walked with nothing along the Beijing streets. It was pitiful. No, it wasn't even that—even the pity was faked. I had nothing, I walked down the street. Every once in a while, a few drunk foreigners passed by; I wondered what could have tempted them to come this far just to stumble around intoxicated.

"Motherfucker!" I swore as I stood alone under a bridge. There were no fresh profanities available. Standing and swearing in such a desolate place in the middle of the night, I lacked even a body to swear at. Could Aygelin imagine me this way? Even I had a hard time believing what I had become.

I was always afraid that Beijing would want me; clearly, that was all bullshit.

This city has never "wanted" or rejected anyone.

––––––––

I am a failure.

The teaching example I had used was, "How do I get to Wangfujing Street?" They would never in their lives get to Wangfujing. As I recalled the earnest excitement with which they had practiced the sentence, I felt I was a failure.

Talk to Aygelin about liberty and democracy? About Kafka?

She had no use for liberty or democracy. Her life was so simple that all she needed was for the man she loved to stay with her.

Her man couldn't do it.

Aygelin, you smell of milk. Even though that is a woman's most precious smell, even though it's a smell I'll never forget.

Yet I couldn't possibly have stayed.

––––––––

I was afraid. It was the first time I'd realized I was afraid.

I was afraid people would greet me with "Welcome to China."

I'm afraid of standing out. Not because I'm different, but because I feel empty here in the city.

Fear feels like abandonment. My Kazakh mother abandoned me among these skyscrapers. I'm afraid that one day the city will abandon me. This is totally unreasonable. But I'm still afraid.

I'm sorry, Aygelin, I'm a failure.

Or perhaps not. Perhaps everyone in the city lives with fear and emptiness, and I simply focused too much attention on the reasons.

I dreamed of my girlfriend. How I longed for her to hold me in her embrace the way you did, give me the same comfort and beauty. Yet nothing like that occurred.

She merely said I was a good person and left.

XIII

Even if Aydana works hard, okay, she'll still only be a head waitress. What dreams could she possibly have? Her dream was to know something, and to be able to communicate.

Kaysa and Kaylat. When I asked the students if they had met lots of nice Han people, why didn't they nod as well? They sit in their little restaurant amid a sea of Chinese. They will be silent their entire lives, unable to understand what people around them are saying.

But do urbanites not fail?

The city always keeps its distance. Whenever I hug my friends the way Kazakhs do, they say, "Whoa, dude, I'm not gay. Personal space, personal space." How could someone who's never really been hugged before be happy?

Just as several of my friends responded after hearing my story: "What is not failing? If Aydana goes to Peking University, will she be not failing? Everything would be exactly the way it was."

In reality, we are each surrounded on all sides by failure.

I hope to have a daughter someday, and to continue living in Beijing. I frequently wonder if her body will carry the Kazakh smell of milk. Will she be like you, Aygelin, or like that girlfriend of mine? Will she know what love is?

I'm not sure.

I don't know if I'd rather she smelled of milk or of French perfume.

I may walk the streets of Tokyo, Paris, or London. But I will certainly never walk through that small town again. You'll be married by then, won't you? Married to some herder. Will he drink? Will he love you?

Will you think of me on your wedding day? The night you held that Beijing boy in your arms?

———

I'm a Kazakh, really. I love you, Aygelin, but this is the world we live in. It doesn't care that a man left your embrace and went to Beijing. None of it should have been that way.

One day, our people will move to the city, or machines will bring the flavor of the city into the countryside.

One day, Aygelin, your granddaughters will smell like perfume.

Maybe then you will understand me better—or, perhaps, less well.

———

XIV

It's 4:00 A.M., and I am in the Central Business District. No one is at work. Beijing's most luxurious district is now as quiet as a tomb. Here at the tail end of night, I hear a girl howling in anguish. I follow the sound. I see a smart-looking young woman in well-cut business clothes sitting on a park bench bawling her eyes out. She is very attractive.

Her head is lowered, and her hair shakes with each sob. I finally understand this superficial truth: there are unhappy girls even in Beijing. Everything is only life, and life is life. Whether we are wearing pink skirts or business suits, rags and tatters or Italian brand names, we will feel anguish and failure.

I give the woman a small pack of tissues, and she repays me with a sweet smile. For an urbanite to smile that way while she is crying is no easy task. I want to comfort her, but she doesn't dare cry anymore. She gets up and hurries away.

When people in need are finally offered aid, they react with shame and exclusion. As if they can only feel liberated and at ease once the aid is gone? What follows is a feeling of abandonment, then the fear of being alone, until they need help once again, and are finally offered it . . .

I don't want to keep analyzing. The sun's almost up; I stand on a footbridge, face the rising sun, and sing that Kazakh song:

> I love the one I hold, may all things rest
> Do not believe the world   has only beauty
> When you believe everyone   in the world is lovely
> Don't forget that earthly beauty   is only in the mold

Galloping toward the mountain pass
The pass is right before your eyes
Sitting at table with family and friends
Happiness is right before your eyes

A star on my steed's brow, I've come to see you
I built a railing around the well, afraid you'd fall
I come purposefully to your door, O my girl
Don't pretend not to know me, and turn on your heel

Galloping toward the mountain pass
The pass is right before your eyes
Sitting at table with family and friends
Happiness is right before your eyes

The sun rises. All is quiet, unbelievably quiet, as if this weren't Beijing.

Aygelin, the man you loved could not have stayed with you; children from the grasslands will never see the diverse world; my first girlfriend found knowledge and morality, but will never get the tree of her childhood back; my Han girlfriend dates and breaks up with that same calm smile, yet has never been happy.

All this can't help but make one feel depressed.

———

Aygelin, perhaps one day I will turn into a Kafka, perhaps not. I don't know what it is to be a good writer. But I do know that no matter what I gain, I will always be failing, because I once lost you, we lost each other.

Aygelin, I never told you that I love you deeply.

———

Because in you I saw something that allowed me to fail gently, intimately.

Because I failed, I fell deeply in love with you.

Because I failed, I left you.

———

Gazing at this blazing orange sun, I suddenly realize why the Kazakhs love it so much.

Perhaps, in the face of such a dazzling sun, we are all failures.

The song of my Kazakh ancestors rings through my head.

I understand:

There is nothing we have to fail at, and nothing we can't.

Dust

By Chen Xue

TRANSLATED BY HOWARD GOLDBLATT

I

The drapes were tawdry, and a clutter of books, magazines, and comic books, as well as a safety helmet, a raincoat, and some tote bags, filled the space on both sides of a twenty-one-inch TV sitting on a black entertainment cabinet whose faux leather top had curled up in spots. The three-cushion sofa with two mismatched throw pillows was neat enough, but the nearby armchair was occupied by a pair of stuffed toy cats. I'd been in the room for a little more than three hours and, owing to an occupational predilection, could not have helped noticing among the chaotic piles of odds and ends a roomful of things that needed to be thrown out. I could imagine the kind of life led by the people who lived there and could guess the sort of mess that lay in the rooms behind all those closed doors. Of course, they could just as easily be as neat as a pin, all the junk having been tossed into the living room and hallway. Your typical shared apartment.

Anna was walking toward me with an armload of shoeboxes, looking as serious as a housemaid busy with her domestic duties. Those boxes, which came in all sizes and in a mix of blacks and browns, exuded an aura of mystery. "May I ask a favor?" she said.

A pink blush peeking through light makeup betrayed her shyness and lent her skin a sort of translucence. Though she was a grown woman of thirty-two, there was a girlish quality to her simple request.

"What is it? I'm happy to do whatever I can," I replied, scarcely able to keep from reaching out and stroking the slightly flushed skin, yearning to see it in its natural state, imagining it to be dotted with freckles and less than perfectly smooth—in short, to see what her face looked like without cosmetics. We weren't lovers at the time, and that thought makes me somewhat uneasy. I was pretty sure I liked her and hoped she'd like me.

"I need some advice on putting my things in order," she said. Over a period of two months, I'd learned that Anna was more reserved than other girls, and that it often took more than one attempt for her to say what was on her mind, a trait that seemed wildly inappropriate for her day job of fielding customer complaints over the phone. But maybe she simply talked herself out at work. So I patiently waited for her to explain what she wanted. "What I'd like is for you to help me organize my things. I moved in about six months ago, and I still haven't finished unpacking. That makes finding anything just about impossible." By the time she finished, her face had turned red.

We'd met on an Internet dating site, exchanging messages and an occasional phone call; that gradually led to nightly text messages. After about six months of that, we met face to face. Anna was an attractive but not beautiful woman, with rounded eyes, a small nose, and thick lips. Full-figured—what these days would be considered pudgy. She may have been unhappy with her appearance, but she looked good to me: full cheeks, dimpled wrists, clumsy makeup, and inexpensive clothes. Most girls these days are too skinny, and a little too shrewd; she, on the other hand, had an earthy sex appeal that gave her an intense vitality. She brightened up even the squalid room we were in.

I phoned to ask her out the day after we met, and over the next two months, we got together every weekend, usually on Saturday afternoons, to take in a movie, go out to dinner, or stroll in the park, before I saw her home. On this day she wanted me to stay for dinner. She had prepared a fruit salad, vegetarian spaghetti, and cream of mushroom soup. I supplied a bottle of red wine and a homemade cheesecake. Her roommates in the three-bedroom apartment, which had a dining room and a living room, were out, and the room we were in was a mess, a poor excuse for a place to entertain a date. After dinner, we washed the dishes, and before we even had a quiet moment, she gave me a job.

"No problem," I said. "I'll take a look." Anna laid the boxes on the floor, crouched down, and opened them one at a time. They were filled with junk. I crouched down, and she stood up, as if concerned I'd say something unkind. "I'm terrible at organizing, so everything's a mess," she said. "I'll take a look," I told her as I began taking things out of the boxes: an unmarked medicine card with two rows of pills, a couple of ointment tubes, three eye drop bottles, a small jar of cotton swabs, five hairpins of various sizes, three hair clips, four scrunchies in different patterns and materials, and an assortment of odds and ends—hand mirror, cell phone battery, phone charger . . . not to mention a pair of goggles and a swimming cap. Box number one. The second box held some cold and flu caplets, three packets of allergy medicine, two combs, a pair of nail clippers, a sewing kit, six cassette tapes, a bunch of cell phone straps and hangers, dozens of Hello Kitty magnets, which had been all the rage in convenience stores years earlier, and five vending machine toys (including the comic book figures Naruto and Pirate King); but taking up most of the space were feminine napkins in a range of sizes and brands.

The contents of the remaining three boxes were about the same—a mix of daily necessities and tchotchkes—and once it was all out in the open, I saw that there were some duplicates. After emptying the boxes and wiping them clean, I spread everything out on the floor by type: medications (for both oral and external uses, one box each), cosmetics and hair ornaments (I waited to put these into boxes until I'd finished with her beauty products), and tchotchkes. That's when she told me there were two more large boxes filled with stuff in the storage room. I looked her in the eye, but before I could say a word, she paled from obvious anxiety.

"Don't worry about it, we'll take our time," I said to comfort her. I liked her as much when she was pale as when she blushed.

She stood there looking down at me, and from that angle she appeared tall and slim. Though she did her best to mask her nervousness with a smile, it wasn't enough. We hardly knew each other, and yet she'd laid out highly personal objects—sanitary napkins and cold medicine—for me to organize. But organizing strangers' households is what I did, wasn't it? It was what I was good at.

———

There is a radiance to the ocean, and there was a radiance to Anna. Laying her most private possessions out that way gave me a glimpse of the ocean in her heart. Knowing that she needed me both pleased and disturbed me. Was I capable of straightening out my life as easily as I did her room?

———

II

———

Organizing, ordering, cleaning up, and discarding were what I did best, and what I did for a living. I was paid by the hour to clean people's houses. My college degree was in philosophy; after graduation I worked for a while as a reporter, I wrote advertising copy, and I ghostwrote autobiographies, but I never felt a personal attachment to any of my jobs. They placed demands on only a small part of my body, leaving everything else to shrivel up. I could muster the energy to get by and meet the basic requirements of a job, but nothing filled the emptiness in my withering heart. Eventually I fell into a depression whose most notable symptom was a loss of appetite. During the year I took off to get better, friends kept after me to do one thing or another, fearful that I'd get worse by locking myself away at home. A pair of newly married friends asked me to help them turn an old house into a home for newlyweds, a project that occupied a lot of my time. When it was done, they praised my natural ability to, in their words, "turn water into wine." What the experience taught me was that I might be able to make a living in the housecleaning business. So I applied for a job at a housecleaning service, got it, and worked there for a couple of years, eventually moving up to team leader in charge of training. While there, I learned many tricks of the trade and got to know lots of people in the business. As time wore on, though, I became restless and felt that there had to be something I'd like better. So I left the service and, with a couple of friends, opened a small-scale housecleaning service in which I could pick and choose the jobs I wanted. Surprisingly, I found myself welcoming the most difficult tasks and challenges, which in turn made me the company's poster girl. After three years of operation, we were charging somewhat higher fees than other services and additional costs for larger items that needed to be trucked away. People called us "sanitation workers," "housework managers," or "storage masters." For my part, I always used "household rescue" online, a sensational headline I devised, thanks to my days at the ad desk, though no one could accuse me of exaggerating.

I set up a blog for our service, where I posted before-and-after de-cluttering and reorganization photos, even affective service logs, and customer feedback. By online and word-of-mouth testimonials, not only did we develop a list of regular clients, but we also formed long-term relations with realtors. We had more work than we could handle. A willingness to get our hands dirty was the key to our success. The dirtier, the messier, the less desirable to others, the better for me, as I viewed these jobs as challenges. Everyone on our team of four had a specialty: Little Wang was strong, Old Liu was experienced, and Lili was as efficient as an octopus, as if she had eight arms. As for me, I was in charge of advertising, meeting clients, handling personnel issues, and making assignments, as well as taking on the most difficult reorganization and de-cluttering tasks. In addition to housecleaning, we also helped with such post-cleaning tasks as disposing of items discarded by our clients. After sorting the objects, we turned junk into cash by sending it either to the recycling station (Little Wang), to antique shops (Old Liu), or to secondhand stores (Huihui).

Our services included organizing, sorting, storage, and discarding in order to return a house that had been swallowed up by junk back to its original state. Our ultimate goal was to leave a home in a clean, orderly state it had never experienced before; housecleaning was simply the basic, first step. I've seen houses that were virtually submerged in all sorts of stuff, a graveyard for things, which I was able to transform by using the cheapest modular storage units, homemade storage bins, or recycled and restored furniture. The response each time was a look of incredulity on the face of the owner and anyone else who saw it. To me, the most important step was discarding, not storage, and that usually led to a tug-of-war with clients, fighting over what to keep and what to toss. If, in the end, they wanted to keep everything, they didn't need our service. What the typical housecleaner failed to achieve was talking clients into getting rid of things they no longer needed and returning their lives to normal. I loved to see clients decisively taking stuff they considered useful (or that might be useful one day) and putting it into garbage bags or cardboard boxes to be taken away. As the useless junk decreased, the house seemed to slowly regain its soul, a process that gave me indescribable pleasure. A sense of calm came over me when I was able to help others regain order in their lives.

No case was too outlandish for us: a mother and father had had enough of their pretty young shopaholic daughter filling her room with luxury goods. A young couple were about to split up because the girl could no longer tolerate her boyfriend's messiness, while he complained about her poor housework skills. After his wife died, a man stopped cleaning for a year, resorting to buying new clothes or wearing the same dirty ones over and over; when he called, he choked up, as if on the verge of tears. Relatives argued over how to tackle the overflowing belongings left behind by a departed elder. Work on a house was repeatedly delayed because no one knew how to get rid of junk in order to make room for remodeling. Houses were full to bursting with odds and ends, even with an abundance of modular furniture. A house was in chaos despite a set of well-organized storage units. A family had collected over a hundred cast-off deity statues, but the children refused to take them after the father's death. A bankrupt collector of bronze and iron objects had to move to a smaller house. One client hoarded old refrigerators; another amassed a hundred and twenty cast-off bicycles.

Every family had its own reasons for, and process of, self-destruction.

———————

As I helped Anna sort and organize the contents of the five shoeboxes on the living room floor, I explained to her in detail why they were sorted this way and what sorting meant. After throwing out all the expired medicine, I found space in her room that was convenient for storage and retrieval, and then I consolidated the books on two bookcases to free up a shelf for the shoeboxes.

Anna's single bed, placed against a wall, was piled so high with clothing that it was hard to see the bed sheet, which was white and sprinkled with tiny blue flowers. This was my first time in her bedroom, but I had no time to entertain romantic thoughts; instead I began planning how to give her tiny room—not even fifty square feet—a complete makeover. In the future, I told her, when she ran into trouble with how to store something, she should put it in a small rattan basket (labeled as temporary storage) in a corner, and I'd help her the next time I came over.

Anna led me back to the living room. The biggest problem with this type of apartment was the renters' tendency to treat communal space as storage space, since no one felt responsible for its maintenance. Anna had most likely had to tidy up the sofa today for us to sit on. Furniture in a wide range of styles filled every corner of the entryway, the kitchen, and the dining and living rooms, with piles of junk inside and out.

She was soon looking at me fondly and affectionately, probably because I'd so quickly solved her problem and made her understand the secret to sorting. We kissed there on the sofa, but I was unable to concentrate owing to the mess in the room. Her body gave off a subtle fragrance of lilies. Though she was horrible at keeping house and moved with childish clumsiness, my feelings toward her had grown steadily from the day we met. The question for me was: What do I do next?

It was getting late, so I got up to leave, telling her she needed her rest.

I sensed that she wanted to say something as I was leaving. "Stay for dinner when you come next week. I'll cook some Chinese food," she said, adding that she wasn't much of a cook. A myriad of feelings, all hard to describe, rose up inside me, confusing me so much that I rushed out the door.

———

Out on the street, I gazed up at her balcony and saw a moving shadow behind the drawn curtain; a size larger than the average girl, it still outlined her lovely curves. What a gorgeous shadow. Not having her right in front of me meant I could study her more carefully. Was that dreamlike figure really her? I imagined how much sexier she would look naked, all quivering flesh. A southern girl, she'd come north to find work, but after working for years as a receptionist at a private company, she had nothing to show for it but a room in a shared apartment. It pained me to see the mess she'd created. All those old things she had trouble sorting were the hard-earned accomplishment of eight years away from her hometown; they were a record of her star-crossed romances and her troubles in finding a good job. I longed to return to her room, where I would place her hand on my chest. "Repair this," I'd say. "No need to sort. Just hold it · in your hand, hold on tight and don't let go."

I shook my head, over and over. I wished I were a smoker, so I could pretend to be enjoying a cigarette under the streetlight, not spying on a woman I was afraid to pursue.

III

I guess that, based on society's definition, in the lesbian world I would be considered a tomboy. In my childhood, I was viewed as neither a boy nor a girl, and was labeled androgynous. None of this mattered to me, because there were more serious problems in life. I had indeed fallen in love with women and would continue to do so, yet I was never sure if there might someday be a woman who would love me as much as I loved her. But at the moment, such dreams were a luxury. I cut my hair short because of the job, but the natural curls made it fluff up messily. Not wanting clients to mistake me for a man, I kept my hair long enough to cover my ears, but it always got out of hand within a couple of months. Most people would see me, a thirty-four-year-old woman, as a typical obasan, but in this occupation, the image of a strong obasan worked to my advantage.

Naturally, I shied away from cosmetics and cared little about my appearance. Though no more than average height, I jogged every day and did two hundred push-ups before bed, since physical strength was my capital. At times I was stared at when I walked into a women's restroom, but so far no one had attempted to chase me out.

What we in this line of work sold was physical labor, so few of us came from wealthy families. Little Wang, a member of an indigenous tribe, had relocated to the city, where he worked for a long time in construction before signing on at a cleaning service. When his antique business went belly up, Old Liu wound up separated from his wife and children; he took up various jobs—first driving a truck and then a taxi, working for an express delivery service and then a moving company. Lili, formerly a caring wife and loving mother, had to pay off her ex-husband's credit card debts after their divorce by peddling credit cards and then insurance policies. When all her personal connections dried up, she employed her former homemaking skills by becoming a professional house-cleaner. As people with diverse backgrounds from different parts of the island, there was no way we ever could have gotten together had it not been for the work we did. You can say it was karma, but I prefer to attribute it to how our specialties complemented each other. None of us could have accomplished anything individually, but when our talents were combined, we excelled in what we did. Day in and day out, we worked hard, dripping sweat, and then went home alone. In a big city like Taipei, it was nearly impossible to find a decent place to live, so I rented an old house that couldn't be sold or remodeled because of a dispute over property rights. We were half renters, half caretakers. With some refitting, the place served as both our office and our living quarters. Recycled items awaiting further disposal often took up most of the yard, but inside, the place was clean and tidy enough. Later Lili brought her son, Dongdong, who was in elementary school, to live with us. It was a run-down old place, furnished with discarded items from clients, but we had a roof over our heads and spring mattresses to sleep on, and you couldn't ask for much more. With all of us together, there was never a dull moment; we sometimes got a hot pot boiling, offered sacrifices on various deities' birthdays, and barbecued in the yard. Old Liu adopted a dog to add to our number.

I never brought a girl home, even though you couldn't call the house shabby. To outsiders, this place was like a homeless shelter. Every single girl I met online backed out when she learned that I was a housecleaner. Anna was the sole exception. She said her job was also a kind of cleaning business, one of "sweeping away customers' dissatisfaction." I found her unusual, but not special enough to bring home.

I had enough money to rent someplace nice where I could have normal dates, but this place gave me a sense of ease and comfort without the need to examine my life. Here I could focus on playing "team leader" and tackling clients' problems. TV call-in shows were always on in the living room, and Lili seemed to have something going with both Little Wang and Old Liu, which led to an occasional argument, but the two men were political junkies and loved drinking coffee with Whisbih. They truly were like sworn brothers. On our days off, I often took Dongdong for bike rides in the park. Sometimes Lili, Dongdong, and I would go supermarket shopping like a family. Lili once took my hand and said, "Why don't we get together, you and me?" "But we *are* together." I let go of her hand with a laugh, and her face darkened. "I know you're from a different world," she said. The note of resentment was unmistakable, but she quickly recovered and patted me on the back as if nothing had happened. "I was just joking, College Girl, don't give it another thought. Besides, I prefer men anyway." When there was no work, the four of us would sit around drinking, playing cards, and watching TV. The year before, when we had a long New Year's holiday, we had all gone to Mount Ali.

Sometimes, when I surfed the Internet in my room, the noise outside comforted me. I shared no blood ties with these people, and they had no inkling of how I felt or where I came from, yet they trusted me and were happy to live with me. To me, we were a family of sorts. In bed I revisited books I'd read many times as a young girl, but only now truly understood. I could fall asleep in peace. Snippets of light and shadow, sometimes in color, sometimes in black-and-white, and always with no story line, played in my dreams.

IV

On Sundays I went to see Mother in the temple-run nursing home. A tight-fisted woman who loved money more than anything, she had nevertheless donated a large sum toward the construction of the temple, saying she was accumulating good karma to forestall retribution for us; yet she was the only member of the family who believed in heaven and hell or past lives. When she ended up alone, it was this temple that took her in, though we continued to pay her expenses, of course.

My brother, whom I hadn't seen in more than two years, came to visit in mid-June, the day after I first met Anna. His hair was longer than Anna's, tightly braided in cornrows after the newest fashion. He'd just returned from Africa, and was predictably dark. I knew he was an artist, but I couldn't say what it was he was good at, except that it had something to do with the the-ater. Then I heard that he was a singer, and that he'd recently taken up African drums. A handsome man with a great sense of humor, he was also agile and lithe, exactly what I was not. He moved fluidly between Mom, Dad, and his girlfriends, and between the countries he traveled to, smoothly and effortlessly.

"Mom had a stroke," he said. We had little to say to each other when we met, but still it was a strange opening line after two years. On the other hand, it seemed perfectly fitting. He lived with Mom in Taipei, but spent most of his time traveling around the world. Mom paid for his upkeep as an artist, and he repaid her by living with her, even if it amounted to little more than nominal companionship.

He was in a hurry to leave after telling me about Mom, and I didn't try to make him stay. "Nice haircut," he said, probably hoping I'd say the same about his. "Why don't you put some stuff together and come to the hospital with me?" he added.

Wordlessly, I returned to the dining table to finish my tea, while wondering how serious the situation was. Mom had had a stroke. Sixty-five at the time, she'd lived her life as if her battery were always fully charged. And still she'd been laid low. Father had long since emigrated to Canada with his new wife, and my newly returned brother could pick up and leave at any moment, so I'd probably end up taking care of Mother. I packed a small bag and left with him for the hospital.

———

My parents separated five years before they formalized the divorce, mainly because Mother refused to sign the papers. She remained in a house overflowing with junk until she was the only one left.

Mother worked for a state-run business; Father was a bank clerk. They'd been married five years when they took out a mortgage on a fourth-floor apartment in Taipei. It was about a thousand square feet in size, with a large master bedroom, two small bedrooms, a small storage room, and front and back balconies. The living room was smallish, but it actually came with a separate dining room and kitchen, a perfect flat for a family of four. Even before housing prices skyrocketed, it was considered a nice, quiet residence convenient to transportation. Mother dealt with public accounts at work, and Father's job was also related to money and numbers. I could imagine how their dates (if they ever dated, that is) went: first a movie, then discussions of account statements. (Or they might have avoided the topic of numbers altogether.) In any case, as far as I can remember, they seldom talked to each other. Father was an extravagant spendthrift, and Mother was frugal, even somewhat miserly; he loved fame, while she loved money. Obsessed with golf, a sport that was above his social standing, he was fixated on working his way into elite society. Mother, on the other hand, never wore makeup and spent whatever time and money she had on savings clubs, plus picking up stuff all over the place. Even when she was young, she had the figure of an older woman. Her love of objects gradually led to the eccentric habit of hoarding junk no one wanted. They'd looked like a decent match when they were first married, but in less than ten years they were like total strangers.

It started with small items: ten towels that cost a hundred NT, a pair of twenty-NT cloth shoes, a desk lamp discarded by the side of the road, a rattan chair left at the community dumpster; it eventually degenerated into landfill "recycles." "I'm protecting the environment, don't you understand?" she'd argue. "All this needs is some minor repair," she'd say as she picked up some random object. She was unalterably opposed to "tossing away anything that still had some useful value," so why spend good money on new things? "Why do you buy so many towels?" Father once asked her. "Because they're so cheap. You can always give them away as gifts," she replied. "We're not preparing for a funeral!" Father retorted angrily with a dark look before storming off. No object was off limits. One of the many items she picked up was a semi-intact old-fashioned "red bed," where the great-aunt of one of Mom's colleagues had breathed her last in the countryside. She hired someone to carry this "treasure" up the stairs, but Father would not allow it inside, so it was left in the stairwell, generating constant complaints from the neighbors.

How and where she developed her obsessive hoarding was a mystery to me. I was in middle school when I noticed that she was coming home late, utterly exhausted. Part of what tired her out was a part-time after-hours bookkeeping job for a small company, but what really sapped her energy were the incessant visits to garbage dumps, where she'd pick up furniture, or trips to all the secondhand markets to purchase cheap goods that were worth more than she paid for them. Like a junk collector, she'd haul and drag and pull stuff either on her bicycle or on a hand cart, some of it hanging on the handlebars. She looked like the Pied Piper followed by a swarm of rats.

And that was how our apartment became a trash receptacle.

———

Father was the first to walk out, with good reason and no regrets. Looking at Mother as if she were a madwoman, he complained, "Who can live in a home like this?" After putting up with her behavior for years, he'd finally told the truth, but I sensed that it wasn't that simple. Then my older brother found an excuse of his own and left. Mother's collection migrated into their rooms before she herself moved into my brother's room, because the walls of the master bedroom had water damage. Ultimately, even my brother's room was lost to the junk, so Mother set up a bunk bed in my room, which she shared with me. A year later, I moved out.

Those unsettling, chaotic years are now like illusory shadows, but after all these years I still can't understand why she was that way. A few years back, when I was seeing a doctor for depression, it dawned on me that Mother might have been afflicted with a mental disorder that caused her to make absurd decisions even with full knowledge that her actions would lead to the breakup of our family. Yet even after that epiphany, I still found it hard to get close to her; I was powerless to improve the deteriorating relationship at home. After we'd all left, I was the only one who continued to see her on a regular basis. One day she withdrew all her pension funds to invest in stock and real estate, and suffered a huge loss when the bottom dropped out of the market during the financial crisis. That gave her even greater justification to retreat into a world of junk.

After I moved out, during my first year of college, my brother returned home from his world travels with a mountain of credit card debt. Everything turned topsy-turvy. He moved into the room I'd shared with Mother, and over the next two years, each time I went back to see them, I noticed that the junk had continued to accumulate, and the place had such a terrible stink that I thought I'd go mental if I stayed another minute.

My headstrong, eccentric, willful mother, who had banished herself to a solitary wilderness, finally fell apart.

———

She spent a month in the hospital, the left side of her body virtually paralyzed. We hired a caregiver, but she complained about the cost, so eventually someone from the temple took her to the nursing home. Over a period of two months, she recovered enough to get around with a walker, but she had yet to recover her speech, and could only make unintelligible noises.

I went to see her every Sunday with a carton of vegetable congee and lots of fruit, plus money to settle her expenses, which I kept secret, since she assumed that the temple was giving her free care. I opened the carton and fed her the same vegetable congee she'd often made for us when we were young. The food tasted good, I knew that. I was adept not only at housecleaning, but also at preparing common dishes. As with a child, I had to coax her to eat, with patience I didn't know I had. If truth be told, she'd been a terrible mother when she was her hyperactive self.

Maybe it was because Mother would never nag me again. Prior to her stroke, she'd either nag me to go on matchmaking dates or try to find me a job; either that or she'd thrust bags of cheap toilet paper or tonic pills at me as I was leaving. She always wanted me to stay for dinner, but the food she put on the table had a suspiciously stale taste. An excellent cook in her younger days, she'd let her skills rust away with the passage of time.

Vegetable congee was Mother's final signature dish, perfected just before she entered into full-blown eco-protection and garbage collection. She was hoarding food, and so she cobbled leftovers together into a soupy rice porridge, which at the time tasted great, but later, when I thought about it, was closer to pigswill. Mother loved it; a frugal woman all her life, she believed she'd be rewarded with good karma by eating food like that.

Mother muttered something, probably grumbling as usual, but to me it was gibberish. Like a clinging child, she was afraid I'd stop coming to see her if she upset me. The docile look on her face always made me feel uncomfortable.

I fed her, pushed her around in her wheelchair, took her to physical therapy, went over the various things she'd written down for me to do in her messy handwriting, and watched TV with her. Then I left, but only after the usual battle to get her to let go of my sleeve.

Located in a suburb, the temple could only be reached after changing buses several times. On that day I was parched as I sat on the bus, rocking along uneven, traffic-jammed streets. The scene outside was a visual abomination; there seemed to be no end to the construction projects.

Roiling dust left a light-gray film on the streets. I longed for a large ice-cold soft drink, feeling as if I'd swallowed a lot of dust. I recalled Anna's bedroom, her soft lips, and her parting gesture, as if she'd wanted to say something more. Maybe she'd hoped I would stay the night. Would we then have entwined our bodies on the narrow single bed in that messy bedroom infused with a woman's perfume? Would I have had the courage to take off her clothes, her bra and panties, before burying my face between her full breasts or her supple, moist legs? Did I have the ability to make her happy?

Suddenly I felt stabbing pains in my chest. Pressing my hands over my heart, I tried to regulate my breathing. Was it love I was feeling? I didn't know. How could I be in love when everything beyond the bus window was the same as always?

V

We spent a week cleaning up the Lin family house. It was a tough case that required the efforts of all four of us. The old house was all but deserted and was falling apart. We'd heard it was an unlucky house in which people kept dying in unusual circumstances. Before we set out, Lili forced an amulet on every one of us. Grizzled Old Liu had such tough karmic protection that no demons would dare go near him. Little Wang, only twenty-five that year, wasn't the least bit superstitious. Years of work had inured me to this kind of thing. Lili loved money, her favorite motto being "Money can make even a ghost turn a millstone." She was always bringing us amulets, which, along with spirit money tokens and even Japanese guardians, hung in abundance from the company truck's rearview mirror.

When we arrived, I recalled a news story from ten years earlier about a murder-suicide. An ex-boyfriend had sneaked into the house and hacked his former girlfriend and her brother to death before killing himself. It was such a shocking event back then that fanciful rumors swirled for some time. I recalled the tragedy because a photo of the house, a serene, pretty place with pine trees in the yard, had appeared in the paper.

The house, which belonged to the Lins, a local gentry family, was more than half a century old. The architecture was a hybrid of Chinese and Western styles, complete with a spacious yard and groves of towering trees. Every room in the two-story building was equipped with a balcony and stone posts; there was also a third-story garret with a red brick and stone facade, and Chinese-style carved dragons and phoenixes. White marble sculptures of human figures stood in the yard. Black and green terrazzo tiles covered the ground-level floor; an ornate crystal chandelier hung from the entry hall ceiling. Everything about the westernized Chinese décor was proof of the owners' costly efforts, but now the place was like a withered, balding old woman with loose teeth and gray hair. Hidden in a yard overgrown with weeds, it looked to local young people like a haunted house. No one knew when exactly it became haunted, but rumors certainly added a hint of mystery. People said that a longhaired dark shadow in white drifted all night long on the second floor, prompting plucky young men to check it out. In the process, they broke windows, walked off with various items, and left trash behind, making a mess of the house. Graffiti and personal messages covered the walls, and the yard was littered with barbecue tools and empty beer bottles.

A realtor we knew contacted us about the cleanup job; the pay was good, but with unusual conditions. A potential buyer was unconcerned about the rumors regarding the house's frightening past. The owners could have hired a run-of-the-mill cleaning service to empty the house of its contents and clean it up, but they wanted all the usable items sorted and returned, though they themselves were unwilling to set foot in the house. That was why we were called in, a common enough occurrence that I was not surprised.

On the first day, we tackled the yard, trying to separate the original owners' possessions from the trash left behind by "visitors." Little Wang and Old Liu busied themselves with carting away the larger items and removing the garbage, while Lili and I advanced inside fully armed, wearing surgical masks, caps, long pants, and long-sleeved shirts.

———

I was surprised by how tired I was when I returned home at the end of each day. This wasn't the toughest house I'd ever dealt with, but there was something about it, like a stubborn thought, or a persistent entanglement, but which I refused to call ghostly. Yet there was a presence of spirit and will that seemed to embroil our work in an eddy of futility. The owners appeared to have fled the house overnight, leaving everything behind, including all the furniture and everyday items, even a motor scooter and bicycles in the yard. In the cupboard were food items so old they crumbled at a mere touch, as well as overturned cups and plates; neatly folded clothes remained in the dressers—altogether overpowering and disconcerting signs of life. A sense of the living was missing, but so was the finality of death. It was as though everything were hanging on by a thread, awaiting its moment to be reborn. The house was like the living dead.

And that reminded me of our apartment, where the smell of death was also pervasive. That smell lingered for years and numbed anyone who came in contact with it. The dank smell of mildew on the cheap goods Mother bought or the junk she collected merged with body odors, a seeming tug-of-war waged between what was decaying and what refused to decompose. Tiny powdery flecks were forever settling around us; they could have come from termites or moths or disintegrating objects. Touching them with my hand gave me the feeling that I was wiping away the molting remains of time.

———————

For our second date after the kiss, Anna asked me to go with her to buy an armoire at IKEA. Pushing a cart down the aisles, we roamed from one section to another. Excited over the expertly decorated fake rooms and floor samples, she tried every sofa she saw, and even lay down on the beds, unconcerned about appearances. She touched the cheap, minimalist pieces of furniture as if they were rare treasures. The other customers were mainly young couples, a man and a woman, two men, or two women. Anna held my arm as if we too were lovers.

She reminded me of my first love, another girl with luscious curves. In high school we were inseparable; we went everywhere together. She even sneaked into my dorm room to share my tiny bed, where we clumsily explored each other's body. But when we were back in the light of day, we acted like good friends, as if nothing had happened. She broke off contact with me after graduation, and I was struck by the realization that my feeling for her was love, the kind of love that made me aware that the object of my desire was someone of my own sex. When she got married, she sent me an invitation with her wedding photo; I barely recognized the tall, slender girl.

Many years had passed before I stopped missing her. And after several failed relationships with different girls, I stopped feeling sad and felt no new attractions. To put it bluntly, I had no intimate relationships. It was only when I was managing my company blog that I occasionally visited online dating sites, but even those visits were limited to chats. Anna was the first girl I'd gotten close to in a very long time. A girl from the countryside, she retained an air of simplicity in the way she carried herself and spoke, but I liked everything about her. She told me about past relationships with both men and women, all of which had ended painfully. "I'm a magnet for jerks," she said with a sad smile. No one, man or woman, had ever truly loved her. On this day we strolled around the brightly lit store like a married couple, or young lovers, and even though we bought nothing, we were infected by an illusory happiness. Holding hands, we acted like newlyweds who were about to decorate their home together. At that moment, I really did feel that I could marry her and take care of her as long as I lived, if there was a way for us to pull that off.

Indulging in my fanciful thoughts, I watched with a smile as Anna merrily roamed the store, until a father and son passed in front of us, instantaneously freezing the ambience around us, changing even the smell in the air. No matter how you looked at it, their clothes and demeanor betrayed the fact that this was not a place for them. The father's faded old shirt was splattered with paint or some kind of dye, his suit pants had lost their shape, and on his feet were plastic sandals. The boy, who looked to be seven or eight years old, was small, scrawny, and dark, with large eyes. His clothes were as tattered as his father's; his slippers made a flip-flopping sound as he walked. With a plastic canteen slung over his back, just like his father, he ran and jumped around the showrooms, his loving father following close behind. Many of the shoppers, alerted by the noisy jumping boy, looked in their direction; like us, the father and son were enjoying a simulated tidy and comfortable home life, but they were drawing quite a bit of attention, too much, even. Without warning, Anna clasped my hand with such force that her nails nearly dug into my palm. We stood still and watched as the father stopped the overactive boy; then they both uncapped their canteens for a drink of water, after which the father wiped the boy's mouth with his sleeve, and the youngster tried not to make noise as he carefully climbed into a room decorated for a boy. It had a desk beneath an elevated bed and other beautiful objects he'd never seen before. Their happiness made the artificial coziness around us seem empty and false, as if they were being denied even these simple pleasures. As though sensing the stares from people around them, the father quickly dragged the boy down from the bed.

"I'm tired. Let's go, can we?" Anna said.

We went to bed that night. I thought she'd want to tell me about her apparent life of poverty in the countryside, her lonely days as a young girl, or her failed romances, but she was quiet when I touched her, moaning softly as though she were sobbing. My unpracticed movements could not hide my excitement; I did everything I could, trying to enter deep inside her, but of course I didn't want to hurt her. My gentle touch made her cry out with pleasure. My beloved Anna, it appeared, had never been truly happy before.

After the passion subsided, she laid her head weakly on my chest and whispered, "Be nice to me." Then she fell asleep with a sweet look.

Her long hair spread out over the pillow. The white ridges where her back met her waist, which people call "love handles," were like a hiding place for secrets. The soft glow of the nightlight rose and fell with her body. Her creamy, porcelain-fair skin sent shivers through my fingertips. With her warm head resting on me, she slept, breathing evenly; the weight on my chest was so real, so solid, that tears streamed down my face.

VI

Over the next few days, I redecorated her small apartment, but she ended up spending more time at my place, not bothered by the simple, unadorned living space and getting along well with everyone. The Lin family housecleaning took longer than we'd planned, and we still hadn't finished after two weeks. Over that period, Little Wang fell and broke his leg, Old Liu's dog died, and Lili's ex-husband tracked her down. Everyone suffered a setback, everyone but me, who basked in the joy of being in love. Anna would prepare boxed lunches for the next day when we returned home from the job, and fix a steaming-hot breakfast for us each morning. She even did our laundry and took over all the household chores, something she'd never been good at. When we returned in the evening and unloaded ourselves from the truck, we'd see our clothes drying on bamboo poles like banners at dusk.

Had the wind of good fortune finally begun blowing my way?

We continued cleaning up the house until the job was finished, which was when we encountered the old man.

Barefoot, with a long tangle of white hair, he sprang out of a nook reserved for spirit money next to the sacrificial table, wearing only pajama bottoms. He drew a scream of fear even from Old Liu, who could usually remain calm in the face of danger. The day's work was nearing its end, and it was getting dark outside, but I knew this was a man, not a ghost. No ghost could get close to someone in love.

In fact, everyone screamed, including him. But after we calmed down, we saw that he was a pitiful-looking old man, covered in filth, all skin and bones. Unafraid, I walked up to him. "Uncle," I said, "what are you doing here?" The animal expression on his face seemed to indicate he had no idea what I was saying, but then he pointed to the cigarette in Old Liu's hand. I handed it to the old man, who took a few deep drags before mumbling, "Thirsty."

I signaled Lili to get some water and food, while Old Liu and I put the old man in our truck, wondering where to take him, the police station or the homeless shelter. After consuming some rice balls, soda pop, a hot dog, tea eggs, and a can of milk, all brought back from a convenience store, the old man finally began to talk. "Your work is done, so you can take me home now." The mystery was solved. He was the Lin family's second son, who had moved in on the first day we came to work in order to make sure we didn't steal anything. He wasn't crazy, he'd just abandoned the life of a normal person. He spoke in code, and very little of that; I reached my conclusion by inference and by putting the pieces together. We took him to the real estate office, where we waited for someone from his family to pick him up. And that is how I finally met the owner of the house, Old Mr. Lin, who was older than the white-haired man. Old Mr. Lin was perfectly normal; he had a stern face on a square head with big ears and a sturdy build. Picking up his younger brother as if he were handling a chick, he nodded his thanks before walking off.

The white-haired man was likely the rumored ghost, I said to myself. But the house seemed truly haunted, so I asked Mr. Wang if the new owner would be afraid. He said no, since it was a religious group that would use the place for Taoist rites. They could hold the ghost at bay.

"Why did the original owners want all their stuff back, then?" I asked. "Wouldn't it be better to start from scratch?"

"They want to burn it," Mr. Wang told me. Before her death two months before, Mr. Lin's wife had told her husband to sell the house, then reclaim everything and burn it. Clean out and clean up to start over, since their younger son, who had been sent to the U.S. after escaping the unfortunate event, was now grown up, married with children, and planned to move back to Taipei with his family.

"Burning everything makes for a clean break. It's good for everyone," Mr. Wang continued as he handed us our fee and some extra money in red envelopes. "You've done a good job." He smiled.

I received news that very night that Mother was dying.

She hadn't believed in god or ghosts until late in her life, when she became a devout Taoist. I'd always thought she had entered a twisted world after Father left, and no one could draw her out. I recalled how, when I was in high school, she refused to throw anything out; she'd even wash and store used Styrofoam bowls. Like a scavenger, she collected paper bags, empty bottles, dishes, and plastic bags, creating mountains of junk in the house. She continued to go to work every day, properly dressed and nicely behaved, but she'd come home with bags of stuff. Lying to her coworkers about doing charity work, she asked them for donations; she then brought home discarded toys, baby strollers, old clothes, instant noodles, crackers, free department store samples, electric cookers, electric fans, microwave ovens, and waffle makers, dragging them back day after day, mountains and mountains of the stuff. At first she sorted the objects and put them in the cupboard or the closets, but when she ran out of room, she simply let them spill out into any available space, introducing an indescribable odor into the house. Like mold on walls, the stuff spread cancerously, with objects of various kind and size overflowing chaotically from storage, until they quietly and slowly took over the house, like creeping vines, dark shadows, or monsters.

And I continued to clean up in secret, stealthily tossing things out.

It was impossible to sort, organize, and store everything; all I could do was throw the moldy food away and do my best to clear paths between objects. I gathered up things that I could handle and whose absence would go unnoticed, such as broken desk lamps, odd photo albums, and rotting rattan chairs, and dragged them down many streets so Mother would not find them and bring them back into the house. Sometimes I even delivered the items to a suburban recycling station on my motor scooter. I probably looked like a scavenger myself with my late-night activities.

———

Father wasn't there when I got to the hospital late that night. I suspected that he loathed Mother, but I didn't know if Mother felt the same way toward him. After he left, I no longer had any feelings for him. His lawyers repeatedly delivered divorce papers, but Mother returned them each time unsigned. So why did she finally sign them? I'd heard that it was because Father's new woman had already had a child. In the end, Mother got the junk-filled apartment, Father got his freedom, and my brother and I each received 200,000 NT.

My brother rushed over early the next morning, trailed by a hip-looking blonde girl. I wondered what had caused Mother's second stroke. The temple staff told us that she'd been revising her will, and they weren't sure which was the final version. We were told to wait outside the ICU for a brief visit with her. After an earlier surgery, she seemed to have shrunk. She was still unconscious and in critical condition. The small bedside radio was playing the Great Compassion Mantra over and over. We went to the family members' waiting room, where Auntie Zhang, from the temple, took out two copies of Mother's will. The contents were about the same: I'd get the apartment, and my brother would get the cash and her insurance policy.

We went in to see her early that morning. She lay motionless, as if asleep. When I rubbed her hand, I found the palm still warm to the touch. Each time I called out to her, I thought I saw her eyelids flutter. I was reminded of the last few years we'd lived together, when I'd stopped calling her Mom and we rarely had anything to say to each other. She'd sleep in the lower bunk while I read in the bunk above her. She'd toss and turn all night, and sometimes she'd get up to rummage around in the living room, as if she felt comfortable only among her junk. For a teenager, it was beyond comprehension, and I felt nothing but anger. My brother looked grief-stricken that morning in the hospital. Being Mother's favorite, he'd always gotten what he wanted from her, and they'd formed a symbiotic, mutually repellent relationship that excluded me. I had always thought of him as selfish and willful until that day, when I saw him acting the role of the older child. Sitting by her bed and holding her hand and mine, he told her, "Don't worry, Mother. We'll follow your instructions, and we won't fight over the property." I wondered why she'd left me the apartment, which had become quite valuable, even if it was brimming with junk. Then it occurred to me that she knew my brother would simply squander whatever value it had. I wouldn't. But was she sure she knew what I was like? Was I the right keeper of that place?

She breathed her last the third morning at eight o'clock.

There was no sign of a struggle or resentment. I felt as if she'd left in peace, but that may have been wishful thinking.

Finally I had come in contact with the real smell of death. There is still a hint of life on the newly dead. Living people don't smell very good, with all the eating and excreting. You can even say there is a putrid odor that goes along with being alive, though it is very subtle, nearly imperceptible. Maybe it has something to do with a person's weight. Alive, Mother had owned as much as she could afford to amass, but now that she was dead, she didn't even own the clothes on her back. I wondered if death helped release her from the baggage of all that stuff. What I'd detected in the house wasn't the decaying odor of near-death or slow death, but the weight of her being.

VII

The four of us spent a week in the apartment. Sometimes I was so lost in thought that I actually fell asleep on my feet, and they had to wake me up. All the diligent work I'd performed for other people now appeared to have been a rehearsal for this clean-up job. I could tell what needed to be thrown out with my eyes shut. As if we were opening a vein in a mine, we had to dig through the piles to reach Mother's core. I'd always thought that she had her own logic hidden in the messy stacks of objects: When Mother and Father were newly married, they lived in a small room that had been added onto a relative's house. They had so few possessions that the only things decorating the walls were their crudely framed photographs. Father, who had vowed to rise up out of the rubble, managed to buy an apartment after rows of old houses had been razed and rebuilt. They were a loving couple back then, when I was born. Mother grew up poor at a time when most people had nothing, so she wanted to own something, anything that would make a house a home, even if that meant accumulating more than she needed. To me, this garbage dump was Mother's private museum; it was a pity that we'd failed to decode the secrets she had hidden therein. I couldn't understand her logic while she was alive, and now that she was gone, I couldn't keep her stuff around. We followed our usual practice, throwing away what needed to go, selling what we could, and giving away what was usable. Ashes to ashes and dust to dust. Everything had to be accounted for. I kept the cabinets in the living room, a rattan sofa, and a dining table, all furniture from my childhood, before the place went to pot, the old possessions when they first "started a family." The bunk bed was the only item I kept from Mother's late collection; I left it in my childhood bedroom.

I asked Anna if she wanted to move in with me. When I told her I loved her, she broke down and cried over the phone. "Let me know when you're ready and I'll come get you," I said. But she just kept crying.

After hanging up, I sat on the old rattan sofa for a long time. A strange fragrance lingered in the quiet room; it was from the cypress furniture and beech wood flooring. The slanting sun shone on the glass-topped tea table, giving the dust motes in the light a cheerful look, and casting a shadow on the wall that looked like a human silhouette. I felt Mother's lingering spirit, and that gave me a sense of comfort.

The Curse

By A Yi

TRANSLATED BY JULIA LOVELL

A chicken can disappear as easily as an insect. The owner of this particular missing chicken, Zhong Yonglian, had deduced that her neighbor Wu Haiying was responsible for the disappearance. There were two pieces of incriminating evidence: first, there was a trail of claw prints ending in Wu's vegetable garden; second, her house smelled of stew. Wu Haiying was not a woman you wanted to get on the wrong side of: she enjoyed a fight, and would coolly set fire to your house if she felt like pursuing the quarrel. If only Zhong Yonglian's son, with his dark murderer's glower, had been around, she thought to herself. But he hadn't phoned in ages, or sent any money home.

As dusk approached, two aspects of the problem occurred to Zhong Yonglian: one, it was Wu Haiying who had sabotaged their ostensibly harmonious relationship, and it would take more than Zhong's own nonconfrontational nature to mend fences; and two, although the disappearance of a chicken was not a disaster of the first order, it could not be overlooked. If Zhong waited till tomorrow, her moment would have passed. And so she decided to take a walk around the village. "Have you seen my chicken?" she asked everyone she met. "Where could it have gone?" "It was last seen on the east side," she told anyone who seemed interested. She'd learned this tactic from her husband. You need to prepare your ground first, he'd instructed her, near the end of the long illness that eventually killed him. Finally, Zhong Yonglian advanced upon Wu Haiying's house: "Who could have stolen my chicken?" she sang out three times.

"What's wrong?" Wu Haiying asked.

"I'm trying to find out which lowlife took my chicken." Once the words were out, Zhong Yonglian felt almost dizzy at her implicit declaration of war. "It'll come back in its own time," Wu replied. "What if it's already dead and eaten?" Zhong renewed her provocation. She quickly looked away. Wu Haiying at last caught on. "You think I stole it?"

"You tell me," Zhong Yonglian pronounced, turning to leave. Wu Haiying pulled her back by the sleeve. Zhong shook her off: "Fuck off and die."

"Are you saying I ate your chicken?" Wu Haiying screamed.

"No. But you just did."

"When?"

"To eat a chicken's an easy enough thing. And tidy—no evidence left."

The rain was coming down in sheets. Wu Haiying grabbed Zhong Yonglian—a thin, weak woman—by the collar, stared fiercely at her accuser's face, then slapped it hard. Zhong Yonglian's eyes and nose began streaming tears and blood, her face contorted from the double humiliation. As Wu Haiying prepared to administer a second blow, Zhong remembered her deceased husband and—with a sob of melancholy outrage—charged at Wu Haiying, who lost her balance in the surprise assault. Scrambling back to her feet, she grabbed hold of Zhong Yonglian's hair (as easily as if it were a bundle of grass) and twisted hard, pulling her to the ground. When witnesses reached the scene, there Zhong lay, screeching for her dead husband and her absent son, with Wu Haiying standing alongside her, ignoring her husband's calls for her to go back inside the house. "She started it," Wu explained. "She said I stole her chicken." Zhong Yonglian beat the concrete with her fists: "Shameless bitch." A few of the women tried to pull her up, but she refused to get up. Her hands and feet started to spasm.

"She's faking it," Wu Haiying said.

"Just shut up," her husband suggested. She wasn't finished, though, even as he dragged her inside. "You all heard her: she said I stole her chicken. Strike me down if I did." Zhong Yonglian sat up and stabbed a finger in her direction: "If you stole my chicken, I swear your son will die this year. If you didn't, my son will."

"If I stole it, my son will die." Wu Haiying accepted the terms of the curse.

"I still don't believe her," Zhong Yonglian muttered. Even as she cried herself to sleep that night, she felt that having the last word had mitigated some of the injustice of the encounter. The next morning the chicken came home, slick with rainwater, like a shabby hermit back from a retreat, scrabbling away at the ground, a red rag tied around its leg. She carried it inside and quietly killed it.

Zhong Yonglian felt guilty whenever she saw Wu Haiying, until one day she realized that even if Wu Haiying hadn't stolen her chicken, it didn't mean she was a good person, or that she wasn't a thief. She remembered the salty bitterness of her blood and tears, of Wu Haiying pulling her down to the concrete by her hair.

Whenever the two women encountered each other, Zhong would strive to match her antagonist's look of contempt. She stretched some plastic sheeting over the fence around the chicken coop, to prevent the birds from flying away, and asked her son-in-law to write "Death to thieves" on the strip of red cloth wrapped around every chicken's leg.

The two women took care to have nothing to do with each other.

As the final month of the lunar year came around, the village spoke of nothing except the return of Wu Haiying's son from Dongguan. He'd come back driving a white Buick that had rolled noiselessly over the frozen grass and stones of the road into the village. He pulled on the hand brake and slammed the door shut behind him with perfect Politburo swagger. He tapped the remote control, and the still car yelped, as if with fear. A girl—no local, for sure—somewhere in her early twenties also emerged from the vehicle, gazing adoringly at him. Her soft, white face could have been caught in a single handspan; her eyes shone with the luster that the villagers associated with foreign, not Chinese, girls. Her hair—dyed sunset-red—was cut in a dense crop. Although it was winter, she wore nothing but a tight gray T-shirt and a pair of black leather trousers, her clothes clinging to her slim curves and long legs. She smiled guilelessly at her audience, revealing pearl-like teeth.

"In you go, Xixi," Guohua said to her, and she obediently disappeared into Wu Haiying's house. She was easily the most beautiful thing the village had ever seen. That whole day, the villagers were troubled by a curious sense of emptiness, of vexed enchantment. Guohua kept her shut up at home until Wu Haiying told them to make a tour of the village, after which he finally took her to see a few of their relatives. Wu Haiying, by contrast, always seemed to be out on calls, her face radiant with delight. Knowing what she'd come to hear, her hosts all hastened to compliment her on her good luck. "Her parents haven't agreed yet," she'd reply, in an attempt at modesty. If her interlocutor failed to say something along the lines of "sooner or later, then," she'd quickly interject: "They've exchanged rings, you know." She was so euphoric that she even forgot to sneer at Zhong Yonglian, who consequently felt that her humiliation was now complete.

Zhong headed off to the country town, where she asked the proprietor of a public phone stall to call the number on the piece of paper she gave him. She wanted to tell her own son, Guofeng, that he should bring a girl back with him for New Year's—even if he had to pay her. After several attempts, there was still no answer. "Try again," Zhong Yonglian urged the man. "Did you dial a wrong number?" The next time he tried, whoever was on the other end had turned the phone off. Guofeng had always been a loner: he never told his mother where he was working, nor rang home. "I don't care about *you*," he'd say if she ever admitted to being anxious about him. "Haven't you got better things to worry about?" Almost every year he'd go into town for New Year's, wandering back long after dark: barefoot, his face bleeding. He'd never tell her what had happened. One year he hadn't gone to town because he was helping his uncle with some haulage work. When the uncle fell ill, Guofeng went AWOL with the van to Anhui over in the southeast, eventually calling home to say it had broken down. Off the uncle went, hundreds of miles across China, and found the van with the door open, the keys still in the ignition, but no sign of any driver. "You should have thrown that pile of junk away ages ago," was all Guofeng had to say about it afterward.

Zhong Yonglian went to the police station, a scarf wrapped around her head. A member of the joint defense squad asked her what she wanted.

"I've come to report a crime."

"Name?"

"That doesn't matter." She cupped a hand around her mouth and whispered into her interlocutor's ear: "Guohua's back."

"Who?"

"The one who ran away after the gambling bust." She had another idea. "He's brought a woman back with him. I'm sure she's a whore."

"Thanks."

The police station only covered its operating costs through fines. Every one of the gamblers caught last year had paid four hundred yuan, except for the absent Guohua. If Guohua didn't pay, people had begun to mutter after he ran away, why should they?

A few days later, the station sent a policeman, a driver, and a member of the defense squad to catch their prey. They dragged Guohua out, struggling like a snared rabbit. Xixi pursued them all the way to the car: "Why? Why?" she was sobbing, just like one of those women in the soap operas.

"Fuck off," the defense squad man—who seemed to have styled his moustache on Stalin's—shouted back at her. Xixi began pounding him with her fists, screaming obscenities in her beautifully accented Mandarin. She bit hard on the inside of her cheek: right on cue, the tears came. "What right do you have to arrest him? Doesn't the law mean anything to the police?" Distracted only momentarily by her adorable naïveté, they carried him off in a cloud of dust.

When Wu Haiying came back from cutting pig fodder and heard the news, she fainted, while Xixi squatted beside her, weeping. Observing them through her window, Zhong Yonglian smiled to herself. Serves them right, she thought. Serves them right, she repeated out loud, pacing around her house.

Half an hour later, Guohua returned, having somehow escaped his captors. Kissing Xixi on the forehead, he ran upstairs to hide inside the grain measure in the threshing room. "Just tell them I've gone to the mountains," he said. By dusk, the investigation team had circled back around to the village. They barged into the Wu residence and began carelessly searching the place. "Where is he?" they barked at Wu Haiying, grabbing her by the collar.

"I don't know."

"You're lying."

Wu Haiying looked away.

"He ran off to the mountains," Xixi sullenly told them.

"Run away, has he?"

"That's what I said."

The man with the Stalin moustache pointed his flashlight directly at her. Closing her eyes, she bit her lip. Her face—skin pulled taut, eyelashes casting a long shadow over her cheeks—twitched.

"He's run off, has he?"

"That's what I said," she repeated, a little more boldly.

"Where's your temporary residence permit?" the man asked.

"I don't have one."

"You should have one."

"I don't have one."

"Then you're coming back with us."

"Why?"

He struck her hard with the flashlight. She crumpled to the floor. "Drag her out," the policeman said, and they started to pull her inert body by her high leather boots. Her face was a mask of despair, as if she were a fish on a chopping block eyeing the gutting knife. Wu Haiying's relatives—who'd gathered around to watch—melted away home. But by the time the police had pulled Xixi into the yard outside the house, the clan had returned, brandishing brooms, poles, truncheons, even tobacco pipes. The police were surrounded, and the beating began. The thin, reedy voice of the policeman tried to plead for calm, but it was too late. Eventually a voice shouted at them to stop. The crowd parted to let the young master—the young master who had returned triumphantly home in a Buick, the young master who had taken refuge in the threshing room—through. Kitchen knife in hand, he charged into the throng like an avenger, plunging his weapon into the arm of the man with the moustache. Everyone closed their eyes, momentarily terrified by the new logic of the situation. Even Guohua seemed unable to believe what he'd done, pausing after he pulled the knife out. Only Zhong Yonglian—inside her head—screamed at him to go on: "Go on! Stab him again! It'll be the death of you, too!" Guohua stabbed him again.

There was no blood. No sound, even. The killing process seemed unbearably protracted, even to the victim, who grabbed at the knife, urging his murderer to stop using the back of the blade. Suddenly conscious of how humiliating his incompetence was, Guohua snatched up a wooden spear instead. Before he was ready to deliver the final blow, though, the three representatives of law and order struggled free from their attackers and scattered like terrified pack animals out of the village, disappearing along a dark maze of paths and byways.

The police never sent anyone back. A relative of Wu Haiying's in the provincial capital rang the Provincial Party Committee; the committee had a word with Public Security, and Public Security canceled the eighteen-man militia detailed to the village. When Public Security told the local police to leave Guohua alone, Wu Haiying's relative agreed to leave Public Security alone. All the same, Guohua and his terrified girlfriend couldn't get out of the place fast enough.

The village's migrant laborers drifted back home for New Year's, bringing marvels such as singing cards, golden mobile phones, and smokeless cigarettes. Zhong Yonglian hung around the entrance to the village, waiting in vain for a glimpse of her son's tall form. She asked the other returnees if they knew where Guofeng was working; no one did.

She went back to the county town to try Guofeng's mobile again; the number was out of service, the man said. Which meant, he explained, that no one was using the phone anymore: maybe they hadn't paid the bill, or maybe it had been stolen. Guangdong was full of motorbike-mounted pickpockets who'd mug you as they dragged you along the ground, sometimes for dozens of meters.

Exhausted by sleepless nights, one day she dozed off in a chair. She dreamed that Guofeng was a little boy again, but his face was bleached white, his voice barely a whisper. She ladled him out some porridge, stirred in some medicine, and told him to eat it up. But Guofeng just stared at her wretchedly, shaking his head. Anxiety clutched at her heart. After she'd put the bowl away, she discovered that a huge squid-colored creature was sprawled across the bed, its emaciated chest inlaid with fibrous tendons and bones, its limbs like flayed rabbit legs. Some of its heaving internal organs had been punctured, and dark blood was dripping down onto the floor. Now it was half-squatting, its right hand flat against the bed board, its bowed legs buckling as it tried to lever its exhausted body up, while the cotton quilt covering it slid off. Its enormous cobble-shaped head was almost hairless and featureless, except for a vast, panting, stinking mouth, armed with long, sharp teeth. As it struggled for breath, its cheeks inflated, then deflated. Swaying as if it were about to fall, the creature suddenly reached out to grab her. She woke up. There was a cold aching in her wrist.

Rushing over to her daughter's house, she found her son-in-law playing cards in the sun.

"I still haven't heard anything from Guofeng. I had a horrible dream: he'd grown wings and a tail, and he was dripping blood." Her son-in-law said nothing. "Will you go and find him for me? Can't you see how worried his sister is about him?" The son-in-law glanced at her, deciding not to say whatever had been on the tip of his tongue. "Please. You're his brother-in-law, and he's my only son."

"How am I supposed to find him?"

"I'm sure you can think of something. I'm begging you."

"China's a big country. I don't even know what province he's in."

"I know you can find him. You young people are so clever. Bring him back for New Year's. He can do what he likes after that. I'm worried sick: I just want to see him."

Her son-in-law stood up. Zhong Yonglian suddenly clung to his knees, her face wet with tears. "I'm scared he's dead."

"What the . . . All right," he agreed, spotting his wife approaching.

"Swear it."

"I swear."

After taking five hundred yuan from Zhong Yonglian, her son-in-law spent a day in the provincial capital, then came back, the money unspent. He'd bumped into Li Yuanrong from the village over the way, he lied, who'd had a letter from Guofeng saying he'd be back in a few days. When Zhong Yonglian refused to believe him, he called Li Yuanrong, who told her himself that "Guofeng'll be back soon. He's on a job that pays a thousand a day—he's trying to earn as much as he can before he comes back." A few days before New Year's, a villager named Guoguang—who'd been working in Guangdong—came back and corroborated Li Yuanrong's story. Guofeng was in the factory next door, he said, and had been on overtime the past few days. They were paying him several times the going rate—four hundred yuan a day. Guofeng had asked him to pass on the message that he'd be back on New Year's Eve.

"How is Guofeng?"

"Still not much of a talker. He's grown his hair out—like a poet."

Zhong Yonglian knew why Guofeng was so desperate to earn money. Every New Year's Day, migrant workers back for the holiday converged on a temple in Yu, a nearby village, to play cards. The bets started off at a few hundred or a few thousand yuan, then quickly escalated to tens or hundreds of thousands. Most of them gambled away all the money they'd worked so hard to earn all year, then borrowed a bit of cash to buy their train ticket back south. Last year, Guofeng had cleaned up over the first four days, then lost everything on the fifth. He'd come home red-eyed, eaten a bowl of rice porridge, then left.

On the morning of the last day of the lunar year, Zhong Yonglian stewed chicken, goose, beef, and pork, prepared the vegetables, and made bean curd soup. By midday the food was all cold, but still she waited, like a woman expecting her lover—too fragile with hope to go out and look for him herself. She was waiting for him to rush in and call out her name; she was waiting to turn and smile at him.

"Guofeng."

"Mother."

Those two words were all she wanted to hear. But as the sun sank and the dust on the road congealed, nothing disturbed the New Year quiet—the village was silent except for the muffled crackle of children setting off firecrackers. Darkness fell, as if a bucket of ink had been dropped over the village. Zhong Yonglian sat on her threshold, weeping.

At eleven o'clock, when all the other households had bolted their doors, and Zhong Yonglian herself was about to lock up for the night, a pair of headlights glowed weakly on the horizon. She stiffened as they approached, clearly headed in the direction of the village. Eventually, she allowed herself to grow excited. She began to jog toward the light, then accelerated to a sprint.

The van drove right past her.

She sat by the roadside and began to cry, her body aching, the soles of her shoes broken by stones, her knees grazed from a fall. Her son wasn't coming home. But just as she had abandoned all hope, the van turned around, returned to the village, and stopped outside her house, the engine still running.

She ran home.

Guofeng emerged carrying a cheap bag, which he dropped to the ground while he took two hundred yuan from his trouser pocket and gave it to the driver. He was as impassive as always. Picking up the bag, Zhong Yonglian asked the driver if he wanted something to eat. He drove off without an answer.

"Why are you so late?" she asked.

Guofeng seemed impatient: "I've been on a train for the past day and night, and I had trouble getting a taxi."

"Are you hungry?"

"Yes."

"I'll heat some dinner up for you."

"I'll have some rice porridge."

"Porridge, for New Year's?"

"I already told you."

His voice was weak, but still commanding. "I'm tired," he said. "Tell me when it's ready." He walked off to the bedroom and lay down on the bed, his eyes closed. When she was finally sure he was asleep, Zhong Yonglian pulled the quilt out from under him and covered him with it. Empty with relief, she set about making the porridge. She washed the pot, rinsed the rice, then added the water. She knew that her son liked his porridge as thin as broth: the clearer and blander, the better. She fiddled impatiently with the gas. She lifted the lid on the pot to see if it was done: after the steam had cleared, she discovered that the rice in the ladle was still hard. When at last it was ready, she ladled out a big bowlful. She carried it into the bedroom, not even minding how hot the bowl was, and called out to him. Beneath the quilt, his breathing was barely audible. He moaned faintly.

"Sit up and have some porridge."

He didn't respond. She sat on the edge of the bed, waiting. He must have traveled thousands of miles on the train, and it was at least another sixty from the country town. She gently tucked the quilt in around him. Heavy snow began to swirl outside the window. The snow is falling, she thought; my son is fast asleep. The world is at peace.

She called out to him again: "Feng."

Again there was no answer.

She drew her face close to his: "Feng," she said softly, "sit up and have something to eat before you go to sleep." Now she was worried: his face, when she felt it, was as cold as ice. She put her hand in front of his nose: he was hardly breathing. She shook him, she tugged at him. His hand fell out of his sleeve, and she pushed up the material to grab hold of his wrist. It was as if there was nothing left to grab.

After a moment of paralysis, she burst into tears.

She might as well have been holding a dead fish. Her fingers were slippery with stinking, decaying matter. Her thumb gouged into her son's destroyed wrist, straight to his hard white bones. His arm had rotted purple—eggplant purple. She pulled up his wool shirt: his torso was the same, his chest criss-crossed with canal-like purple veins. When she tried to lift him from behind, his head hung down as if detached from his body; a rank odor of chemicals belched out of his open mouth.

Three minutes was enough for the doctor in the county town. "Your son's body has been destroyed," he told her when he emerged from the ward—he seemed angry about it. "Everything: organs, skin, bones. He rotted to death." She rented a car to take Guofeng back to the village and quietly buried him.

After the spring had come, an ambitious intern from the provincial legal aid center came looking for her. Zhong Yonglian—her hair now completely white—gazed uncomprehendingly at him as he explained concepts like lead poisoning, maximum workload, and health and safety. Changing tack, he tried an analogy to help her understand Guofeng's death: think of the chemical warfare plants that the Japanese built when they invaded China—the place your son was working in was much more poisonous. Zhong Yonglian simply walked away, shaking her head.

"I just want to help. It won't cost you anything."

"No."

"Are you going to let your son die for nothing?"

"I don't need your help." She made her way over to her neighbor's house— ever so slowly, as if she were convalescing from an illness. Seeing Zhong Yonglian carefully sit down on her stone threshold, Wu Haiying brought a stool for her to sit on. "The ground's too cold to sit on."

"I was wrong about the chicken."

"Shush now."

Wu Haiying squatted down and stroked Zhong Yonglian's hand. The tears ran silently down Wu's face, while Zhong stared stolidly into the middle distance—like one of those socialist realist statues of the revolutionary martyrs. A migrant laborer who hadn't yet left for the south was playing an American pop song in one of the houses near the mouth of the village.

> Everywhere I'm looking now,
> I'm surrounded by your embrace.
> Baby, I can see your halo,
> You know you're my saving grace.
> You're everything I need and more,
> It's written all over your face.
> Baby, I can feel your halo,
> Pray it won't fade away.

They sat there, listening.

Unfinished—To Be Continued

By Li Zishu

TRANSLATED BY NICK ROSENBAUM

After passing through many places, after coming to recognize numerous cities and towns by means of your own stories, you arrive, at last, at this city.

You use the word "arrive," not "find." This is correct. Though you've walked many a road to get here, this is not a place that can be found. It does not exist. Or perhaps one might say, it merely exists in those impossible parts of the world. It is fictional, only a place at which to arrive.

But it might not be easy to see that it is fiction. The people in this city and their lives are supported by definitive evidence; the structure of each cityscape rests on ample foundations. You find it hard to say what exactly in this city is artifice. It isn't even a reflection of the real world: every counterpart here is endowed with its proper temperature and texture; each possesses its own historical record, its loves and hatreds, affections and enmities. You can't even say whether the people who live in this city have other halves living in the world outside; at the end of the day, this place does not exist in parallel to the real world. You can only say it is purely the invention of some woman (she probably is a stickler for wording) and is the most complicated piece, the most comprehensive statement, she has ever created.

Because this is her city, it has been labeled and named by countless tales. You should be able to recognize these labels, as you've read her seven books of stories. You've read them over and over, read and reread them so many times that you feel you've read through an entire atlas. You've memorized almost every street in the city, every corner, every telephone pole. Where the old buildings are, where old houses stand, where a mosque can be found. Ah—and also, you know where to go to read about its history, a history half of which is spread open in daylight, with the other half written in wavering shadows. The woman always writes history this way, hanging books out to dry as if they were wet clothes, or ripping out pages and spreading them out over the pavement, fashioning them into the backdrop of all of her stories.

But these things are not what make you recognize this city. First and foremost, you can't help but recognize this rain. The rain is unending, as if it's fallen for hundreds of years. Perpetual rain makes the entire city look sickly, as is written in the stories. Nearly all of the woman's stories contain rain; every letter is waterlogged, the stories are soaked, but there isn't even time for mold to grow. Immediately another rain, and then another story, lights up the scene like a streetlamp. The characters open their umbrellas one by one; some pull on raincoats, pushing their way from this story into that story, then drive cars with streaming fog lights, wipers brushing the rain aside, stuck in a cavalcade of cars circling slowly, slowly, to return again to this somehow familiar story.

You also recognize other things within this rain: streetlamps, lighting up one by one like cigarettes; a gray pigeon, two gray pigeons, ascending slowly, wings flapping; a window, with a hand reaching out to close the shutters; a sparrow or a crow or a magpie on the windowsill, craning its neck as it preens; the still-dripping shadow of a shirt hung on a wall to dry; a cat watching the world with cold eyes from the window; a child with heat streaming from her nose, both palms glued to the windowpanes, silently focused on the street below. Too familiar. You've relived scenes like these time and again through the woman's stories. You even suddenly feel that while walking these streets, which are bustling with activity but full of silent, wooden-faced people, you've caught a whiff of that woman's tropical essence.

Regarding her warmth, of the stories you've read, it is most instructive to consult "Zhang Wang's Shadow."

(. . . warm pearls of sweat bead across her back, across her chest, across her armpits, across her inner thighs. Her flesh, like a flower, like jade, studded thick with rain and dew. At this, their first meeting, the woman is unashamed, not the slightest bit coy; in bed, she is a bramble in full bloom. Later, Zhang Wang could never recall how they walked from the airport to the hotel. It seemed that neither held the other's hand; it seemed that the woman led the way, two or three paces ahead, occasionally turning her head to offer him a smile.

He wanted to grab hold of her hand. This scenario he has envisioned hundreds, thousands, of times, from the day they first agreed to meet all the way up to his fitful half-sleep on the plane, waiting for an eternity, his imagination restless. Zhang Wang had expected that the moment they met, they wouldn't be able to stop themselves from embracing in the terminal, even kissing passionately. In preparation for landing, he brushed his teeth in the plane's tiny bathroom, wiping his face with the towel he had brought along. But the arrival hall was immense, much larger than he had expected, and surprisingly cold and still. Several people in painstakingly ironed clothes held up various name cards, bodies crushed together as if huddling for warmth. The woman stood behind them. They recognized each other at first glance, but at the instant their eyes met, the woman turned away, bashful, her gaze fixed on the reflections of people on the marble floor, as if ashamed, unwilling to recognize him.

Now, at the hotel, she seems another person entirely. Perhaps she has finally relaxed, as if she was anxious that someone might be hot on her heels. The door closes and she kisses him, arms around his neck, encircling him like twining snakes. Zhang Wang, flustered, returns her kisses, his mind flashing back to a picture of the Indian serpent-goddess Naga that he saw while practicing painting in the countryside as a child. Her kisses are passionate, the woman's tongue more greedy than his, and very quickly he feels that he cannot breathe; the room is spinning. If not for the clothes holding her body in, the woman might very well have insinuated herself into the spaces within his chest, might have enshrined herself between his ribs. —"Zhang Wang's Shadow")

You recall that in another one of her stories, a frigid woman turns away, and her slender silhouette murmurs: *People are always asking, when is the rainy season where you are?*

The rainy season is now, is always. Thus this city has long since lost its rainy season. Such a city fits everything you've imagined about the woman's books. Here, the only thing that is difficult to imagine is your father. You know that every year he would come and spend several days here, just like Zhang Wang in the stories. Every year, precisely during the dry season where you all lived, your mother going crazy managing the family's water use while at the same time trying to keep the plants in the courtyard alive, your father would find some excuse to take a long trip abroad, and he would always find his way here, coming to live in the woman's stories, sometimes at a hotel, sometimes in a small building with two windows, under different guises and names, to spend a few days in tender companionship with this woman. Even near the end of his life (your mother says that by that time, in the bedroom, his spirit was willing but his flesh was weak), as long as he could still move, he always made it here, year after regular year, to this story.

The father you knew was a man of few words, unattractive, thin as a shadow. When he was young, he studied painting unsuccessfully and dropped out of art school, taking up actuary work and computer science. Industrious and frugal until the day he died, he drifted into a few small investment projects, but he was never the type to chase after money. He was practical to a fault, and lived a life devoid of the merest hint of the romantic. Your mother was always a bit careless, with no eye for details, and never worried that a man like her husband would ever go astray. So she never took any precautions, and couldn't put a date on when your father began to carry that "happiness" key ring, much less came close to growing suspicious of it.

In point of fact, if you hadn't read those seven books your father left behind when he died, you wouldn't have found that key ring in any way dubious. But after your father passed, all of your suspicions finally crystallized around that short story, no more than a thousand words long, finding in it what amounted to ironclad proof. Your father had the same key ring. And it was quite literally the sign of his own broken happiness.

(. . . for these two or three minutes, she and her husband, as well as that woman with the "happiness" key ring, sit peacefully on the park bench. Several pigeons fly past, landing by their feet. She draws her body closer to her husband, and very gently empties the birdseed she has brought him into his palm. The man is very happy, it is clear. His disease has finally progressed to the point that he has forgotten his entire family, and coming to the park to feed the pigeons has now become his favorite part of the day.

He gives every pigeon a name, chats with them, treats them like old friends. But he can't remember people's faces. Sometimes upon waking in the morning, he stares at her with wary eyes, as if sizing up a stranger. Nevertheless, from time to time he still pulls out his key ring and toys with it, staring at it, his heart pounding.

A single xi, 喜, shaped like a half-circle. "Happiness." Silver-gray, some metallic alloy.

Many years before, when her husband was transferred abroad to work for two years, he brought back this keepsake. The xi appears to be magnetic, and she can guess that it was once connected to another matching half-circle. Half of a shuangxi, 囍—"double happiness"—its other half missing. She suppresses the urge to ask, but surreptitiously scrutinizes his movements and bank accounts for quite some time. She finds nothing out of the ordinary, and decides not to bring it up.

In the past ten years, they have moved three times. But no matter where they go, no matter how many locks they have changed, her husband always uses the same key ring. Half of double happiness—one incomplete happiness. When clustered with other keys, it too looks like a key, a key that opens a dark room she cannot know. —"Key Ring")

The woman who wrote this story clearly overestimated your mother, imagined her as much too big-hearted and gracious. But the kindness revealed in such a story makes affection for the author well up within you. Maybe it was for exactly this reason that you managed to sit through all seven collections of her stories. You have tried to find in these books the father you never knew, but the woman's style is opaque, often stopping just short or sidestepping the most crucial of questions, so no matter how many times you read or how hard you try to piece the facts together, what's left is always incomplete. Your father, incomplete. The woman, incomplete. Time, desire, love, all incomplete.

Even years afterward, you often imagined one day meeting the woman who wrote these stories. Some nights, unable to sleep, you couldn't help but take her books out to reread. You weren't aware that you were already imagining her, hadn't even realized that through your imagination you were acting out the role of your father, entering her body through her words, making love to her again and again.

These are your dreams over the past few years, not for anyone else to know, tinged with a shameful quality akin to incest. But precisely because of the shame that surrounds these dreams, that feeling of sin, you sink deeper and deeper into your indulgence. Your wife is a delicate, sensitive young woman, but she has not discovered your perversion. As for those seven books, because she doesn't know Chinese, apart from hearing you mention and hence having some idea that your father might have had a history of womanizing, she hasn't noticed that you are always departing upon journeys, always imagining your encounter with the city at which you will arrive.

———

You linger in this story world where rain falls all day long, slowly discovering what makes it unique. This city's hustle and bustle is merely a facade; its true population is not nearly as large as you have seen: each person is double-cast as yet another person. The woman likes to remake everyone she knows, including herself, in her own particular way, melting them down and then folding them into her imagination and words. Reproduction and re-creation, like creating an Eve from a rib.

Or, as you painfully discover, this city can no longer house any complete person. (Clearly this is not your own phrasing; it is a sentence from a story called "A Short Song," spoken by the protagonist Chunli to her lover.)

Out of all seven collections, this is one of your favorite stories.

(. . . though she sees him lugging the awkwardly large suitcase, at the same time shouldering a rucksack so large it looks like a turtle shell on his thin frame, stumbling a little in the process, Chunli makes no move to help. She merely crosses her arms and stands by the door, blankly watching him go. As he waits for the elevator, he rattles off another slew of reminders: *Weather's been pretty chilly lately, you better take good care of yourself, you little tropical fish; be careful when you're doing chores now, don't twist your ankle again or hit your head,* tired phrase after tired phrase.

Being on your own here, it'll be so lonesome.

Chunli does not reply, just keeps nodding her head. It's autumn now, only about 20 degrees Celsius during the daytime, and Chunli is already wearing her only sweater. The sweater is a murky green, very loose, with especially long sleeves. Chunli likes to cross her arms, sticking each hand into the other sleeve, sometimes even leaning on the doorframe with a silly look on her face, like an old-fashioned village mandarin. She looks simply adorable when she does that, he thinks. Just looking at her, he can't stop himself from hugging her to his chest, saying, *Oh, you . . . how can you still act so childish?*

Actually, both of them are getting on in years; he is just a little older than Chunli. But their two years together in this little building have been so sweet, laughter from dawn to dusk, Chunli bursting with energy all the time. They really have been just like two big kids, strangers to sorrow. But of course, this bliss is all hollow. Last night, in the midst of lovemaking, Chunli felt a sudden sadness, as if amniotic fluid were bubbling out of some hole in her body. She said nothing, biting her lip, her tears trickling forth in silence. Sex continued in the dark. He was startled when he realized that Chunli was crying, and their fun abruptly ended.

He thought he'd hurt her. God, can it hurt that much? Trail upon trail of tears streaked down Chunli's face. She saw him stop and knew she could not keep quiet anymore, and she finally let go, sobbing uncontrollably.

She ended up crying all night. The candles burned down before her tears dried. Today Chunli's eyes are swollen and her heart is wooden. Watching him shoulder the rucksack, lug his big, heavy suitcase, squeeze his body awkwardly into the elevator, she makes no move to help, not even giving him the benefit of a *take care*, or a *have a safe trip*. When the elevator doors close, he shouts from within, *Chunli!* Chunli stands, hands clasped together, still in a daze. She is counting down mentally, tenth floor, ninth floor, eighth floor, seventh, sixth . . .

Once she reaches "first," she imagines him dragging the suitcase from the elevator. After leaving the building, he will still need to follow the winding flagstone pathway around the courtyard to reach the gate. Chunli waits for a moment, then turns around and locks both doors. She has already decided that, no matter what, she will not go look. But she paces back and forth through the living room, agitated, hands shaking, index finger tapping against thumbnail. A sadness that her tears should have depleted now wells forth like an undercurrent. Chunli lets out a teary gasp and flees to the bedroom, jumping straight onto the window seat. Like a child, her palms and forehead glued to the windowpanes, she watches wide-eyed as dust blows across the road outside the apartment complex, as a taxicab pulls slowly away. —"A Short Song")

"A Short Song" is set in a place called Hometown in Mainland China, which is located in this city. Actually, by the time you read the book, you already know what's coming. The woman's descriptions are ever so precise; that little apartment with the window seat is a near-image of one of your father's many small-scale investments in China, rented over many years to various tenants. One year, a developer snapped it up at a premium, and you accompanied your father there to help clean the place up.

Of course, by then the woman was no longer there. At the end of the story, Chunli leaves, setting the key to the apartment on the bed, and taking her lonely "happiness" key ring with her. Where will she go? She can always find shelter in the next story. But the next story always takes place in this city. You look around. Every woman on the street carries a shadow of her, or resembles her slightly; even the schoolgirl walking past wearing a backpack faintly evokes the woman's childhood. You know she is in this city, and you know that everyone to some degree symbolizes her. But with the dissolution of her selfhood she is gradually disappearing from the real world, and you are unable to reconstruct her from these scattered elements.

Yet of all the characters in her books, there must be one who has been allotted something more of her than the others. After all, this self-replication cannot be a uniform process. Someone must have inherited more of her background and upbringing; someone must have shared more of the moments she has lived; someone must have met more of the people she has met, must have shared more of her joys and virtues, borne more of her terror, pain, sin. In such a multitude of characters, there must be one who was created most in her image.

Because you so strongly believe this, the woman responds to your searching eyes, and walks forth from her story.

Unbelievable. You catch sight of her amid the shifting scenery, in the same way that it is impossible to miss an incandescent body in a mass of dark shapes. The woman stands across the street, in front of a small convenience store that shouldn't exist: aging shelves stacked full of dark masses of wholesale goods, colors faded from nearly all of the woven dustpans, wide-brimmed hats and palm-leaf fans, iron-backed wall calendars painted with cheongsam-clad beauties, paraffin lamps, vinyl records, and cassette tapes . . . everything, including the store itself, faded into grayscale, with a hint of sepia, like scars slowly seared onto the skin of time.

The rain falls harder and harder. The woman looks up at the sky, suddenly raises her arms in the air to open a brilliant crimson umbrella. On this street, in this encroaching darkness, her umbrella looks like a blazing tendril of flame.

Everyone on the street sees it, a crown of radiant fire filling their vision as they hurry along their way. What a showoff. You recognize her immediately: she is a character she has written herself, most likely a woman from a certain short story who sits on the window seat every morning, watching and pining from afar for some young man.

She is aware of you immediately, too, because your body is suffused with a flavor not of this story. Tides of people flow down the street. They don't speak, the cars don't sound their horns. But hovering above the street is a colossal inaudible cacophony. You stand on the other side of the street, leaning against a bare telephone pole, wearing a hooded raincoat. The air surrounding you seems to thicken, and the people shrink back ever so slightly as they hurry around you. She cannot recall in which story she wrote someone like you. Could it be that you were only a child in one of her stories, and you escaped from it after its conclusion, to grow up alone in the outside world, slowly completing yourself?

Yet the woman knows that you are not a secret danger hidden in her soul, not because you are no longer a character from a book, but because she is no longer the person she was when she wrote her stories. Over those years of writing, she has broken herself into piece after piece, then ever so carefully kneaded the fragments into layer upon layer of fiction and reality, until she completed all of her stories. "She" no longer exists. Instead, she has become a collection of shadows cast from many directions by characters from countless stories.

"This is only a story, it's not real." She rubs one eye, then the other, wiping you out of the world of her story.

You fade away into the rain.

———

The woman sees tidy curtains of rain streaming down over the rim of her umbrella. Beyond the sheets of rain there is more rain, as far as the eye can see, pitter-pattering. She cranes her neck and the city stands at attention, the buildings raising the overcast sky higher and higher, and she feels like this place is a gorge, or a deep well. Rain pours down, millions upon millions of pearls of water, pattering upon the asphalt of the road, upon the roofs of cars, breaking again and again over people's sullen gray raincoats and pitch-dark umbrellas, a snow-white steam rising like mist from the street.

In her books, whenever there is a story, it is accompanied by this kind of rain.

Also, there is always a mangy wretch of a dog, all skin and bones, limping on one leg, walking the wrong way down a one-way street, soaked from head to toe but totally unperturbed. Wedging himself into the waves of people coming home from work, he waits until the light turns green and hobbles across the road, a grizzled veteran of the city. When he passes the woman, he seems to

be giving her a sidelong look, and in that glance there passes some tacit understanding. This is how this city is, buildings crammed too close together, and
people with nowhere to go, pushed onto the streets like refugees. Apart from
the red, green, yellow lights at each intersection, all else is as written in the stories. A desolate cityscape, all color nearly washed out.

The rain falls endlessly, resentfully, like music both plaintive and querulous.
All of her stories are soaked completely through. Why? The rain is no longer
linked to the monsoon season. She remembers that long ago, when she was still
young, the comings and goings of the rain could be calculated and predicted, as
in April, during the Qingming Festival, or during September's Nine Emperor
Gods Festival. The rains fell on schedule, year after regular year. But now, like
the waves of desire that began to pummel her after she turned forty, the rains
are unending in their appetites, day and night, intermittent yet uninterrupted.
It is no longer possible to say whether they are the epilogue to the last rain or
the prelude to the next.

Back then she was so young, her literary talents were astonishing, her imagination surging. She could label every kind of rain with a different story, or
record every story with a different kind of rain. But her genius is no more. Her
memory wanes. Her thoughts are gummy, her head is filled with sludge. More
and more often, and more and more clearly, she hears voices drifting from that
faraway world. The rain becomes more nondescript, losing its character just
like the city she lives in. Sometimes she wonders if it is because she has written
and rewritten this city so many times that it has lost its passion, become a typical city. If it weren't for this strange but routine rain, would this city still have
value, still need to be remembered? Would it still warrant a pin in the map, a
foothold on the world?

She sometimes wonders if all the people who have passed away around her
weren't cursed by her pen. Her parents, friends, colleagues; her lovers and part-
ners. As she lives, she can't help imagining their misfortunes, calamities, and
deaths, spinning stories out of their misery. Her father's reflection surfaces most
often in her work, and because of this he lived in suffering and died alone. And
then there's that man from far away. She has never written about him explicitly,
but she knows that his shadow flits among her words, between her lines: tall,
lanky, rail-thin, back slightly bowed, assuming different names, his features
blurred. At first she obscured him intentionally in her stories' twists and turns,
but the passage of time has become the moth in the bookshelf, eating away at
the secrets buried deep within her memories. She almost hasn't noticed that she
is unable to recall the man's face.

Yet the woman knows that there will be a day when she remembers, perhaps
on her deathbed, when memories lost like pearls in the crannies of her mind

will float to the surface one by one, stringing themselves together. Will this come to pass? Without a doubt. She has written this ending into so many of her stories. If such a thing truly can happen, then in the last moment of his life that man must have seen her, seen emerging from the chaos all the wondrous things from those years so long ago.

You watch the woman. Her eyes are wide open, but she walks down the road like a sleepwalker. Her red umbrella looms enormous over her head; it's unclear whether it's blocking her face or your line of sight. But that red is an eye-catching marker, making her unable to cover her tracks within the world of her story. She walks on that side of the road, you walk on this side; there are many cars in between, as if what separates you is the space between truth and fiction. But at least for a moment, your worlds move in parallel.

The woman has not noticed that you are here. Didn't she already erase you from this story? With no way to leave or return to this city, all she can do is follow the path before her, imitating the pace of everyday life. The scenery surrounding you isn't pretty: on the right, a six-lane highway flows like a river, cars surging past in an eternal torrent. From this side you can't see any overpass or crosswalk by which people could reach the other side. To your left is a wall covered in graffiti, stretching unbroken in both directions. Apparently this was the perimeter of an old prison—apart from the twin doors that bar the entrance, it appears to be an endless circular wall.

The woman can't recall in which book she wrote about this prison. She once thought about walking around the entire thing, leisurely taking in everything drawn on the wall. The things painted on its surface are unremarkable, just a great mess of block letters and crude depictions of people. Swearing and mocking, advertising and proselytizing, good and evil canceling each other out. God loves the world; fuck your mother; every man's dream drug; 100% money back guarantee; die, earthlings; O Merciful Buddha; legal loan hotline, 1234567; Chen so-and-so, screw your entire family . . .

Ever since the woman stopped writing stories, she has found herself drawn to this area, finds herself frequently walking down this road. She is already tired of the graffiti, so she tries to imagine what is written on the other three sides. She remembers that once, as she walked down the street, a man claiming to be from the True Christ Church wouldn't stop following her, and amid his proselytizing he told her the story of this wall. Back when it didn't rain all day long, he said, there was a prisoner who walked around the perimeter painting the world's longest mural. But before he finished the entire wall, his sentence was up and he was discharged. Afterward, though he specifically requested to be allowed to finish the mural, even offering to buy his own supplies and paints, he was not granted permission, not even when he was dying from cancer.

That story was an utter fabrication, full of fatalist overtones and designed to intimidate, concocted in just as hackneyed a manner as the missionary's tired preaching. He wanted to convince her that living is great misery, that her life was incomplete, that she wasn't happy. The woman couldn't be bothered, so she picked up her pace, hurrying through the rain, her red umbrella an enormous shield careening wildly down the street, not even sure what she was trying to fend off. Even though the True Christ missionary stopped following her, he stood in the middle of the street, legs planted wide apart, shouting after her: *It's no use! You can't run! The Kingdom of Heaven is upon us!*

After that experience, the woman can't help feeling nervous whenever she walks down this stretch of road. She holds up her red umbrella to give herself cover. No matter where she goes, rain streams from her umbrella. It attracts rain in the same way her pen attracts disaster. Bearing down on her umbrella is not the heaven the True Christ missionary spoke of, but memory, suspended in the air like smog. She raises her head. Above her there will always be a girl watching from on high, her palms and forehead pressed against the window-pane, always a sulking child. The woman knows that this is only a fictional image from her stories, but in this city, though stories are always told slant, they are the most honest witnesses possible, their testimonies overruling all other truth. They are clearly saying to the woman: *It's no use, you can't run.*

Just like the rain, no matter which corner of the city the woman winds up in, she will always hear the cries of True Christ. You can't run, you aren't happy. At this very instant, she hears that voice lingering like wind and stops in her tracks, suddenly not sure which story she inhabits, or which story she should go on to next. The endings of all these stories are inevitable; she is well-versed in the fates of everyone here, in her own fate, in the machinations that pervade every so-called impermanence, and the subtle coupling between fate and fate.

How depressing. The woman thinks she might as well circle around and take a look at the scenery on the other three sides of the wall, but today the rain is falling as thick as paste, sapping her energy. She walks down the road, her shoes soaked, her clothes lashed by the rain. She feels tired and suddenly wants to go home, and by the side of the road a bus stop appears. There are lots of people waiting. The woman tries to push under the awning, but no one wants to scoot over for her. She can't get in; all she can do is stand outside in the rain holding her umbrella. This rain immobilizes everyone under the awning. A mangy mutt, half-lame, saunters over like he owns the place, a big bone in his mouth that he found who knows where. As he walks past the bus stop, he eyes the faces crammed inside with fascination. As his gaze settles on each face, it freezes in place. Only the woman hides under her umbrella, so that no one can see her expression. The dog doesn't press the matter, and walks away nonchalantly.

This is how stories are meant to be crafted: she and others painted into an oil painting, pigments daubed thick on the canvas, mottled like butter and choc-olate-hazelnut spread smeared on toast for breakfast. The brushwork is bold, and each person is assigned a meager amount of space. But no one can escape unharmed: each person must give up all of their qualities, all of their details.

This oil painting was at one time hung on a wall in your house, right inside the entrance, over the shoes, facing the door. The painting depicts a bus stop crammed full of people, a rainscape meant to be appreciated on a mostly emo-tional level. Vacant, indistinguishable eyes stare out at the world beyond the picture frame. The woman's red umbrella looks like a single exotic flower, blooming alone at dusk.

No matter how dazzling the outside world might be, the woman under the umbrella will not raise her head.

You found this painting among your father's old belongings. He painted it in his workshop when he was at home recovering. Your mother remembers how when he was young, he felt that his talents couldn't compare to those around him, and he decided to quit school. Afterward, nobody saw him so much as pick up a brush. Later he fell ill and was unable to work, and with nothing to do at home, he was suddenly inspired to paint. You saw him when he was paint-ing this picture: it's unclear whether it was because of the pain of the disease, or because he had been away from the brush for too long, but he clearly wasn't up to the task. He shut himself up in the studio, sulking, even talking about quit-ting: *Enough, enough.* But just a few days later, he would be back in front of his canvas, painting in silence. This cycle repeated itself again and again, and god knows it took him long enough, but he finally managed to complete it. After-ward, though, he lost all interest in continuing to paint and just sat in front of the painting, lost in thought. Later his health declined even further, and he lay in bed fading in and out of sleep, until he finally passed away. The picture lan-guished in the corner of his workshop, attracting no attention.

Until one weekend, while cleaning out the house, you went into your father's workshop and remembered that you still had to deal with the things he left behind. Your father was frugal by nature, counting pennies till the day he died, even a bit of a packrat. Somehow in the course of several dozen years of modest living, he managed to amass a huge amount of ephemera with no practical use or value. It was hard to tell how these objects were related; the collection was quite incongruous. But they were all locked up, suspiciously, in the same drawer of a steel filing cabinet.

These were not the sorts of things so valuable that one would want to collect them: seven books printed in traditional characters; a story collection with yellowing pages; a beautifully embroidered gift box that once held teacups or a vase but now contained several random objects, including two cell phones your father used until they were unusable, lying together in the box like a pair of specimens; a few dollar bills and a handful of coins from a small, distant country; and a heavy, unwieldy-looking square mug with a round handle, painted with a twining red flower with green leaves, as breathtaking as a whole-body tattoo.

You felt instinctively that there was something fishy about these objects, especially the books. Your father didn't put them on the small bookshelf in his workshop, didn't allow them to coexist with his tomes of computing diagrams and actuary science, his two English dictionaries, his thoroughly antiquated collection of world maps. Instead they were sequestered in that drawer, a world unto their own. His having hidden them away like that seemed extremely unusual. Moreover, those seven books were written by the same obscure author, a woman. You noticed that every few years, on each book's date of publication, the author signed and dated the title page. Though the inscriptions weren't made out to anyone and nothing else was written, each time the author published a book, she remembered to send your father a copy. The sentimental implications did not escape you.

You knew that your father was interested in classical poetry, and because he studied Chinese painting, he had a bit of an aesthetic fixation on traditional characters, even seeing to it that you studied Chinese. But he was never an avid reader, and he was certainly not the type to read novels. Moreover, nobody knew he had a friend who wrote books. These facts made those seven books of mysterious origin seem even more shady. The lack of words on the title page began to remind you of the empty space in Chinese ink paintings, fertile ground for idle imaginings, intimating things not meant for the eyes of others.

On the back flap of each book's dust jacket was a blurb about the author, no more than two or three cursory lines of text, explaining that she was born on a small island, is younger than your father by a few years, is a talented writer, and has won a few fairly trivial literary prizes. The name of the island was a mouthful, like syllables produced by a string of bells. You couldn't stop yourself from reading it out loud over and over, and once you finally read it smoothly, you realized that it was the sound of rainfall, meant to be read pitteringly, patteringly, plashingly, incessantly. And just when you got it perfect, thunder boomed outside the window. That year there had been a six-month drought. Precisely on that day, the sky let loose its first torrential storm.

The rainy season that year was very unusual. As if adjusting itself to the pace of your reading, the rain stretched out for much longer than it had in years past. You read the books one by one, in the order in which they were published. The woman's writing is dense, viscous, her tone languid and lethargic. There is much more description than narration—too much, in fact, as if what you're reading is not a book but a string of still-lifes. And she is painting in oil, an oil paint that never dries, forever soaked in rainwater. To read such a book is to be short of breath, the feeling of a swimmer about to drown above a vast coral reef, an exquisitely gorgeous kind of despair.

You don't know how you made it through book after book; perhaps every time you felt like quitting, you caught a glimpse of something between the lines. In many stories you notice that cup painted with the red rose; in two of her works, spaced quite far apart, you encounter the same key ring, its fate the same: two halves in a set, each half ending up alone.

You even saw yourself in one of the books. Perhaps it was "A Short Song"? (One night, the man gets a little drunk, perhaps truly unable to hold back any longer, and tells Chunli that his son, who lives far away, has earned outstanding marks and been admitted to university. The man rarely brings up anything from that life. Chunli rests her cheeks on her wrists as she listens, forcing a smile. Though she is pleased for him, seeing the light in his eyes and the pride written on his face, she also feels an immense, lonely envy . . .)

Though her books are all reconstructed stories, though the characters in them have had their names changed, their ages altered, their appearances modified, taken together they constitute hard, self-referential evidence, evidence that corroborates itself again and again from one story to the next, like a trail of clues linking every plot. The woman has said everything, but has taken the utmost care not to reveal anything.

———

You take your left hand out of your pocket and open your palm.

"I know you still have an unfinished story in you."

There are barely any people left at the bus stop. After you walk over, braving the rain to stand next to the woman, she begins to erase the people nearby, one by one, at random. She originally thought you were another emissary sent by True Christ to proclaim the end of days, but your steady, quiet demeanor, not of this fictional world, made her quickly realize that you are not any character she has created. You are merely a reader who has followed the stream to its headwaters. She looks up from under her umbrella. Actually, the rain has stopped. Only her red umbrella continues to stream down its curtains of rain.

The woman sighs, and takes the keepsake from your hand.

(A year ago, when the doctor pronounced him sick and counseled them to make the necessary preparations, she finally couldn't restrain herself any longer. *Is there anything you need to say?* The man shook his head, but at the same time stuck his hand into his pocket, as if looking for his key.

At the thought of him suffering silently, she caves. She stands up, tells him she's going to go freshen up, and gives the bag of birdseed in her hand to the woman, saying, my husband isn't in his right mind, please look after him for a little while.

Ten minutes. I'll be back in ten minutes.

She doesn't go far, but doesn't stay too close. She returns ten minutes later on the dot; the woman gives the birdseed back to her and leaves without saying a thing. The woman looked so kind and serene, he still looks impassive, and she can't help but wonder if this was purely some kind of misunderstanding. Several days later, she discovers that his key ring is missing that half of double happiness. Because the man has forgotten it existed in the first place, she is unable to pursue the matter any further. —"Key Ring")

The woman puts away the key ring and her umbrella. The rain really has stopped. Did she write that into the story? She can't quite believe it, standing there watching the street empty of people except for the two of you, the cars on the road vanished without a trace. The wall that symbolizes the prison still stretches across the other side of the street, graffiti unchanged, crows resting on top. The woman understands that this is the boundary of the world she can will into being; she is at once unable to remove it, and forever unable to scale it.

The prison, the front and back sides of this world: these are the ingredients for her next tale. Seeing as the two of you are the only ones left in the city, and the next rain hasn't yet caught up with you, the woman takes your arm and says, let's go, we'll take a walk around that wall across the street, see if there's anything written by your father.

You don't resist. You know that before this fantasy disintegrates, all you two can share is this tiny indulgence. So you step out into the road together. Even though there are no more cars passing by, the instant your feet meet the asphalt, a crosswalk as straight as a brushstroke springs into being below.

Now that there's a crosswalk, a mangy creature who has escaped intact from another story, dragging one crippled leg behind him, limps slowly toward you across the street . . .

Philosophy in the Boudoir

By He Wapi

TRANSLATED BY NICKY HARMAN

I. Poem

Milly and I entered the gloomy room, and I suddenly felt as if a snake had coiled itself around my neck. "Do you like it here?" she asked. I frowned. The double bed smelled old and musty. I think it was at that moment that I sensed how it was all going to end.

Before we went out that evening, she said: "You're really pretty." I pulled the zipper up on my dress and looked at her in the mirror, standing behind me. She leaned against the door jamb, her arms folded across her chest, squinting at me. I wanted to look at myself again but found that I couldn't focus. "But I don't like your figure," she went on. "I like full breasts and a big ass. I had a Greek friend when I was at school in France who was like that. She had blue eyes, too. I may be a woman, but I still wanted to fuck her."

Every time those words come back to me in the dead of night, I feel a nerve twitch in the right side of my neck, as if it's going to leap out from under my skin and roll around on the dusty floor.

Everything's alive. It's only me who died.

After Milly swore to me that we never killed Chen Mengla, I started to wonder if I was going stark raving mad. But here's the paradox: I can't be normal because I know I'm crazy; but I can't be crazy because crazy people don't know they're crazy. So what the hell am I?

In the Don Juan Bar, Milly pulled out two pictures she had painted just before our trip to Burma.

One of them consisted of seven large breasts, flushed faintly pink under white skin, gathered around a table as if they were at a conference.

"This is called 'Wei Xiaobao's Family Photo.'"

I laughed. "So what's that, then?"

The other painting was of a pile of male genitalia, in all shapes, sizes, and colors. "That one's called 'My Penis Collection.' I'm planning to give it to Louis Vuitton to use as a bag logo," she explained, completely straight-faced. "These two pictures represent my genitalia expressionist phase."

"I will organize a world touring exhibition for you," I said.

Milly eyed the piece of bacon on her fork like a fighting cock, and recited:

> This piece of meat is still alive
> But it has no future
> Because I'm going to eat it up
> Just like life eats us up.

Every time she made up a poem, I had a feeling of superiority. At least there was something I was better at than Milly.

Just then, however, I was distracted by the feeling that the zipper down my back was coming undone. So I was completely unaware of Chen Mengla crossing the smoke-hazed room and coming toward us.

At that moment, I was still alive.

I have never regretted anything that happened after that, because after I got drunk, my body seemed to take on a life of its own, so my consciousness is not to blame. What I do regret is that when Milly told Chen Mengla to sit next to me, I didn't refuse. The result was that my nostrils were filled with the odor of his body under his pale-green uniform. It was such a calming smell, it made me tremble, and I suddenly wanted to obey his every command.

We had arrived in the town of Xiaomengla only the previous morning. We hung around in the frontier market for a while, and Milly spent ages browsing through porn DVDs at one stall until we saw a police car come by and I dragged her away. Then we got permits and walked across the border to the Myanmar side. The June heat was stifling, as you can imagine. Even in the evenings there wasn't a breath of wind, and my cotton skirt clung to my skin, making me long to strip down completely. As we walked down a scorching, dusty road, an old-fashioned Mercedes-Benz—the kind you see in 1980s Hong Kong films—drove past and then stopped. Someone whistled at us.

The two men, father and son, ran a chestnut farm in Guizhou, and they offered to give us a lift back to Xiaomengla. The son, Guo, was in his early thirties, and wore a red T-shirt revealing blurred tattoos on his bare arms. He said he had just gotten back from Guiyang after seeing off his girlfriend. He'd had enough of her.

"I'm not the kind of guy who ditches old friends, but she's been with me for three years, and she's so dumb, she never did anything except gamble here, day after day. Just the day before she left, she lost 90,000 kuai of mine," he said.

Old Guo, a scrawny little man, gave a snort of derision.

We got into the air-conditioned car and drove through the main square past the food stalls. "Three years ago, the market was just as big as this, but you know what they sold?" The younger Guo smiled, showing a gold tooth. "Guns, drugs, and Russian slave girls!"

We crossed a bridge, and he went on: "If you come out tonight, you will see forty or fifty prostitutes, all waiting to be screwed. The casino we passed a couple of miles back has a show tonight. Do you want to see it? They're four retired ladyboys from Thailand. Have you ever seen ladyboys?"

I looked at Milly, who was gazing abstractedly out the window at a large makeshift shelter under the bridge.

"What's that?" she asked.

"Oh, that's the cockfighting arena."

II. Cockfighting

When I raised my camera, people rushed at me from all sides, yelling: "No photography!"

They believed that pictures took the soul away, and their cocks wouldn't win the fights.

A scrawny black cock was pacing around its cage, whether from anxiety or excitement, it was hard to tell. Its owner, a young man as bald as his bird, put it into the ring, where there was another cockerel, a red one. The afternoon heat must have made the birds drowsy, because they didn't look interested in fighting. They stalked around the arena, stopping from time to time to preen, as if they were dancing a friendly cha-cha-cha.

The owner of the black cock threw a cup of cold water over it, whispering encouragement. "Look how arrogant it is! Don't you want to beat it up? Aren't you jealous? Don't you want to win the prize? Don't you want a nice dinner tonight? Don't you want me to give you the most beautiful hen in the coop? Don't you want to step on its head, and enjoy the sweet taste of victory?"

Under the blue-and-white-striped nylon awning, the air was filled with the reek of bird shit, sweat, feathers, fury, blood, alcohol fumes, and urine. I began to find it stifling. I looked around. Where was Milly? Milly was walking around the edge of the ring, peering in, as excited as the locals and shouting encouragement: "Go on! Go on!"

At that moment, the space lightened as someone pulled aside the curtain and entered. No one paid him any attention—there was nothing unusual about him—but I gave him a long look because he was wearing the same light-green uniform we had seen at the border controls that noon. He met my eyes as if in greeting, and came and stood beside me.

I knew how conspicuous I must be among all these gamblers.

The black cock suddenly woke up, its owner pushed it forward, and it hurled itself on the red cock. Cockerels have no facial expressions, but I got the impression it was not feeling very brave. It looked as it wanted to weep and beg for mercy but was forced to go for broke anyway. Sometimes we have to win or die, there's no avoiding it.

How can I get out of fighting you? it seemed to be saying.

Even without facial expressions to go by, I'm sure cockerels can read each other's minds. The red cock could tell that its opponent was a coward, so it turned pitiless and, without a moment's hesitation, flapped onto the black cock's back. There it crowed loudly, clawed at the sparse feathers, and pecked at the black cock's eyes with its orange beak. After a desperate struggle, the black cock, blinded and streaming with blood, collapsed to the ground like a shadow puppet whose stick had been removed. Little by little, the red cock stripped its opponent of its remaining plumage and started to feast on the tender meat at the side of the long neck. This was a lot more delicious than its evening chicken dinner. This was the real taste of victory, not the kind of stupid thing its human owner promised.

The red cock stood there, a great strapping bird with its chest puffed out, instantly the star of the show. In the excitement of the moment, its wattles swelled and turned a reddish-purple, just like an engorged penis. Under its claws lay the twitching body of the cowardly cock, its pathetic victim.

At that moment, the man in the green uniform looked at me and asked: "Are you on holiday?"

He was as swarthy as the other locals but wore a pair of incongruous gold-rimmed spectacles.

He looked over at the cock owners, who were arguing noisily, and asked again: "Are you on your own?"

"No, my friend's with me." I pointed to Milly, who was walking toward us.

"Two girls on your own . . . you should be careful where you go. This is a rough area, you know. Where are you staying?" Then he went on, "I'm taking you with me."

At that instant, despite the stifling heat, I suddenly experienced a kind of physical excitement. I wanted nothing more than to hear this stranger repeat, commandingly, "I'm taking you with me!" And to see him take out his hand-cuffs and his rope and his deadly weapon.

Obediently, I stood up.

He put us in the back seat of his car and drove off without a word.

"What's your name?" I asked.

"Chen Mengla."

I saw Milly bite her finger and smile, and stealthily pinched her sweaty knee.

"My parents were educated youth, sent to the countryside," he added. "They're not from around here."

He was not robustly built; in fact he was rather scrawny, and his uniform hung loose on his body. His delicate sunburned skin gleamed with moisture, and I began to imagine how the sweat would pour from his back when he made love.

He didn't smile much. I preferred serious men; it made their smiles all the more precious.

III. The Gecko

There was a very annoying gecko in our room. It smacked its lips like a baby and chirped like a fledgling bird.

"I'm going to pay a girl a hundred yuan to spend the night watching our beds and chasing the gecko away," I said.

I got off the bed, took out a knife, and sliced open a red-skinned mango. I gave some to Milly, but she did not take her eyes from the laptop screen. I leaned over to take a look and saw a man tying up two thin, dark-skinned young Southeast Asian women. He was using yellow tape to gag them and had one tied to a chair with her legs splayed open, while the other was sprawled across the desk with her ass in the air. He took off his belt and began to beat them, and then fuck them, one after the other.

I muttered to myself, "This isn't just a porn film . . ."

"What d'you mean?" she asked.

"Because, look, they're bleeding." I pushed my face closer to the screen and pointed to the girl bound to the table. "Look at her expression."

The girl was frowning, apparently in real pain, and making whimpering sounds.

"It's just play-acting," Milly said impatiently, brushing my hand away.

At that point, the man, whose face we couldn't see, tore the gagging tape from the mouth of the one girl. She went into coughing spasms, choking and crying. He ordered her to put a small wine cup in her mouth and went on fucking her from behind. He was so rough with her that the cup fell from her mouth and smashed on the floor. The man was furious; picking up a fragment of the broken cup, he slashed her back with it. The girl gave a shrill shriek.

"That's real!" I yelled.

I grabbed the mouse and slid the progress bar back to replay it. Blood was pouring from the slash on the woman's back. Her ears were soaked in blood, too. Finally the man put a plastic bag over her head . . . she continued to struggle, and her legs pedaled frantically.

"He's killing her." I was open-mouthed with horror.

But at the last moment, the two women suddenly made a dramatic appearance back on the screen.

They were nude and giggled and chattered in broken English, saying how much they'd enjoyed it all.

"I told you it was play-acting," Milly said carelessly, finally taking a bite of the mango in her hand.

"No, look, that's not the same woman!" I jerked forward and hit the pause button. "The one on the left is the same, the one on the right isn't. The one that was slashed and suffocated with the plastic bag has disappeared . . ."

Milly abruptly shut the laptop lid down. "Did it get you excited?"

"What?"

"Look at you, all red in the face and breathing raggedly. I know you like these feelings. I like having sex in the woods, you like doing it shut up in a windowless cell; I like handcuffing a man to the bed, you like being tied up. Why don't we give it a try? We can get hold of that young guy, Guo. He looks like he's got a great body. The three of us can have fun."

"Guo?" I smiled in embarrassment, remembering the way he talked, spittle flying.

"Yes, Guo. Every time I go somewhere new, I always enjoy sampling the local produce. Guo's real local produce, don't you think? With his crude talk, his gold tooth, and his lecherous leering. And the way he looked when he talked about Russian slave girls and his yellow fingernails . . . in Hainan you eat coconuts, in Cuba you see Che Guevara, in Mongolia you eat barbecued sheep. And how else do you think you're going to amuse yourself in Xiaomengla?"

In my view, muscle-bound men and crude language were not sexy at all, merely comical. I liked cold things, and men who were shy, gentle, calm, and sweet-natured. It was as if only coldness could make my terrors erupt. Terror was uniquely erotic—and the most delicious part of terror was always the moment when you waited for the whip to fall. However, I did not say that.

"We can play king and girl slaves," Milly went on. "Or if you don't want to do that, cops and girl robbers. Yeah, that guy who brought us back this evening, Chen Mengla, he can be the cop. He's not really a policeman, but I'm sure it wouldn't be difficult for him to get hold of a pair of handcuffs to satisfy your cravings. We can make a porn film and sell it to this company." Milly turned the DVD case over and looked at the text on the back.

"It's a great idea, but going across the border again wasn't part of my plan."

She traced circles on my flat belly. "Why are you so unadventurous? You know you want it, and it's within your grasp—and yet you still refuse it. Why? Who are you putting on an act for?"

Just what kind of a person am I? Even after all these years, when I think back to that evening in Xiaomengla, I feel like I'm suffocating.

Back then, I was a puppet. I was the black cock staring death in the face. I was the towering memorial arch. I was always just missing out on an orgasm. I was Milly's shadow. I was a murderer.

Suddenly I longed to see Chen Mengla again.

IV. The Cop

He emerged naked from the bathroom in clouds of steam. He had a big erection, though it drooped almost defensively. As he rubbed his hair dry, he asked casually: "Can we start?" I discovered then that I was unable to speak. I had been gagged with a strip of coarse material. I tried to sit up but found that both of my hands were stuck behind me, and I could only struggle upright using my shoulders.

He knelt on the bed sheets and silently, gently kneaded my buttocks. It reduced me to lamblike bleats of pleasure. Suddenly he leaned over me, and a jab of pain made me cry out. The pain seemed to come from my breasts. Like a drowning woman, I struggled to break free of the handcuffs without losing my balance, only to find myself in even worse pain.

He pulled his trouser belt free and snapped it against the palm of his hand, then suddenly lashed the bed sheet beside me. It terrified me, and I whimpered my resistance. But the next blow of the belt landed on my tautly stretched body.

The searing pain quenched all my feelings of sexual arousal. I was like the black cock being splashed with cold water, instantly alert to the fact that I was staring death in the face.

This was not a porn film. I couldn't put a stop to this just by saying "That's enough, get off me." A filthy piece of fabric was blocking the fresh air I needed to breathe, and I couldn't even gasp as each blow fell.

He stopped his whipping and kneading and dropped his boxer shorts. His penis stood angrily erect, just like the vicious red cock. At that moment, I grew really afraid and started to tremble all over. I couldn't shout "Stop!" through my nose, but my tears begged him. Things were going to happen to me that I couldn't prevent: I'd be cut with a shard of glass, have a plastic bag put over my head, be devoured . . .

When I was ten years old, I was playing hide-and-seek with my younger cousins. They took off, leaving me in my granny's cupboard. I couldn't open the door from the inside. I became hysterical as I struggled to get out, cried and beat on the door. It nearly gave me a nervous breakdown.

Once I was having my teeth cleaned and found myself suddenly unable to breathe. When I panicked, the blonde, blue-eyed nurse calmly told me I'd be fine if I just breathed through my nose, but I couldn't. I put my hand up to stop her, but she carried on with the cleaning. I waved my hands, pushing away the instrument she was using and making her cry out in shock.

Another time, on a thirteen-hour flight, my nose was blocked from a cold, and the cabin pressure made me temporarily deaf. I panicked and kept pressing the call button, begging the cabin attendant for help. She showed me how to take deep breaths through my open mouth, but it didn't do any good, and I wailed that I wanted the plane to land, or else I'd die. "You're not going to die," she said. No, actually this was more terrifying than dying.

I remember every single time I've felt like I was choking. It's like layers of plastic wrap wound around my face. I'm imprisoned, cut off from the rest of the world, I can't communicate. Being deprived of air feels more terrifying than dying. Maybe this is what loneliness is. I'm in this world, you're in another one. I'll never be able to get to you.

He undid the handcuffs so he could push himself into me, and reattached one wrist to the bed frame. But the other hand . . .

Only my death would free me.

Or his death.

I felt under the pillow for the knife, which was sticky with mango juice, and stabbed him in the throat. There was a great spurt of red, and I couldn't see anything anymore.

V. The Grave

Afterward, I asked Milly: "How did you and Guo get rid of the body?" She looked at me, confused. "What body? What are you talking about?"

The last scene is crystal clear in my memory: Milly was rushing toward the body, which had fallen heavily backward. His throat had been almost completely severed. Crucially, all the blood had spurted out in the room. That was a good thing. The bed, the side table, the bedding and mattress, shoes, bowls, and chopsticks, absolutely everything was dyed the color of chicken's blood. I was the red cock. The victory was mine.

"Think about it . . . how could I have possibly washed the whole room clean of every blood spot and stain?"

"Right, it would have been impossible."

"So it didn't happen. You were just drunk, pissed out of your skull. Really, you've been reading too many novels. There's a scene like that in *Philosophy in the Boudoir*."

———

The next afternoon, we left Xiaomengla. I sat on the bus nursing a splitting headache. I looked over at Milly, who was sitting on the other side of the aisle, her eyes shut, listening to music, a contented smile on her face, the sun blistering down on her pale thighs.

As for me, I hurt all over. My right arm ached oddly, and quivered. That was proof that I had killed someone. There were other clues. Why had my copy of de Sade's *Philosophy in the Boudoir* disappeared? Why, in the weeks after our return to Shanghai, did I keep hearing Milly on the phone outside the door, in whispered conversation with Guo? Why did I have absolutely no memory of packing my suitcase and checking out of the hotel?

"What really happened that evening?" I asked Milly.

"You were a spoilsport. You got so drunk in the Don Juan Bar, Chen Mengla and I had to help you back to the hotel. Since you couldn't control yourself, and you were puking, too, we left you in your room and went down to the river to have sex."

"What time did you come back?"

"We went to a casino after that. By the early hours, we had lost all our money and were just about to leave when they offered us a room for free. It was a nice room, too, with real fresh flowers by the bed, and condoms and massages. When we got back the next afternoon, you were still asleep. I packed our suitcases and then woke you up. Mengla performed like a stallion when we had sex down by the river. True, he wasn't Guo, and we ended up doing it because you got so drunk, but I never imagined he'd be so virile."

"Do you still miss Guo?"

"Guo?" She snorted out the cold water she'd been drinking. "If I ever saw a gold-toothed guy driving an old Merc in Shanghai, I'd think he was a freak, a head case. I have no interest in Guo."

"But you've still got his number in your phone, but not Chen Mengla's."

She snatched the phone from me. "Don't you know I delete every man I've fucked from my contacts?"

She delicately wiped the traces of the sashimi we had been eating from her mouth and, looking me straight in the eyes, said:

"I'm going to swear to you one last time: you never killed anyone, and you're entitled to live a happy life with a clear conscience."

———————

Who should I believe, Milly or my memories? I kept on looking for Chen Mengla, writing to every organization on the southwest border that dressed its employees in light-green uniforms. But they all said there was no such man. Not that he'd died or disappeared, but that there had never been anyone with a weird name like that.

When Milly wasn't looking, I got her mobile and found Guo's number, but it had been disconnected. He'd probably been bumped off by his gambling mates.

It was not that my memory was blank; I retained everything. But the answers my memory gave me were different from everyone else's.

Finally, all I could do was make a small grave mound in the back yard, to be Chen Mengla's grave. I used to go and visit it, to tell him that that night I had almost fallen in love with him. But how could I have known that fear, not death or pain, but fear itself, would be so terrible?

VI. The Boudoir

Two years later, on my birthday, I found a present from Milly at the foot of the bed.

It was a copy of *Philosophy in the Boudoir*. There was a trace of dried blood on the cover. My heart skipped a beat, and tears welled up in my eyes . . .

But there was a scrap of paper, too, on which she had scribbled: "This is not the one you lost. The red streak is acrylic paint. Happy birthday."

There was a sketch folded up inside the book. It was of me sitting on a riverbank, wearing denim shorts and a T-shirt. It must have been the first time Milly had drawn someone with their clothes on. The intent, clear-eyed gaze of the girl in the sketch made the color rush to my face. No descriptions of sex or obscene pictures of flesh had ever made me feel the shame that overwhelmed me at that moment.

And I'm afraid to admit it, but that feeling was unexpectedly pleasurable.

INTERLUDE

An Education in Cruelty

By Ye Fu

TRANSLATED BY A. E. CLARK

Is human cruelty an instinct of our animal nature or a genetic trait? Is it a dysfunction forced on us by a particular kind of society, or does it arise from an individual's education and upbringing? Can we adapt Tolstoy's celebrated dictum to say that all good people are basically alike, but every cruel person is cruel in his own way?

Long ago, while I was incarcerated, my mother wrote to tell me that my daughter (who at the time was not quite six years old and didn't know her father) had undergone a troubling personality change. She would take a kettleful of boiling water, for example, and slowly pour it into the fishtank and watch the fish struggle desperately with no way to escape, till at last they were scalded to death. My mother was afraid the child's play revealed a cruel streak. The news shocked me, but I realized on some level that almost all human cruelty partakes of the nature of a game, and in a great many games there is an implicit cruelty.

I didn't hold it against my daughter. Her behavior could be attributed to immaturity, the lack of a father figure, and the fact that she had not yet been taught any precepts about safeguarding life—precepts more or less religious in origin, but typical of civilized society. She was still in a state of primitive barbarism that recapitulated the early history of the human race. But then I thought back to the rough childhood I had endured in a remote small town, and it dawned on me that by growing up in this country, I had received a whole education in cruelty. Considering that adults still play (or at least tolerate) all kinds of sick, cruel games, I'd be ashamed to judge a child harshly.

That famous period of ten years commenced when I was four years old and found me in the state of nature. There was at that time no regular kindergarten or preschool instruction, and naturally there was a complete lack of educational pastimes. The first game I learned from the older boys in the village was to catch a toad out in the fields and make a little kiln of mud, inside which we'd spread a layer of quicklime. We'd put the toad inside and seal up the kiln with thin streaks of clay, leaving a little hole on top through which to pour cold water. On contact with water, the quicklime was energized and generated a great deal of heat, and as the steam curled up, there rang out a croaking cry of tortured pain, first very strong and then fading away. When the steam and the noise were both finished, we'd rake open the mud kiln to find that the toad's ugly skin had peeled off, exposing the trunk of its body, translucent and glowing like the flesh of a newborn child; for in death the toad revealed a beauty of extreme purity.

Who had invented so cruel a pastime? The children must have come to it by imitation, but what exactly were they imitating?

––––––

For years I have had a recurring dream in which I am standing naked under the blue sky of late autumn, trying to soak up enough sunlight to survive the winter—for the winter is going to be exceptionally cold. The rays of the setting sun slant over the high wall behind me, casting an enlarged shadow of me on the wall in front. The shadow of the electrified wires just happens to cross at my neck, making the silhouette of my head look like a wild fruit overripe amid a tangle of withered vines.

This made me realize that if immersed in a savage reality, the heart becomes inured to cruelty: it has to. This scene, which I had actually experienced, was so frightening at the time that later, during a long spell of ordinary life, it was fashioned into the image of a recurring dream. I would like to identify the moment when I began taking cruelty as a matter of course. When did we start to accept malice and violence as a part of normal life, excusable and unchecked by any law?

I was six . . . yes, I was six years old and in the first grade. Early autumn, 1968. At the end of the school day, we children were called together, and a peppy teacher took apart a big broom and gave each of us one of the bamboo stems. Then we lined up and headed off to administer a beating to a thief. When our troop of scouts came marching down the street, the townsfolk who had surrounded the thief raised a jolly cheer. The thief had been made to stand on a cement culvert pipe. His shirt was tattered and his trouser legs had been rolled up over his knees as if he had just come in from the paddies, and he was shod in straw sandals. These particulars are etched in my memory because our height reached just about to the man's ankles. The grown-ups were loudly urging us on, "Beat him! Beat him!" And thus the small town's Carnival of the Thief got underway.

We schoolchildren from the village ranged in age from six to sixteen, and, giddy at being for the first time encouraged by adults to beat up another adult, we didn't hold back. Lashed like a top by countless bamboo rods, that middle-aged thief began to hop and prance along the pipe in a dance that never let up. There was no escape. To whichever side he was driven, a dense screaming throng was waiting to whip him. I distinctly remember the coarse skin of his calves, still a little muddy, slowly turning from red to purple, then gradually swelling and turning white and translucent like a turnip. He kept uttering little cries and desperately flailing his hands and feet. The drops of his sweat fell like rain, and there shone from his eyes the cold light of death. I swung at him a few times. Then, frightened, I held back, but the grown-ups and the other children were still engrossed in the delightful sport they had devised. Finally I noticed that he had grown so hoarse that he could only open and shut his mouth soundlessly like a fish, and his body was shaking like a kite off-kilter, and when one more blow came, the blow that was one too many, he fell with a crash . . .

When first summoned round him, we had learned from the grown-ups' execrations that he had been caught trying to steal three feet of cloth from a tailor's shop: that was all. He was a peasant come in from the country to attend the fair. In later years, remorse would haunt me. I kept thinking that life had prepared the same winter for us both; doubtless his kids, about my age, wore rags, and he didn't have the money to keep them warm.

And on this day he had spied those fatal three feet of cloth. Each time I recall the scene, the pain reaches a little deeper. Having written thus far, I find tears running down my face, and I realize that this was the beginning of my education in cruelty.

————

It's often hard to identify the moral quality that makes some hurtful acts cruel. If in a room full of mosquitoes we were to shut the doors and windows and light a coil of insecticide in order to exterminate the pests, no one would condemn us. What about mice? Well, they spread disease and steal food, so they too deserve to be exterminated. As for the means employed to exterminate them, people don't usually inquire too closely.

When I was about ten, my mother sent me to the coal mine because my father was being punished in all sorts of ways after being "knocked down." It had proven too much for one of his colleagues, who had already committed suicide. Mother was worried and sent me to keep him company, thus introducing me to the real life of the working class. There were many rats in the mine, and the men who risked death in the pit had nothing in the way of entertainment, so in their moments of free time they set about exterminating the rats for fun. They'd use all their wiles to capture a rat alive. Then they'd stuff raw soybeans into its rectum and sew up the anus. The soybeans would expand inside the rat's body and drive it mad with pain; then they'd let it go and watch it run around in a frenzy, careening back to its home, where it bit and scratched at its own kind, creating a rousing spectacle of mutual annihilation: this trick was more devastating than any poison. Or they would tie a wad of cotton soaked in gasoline to a rat's tail and release it after setting the cotton aflame, and then watch with pleasure as the little fireball ran around crazily. These scenes frightened me. Nothing but disgust and hatred made them torture rats so: was this the human race's idea of justice?

And what of how humans massacre each other? The Nazis' hatred for the Jews, and the genocide they perpetrated, are too well known to need recounting here. The hatred we once harbored for what was called the exploiting class seems practically on the same level. In my part of the country there was a major landholder named Li Gaiwu; in the era of land reform he was crammed into a cage by angry peasants who then propped him over a fire and roasted him alive. Such a drawn-out, hideous death: none of us has even an inkling of the pain. If we review our penal history with its "death by a thousand cuts" and violent forms of sterilization and other such punishments, it is hard to believe we are a people under the guidance of reason.

A lesson taught us from our earliest years was that "Kindness to the enemy is cruelty to the People," and this political ethic has always guided our social life. A maxim which Party members consider the Golden Rule demands that we treat comrades with the warmth of springtime, but to the enemy we must be like the autumn wind that blows away dead leaves without mercy. We recognize empathy as a basic element of human nature; the Buddha said that only with compassion can living creatures exist. To be without empathy, to be ruthless, means we need only take a political stand and can dispense with fundamental human considerations and instinctive sympathies. When dealing with outsiders (i.e., enemies) we may take any measures, however extreme, to punish them.

In the natural order, it's hard to distinguish between noxious insects and those that do some good. How accurately, then, are we likely to differentiate between enemies and friends, when all are of our own kind? The final decision will inevitably be based on power. When the highest authorities declared that sparrows were pests, these innocent creatures had to be exterminated by the entire people acting in concert. For these little birds, the sky suddenly shrank;

they were massacred; they fell in droves, dead from exhaustion as they struggled to flee the country. If birds fare thus, how can men endure? When we calmly look back on the whole twentieth century and consider all the people we called enemies and the animals we called pests, how many of them look entirely evil or destructive from today's vantage point? Those poor teachers, or fellow soldiers, or relatives and neighbors might flourish at morn to be cut down at night, as the highest authorities inscrutably blew hot, then cold. Is there anyone who has not tasted this cruelty?

In 1976 I was a student at the junior high school in my small town. That year in our country there was a great deal of grief and laughter, emotions that took many forms and were seldom openly expressed. Historians later saw this as a year of transition. That winter, we students were taken as a group to participate in a public trial and sentencing at which a counterrevolutionary named Yang Wensheng was to be shot. From what we could make out of the incoherent verdict, this was a man so bad that even his death would scarcely suffice to appease the People's wrath. His crime was that when high authorities had arrested the Gang of Four, he insisted that—based on the principles and examples of historical fiction—this had been a palace coup. He was constantly making speeches and pasting up large-character posters opposing the Central Government under Hua Guofeng. He called on people to guard the heritage of Mao while resolutely opposing the return of the capitalist-roader. Prior to this, he had been well-known in town as part of the extremist faction of the Red Guard and had, to be sure, persecuted some of the local cadres.

In those days, many of the ancient formalities were still observed while a prisoner awaited execution. The man was tightly bound with ropes, and once the sentence had been read aloud, they thrust down the back of his shirt a sharp stick on which the name of his crime had been written. I saw him grimace with pain then, but he was bound so tight he couldn't cry out. A few of us kids were bold enough to hop on our bicycles and chase after the prison van to some undeveloped land outside the town limits. There he was lifted down out of the van and kicked to his knees on the frozen ground. From less than a meter away, the executioner deftly fired at the man's back, and he pitched forward. Though his crumpled body shuddered a few times, he soon became still as the echo of the shot reverberated off the surrounding hills. A throng of all ages, male and female, had gathered to watch. In a society rife with tedium, an execution served much the same function as a wedding banquet: the man's death provided a little zest for the masses. A grown-up went and turned over the body and loosened the clothes, and we were startled to see blood still flowing from the bullet hole on the left side of his chest, as the last of his body's warmth dispersed upon the wintry earth.

Thus was a life disposed of. Some time before, in the north a woman named Zhang Zhixin had been put to death in an even more brutal fashion. These two people were charged with the same crime, though in substance their actions were diametrically opposite. We could say that Zhang died for her wisdom and clear vision, while Yang died for his folly and stubbornness. What got both of them in trouble was that at that stage of history each was a person who stuck to his convictions and expressed them; how the world later gauged the validity of their beliefs is irrelevant. They were punished as criminals for nothing but their expressed opinions: they led no rebellion, committed no murders, burned no buildings. Every civilized country writes freedom of speech into its constitution as the citizens' right. Yet for attempting to exercise this simple right, Zhang became a tragic hero and Yang remains forever a fool.

As we wander through this world, the fleeting pleasures of the senses make us cling to life, and the religious ideal of self-sacrifice presupposes heroic virtue. To survive we must vie with other species for the means of life, and if an instinctive animosity arises from this situation, it is hard to fault men for it. But when there is a life-and-death struggle of one man against another, or of tribe against tribe and nation against nation, and we must plot against one another and fight at close quarters: what moral criteria are laid down for human nature then? Can't some principle always be found, such as individualism, nationalism, or patriotism, that will let us bend the rules and justify our violence?

When I ask these questions about the history of individuals, or the background of my relatives and friends, or the stories (both factual and imagined) of our people, I usually find myself unsure what moral standards should be applied. The common people worship Heaven and Earth, and this teaches them reverence. The gentleman stays far from the kitchen and thus cultivates compunction. Reverence leads to awe, and compunction leads to love. Now if everyone were imbued with awe and love, perhaps there would be no need for religion, and we could still manage to live saintly lives. The difficulty comes when you dwell in an atheistic country where constant propaganda has exalted scientific fundamentalism into an overarching value, and where revolution and violent rebellion (as led, for example, by Li Zicheng and Hong Xiuquan) are the stuff of heroic legends. Is it possible to feel any awe under these circumstances? Can all the laws in the world check the malice latent in our nature, especially since it has been repeatedly encouraged and sanctioned?

In the perilous year 1949 my father, the son of a small landholder, sought safety by joining the new government. Calamities befell his family during land reform, but he became a hero—in another county—in the fight to suppress the "bandits." My father always tried to avoid discussing his past, much as a bitter old man who has failed in life will fear to encounter a woman he loved in his youth, but I was able to piece together his story from the recollections of some who had known him back then. In that cruel time, he had to be particularly ruthless, since otherwise his loyalty would have been doubted on account of his background. When I think how he trapped and killed those fierce brave men of the highlands and signed death warrants for landlords who had worked hard (like his own father) for everything they had, I am sure that this was not how he wanted to act. He was not stupid. He couldn't have thought he was being fair, but he knew that if he revealed even a hint of human kindness, it would give others a reason to mark him for liquidation. It was like the organized-crime families in which junior mobsters must commit a murder as soon as they are recruited, to give proof of their staunchness. He had no choice.

After the Uprising of the Three Townships had been quelled, his pacification squad took about a dozen prisoners. From the county seat came orders to bring them into town, but my father had only two armed men with him. With their hands tied behind their backs, the bandits were marched toward the city, but they dragged their feet enough that nightfall found all of them still in a desolate part of the country. It was a dangerous situation. My father's two subordinates suggested that they kill the prisoners and report they'd been shot while trying to escape. He was in charge; it was his call. For his men's safety, he consented. The prisoners' bonds were untied, and they were told to run for it and take their chances. The three militiamen opened fire on the scattering fugitives in the moonlight, and hardly any managed to get away alive.

This was the cruelty that the revolution required. Long before, our Leader had used a series of parallel sentences to explain exactly what is meant by revolution: "an act of violence." In our childhood, this startling passage was popularized as a song whose terrifying refrain echoed through the land. To its melody, kids gracefully brandished belts (and whipped their classmates who came from bad class backgrounds), forced their teachers to eat excrement, raided homes and pillaged them, and hounded innumerable innocents to death. I reckon that few in my generation were squeamish at the sight of blood, because we had seen so much of it. We had grown accustomed to all of life's cruelty, and nothing shocked us anymore.

Apart from cases in which people are *forced* to be cruel, I am often unsure whether cruelty stems from ignorance or hatred. Or could there be other causes than these two? After reading the letter from my mother, I remembered something that happened when my daughter was even younger and we lived together for intervals. She was just over a year old and still didn't get along very well with people she didn't know. Though her father, I was much like a transient visitor, and her tantrums left me at a loss. The best I could think to do was to carry her in my arms to the fishtank. It worked: the swaying, glittering fish caught her attention and she stopped crying. At first her tearful eyes tracked the soundless dance of the fish, and then when the fish tired and stopped moving, she reached out her little hand to slap the glass and stir them up. Startled, they broke in all directions and bumped into the glass as they fled. Only after some time did peace return. Then she'd bang the glass again, and once more the fish would flit around wildly. Eventually my daughter smiled through her tears. Perhaps she realized her power to tease these magical little elfin creatures and was pleased with herself.

When the game staled through repetition, she required more stimulation and ordered me to hold her closer to the tank. Then she surprised me by reaching into the water and grabbing at the flustered fish. She was brazen about it and seemed perfectly confident that these small weak animals could do her no harm. What if they had been scorpions? What makes a child know instinctively whether it is safe to tease a particular kind of animal? Do we have an innate ability to infer from the aesthetics of a creature's form whether it is innocuous? The fish could not long evade her grasp, and when she'd got one, its panicked wriggling startled her and she threw it on the floor, where it flopped about like a mechanical toy before lying still. She burst into laughter.

Thus I realized that although my daughter, like me, was fond of fish, she expressed her love by tormenting the object of her love. This amorous baiting, as well as the full-blown cruelty to which it can lead, is often seen between grown-up lovers. Milan Kundera says in one of his novels, "They loved each other, but each put the other through Hell." Cruelty that arises from attraction or love may be hard to understand, but it is all around us. My provisional term for it is "affectionate cruelty."

————

From its origin to its dying-out in our society, the term "rectification of styles" has a history spanning no more than half a century. Yet this term—not, on the face of it, a harsh one—laid waste the spirit of our people, and to this day one can discern the scars it left behind.

For my generation the fear wrought by this term, a terror from which there was no escape, started in elementary school. At that time I had no inkling where the term came from; I didn't know it had been invented at Yan'an and could make our parents' generation blanch with fear. But when the term came back and repeatedly invaded our childhood, it inspired a dread that lingers with me to this day.

I don't understand how those who crafted this country's educational system could have wanted to introduce the cruel ways of adult factional strife into the lives of inexperienced children. But I know that each semester, I quailed in anticipation of the Rectification campaign. The program adapted for school students employed the same kinds of threats and blandishments as the adult version and taught a swarm of naturally kind and honest children to betray and denounce one another. Although the substance of those accusations now sounds absurd—indeed, ridiculous—the seed of malice was being sown in our young hearts. When you saw a trusted friend step forward to denounce you to the authorities, righteously, for some trifling naughtiness the two of you had committed, you could not help feeling that human affairs and human nature were treacherous. In the train of betrayal and denunciation always came criticism and mockery, as every child lost all sense of decorum in an orgy of back-biting. Children's innate sense of dignity and sincerity crumbled, to be replaced by a grown-up cunning and the skill to make others take the blame. I can still remember a girl from high school, a lovely and gentle girl with a thick dark braid. Perhaps because her parents came from the provincial capital, she was intellectually and emotionally more mature than the rest of us. In the course of one campaign for the Rectification of Styles, her closest girlfriend turned on her and reported hearing her say that she loved to look into the limpid eyes of a certain boy and often dreamed about him. The informer announced this in a tone of the strictest propriety, and the whole room rocked with laughter. Stunned, the innocent girl turned very pale, and then her face and ears flushed crimson and she ducked her head under her desk and cried in anguish. She wept in despair like a widow who has been caught in the act of adultery, and it made me and my peers, all equally confused about our teenage crushes, shiver with fear. A scarlet letter of shame was etched into the heart of a thirteen-year-old girl. She could not possibly remain in that school. Her family pulled her out and sent her to live with relatives in Wuhan, and later she was married off at an early age and became a housewife who sold snacks at a counter. After seeing how quickly a beauty and her youthful innocence were trashed, who could put any trust in childhood friendship?

Informing, denunciation, betrayal, even entrapment: these defined the ethos of my world from childhood on, and there was no defense against them. What kind of a motherland would wish her children, at what ought to be a tender age, to learn such ruthless arts of survival? In today's society I sense insecurity and constant danger everywhere, and most of it is rooted in the atmosphere of conspiracy and treachery that was fostered in our education.

What clings to all my memories of the time before 1976 is the smell of blood. I remember, when I was about eight, passing through the courtyard of the District Office at Wangying Town as dusk fell. Suddenly I saw some townsmen tie a peasant's hands behind his back and hang him by the arms from a pear tree. The pear trees were then in bloom; the air was filled with their soft scent and the peasant's screams. The rope that bound his arms passed over a branch, and another townsman gripped it from below. When the rest of the group roared, "You're not talking yet?" the rope would be pulled, the peasant's feet would rise higher off the ground, and the ripping in his arms would grow more excruciating.

When he had been hoisted all the way up among the flowers, his sweat fell like rain and his face turned as pale as the pear blossoms. While he writhed and pleaded, he shook the tree and released a gentle fragrance as petals fell to earth. I stared blankly at the tableau; to this day I cannot fathom the cruelty necessary to take a stranger, tie his hands behind his back, and hoist him by them into the air.

When I became a policeman, a veteran officer cheerfully explained to me that this kind of interrogation, in which the hands are tied behind the back and the prisoner is hung by them, usually should not be protracted beyond a half-hour. Any longer than that and the suspect's arms will be permanently crippled. I found his well-intentioned advice horrifying, and it brought back the memory of the scene I'd witnessed as a child. It occurred to me with a chill that this rule of thumb must have been distilled from many years' worth of experiments.

But did this technique of interrogation through torture ever cease being used? In a precinct house where I was assisting with a case in 1988, I was forced to witness a comparable scene. The Chief, who was quite experienced, took heavy iron shackles and placed the suspect in an awkward position named after a martial arts move. His hands were shackled together behind his back, one reaching down with the elbow over the head while the other reached up from the waist. In this position the suspect was forced to kneel for a long time, and the Chief left me to keep an eye on him. Being new to the profession, I was in no position to interfere and watched helplessly until the suspect passed out. Then I went to call the Chief to come take the heavy cuffs off him. The Chief exchanged the position of the two arms and continued the treatment.

I am by no means of a cruel temperament. How, then, could I witness a scene like this and—though I felt some sympathy—act as though nothing was out of the ordinary? Later on, when I myself had become a convict, I thought about this a lot and realized that the training in cruelty which had begun in our childhood had worn a callus on our souls. This callus played a trick on our conscience and made us gradually numb to human suffering. What's more, our cowardice overwhelmed the little pity we could still feel, so we lacked the guts as well as the ability to change the system to which we'd grown habituated. When I heard the cries of a man being interrogated under torture, I didn't dare put a stop to it, because I submitted to the uniform I wore. The uniform short-circuited my conscience; for a while I ascribed to it a supernatural power. Consequently, when one day another man wearing that uniform struck me in the forehead with an electrified baton, there was nothing I could say. Neither of us felt any personal animosity; it was only that his education led him to treat me as a foe.

Who, then, was the unseen Founder behind these countless acts of cruelty? Can we blame oppressive officials, those stock figures who have been passed down through the generations in a certain style of biographical history? Or is the toxin of this cruelty contained in the cultural traditions of our people?

———

The elementary education that my generation received had hatred as its starting point. Teachers invented for us an unspeakably evil Old Society, and made everyone sing each day, with grief and indignation, the song:

> In the Old Society, whips lashed my flesh,
> And Mother could but weep.

And now it was necessary for us to

> Seize the whip and lash the foe.

This is how the violence and cruelty of youth were ignited, and the force thus released spread inevitably to the whole of society, polluting the manners and morals of that era down to the present day.

When the superintendent of a Detention and Transfer Center can incite the common people who've been locked up there to abuse each other so badly that some of them die; when street-level Code Enforcers can wantonly chase down a peddler with their clubs, and go so far as to beat to death a bystander who photographs them; when soldiers can open fire on students and kill them without compunction, without any misgivings at all . . . could all these unconscionable acts of wickedness reflect the impact of education throughout society?

These days, I can find on the Internet a great many angry young men who rage against Japan and are itching to attack Taiwan. *Rape them, kill them, nuke them,* they roar against those who—in their minds—are enemies or traitors to China. It makes me very sad. These kids were untouched by the Cultural Revolution. They don't even know about 1989. They didn't receive the barbaric education that we got in our day. Whence came this cruel mindset? If an evil administration were to take power, arising from and supported by people such as these youths, who knows what hideous crimes this country would inflict upon the world?

Clearly, some system that inculcates cruelty is still at work in our society; it has always been at work, spreading its influence unseen. The tension between oppressive officials and violent mobs grows ever worse, and the worst in human nature is brought to flower. For it is easy to cultivate hatred and cruelty among men; to propagate love, alas, is hard. When I consider the dreadful possibilities, I have a feeling that the peace of this night will prove fragile and short-lived. I can only guess what lies out there in the dark, but this vast city cocooned in insatiable self-indulgence makes me shudder with fear.

Notes

---

203   *That famous period of ten years:* The Cultural Revolution, 1966–76.

207   *1976:* The year of Mao's death.

207   *the return of the capitalist-roader:* Deng Xiaoping made two comebacks from an official obloquy tantamount to banishment.

208   *Zhang Zhixin:* A staunch Party member whose criticisms of Jiang Qing, Lin Biao, and Mao himself early in the Cultural Revolution led to her arrest in 1969, followed by six years of maltreatment in a Liaoning prison. In April 1975 she was impaled and decapitated; some accounts say that in preparation for her execution her larynx was slashed lest she make a statement on the execution ground.

208   *The gentleman stays far from the kitchen:* From the *Mencius,* book 1, part 1, chapter 7: "So is the superior man affected towards animals, that, having seen them alive, he cannot bear to see them die; having heard their dying cries, he cannot bear to eat their flesh. Therefore he keeps away from his slaughter-house and cook-room." (Trans. Legge)

208   *Li Zicheng and Hong Xiuquan:* Leaders of violent nationwide revolts in the seventeenth and nineteenth centuries, respectively. That they were responsible for the deaths of millions makes it all the more relevant that Mao admired them and that they are depicted with respect in modern pop culture.

209   *Uprising of the Three Townships:* A popular revolt against land reform that broke out in three townships of Lichuan County.

209   *"an act of violence":* The "parallel sentences" to which the author refers form a celebrated passage in Mao's 1927 *Report on an Investigation of the*

Peasant Movement in Hunan: "A revolution is not a dinner party, or writing an essay, or painting a picture, or doing embroidery. It cannot be so refined, so leisurely and gentle, so temperate, kind, courteous, restrained and magnanimous. A revolution is an insurrection, an act of violence by which one class overthrows another."

210   *Milan Kundera says . . . :* See Milan Kundera, *The Unbearable Lightness of Being*, trans. Michael Henry Heim, II.27 (p. 75 in the Harper & Row edition): "In spite of their love, they had made each other's life a hell."

211   *Rectification of Styles:* Mao's campaign to purge some of the Communist intellectuals at Yan'an in a climate that came to resemble a witch-hunt. Especially in its final phase during 1943–44, there were forced public confessions of error, daily self-criticism, and accusations that led to the death of thousands of Party members. The campaign instilled a lasting insecurity in Chinese intellectuals and cemented Mao's dominance.

213   *In the Old Society, whips lashed my flesh . . . :* From a propaganda song, "A Folk Song for the Party to Hear: Comparing the Party to My Mother" (唱支山歌给党听, 我把党来比母亲), associated with the 1962 "Learn from Lei Feng" campaign. Words by Yao Xiaozhou (1958).

War among the Insects

By Chang Hui-Ching

TRANSLATED BY LEE YEW LEONG

Firefly

The bees have decreased in number. Before the bees, the fireflies decreased in number. One day, a pink flamingo (bending its long neck, standing on one leg, as if about to doze off) appeared in my dream. From that one bird, innumerable others suddenly multiplied, assembling in neat ranks, like a matrix. The flamingos spoke soundlessly: We must reclaim our pink from Hello Kitty.

To the right, red; to the left, white. In the middle, pink. A color cheapened from indiscriminate use by young girls and their imitators. A color now calling to mind *Sex and the City*. Desiring glamour, but also purity; not daring to be "Red Rose," but not content to be "White Rose," either. Pink flamingos, if you seek redress against those who have stolen your hue, I'm afraid you'll have too many enemies.

At the time the following story takes place, very few colors belong to mankind. Pink is not among them.

Nights are still very black in these times; the stars in the sky are plainly visible. Not one by one but in constellations: the beast, the dragon, the bird, the woman, the fish, the hunter. No other light exists. Except for lamps inside homes, fires at city gates, and the infinitesimal glow of the few species that emit light in the wilderness outside the city, night is pitch-black. Come night, more tangible entities can be seen in the realm of the sky than on land.

Fireflies are lights delimiting the visible. On riverbanks where water and earth mix, in swamps and in wetlands, animals hesitate, vacillating between the use of gills, the use of lungs; the need to swim, the need to walk. In terrain marked by ambiguity, the faint light of insects can be seen. Their glow absorbs the darkness surrounding it, softens it, then penetrates into its deepest interior. Man can take heart: in Night's darkness, the source of light is yet contained. Even under a cloud-covered sky, one can see the star mimicked by a firefly. Cool twilight. A physical body in the midst of the unknown. The man in this story has seen this firefly. In the empty spaces of his own body, a light seems to flash as well. The firefly copies the star, the cells in his body copy the firefly.

Farther from the riverbank there's another kind of light. Marsh lights—will-o'-the-wisps. There, the earth has left the shore behind. Life—having transcended the vacillation between habitats, having grown the corporeality required for Earth's gravitational atmosphere—becomes resolute. The man now looks at the distant marsh light with the same pair of eyes he used to look at the firefly. A corpse lies below it, he knows. Although from this distance, in the night's blackness, the corpse's white bones are denoted by mere light, flickering intermittently like a faint smell. At times, he thinks: It's not life but death that is bright. Life is in darkness.

He knew that skeleton. He knew it when it still had flesh, blood, and a name.

Locust

Man does not decide who gets to be man. War decides. Which ones get buried under the ground, whose story gets recorded as History, which women get to keep the children they have borne.

That year, the locusts came from the East.

"A conceptual attack. Afterward, the real battle of the flesh."

A lone green grasshopper perches on a reed, munching leaves. A child reaches out and plucks it gently with his fingers. He plays with the grasshopper. When his mother calls out "Dinner!" the child crushes the insect and throws it away.

One day—nobody knows when or why—the grasshoppers multiply past a critical point; en masse, they mutate, go mad. Having grown ferocious trampling limbs, these newly aggressive insects will even eat animals. Unrecognizable, a new species. Overpopulation (and with it, increased friction among grasshoppers) has emboldened them, causing a change in their very nature. They become something different altogether, just like the city dweller is unlike the human being of the underpopulated plains.

"Such is the stubborn resistance you shall face. In reaction to the victory of the Kingdom of Qin, the six kingdoms in the East will band together. These dust-like Easterners will form one hybrid beast: an animal with the wings of the Yan Kingdom, the body of the Chu Kingdom, the eyes of the Zhao Kingdom, and the bones of the Qi Kingdom."

Yingzheng, at the age of fifteen, had a logical solution to this problem—it involved taking matters into his own hands.

Bird

An eagle, suspended at a height. Buoyed by air currents. Waiting, or watching. Maybe neither. Being in midair—that's its entire existence. Just as mating is sometimes an animal's only raison d'être. The eagle in flight can perceive the direction of every feather, and the directions of the different air currents lifting it up. It senses, too, the empty spaces in its body, in conversation with the immense space of the sky outside. Space translating space.

It hears coming from all directions, above and below, the sounds of other bird species. Among these others who travel in the same air, some have small wings, flying at low altitude, disturbing the air at greater frequency, shrill, noisy. Bigger birds fly at higher altitudes; their wings, which beat only occasionally, nevertheless control the direction of air currents, as if leaving a claw print in the air. Thus the eagle merges its body into the air current, flaps its wings a few times, thereby signaling its respect to the giant condor in the distance.

After gliding past the mountaintop, the eagle begins its descent. At touchdown it metamorphoses into a man, with a head of white hair but a youthful face.

At the very beginning, the ancestors of the Qin people lived in the East and kept watch over sunrise. Later on, they moved to the West and kept watch over sunset. The ancestral spirits of Qin became a flock of birds, scattering between the East and the West. Each one of these birds, wherever it was, kept watch over its own meridian line where day changed into night. Time is a seam. Where you stood—east or west of this line—might yet determine the course of an entire civilization. At its easternmost point, the birds welcomed daybreak; at its westernmost, the birds welcomed night.

The flock had heard that on the other side of the mountain was another God watching over sunset. This was not merely hearsay; the birds themselves sensed it. So they each kept to their own territory, careful not to overstep their boundaries out of respect for that netherworld God of whom they knew nothing, only that He was completely different from them, so completely different that they could not both exist on the same mountainside. Keeping one's distance seemed the best way of showing reverence.

There were several rumors about who this Western God might be. Some said He was a tiger. Some said the Golden People. Some said He was the God of Autumn, the God of Death, the God of Executions. The day He appeared, true and false, right and wrong, were born. With truth came the possibility that man could commit wrong. No one could be right forever. Thus man would always live in fear of severe punishment from the Gods. No one escaped; no one could forgo the process of maturation, of getting old, of dying that the Gods made mortals go through. Once he became an adult, Man would be held accountable for his wrongs. Then, when he became old and afflicted with sickness, he would feel, as death approached, that he was being punished. At his death, he would at last enter the netherworld. What happened thereafter could no longer be discussed among men.

Some say life and death are blurred. It's possible to die without realizing it. No voice has ever returned from that place. The dead leave their voices behind. Their voices echo back and forth in the valley of the dead, awaiting the arrival of those they stood up in their past lives. There, there'd be no other place to go; no one would miss their appointments.

The ancestral spirits did not know what would become of the Qin Kingdom, the situation having unfolded beyond the understanding of these Gods-turned-birds. The spirits of all Qin emperors before Yingzheng were now part of the flock; only momentarily did they become men before transforming into birds.

There was something about this Yingzheng that prepared him to overturn ancestral etiquette, all the past emperors knew. But what, exactly, none of them could say. They only knew time, the fact that with time all life goes to seed. That the soul would return to the flock, its time on earth having been merely a field trip to gather data, to add one more computational variable to collective knowledge.

Keep watch, that was all one could do. And to keep watch was simply to wait.

At sunset, a commotion arises in the West. The man metamorphosed from the eagle stands on a ridge, pricking his ears. He seems to understand, but also not to understand. The voice has come from the opposite side of the mountain, from the land of the dead. The dead: those who stubbornly keep watch and wait endlessly while their voices echo back and forth within the valley.

Can Yingzheng resist repetition? Can you? Can Man resist repetition?

The man jumps off the mountain ridge. His body, like a drop of rain falling into the ocean, merges with the air currents of the mountain. His arms transform into wings. He is an eagle again.

Man

At thirteen, Yingzheng inherits the throne.

Before power comes death. The throne by necessity a product of death. After all, only when Yingzheng's father dies does he stand to inherit it.

Too young to be king? Not really, since most matters are overseen by Lü Buwei. Lü, who has supported him, even killing, for his sake, Yingzheng's half-brother born of a different mother. Because—and he read this from Lü's gaze—no one must stand between Yingzheng and his rightful throne.

Rumor has it that Yingzheng's younger brother was killed because he was not the emperor's biological son, but rather a bastard who resulted from his concubine mother's straying: a walking time bomb of scandal each day he was alive.

"Must have been Old Lü's doing, this rumor," Yingzheng thought the first time someone told this to him. Lü couldn't care less about the purity of the throne's lineage or a woman's claim to chastity, he believes. His informant was the eunuch who waits daily on him hand and foot. Every morning, as the eunuch dresses him, he also delivers updates on the previous day's events, news of the palace. Yingzheng relies almost too much on this eunuch. But after all, this is the person he has opened his eyes to every day since coming to live in the palace. At night, dreams and visions envelop him; half-asleep at daybreak, he can't tell where he is. It's this eunuch who gets him out of bed. Puts clothes on him, awakens the sensation of touch in his skin. Speaks to him, restores through language his world, his identity, his history, the very rules of his existence.

"According to hearsay, he was not in fact sired by the emperor. Your Highness, if word got out about this, can you imagine the scandal it would have brought your father? That's why Master Lü had no choice but to kill him. The dignity of the emperor must be preserved at all costs; if not, chaos will rule. You, Your Highness, are the emperor's only son. It's you who are the prince!"

Hearing this, he starts. "Must have been Old Lü's doing, this rumor." But he only grunts in acknowledgment, throwing the eunuch a glance. He is surprised and disgusted, but he doesn't show it. *He must be obeying Old Lü, telling me all this. This eunuch is Old Lü's underling.*

Only one second and the glance is over. From then on, whenever he looks at this eunuch again, he feels nothing but indifference.

Yingzheng did not mind having a younger brother. But his grandmother doted on this younger brother; this alone made him more than a younger brother. Now he represented danger; he had to die. Yingzheng has learned that love is dangerous; he must, if only out of self-preservation, eradicate the love he never got.

He still remembers the day he first arrived at the palace from Handan. He was taken to pay respects to his grandmother, Queen Mother Xia. His half-brother was sitting on her knee. Even then, his younger sibling was the one getting all the attention.

At that time, his father, Yiren, a former hostage of the Zhao Kingdom, had absconded back to his own country and ruled it for several years. At Handan, Yingzheng and his mother were waiting for the day they would return to their kingdom and reunite with his father—whether that promise would be kept or broken, who knew. All this while, as they waited, it was constantly drummed into Yingzheng that in a faraway land there was another version of himself, nobler and richer, a Yingzheng who had no need of worry. A princehood, like a piece of stored luggage, waiting to be claimed.

It was during this period of waiting, as Yingzheng counted the days to his return, that his half-brother was born. A child who never lived apart from his parents because he grew up in the palace; a child who even had a grandmother. Yingzheng doesn't have a grandmother. When he was taken to pay respects to the queen mother for the first time that day, and he raised his eyes hopefully only to behold her cold expression, the thought immediately occurred to him: "I don't have a grandmother."

One day, the queen mother made an unexpected visit to the two of them, and his younger brother, despite his age, immediately started talking in a nasal childlike voice, playing innocent, Yingzheng could tell, or playing dumb. The queen mother bought the act hook, line, and sinker. Everything the younger sibling said was met with laughter and praise from the matriarch. The moment the queen mother stepped out, however, he switched back to his arrogant and cold self. This episode marked the first time Yingzheng experienced what others call jealousy. Even though he told himself that it was the pretense of it all that offended him. A pretense by this spoiled sibling who had never gone through his ordeal. Ignoring Yingzheng, the younger brother kept his head down and continued to play with his alloyed toy—a bronze beast.

Love, like any luxury item, ought to be strictly rationed according to a quota system. Love: something that the younger brother received immediately, at birth. Yingzheng knew, however—and this was what Lü wanted him to believe, too—that only *he* had the right to the luxury of love. Transgressor, die.

The Palace of Life

One's right to the throne, one's sexual allure, one's status: none of these is fixed. No power is inherent. All has to be won. I know. From the beginning, I have known. Including who I am, whose child I am: these can all be tampered with. My father—he's a good example.

Yiren, my father, was the son of the Qin prince.

At that time, the prince—that is, my grandfather, who later ascended to the throne—was married to many wives who collectively bore his many children. So many that adding one more made no difference—or taking one away, for that matter. Having more children increases the probability that one's DNA will be passed on. My grandfather cared a lot about increasing this probability.

But for my father, this posed a problem—an existential problem, if you will. Amid the heap of sons sired by my grandfather, that is, amid my father and the heap of his brothers, only one of them stood to become the prince, and thereafter the emperor.

Apart from this prince-elect, any one of the other sons might be offered up for barter.

My father was the kind who could be exchanged for another. His mother, Concubine Xia, was not the first in line (hers was not the womb designated to bear the prince-elect); nor was she the apple of the prince's eye. Far from it, in fact. She had lost her sexual allure. Nor was my father outstanding in any way, since he did not leave a lasting impression on the prince. Therefore the probability of his being elected to the princehood was pretty much nil. One day, at a diplomatic meeting, the Qin chancellor and the Zhao chancellor had a falling-out. As a result, each threatened to use military action to batter the other kingdom's city walls, farmlands, palaces, and temples. Despite threatening each other, they subsequently came to an agreement to blackmail both of their emperors upon returning to their own kingdoms; it was put to each emperor that one of his prince's sons might be dispatched as a hostage to the other emperor.

Over in the Qin Kingdom, the officials from Home Affairs and Foreign Affairs drew up a list of possible candidates and submitted their names to the emperor and to the prince. The most resourceful of the prince's sons had managed to win the affection of both emperor and prince—there was no question about it; their names would not make the list. The second most resourceful were those who had managed to pull some strings; their names would also be excluded. Yiren belonged to the third kind, and so he was on the list.

Before leaving, he went to bid farewell to the prince.

"What's your name?" asked the prince.

"I am Yiren," he said, before adding "Father, Your Excellency."

Being called "father" awakened a feeling of kinship in the prince's heart. He felt shame at having forgotten his own son's name. The prince clasped Yiren's hand, and invited him to drink some wine. The drink caused Yiren to fall into a stupor the moment he boarded the carriage, so that he departed in a daze, without a single tear.

The anxiety began after his arrival in the Zhao Kingdom. If peace had been assured, the hostage exchange would never have happened in the first place. Rumors of war between the two kingdoms had never been far away. Yiren worried that the very moment something went awry, Zhao soldiers would barge into his room and drag him to their torture chambers. In a foreign kingdom, in a foreign land, in a foreign city, he was hard-pressed to pinpoint his value as guarantor. If war erupted, no one would give a damn whether he lived or died. Except himself.

Yiren preferred to perish in the chaos of the battlefield than to die alone as a hostage. A hostage dies a most lonesome death. Before fighting even begins on the battlefield, he is singled out for torture and execution. Being in a group is safer than being alone; it's in numbers that life achieves victory, anyway. Had it not been for his father's sperm swimming en masse toward his mother's egg, Yiren's birth would have been most unlikely. Just as life begins among other sperm, so too should life end among other people. There was something terrifying about dying alone. At least that was what Yiren thought.

The first person to tell him not to obsess about dying alone was Lü Buwei.

"Come now, think again. It's you who should be prince," Lü cajoled. "I know you don't want to die alone, but that doesn't mean you ought to hide among the rest. It's you . . . It's you who are prince." As if Yiren himself could not recognize his own worth. But the image that came to Yiren was that of a sellavision ad. In it, he was the product being advertised.

A trader at heart, Lü had a certain flair. A flair for picking out a good, multiplying its value, then selling it. A flair for seeing into the "future." Known as "the Fisherman," Lü could locate the strange, the rare, and the precious in the commonplace, transforming a piece of rock into luxuriant gold.

Everyone said afterward that Lü had sharp foresight, investing as he did in Yiren. What a fantastic pick. Lü only smiled. In point of fact, Yiren was not his first investment. Concubine Zhao was.

———

Some say that Lü is my second father. Others have said he is in fact my true biological father. I know what people whisper among themselves, that he planted me, like a seed, in a woman's body, then sent that woman to Yiren. Like parasitic wasps laying eggs in other insects' bodies so that their offspring might feed off their hosts. Carrying Lü's DNA within me, I have infiltrated the Qin to become their heir.

They say that Lü did so much for me only because he truly loved me. Who knows. Traders aren't exactly known for putting all their eggs in one basket. Who knows how many other eggs Lü might have planted in other kingdoms? I may simply have been the first to incubate successfully.

(The unsuccessful don't get written up, you understand? For every person who makes it into the history books—those whose eggs have hatched successfully—there are hundreds of thousands who don't!)

We all resemble parasitic wasps. The grand plan conceived for my father, Yiren, by Lü was exactly the sort of strategy adopted by these parasites. He found the crux of the problem: that my father was not special in any way—which is why he became a hostage in the first place. What my father should not have done was to hide among the crowd in the hope that people would forget to kill him—no! What he should have done was cultivate his individuality. "If you desire to live, *be* that special one. Your father's true heir," Lü cajoled.

"How can I be that special one?" my father asked. He who only thought of hiding, not about how to vie for affection.

"Your father has a thing for Madam Huayang. She has no son. Go and be her son."

In my and my father's time, sons can be created artificially, outside the womb. Lü pulled some strings, and before long, Yiren was calling Madam Huayang his foster mother.

First Yiren's biological mother, the Concubine Xia, lost her allure—and with it her husband's affection. Now her son, Yiren, called someone else "Mother." This meant that on the woman's battlefield, she had lost twice. But my grandmother was no ordinary woman. Swallowing anger and hatred, she meekly congratulated Madam Huayang for acquiring a truly excellent heir.

Thereafter, my father, Yiren, became a parasitic wasp, feeding off the prince and Madam Huayang, while his biological mother, Concubine Xia, kept silent. It's not the end of the story yet, so no one can know who the real Queen Bee is.

———

Madam Huayang was originally a Chu princess. One might also see her as a parasitic wasp. A parasitic wasp sent to infiltrate the Qin Palace. Perhaps that was why she was willing to play the role of Yiren's host. They had the same goal, the two of them. Without a child of her own, Madam Huayang knew, she would not hold the prince's affection forever. To procure her own long-term survival, she needed to deposit her future somewhere on the prince's body. Yiren represented an opportunity to do just that. She recognized that opportunity and cultivated it.

It must be stressed that this was as much Madam Huayang's strategy as Lü's. He was the one who sent Yiren to her, but she had to agree to take Yiren in. It was he who planted this egg in Madam Huayang and the Qin prince's marriage, but wasn't she, a Chu princess, also planting a Chu egg in the Qin Kingdom? Perhaps she had known then that this egg would hatch into a monster that would end up destroying her. But she must have been prepared for such a possibility. When I think of it now, it must have been then that the seed of discord was first sown that later grew and bore the fruit of massacre. I am the child of a parasitic wasp, and the executor of that massacre.

The world is about to close its doors. A long era is about to end. Those who know better do their best to find good (read: wealthy) families to host their offspring, so their DNA will be passed on into power and affluence. Breeding, bartering, placing everything on that one bet: anything to gain the upper hand in a new era, anything to win. In Madam Huayang's homeland, the Chu Kingdom, almost the same games are being played, the same parasitic experiments. For example, Chun Shenjun got a singer pregnant, then sent her onto the palace grounds. But he did not succeed. He did not even see that the singer's true love was her own brother. "Their child" was in fact the consequence of incest between the singer and her brother, and the political struggle was only a cover.

The Womb of Death

At this point, you might think to pity me. Even though I don't care for anyone's pity. But you understand now why I hardly knew anything about myself after the fact? I had forgotten where I came from, my true provenance. Which is the correct version: the one in the official Qin records—the story that Lü, my father, wanted me to believe—or what Queen Mother Xia hinted at with her glacial expression? Whose child am I? I don't know anymore. Perhaps I'll ask Mother. Except that she has long since stopped speaking to me because I have had all her lovers killed.

One day I closed my eyes and saw the sea. The sea that I had never before set eyes upon, an endless body of water.

Seeing this image, I suddenly got it. As if someone had projected a documentary on the wall of my brain. A silent film, but I got it all the same:

"What's happening now doesn't matter. Only the future matters."

"Everything I see now will disappear. Everyone I know will die. Only the future, no matter what it brings, will happen."

I want to go to that future. To participate in it. I want to be present for a certain something when it happens. Even if it's death.

From now on, when I see people walking in front of me, people who are alive and moving, I will think I'm looking at the dead future. I already see the deaths that lie in store for them. I shall wear black. I shall make it our official color. Still alive, these citizens of Qin don't know I am paying my respects to them, sending them off to heaven. But death is the end result—nothing to grieve about. At least for me, who knows nothing yet of life's joy.

The joy of life was the first thing Lü taught my father.

"Someone of your status should indulge in more pleasures," he said.

"Women, for example," Lü continued, his nostrils flaring, looking meaningfully at Yiren. "Not any woman. A good woman. Which is not easy to find."

Saying this, Lü slowly undressed Concubine Zhao, one piece of clothing at a time.

A maid, having filled Yiren's wine cup, lowered herself; first she used her fingers to envelop Yiren's penis, then her mouth.

The final piece of clothing slid off of Concubine Zhao.

"Have a look, isn't she exquisite? Not only are Zhao women beauties, they have been groomed to service men and make them feel ten years younger. The kind of woman who can distract men from battle but also make them go to war."

By now completely naked, Concubine Zhao was not embarrassed in the least. Lü put a finger inside her. "See, Master Yiren? Here's a good woman for you. Always wet." Lü set Concubine Zhao on the bed, his finger rubbing her clit.

"I'm over the hill," Lü said, and stood up. "You young people have fun. Make sure that Master Yiren has a good time." He grabbed the maid, who was still fellating Master Yiren, and went with her to the area behind the folding screen.

The bright, smooth body of Concubine Zhao sidled over. He put his arms around her waist. Her nubile body wrapped around him like a summer shirt. With a deft twist of her hip, she slipped inside his robe. Her thigh pressed hotly against his cock.

It felt good. Despite himself, he let a moan escape from his throat.

Wine and food be damned. He pinned the beauty down and began to make love to her.

Lü, still being serviced by the maid, watched over the short folding screen. That old fox, Yiren cursed inwardly, but the depraved voyeurism only added to the thrill. Eyes glazed, Concubine Zhao thrashed even more; he suddenly felt as if he had known her for a long time. Their acquaintance went back further than ancient times—a memory stored in genes, perhaps from the time when the two of them were beasts, no, when they were insects, mating. Just mating. It felt good. Forgetting. Forgetting one's status, forgetting one's kingdom, a kingdom pitted against other kingdoms; forgetting barter, forgetting all these rare, precious things.

The light cast a shadow of Lü and the maid's lovemaking on the folding screen; Yiren could make out from their silhouettes what was going on. Fat Lü had grabbed the petite maid by her waist and was pumping into her, his stomach whacking against her uplifted ass.

Yiren accepted the woman that Lü Buwei gave him and with it his alliance. What Lü knew, Yiren would come to know, too.

One day a Chu envoy arrived, sent by Madam Huayang. He was a young man of aristocratic background, with the self-importance of someone who has never tasted hardship, and the inclination, often seen in someone carrying out his very first mission, to fuss over every detail. At night, Yiren sent Concubine Zhao to entertain him. This time, Yiren played Lü's role—that of the voyeur behind the folding screen, the old hand able to transcend desire's possessiveness, who shares pleasure with others.

The youth went from panic to utter bliss. The next morning, by the time of his departure, he was filled with gratitude toward Yiren for initiating him into this adult world that no one had told him about. Gratitude for Yiren's selfless sharing. An unforgettable experience that would stay with him for the rest of his life. Such a perfect body, and such pleasure it brought! Never again would he find either back in his kingdom. To the very end of his life, he would remember this episode. He turned it over and over in his mind. The memory let him feel that he was different from the dead.

From that time, we return to the present. From Handan to Xianyang, from my mother and the men who moved in and out of her to me. From countless sperm rushing forward to only one—its DNA passed on. Into my body. Into me, at age fifteen, on the eve of war with the six kingdoms, calculating the number of troops, the extent of the power at my disposal. Plotting to increase this power even more. To make a soldier possess more than one soldier's power. How did man evolve to the point where he could have so much power, and need so much power? When we were still sperm, we only knew to rush forward—and only momentarily.

How many enemies?

"Many. Everyone outside our gate is our enemy. As one kingdom, I shall fight six kingdoms; this is not even counting the smaller ones."

"It's an illusion, this idea of a collective," my advisor says. "Every one of these six kingdoms is our enemy. Don't treat them as one. They are six kingdoms. Don't treat them as six kingdoms, either; they are just a lot of people. No matter where you look, you'll see only one man; he's only one man, you are also only one man."

If only it were that simple.

The locusts have come. My servant deceives me, keeps this from me, but I can feel it. From the other side of the sky, like a dark cloud, they arrive. Awakened from my dream, I sit up. The sound in my ears is like oneiric dust, scattered and adrift in air. A demon flaps its wings. They are here.

I shake off my bodyguard and jump onto my horse. I charge out of town. They are here. Massive, red-eyed, and hungry, the locusts swarm at my body and my face. Burrowing into my robe. One after another after another. There is madness in their flight. It's not to eat that they fly like this. Not even to live. It's to die.

I need strength. I need the power to kill these insects, to weaken them, to take away their strength. Soon the power comes. A power summoned from within, like a cloud. When Man really needs power, he often gets it unexpectedly. Or perhaps at that very moment, I changed. Genetically. The way locusts that wreak havoc are no longer insects. I'm no longer a descendant of a Qin emperor, or a bird. I am instead the conductor of a power whose provenance I have never known.

—————

Eagle-Man observes Yingzheng from afar. Yingzheng stands in the middle of a plain, besieged by the swarm. Yingzheng is as mad as the locusts, Eagle-Man thinks. Unbeknownst to Eagle-Man, fighting these mad insects gives Yingzheng even more power. It comes from the other side of the mountain, Eagle-Man hypothesizes—Yingzheng's newfound strength. No matter what caused it, neither he nor the Qin ancestral spirits has any say; Yingzheng is as good as unstoppable. What will this move of his bring the Qin? From the time they were one people, never has a leader taken such a risk. Now they have only to wait and see what fate has arranged.

A fog rises.

Black locusts dive into the milk-white fog. Impossible to tell how much time has passed. Is it day or night? Both the sun and moon are blocked. Light's flaw is that it can be blocked.

A roar comes from within the depths of the fog. Like a tiger. Or a leopard. There's a bestial quality to it, it gives fright. Fright that causes Eagle-Man to abandon his human form for wings and fly away.

The fog induces the locusts to undergo a metamorphosis. Shrouding each locust, the fog tricks it into thinking that it alone showed up for the battle, even though it is surrounded by fellow locusts. Each one reverts to a cowardly, docile plant-eater. Perhaps the docile behavior was always a pretense, which explains why the switch takes place so quickly. Or perhaps it is aggression that is the pretense. These false insects are now drawn to the smell of the swamp rising from the depths of the fog. One after another after another, they plunge into it. On the water's surface, the swift-moving fog suddenly coalesces into a blue python-like form, its mouth open for the locusts to fly into.

That year, the Qin people had a poor harvest, but there were more fish and prawns in the rivers and streams than ever before, and Yingzheng's soldiers received a boost in their protein intake. The combined force of the six kingdoms was easily toppled. As if their souls had first been consumed elsewhere. It is not always on the battlefield that the final outcome is enacted.

———————

No one we defeated knows the secret to our strength. My mother rebuilt the Qin Kingdom like a beehive. At the very heart of the colony is its Queen Bee: Concubine Zhao—my mother. Her sexual history, after coming from Handan, the capital of the Zhao Kingdom, to Xianyang, the capital of the Qin Kingdom. She had countless lovers, countless faces, Mother, who spent day and night copulating. The more her desire was stoked, the longer she could mate; the more frequently she came to orgasm, the better our harvests, the more victorious our battles. She was the goddess of victory, and she was my mother. But I don't set much store by these triumphs. In truth, I don't consider them real, and for that reason, they cannot last forever. After life comes death. And yet, before this realization came to me, I had already used death to rebuild my kingdom.

Monsters at Volleyball

By Lu Nei

TRANSLATED BY ANNA HOLMWOOD

At lunch, forty of us went to play soccer at the field under Chengxi Bridge. It's a perfect square, each side with its own rusty goal. It's a weird place to play. We split into four teams as if playing four-army chess, all chasing one ball. You could shoot into any of the other three goals, but whichever team let in the most goals lost. It looked like a gang fight, but it was just a bit of fun.

As I was going for the ball, an elbow landed squarely on my nose. At first I thought it was snot dripping from my nose, but when I wiped it, my hand came away smeared with blood. I stuffed a handkerchief into my nostrils and left the field to have a smoke. I studied our dreary gray surroundings, the bridge in winter more tattered than my trousers, a row of withered brown dawn redwoods obscuring the river. We were far from the city, and the area was bare except for the morning fog, which had yet to lift.

I sat for a while. Fancy Pants came over to borrow a cigarette. "We're like a bunch of crazies," he said.

Everyone goes a bit crazy in this weather, it makes you feel better. If you don't, it feels like the sun will never come out again.

Pork Belly came over. Pork Belly is fat because of a hormonal imbalance; he weighs more than a hundred kilos. He can't run. How the hell he got into the School of Chemical Engineering's class of '89, no one will ever fucking figure out. More than a hundred kilos! A guy like him couldn't fix a water pump any more than he could defend like Rijkaard. One time when we were playing basketball, he fell on Little Leper and broke one of his ribs.

"Give me a cig," Pork Belly said.

"Get lost, you never buy any," I said.

"Then give me a puff," he said.

I gave him my cigarette. He took a drag and gave it back, but I didn't want it. Watching him suck on the cigarette, it struck me that his lips looked like a pair of butt cheeks. I looked up and wiped my nose with the handkerchief. The blood seemed to have stopped.

We were apprentices on the assembly line of a factory four kilometers west of the bridge, dropped in the middle of total wilderness. In those days the city had yet to expand beyond the old city moat. It was like being in hibernation; everyone stayed inside the city. Every morning we crossed the city and went out to the factory, where we horsed around for the entire day. As soon as the bell rang, we left alongside the worn-out workers, then went looking for somewhere else to horse around. Most people who pass this place think it's being guarded, but Bandit said nobody watches over it, so we brought a ball.

"What's that?" Five Scars came and stood beside me, pointing to a building in the distance.

It was lost in a brownish, sickly chemical fog. It looked like a glass ashtray.

"A sports center for the new part of town," Fancy Pants said. "They built it over a year ago, it was on the news."

"Looks like they built it a hundred years ago."

"The weather's bad today."

"You been? They hold matches?"

"I don't like playing sports, I don't even like watching sports, so why the hell would I go there?" Fancy Pants said. "Think about it, when have we ever had a proper match over here? Apart from running around like fucking idiots, and winning that Workers' City Cup, what matches are there in this city? We've never had one. We just run around like fucking idiots."

"The sports center's finished, maybe they'll have provincial-level matches now?" Pork Belly made a face like a concerned citizen.

"Last year's provincial ping pong championship was held in the city stadium. I went to see it." I looked down and the blood started pouring from my nose again, so I raised my head and continued, "They played well, especially the girls. Still, they have no chance of making the national team here in the Ping Pong Kingdom. It's like ink-brush writing: it doesn't matter how much you practice, your writing's not going to be hung on the walls of the Great Hall of the People. So I'm telling you, you fucking idiot, provincial-level matches aren't worth watching."

At that point Mr. Chen, one of the teachers from our school, came over. Mr. Chen is a young, bookishly pale kind of guy. His full name is Chen Zhenguo, and he used to be a student at our school, too. Now he handles political and ideological stuff, keeps tabs on who's fighting who, who's smoking, and he has to follow us out to this godforsaken place for our apprenticeships. I threw away my cigarette. "For fuck's sake," he said, "you're playing soccer instead of working? You fucking idiots want a workout, huh? Go to the workshop and work your fucking muscles there. I'm confiscating the ball. Big F, where did you kick the ball? Go get it for me. Fucking hell."

We dragged behind him, leaving Big F to run off into the long grass by himself. As soon as we got to the factory, I slipped into the medical room. It was warm in there. I waited for half an hour before the nurse arrived. She asked me what I was doing there. I told her I had a nosebleed and needed some sterilized cotton. She was very sympathetic, but after a long search she still couldn't find any. Eventually she tossed a surgical mask at me and told me to rip it open and pull the cotton out. I wasn't actually still bleeding, so I thought I might as well wear the mask as I headed back to the workshop. As I walked in, I saw Cat-Face and a few of the kids from the local technical academy fighting. Normally we would rush over to help whoever it was crush those nauseating academy kids, but this time none of us stood up; we just watched as they smashed Cat-Face's head. In fact, we clapped and whooped.

Just goes to show what a bunch of fickle jerks we were.

————————

The academy kids were our sworn enemies. The technical academy wasn't a university; they only had one year on us, but in the factory they were classed alongside the cadres. We were workers. They were shrimp among the cadres, but they were still cadres. We were sharks among the workers, but we were still only workers. It was that simple.

Take me, for example. My grades at junior middle school were enough to get me into a technical academy, but unfortunately I applied for the most prestigious finance and economics college, and they required even higher grades than the best academic middle schools. This chemical engineering school was my second choice. If I'd known, I would have applied for the Textile Technical Academy; not only were the required grades low, but lots of girls went there. Just my luck, only getting into the School of Chemical Engineering. Out of a whole class of forty, there wasn't a single girl. As soon as we started, we all fell in love with the beautiful teacher who taught us technical drawing. When she got pregnant, we all cried.

Even so, I didn't want to fight with the academy guys anymore. They were savage, and they had the protection of the department. It didn't matter how the fight started; it was always us technical school kids who got punished the worst. It was like in the Yuan dynasty, we were the lowest of the low, the Han Chinese, and while the academy guys weren't exactly Mongols, they were still above us in the pecking order. I'd been here for two years and was about to graduate; I didn't want this extra trouble right at the last moment.

Big F didn't come back all afternoon, so in the evening I went to find him, to tell him that his least favorite, Cat-Face, got a beating and had to go to hospital for stitches. But Big F wasn't in the mood to talk about Cat-Face. "I went to the sports center this afternoon," he said instead.

"Fun?"

"Really fun. I'll take you tomorrow." Big F noticed that I wasn't too impressed. I was obviously eager to keep talking about Cat-Face's beating, so he decided to give away his big secret: "The girls practice there."

"What girls?"

"The volleyball team, provincial level," Big F said, cracking his fingers. "There must be twenty, maybe thirty. Twelve at least. All really tall, taller than me. Taller than you, even."

I looked at him sympathetically. Big F was a short-ass, strong but short. As if to make up for his shortness, he liked tall girls, like Men Men, who went to the Textile Technical Academy and towered half a head above him.

When I was small, the Chinese women's volleyball team were national role models for battling through adversity. Even my strict mother allowed me to stay up until the middle of the night to watch them play. If I didn't get to see their matches, I couldn't focus on my homework, and then I'd be told off by my teacher. I kind of hated them at the same time. I first went to a volleyball court around the time I had grown to 178 centimeters. The net was taller than I'd imagined; when I jumped, I could only just get four fingertips above it. It was embarrassing. That was when I realized how tall volleyball girls are. I like girls half a head shorter than me. If I were with a girl taller than me by a head— well, I've never experienced it; I don't know how it would feel.

"I'll come with you tomorrow," I said to Big F.

————

The next day at lunchtime, we went back to the field. Following Cat-Face's battering, Mr. Chen was scared we were going to try to get back at them, so that day he let us go play. But who was going to bother getting revenge for a loser like Cat-Face? The gang had completely forgotten about him and were busy kicking up dust on the field instead, enjoying our hard-won freedom. "The girls' volleyball team plays at the sports center," I told them. After that, no one wanted to keep playing; they all wanted to trek through the long grass to take a look. Big F wasn't pleased and swore at me.

The weather was pretty good that day: the mist was gone and the sun was out. As we walked, seeds from the dry, dead grasses floated up into the air. We were doing some serious damage to the grass. The ground was so dry it was soft, the soil was loose. It was really comfortable to walk on. If only the soccer field were this comfortable.

As we approached the sports center, it towered above us like a humungous assembly workshop, with dark-green walls and tea-colored glass. An assembly workshop can never be round, I thought angrily—why did I think of that? How idiotic. Winter weeds were floating all around us, and nearby there was an abandoned worksite. It looked as if they'd been conducting an archaeological dig, and after they finished excavating, they drove in some poles and left the pit open. This place was so different from the city, it was like being in another country. They said lots of foreign companies were advertising jobs out here, and they paid well. A brand-new sports center symbolized new life rising from the ground.

We swaggered in, but it was deadly quiet; there wasn't even anyone at the door. Our gang swaggers boldly everywhere (except maybe the police station), and everywhere we swagger we get stopped (except by the police). It was indeed massive inside. It had high ceilings, with a viewing platform surrounding a court across which someone had strung a volleyball net. There wasn't a soul inside. We were disappointed, and a cigarette started making its way around the group. When it got to me, I stubbed it out. "You can't smoke in here."

"You fucking idiot," Five Scars said, "there's no one here. First you bring us down here and then you don't let us smoke."

"The athletes can't inhale any smoke; it damages their lungs. My uncle said so." They all knew about my uncle. He's a provincial-level fencer.

"There's no one fucking here." Five Scars isn't a very eloquent kid; he repeats every sentence about ten times until he gets fed up and stops.

"Can't you call the volleyball girls to come and play for you?"

"If we'd known, we would've sent you ahead to check first, let you waste your own time," Five Scars continued. "There's no one here, for fuck's sake. I don't even like volleyball. I like soccer."

That idiot liked nothing more than to play one-man soccer, with the sky as his goal. Volleyball meant nothing to him. I ignored him and went by myself to the net. I jumped up and made a swift downward movement with my arm. I was delighted to discover that my elbow reached over the net. I tried again just to check, and I was right. This meant that my spikes wouldn't fly out toward the spectator seats anymore.

"What are you doing, idiot?" Big F had sat down on the spectator platform and was shouting at me.

"I can spike the ball," I said. "Throw me your ball and I'll show you."

"Spike a soccer ball? Are you fucking insane?" Big F said. "You want to give us a show?"

"You don't know shit; last term I could barely reach the net. Now I can already get my elbow above it. That means I can do a smash. I've gotten better at jumping; after all, I haven't grown any taller these past six months."

No one cared. Only Quiff came running over. Quiff was the tallest in our class at 182. He jumped up in his leather shoes and flicked his hand. "What's so great about that? I can do it, too."

"But last term I couldn't reach," I said.

"Last term you got dumped by a girl from the Academy of Light Industry," Big F shouted from afar. "You shrank after that, you couldn't even reach your own butt. But it seems you've gotten back on your feet this year."

Just as I tried jumping up again, I saw a girl appear at the opposite end of the net. She was wearing a full volleyball uniform and was taller than me by about half a head. She had a volleyball tucked under her elbow, and was laughing at me. I froze.

"Last year you were jumping against the men's net. Our girls' net is lower by twenty centimeters."

The court had an echo, so the idiots behind me all heard and bent over laughing.

Their practice was closed to the public, so we were ushered out and went to sit outside the sports center to cool down. We couldn't see through the tea-colored glass, only our reflections. Soon we were bored and out of cigarettes. Big F needed to take a piss, so he ran over to the worksite and peed into the hole. The rest of us joined in. "We should have pissed at the green windows; after all, we can't see in," Wu Bi said once we'd finished.

"And you'd be comfortable taking that tiny dick out in front of people?" Fancy Pants asked.

Wu Bi was the disabled kid in our class. His hair was graying prematurely, he lisped, and he had a really small dick. If you pulled down his trousers, you'd think he was a girl at first. But you only had to hear him swear to know he was a guy. He told Fancy Pants to fuck off at least twenty times. Fancy Pants didn't respond, not even with his fists, mostly because Fancy Pants hardly ever gets into fights. He always tries to maintain a strange sort of dignity, and the rare times he does answer back, his obscenities are so fruity that the other person is already wild with anger before he's even finished. He turned and said to me, "Wu Bi's been drinking some sort of herbal beverages these past few days, Apollo's Salts or something. Apparently the side effects include enlargement of the penis, and apparently that can cause agitation."

We walked back to the factory.

The whole way, Fancy Pants kept asking me about how the girl from the academy dumped me. It seemed his girlfriend might be about to get rid of him, so he was preparing himself for how it might feel. "I can't be bothered to talk about it; ask Big F," was my reply.

"This fucking idiot here fell for a girl at the Academy of Light Industry," Big F said. "I saw her, she was ugly, but she had these dimples like that actress Zhong Chuhong. He stopped dead at the sight of these dimples, like when Five Scars catches sight of a bottle of erguotou. So he went to her school and started trying to get with her. What was her name?"

"Li Xia," I said.

"Yeah, Li Xia. She was pretty good to him at first, and bought him sodas. She was from a town outside the city, didn't talk like us, and lived in a group dorm. This idiot over here likes girls who live in group dorms."

"Because no one gives a shit," Fancy Pants suggested. "But even if you start dating one, there's no future in it. They always go back home to their small towns after graduation."

Big F continued, "Once she took us to see volleyball; the academy has a men's team. We went with her to the court and watched them play. But no one realized she liked one of them, the best-looking one, what was his name?"

"Zhang Min," I said.

"Yeah, Zhang Min. Fucking idiot watched for half a day before he realized Li Xia was looking at this guy funny. He got jealous, marched onto the court in his leather boots, flew past the net, and thumped this Zhang Min in the back. Then he jumps up to block a shot and the ball goes smashing into this face. Smashed right in his face!" He laughed.

"What's funny about that?" asked Fancy Pants.

"You weren't there," Big F said. "I was there. I thought I was gonna go crazy from laughing. Fucking idiot covered his face and lay down on the court. Everyone was pissing themselves, and Li Xia was laughing so much she was nearly on the floor. This idiot was too embarrassed to go see her again."

"That's actually a funny story," Fancy Pants said, his face still dead-serious. "No wonder he was practicing how to spike a volleyball."

"Somebody hit me in the face with a ball, that's all," I said. "Big F, remember the time you got kicked in the balls by Li Xiao? You were both trying to get with Men Men, and he kicked you right in the nuts. Still in working order?"

Big F lunged at me and tried to kick me in the balls, but I dodged behind Fancy Pants. Fancy Pants shook his head in disgust and cupped his own balls for protection. "Don't be so pathetic," he said. A flock of birds flapped up out of the long grass and into the air, swept over our heads, and landed again in the distance. Did we scare them off, or were they just looking for a new place to hang out?

When we got to the factory entrance, Mr. Chen was smoking in the reception area. He pointed at us and said: "Have you fucking losers been playing soccer again? I told you, don't think about Cat-Face. In life, if you get a beating, you get a beating. It's bad luck, that's all. All you idiots do is fight. Don't bring me more trouble, or you're all be expelled."

———————

Cat-Face got four stitches at the hospital and appeared a few days later in the workshop looking like a wounded soldier. We were screwing nuts into the lid of a large basin. The workshop supervisor had handed out twenty wrenches, one for every two students. Once we finished, he collected the wrenches and discovered there were only ten left. As he was hurling abuse at us, Cat-Face walked over, his face wrapped in bandages. His face was big at the best of times, but now it bulged like a gourd. Cat-Face grabbed one of the wrenches and started waving it around. The supervisor was frightened. "What are you doing?"

"The academy kids? Call them in."

"What the fuck's it got to do with me; you want to fight, don't do it here. If you want to start a fire, go burn down their houses."

"Fuck, I was beaten at the entrance to the workshop, and now that I want to get them back, you want me to do it someplace else?"

The supervisor couldn't dissuade him. He thought his bark was bigger than his bite, and Cat-Face deserved it anyway. With only nine of the wrenches—he wasn't going to ask for the one in Cat-Face's hand—he stomped out muttering curses and disappeared from our sight.

Cat-Face called a few of his closest friends over, went to the side, and lit a cigarette. Together they discussed their plan of action. This kind of thing was common at the school: you kill me, I kill you back. It shocked no one. Me, Big F, and Fancy Pants didn't get along with them all that well, so we weren't about to get involved in this sort of bullshit. Fancy Pants said Cat-Face wasn't going to do anything earthshaking. If he'd really wanted to get them back, he would've gone quietly, by himself, with a kitchen knife. He wouldn't gather seven or eight of them and use wrenches. I'd never seen anyone use a wrench as a weapon; it was too much like a propaganda poster. I could imagine the slogan: "Workers Unite!"

That afternoon the three of us slipped out of the factory and went back to the sports center. This time we went a faster way, following the dry, hard winter road. The weather had turned bad again, and it looked like snow clouds were gathering in the haze up above. Sometimes I wonder what would happen if the snow didn't fall gradually in flakes but just crashed down on this goddamn world in one big clump. What a load of crap.

"I've been dumped," Fancy Pants said.

"You were only together a few days, weren't you?"

"Two months. She doesn't like me."

"Did you kiss her?" Big F asked.

"Once. She wouldn't let me a second time."

"Don't sweat it, it'll pass."

"I haven't been smashed in the face with a volleyball or kicked in the nuts, so what have I got to sweat about?" Fancy Pants looked nonplussed. "Let's go watch the girls' volleyball team. Talking to you guys about this stuff is a complete waste of time. You guys know nothing."

But the girls had already left. We had walked for half an hour for nothing. The sports center was empty; not even the net remained. I sat down on the viewing platform and caught my breath.

"Training's over," Big F said.

"What about that tall girl from last time? I've never seen such a tall girl. Big F, you're into tall girls, right? She was taller than me!" I said.

"She was too tall," Big F muttered, depressed. "She must have been taller than me by more than half a fucking head."

I shut my eyes to think for a second, but I couldn't remember what she looked like. She was indeed tall enough, and I kind of admired a girl I literally had to look up to, just the way I admire writers, policemen, engineers. That's a fucking irritating feeling. I even admired Zhang Min, who'd thrown a ball in my face; he was about the same height as me, but his calves were long and so full of spring. He could jump up real high to spike the ball. I couldn't.

An old guy walked in and shooed us out. I went to go see whether there were any more wild birds in the grass, so it took me an hour to get back to the factory. When I got back, I saw a crowd of people standing by the door to the washrooms. They'd run over after the last bell as if they'd been rushing for the winter sales. I'd just seen so many birds take flight, and they'd been so calm, far more composed than any human. Only later did I realize those people wanted to wash and get back to their rooms before the snow came. But the snow didn't come. Cloudy days make people paranoid.

———

Mr. Chen called us to the factory canteen for a meeting. It was midmorning, and it was empty. In a moment of candor Mr. Chen said, "If you're planning on getting revenge, you're going to get expelled. Anyone who gets into a fight will be expelled. Bloody hell, you're just trying to make life hard for my wife, to put me in a difficult situation. Is that it?"

Cat-Face spoke up. "Those academy kids beat me up pretty badly, and not one of them got expelled."

"How do I know what the deal is at the academy?" Mr. Chen said. "I work at the School for Chemical Engineering, I can't expel students at the academy. But I can expel you lot."

"If you want reconciliation, tell them they can buy me dinner. They can kowtow before me and serve me tea. Or else this isn't over."

"Fucking hell," Mr. Chen sighed, "you guys think you're a bunch of gangsters? If it weren't for me protecting you, you'd have been expelled at least twenty times this term alone. Once you're expelled, you can get anyone you like to kowtow before you. You can bring the whole mafia in here and make me kowtow. But till then, no. Fuck."

Mr. Chen left. I felt a bit sad after hearing what he had to say because I've seen Cat-Face be made to kowtow before, and it's not like you just kowtow and everything's resolved. He had his face stomped on. They spat on the ground and made him lick it clean. It's no fun, no fun at all.

"I want to get someone to snap the tendons in their feet." And Cat-Face left, too.

The next day Mr. Chen brought us back to the canteen. "Shit, things are pretty fucking bad. Those guys from the academy are too scared to go to the factory for their work experience. They went to speak to their headmaster, who went to speak to our headmaster, who came to speak to me. If any of you dare do a thing, I'm done for. Fuck it, whatever. You die how you want to die. If you've got it in you to go pick a fight at the academy, I might as well go along and get killed, too."

Cat-Face looked depressed. It wasn't easy to retaliate within the factory walls, but going to the academy would effectively be declaring war. We'd need ten times more people than them, and ten times the weaponry. A wrench wouldn't cut it. For one thing, Cat-Face would never be able to find enough people, and we all knew that even if he could, it'd cost him serious money. Some of them wouldn't even fight, they'd only be there for the free food and drinks. But there's no way you could go over there with a squadron of three. You'd need backup in the form of a whole load of idiots to make it look like a proper battle: the front-line force, the guard patrol, hell, even the song-and-dance troupe and the kitchen staff.

Me, Big F, and Fancy Pants yawned and walked away. The night before, we'd played mah-jongg till morning. We were tired; we couldn't be bothered with work, let alone getting involved in this stuff. In our group only Kuo Bi was itching to have a go. He was a sicko, he only had to see a fight to want to get involved. Sometimes when he saw women having arguments with the vegetable sellers in the market, he would march forward with his fists up. He had raging hormones. "Kuo Bi, you shouldn't be living in China," Fancy Pants said. "You should go to Africa and hunt." We decided to go find somewhere to sleep.

Come lunchtime we were kicked awake. We looked up. It was Mr. Chen. We had no idea what he was doing. "Fucking sleeping, eh? The headmaster's coming. Do me a favor and get yourselves together."

I rubbed my eyes. What was this about? The headmaster, ride a bike all the way down to this remote place? Not likely. Then I realized it was because of Cat-Face. He'd said he wanted to snap the tendons in their feet, didn't he? Us close friends never believe him when he says shit like that; the idiot doesn't even know where the tendons are in his own foot. But to normal people it would sound scary, like a country threatening to drop an atomic bomb.

We lined up and waited for the headmaster. He was short and fat, like Napoleon, and whenever he made inspections, he put on a Napoleonic air. Accompanied by Mr. Chen, he started by examining our faces. Apart from the three of us who'd just woken up, the rest were all right. Once that was over, he crossed his arms and began pontificating on world affairs, the latest news stories, and political trends. After that he had another look at Cat-Face's injuries, implied that a few knocks were nothing, and comforted him with some warm words. Trying to get revenge was not the wisest course of action; we must attempt instead to turn our enemies into our friends, to be strong men. His educator's demeanor was on full display. He was patient and systematic in his explanations. Mr. Chen was standing behind him, nodding, glancing regularly at Cat-Face's injured mug. Cat-Face had never before been on the receiving end of comforting words like this, and he looked like a kitten with its eyes closed in pleasure at being stroked. Then suddenly he started to cry. We all breathed a sigh of relief and thought about how magnificent the headmaster was: he'd exposed Cat-Face as a crazy with such effortless ease.

"In order to strengthen relations between the various light industry educational institutes in the area, including the Academy of Light Industry and our own School of Chemical Engineering, we are going to hold a sporting competition. Sport for friendship. Volleyball, that's a good sport. I am willing to approve a volleyball competition. What do you think?"

We nodded. What else were we going to do?

The headmaster turned to Mr. Chen and said, "You organize it. This group of boys is the core of my school, let them take the court." He patted Cat-Face's shoulder and said, "You take part, too. Use your fists on the ball, not other people." Cat-Face was sobbing so hard he was nearly out of breath.

The School of Chemical Engineering's class of '89 was made up entirely of boys; there wasn't a single girl among us. Some people call this kind of group a "monk's class," or a "hooligan year." When they play ball sports, all that's needed is the slightest contact, flesh on flesh, and there'll be a fight. I once watched Five Scars play soccer. He limped his way up the field, dribbling the ball and yelling, "I'll kill anyone who dares steal the ball from me!" And so he managed to dribble the ball right into the opponent's goal. We suggested that he balance the ball on his nose like a seal, but no one dared tackle him anyway. There wasn't a sporting bone among us. Tackling in soccer gets you into a fight, but with volleyball there's a net in the way, just like in ping pong. If you can't get the ball, you just smack yourself in the face. Our headmaster's a genius, if you ask me; he knew we'd fight over a game of chess but wouldn't run around a volleyball net to beat up the other guys. That would be just too low, even for us.

If the Academy of Light Industry had one strength, it was volleyball. They had an after-school club, and Zhang Min could tip the ball over the net beautifully. Our strength wasn't soccer, or even fighting, but just acting like a bunch of fucking idiots until everyone was disappointed. I spent the whole night thinking about it. Cat-Face had done well out of it, all right; he'd managed to get us involved in a high-level sports match without a hope in hell of winning. I dreamed that I was wandering between the factory and the new sports center, wild birds flying up around me, the snow falling in large, swirling flakes. I was wearing shorts and was freezing. I kept fighting off balls that were flying at me. It was fucking exhausting. Then instead of balls it was wrenches, and I woke up.

On a winter afternoon not long after that, we got on our bikes and rode to the Academy of Light Industry. Mr. Chen took us. The headmaster was going to come, but he had to go to a meeting. Walking into the academy felt strangely familiar. Yeah, I'd been out with a girl who went here, I'd been here loads of times. I almost thought about going to her dorm. The thought was quite painful, my face smarting from the memory of getting smashed by a volleyball.

They were already on the court waiting for us. There are lots of girls at the academy, and they'd formed a brightly colored cheerleading team, clapping and cheering as we entered. Man, I was jealous. The court was a square slab of concrete, perfectly flat and clean with straight white lines painted on it. The net was already strung across. The forty of us cringed. Our team was a ragtag bunch, made up of short, tall, fat, and scrawny guys, each one different. Mr. Chen whispered, "Focus, guys. I don't fucking want to be here, either; the headmaster sent me. Play well and I'll give you a day off." We nodded. Mr.

Chen looked at all of us. "Who's up?" We looked at each other in dismay. "You haven't even talked it over? What the hell are you doing here, then?"

"Waiting for you to choose."

"How the fuck do I know which one of you plays volleyball? Who doesn't play? Choose yourselves. Quick."

The other team appeared, and the first one I saw was Zhang Min. He was wearing an official volleyball uniform in this cold weather, as if the freezing temperature could do nothing to knock the power out of him. He started jumping up and down to show off his physique. He was the king of jumping. In actual fact he wasn't that good looking, just kind of chiseled with a flouncy haircut. It was enough to make him the focus of the court. Of course, all the girls started shouting, "Go, Zhang Min!" Smiling, he ran a lap around the court. They were all flouncy, the whole team, and although they weren't brave enough to wear shorts like him, they were all wearing track pants with two stripes down the legs and athletic shoes. Those two strong, beautiful legs were Zhang Min's sole privilege.

I looked over at our team. Half of us were wearing leather shoes, half knitted cotton trousers, all of us wool sweaters. Even the most imposing of us, Kuo Bi, was wearing a leather jacket. "Fucking hell, what's with the jacket? Dressed for a date?" I couldn't stop myself.

"Who's the idiot in shorts?" Fancy Pants asked.

"Zhang Min, the one who spiked the ball in Little Lu's face," Big F said.

"Fucking idiot," Fancy Pants said. "If we had worn shorts, he'd have had to play with his dick out in order to be satisfied."

We spread out and did some warmups while picking a provisional team. A girl came over to see what was going on, and asked, "Why didn't you bring any cheerleaders?"

"We're our own cheerleaders," I said. "We don't have any girls at our school, so we've brought a bunch of losers. Wanna see?"

"Yeah," she laughed.

"Don't care, not going to show you."

We started choosing the team. It was like deciding who was going to pay the bill: everyone tried to get out of it. I was selected first. I didn't want to play, but I had no choice. I ran a lap around the court to the sound of friendly clapping; they had forgotten that I was the one who got a volleyball in the face. I jumped up to touch the net, and my heart sank: they'd strung it at men's regulation height. I could only get four fingers above it. It wasn't that I thought that all of the guys on the other side could jump higher than me, but that Zhang Min certainly could.

"Short legs! Long torso!" The girls were laughing at me.

I didn't care. I don't worry about girls. Their aim in laughing at me was to get Zhang Min's attention, and if Zhang Min weren't playing, they'd like me. If we were fighting with words rather than a volleyball, they'd want to marry me. That's what I wanted to believe.

The second one up was Cat-Face; he had to be on the team. He stuffed his hands in his pockets. His head was still wrapped in a bandage, and he skulked onto the court, spitting a wad of phlegm. This isn't a fucking soccer field, I thought; who said you could spit wherever you want? Cat-Face couldn't find the three guys who'd beaten him up, so he shrugged and stood where he was, pulled his hands out of his pockets, and cracked his knuckles forcefully as if he were about to start a fight. The crowd started clapping again.

The third one picked was Kuo Bi. Kuo was a bit on the short side, but he'd make an okay feeder, despite the fact that normally he couldn't catch a cigarette, so you couldn't exactly expect him to be any good at catching a volleyball. Quiff was fourth to be picked. He was the best with the girls; he was always talking to them, even as he walked onto the court. Five Scars was fifth, and he immediately went to kick Quiff in the butt to get him to focus. It was important to him to win. As for the sixth, we had no one; no one would agree to play. After a lengthy discussion, they kicked Fancy Pants onto the court. "I hate ball sports," Fancy Pants said loudly. "I'll go, but don't expect me to move a muscle." The crowd hushed.

The referee was a PE teacher from the academy. He grabbed a stool and stood by the net. First came the rules: Best of five, change service after fifteen points. No one understood the stuff about rotating positions. "Whatever, it doesn't matter," Zhang Min said loudly. "They don't understand. Let's hurry up and play, I'm freezing." I nodded and replied, "We don't understand, that's right, and if we delay any longer, those legs will turn into an Eskimo Pie." The referee agreed.

At that moment, I caught sight of Li Xia.

She was a good-looking girl. It wasn't just her dimples that I found attractive; there was a lot I liked about her, but, as with my laziness, I couldn't rationalize it. She was standing at the edge of the court looking at me the whole time. It was cold, and she was clutching a pink hot water bottle, nodding at me with a smile on her face. I couldn't help myself; I ran over to her. "You haven't come to see me in ages," she said. I looked at her dimples, first the left, then the right. Her complexion wasn't too good. "I've come to play volleyball," I said.

"Play your best, I'll be cheering for you," she said.

She was so soft and gentle, and gentle girls like her love to laugh, but I didn't want her to see me make a fool of myself. I wasn't the least bit angry with her.

With a pair of dimples like that, it would be a shame if she didn't laugh. I thought of the time she had complained to me about how boring the academy was, every day from the dorm to the classroom and back again. She hardly ever got to watch TV, just read, and she didn't enjoy that much. I wasn't put on this earth to be laughed at, I thought, but I could be laughed at as long as I was willing.

My neck tensed. Mr. Chen was pulling me back onto the court.

"I'll come see you after the match," I said to Li Xia.

I don't know why she wrinkled her brow. She found a bench, sat down, and nestled the hot water bottle underneath her clothes and against her lower belly. She was watching me, not Zhang Min and his beautiful legs.

"Is that the girl you like?" Fancy Pants asked.

"Yeah."

"She's got period cramps," Fancy Pants said. "I can tell just by looking at her. Period cramps. Bad things, hurt like crazy."

"What should I do?"

"My girlfriend got cramps. We were only together for two months, so I only saw it twice. She said she had to lie flat and use a hot water bottle. That and drink molasses."

I ran over to her and said, "Why don't you go back to your dorm?"

"I'm fine. I came to watch you."

"Fucking hell, Little Lu, what's going on?" Mr. Chen said. I ran back onto the court. As soon as the referee blew the whistle, the ball came flying over, and Five Scars made a tiger fist and punched the ball right into Cat-Face's butt. Everyone started laughing. "Fuck, no laughing allowed," Five Scars said. "Don't anybody get in my way!"

I turned to look at Li Xia. There was a gently pained look on her face. Then she laughed. Because it really was funny. We idiots deserved to be laughed at. I was happy for her to laugh at me, just as she was happy to come see me when she had cramps. A fair swap, I'd say. I couldn't be bothered to play, and by the time we were down 0-5, I couldn't take it anymore. I couldn't hear the laughter. Zhang Min was so cold he was shivering, and he couldn't even jump up to do a block or a spike. He must have remembered me by now. At least I could still fucking whack the ball, I just didn't want to. At one point the ball went flying toward Li Xia—that was the only time I could be bothered to reach out and hit it. Then I looked across and saw Fancy Pants looking sour. He lifted his foot and placed it on the ball to stop it from rolling around. I raised my hand to stop the game.

"I'm hurt," I said.

"Where?" Mr. Chen asked.

"He's got period cramps," Fancy Pants answered for me.

I ignored Mr. Chen's abuse. The whole thing was too fucking funny. Anyway, I'd done my bit, just like my dad with the socialist education movement, or my uncle with the Red Guard movement, or when my uncle on my mother's side helped bring down the Gang of Four. As long as you participate, history will leave its mark on your rear end. And Mr. Chen had definitely left his mark on mine. When I left the court, I saw the remaining thirty-four bastards sitting on the ground laughing. Fancy Pants left the court at the same time. "Those were the ten most fucking boring minutes of my life," he said. He walked off to the bike sheds in the distance. After that, the bastards pushed grizzled Wu Bi and fatso Pork Belly into the center of the court. Everyone was peeing their pants with laughter.

I didn't want to watch anymore, so I ran over to Li Xia. "It's too cold, I'll take you back to your dorm."

"Okay," she said, "I can't take much more."

She stood up, but I didn't dare touch her. She walked really slowly, and at first I walked beside her. We left the court, leaving the mess behind us. I heard Big F shout, "Fuck, I don't want to play!" Big F was kicked onto the court. The team now consisted of a bandaged Cat-Face giving death stares, scrawny Wu Bi with his white hair, dumbass Pork Belly, moaning Quiff, crazy Five Scars, a furious Kuo Bi, who didn't want the game to end, and short-ass Big F, who didn't want the game to begin. Seven in total. All facing Zhang Min's beautiful legs. Distressed, Big F said, "I don't fucking want to play volleyball."

Li Xia and I walked away side by side. "I haven't been to see you in ages. Time really flies."

"Yeah, I graduate next term. I'm going to work in the new part of the city. I'm really happy."

"Me too. The new part of the city has a big sports hall; you can play volleyball."

My heart fluttered. Then it did it again. But I didn't look back. I just walked away with her.

Who Stole the Romanian's Wallet?

By Wang Bang

TRANSLATED BY NICKY HARMAN AND YVETTE ZHU

I

Shuangxi ran down the winding stairs. She hadn't stopped to wash her hands, and the baby oil on her palms made the Edwardian banisters in the Balsam Chinese Medicine and Massage Parlor shine like pig's blood. She hadn't changed her shoes, either. She was wearing flannel tiger-head slippers brought from home a few years ago. The tiger head was still intact, but the rubber soles had been chewed by the landlord's loony dog. She was reluctant to spend money on a new pair: even dead people's slippers from a charity shop would cost two pounds, and she'd rather spend the money on a couple of classes at the "English Corner" Conversation Center. This pair was fine for doing massage, but walking in them was like walking on banana skins, and they were even more slippery when she was going downstairs. She'd just gotten as far as the second floor when she collided with a bushy Christmas tree with sharp, pointed plastic leaves that nearly spiked her in the face.

"Hey . . . Where the hell you off to in such a hurry?" The face that poked out from behind the tree belonged to the Hong Kong maid, Porky, and was as round and brown as an omelet cooked in one of her beloved nonstick pans.

"Porky! What are you doing with that tree?"

"Boss lady wants it downstairs."

"Isn't it last year's tree?"

"We use the same tree every year! It must be five years old by now."

"Let me by, I'm in a hurry!" cried Shuangxi. With a huge effort, Porky pushed the tree against the wall and made two inches of extra space. Then she lapsed into a brooding silence.

"Forget it; you go down first, and I'll carry it for you." Shuangxi picked up the tree.

"Okay, I'll wait for you downstairs." Porky's frown relaxed. She bent down, lifted and eased the great rolls of fat around her ankles, then started complaining that their tight-fisted boss was asking her to cut paper napkins into snowflakes for window decorations, before she finally gripped the banister and took the stairs one step at a time. Shuangxi followed anxiously. Prince William, the black cat, suddenly scurried past their feet on his way up to the rooftop, where he could skitter around in London's first snowfall of 2012.

By the time Shuangxi was outside the door of the Balsam, the Romanian she had been pounding and kneading was sitting dazedly on the tube headed for the airport. After the trauma of the previous night, followed by that last hour of complete relaxation on Shuangxi's massage table, he felt limp and droopy. But he couldn't let himself drop off—he was too uptight about the trip to do that— so he used hunger to stay awake: he imagined delicious things, like his wife's breasts, blood sausage, baked carp, and, oh, those delicious fat pumpkins. "Our pumpkin fries are better than English chips!" Every time he found himself in some nameless canal-side town and was forced to eat at the chips stand, he said this to the sellers, but they just nodded absentmindedly.

Even though the chips in England were barely edible, he had to come back after Christmas to find a new job in a new city. He was over forty, and his CV was mostly filled with periods of unemployment. How would he ever find a better job than the boat repair shop? "That damned Peed. That miserable, goddamned idiot of a dog, destroying my future like that! Fuck! Fuck! Fuck!" He closed his eyes, swearing under his breath. The swearing dispelled his drowsiness, but the pain in his spine returned, the nerves dancing under his thin skin. He began humming his favorite Romanian folk song, "Românește." He liked weepy songs, even when he was in a good mood.

II

Shuangxi chased after him all the way to the tube entrance, her tattered slippers sinking into the dirty snow. She was frozen, but she could see a few hookers, tottering in skyscraper heels, their thighs bare, who were shivering even more than she was. She picked up a free newspaper, folded it into a hat to keep the snow off, and started running back. "Who knows, that rich Romanian may have gone back to the Balsam another way . . ."

But there was only old Doctor Wang standing at the front desk, using an old pair of scales to weigh out dried herb roots that he would pass off as ginseng. Shuangxi hung around a bit, then decided to go back to her room. Just then, Jessica came out of the kitchen with a steaming bowl of Shaanxi beef paomo, improvised from chopped-up pizza dough, vinegar, and chili bean sauce. "Try some!" she cried, then went on to complain, "Business is lousy at Christmas! I only had two customers. I got five pounds from one and seven from the other. He was only going to give me five, but he dropped two coins. I got down under the sink, scrabbled around for a bit, then pretended that I'd pulled a muscle in my back. So he had to grit his teeth and let me keep them. How about you? How much did you make in tips this morning?"

There were eleven masseuses at the Balsam, two of whom Shuangxi took pains to avoid. One was the eccentric Jessica. According to her, she had gone from Shaanxi to Fujian in the 1990s, then from Fujian to England. She came with only a bottle of water, some ship's biscuits, and a bag of diapers, spending twenty-one days in a container ship. Then she walked from Bristol to London, spent six months with only the Thames to bathe in, lived in Hyde Park, where she fought with feral cats for food . . . and survived. The job she was most proud of was as a butcher in a Cantonese restaurant. This part was true. Her fingers were covered in scars that marked her glorious defeats at the hands of Cantonese people, roast duck, and pineapple skins. What was scary about her was not her past but the fact that she was a kleptomaniac. Every month or so, she'd go to the public restrooms in supermarkets and parks to steal toilet paper and liquid soap. Every week, she went to churches and stole candles. She even lifted nonskid mats from children's playgrounds and roses from the squares after Remembrance Day. According to her, the number of men she had stolen from was more than she could count.

Shuangxi didn't want to get involved in a conversation, so she said, "Not much . . ." and turned to go. But Jessica caught her by the sleeve. "Come on, taste this. It's real Shaanxi paomo! Shit, wait till I save enough money to open a shop. You know, Sainsbury sells pizza dough near its sell-by date for twenty pence. One pizza dough makes five bowls of paomo, and at five pounds a bowl . . ."

"You're not afraid of poisoning people?" Shuangxi said indifferently.

"For god's sake, pizza dough can be frozen for up to three years! What's to be afraid of? The companies that sold tainted milk powder weren't afraid. So how much did you make in tips this morning?"

"Two pounds," Shuangxi said honestly, and shot up the stairs next to the front desk.

III

Back in her room, she closed the door and took a crumpled plastic bag from her pocket, inside which was a wallet crammed with bills. She tore the wallet open and sorted the bills out one by one—eight ten-pound notes, six twenty-euro notes, two five-euro notes, and a Halifax cash card. She counted it in dismay. "This is a helluva lot of money! It must be his entire month's salary. How on earth could he be such a fool? I should never have dragged him in here for a massage, poor man. It must be this terrible cold weather that got to him!"

The weather really was bad. There had been snow flurries since early morning, and it was so cold that the stone statues on the street looked as if they wanted to tear the coats off the pedestrians' backs. Even so, Shuangxi had still gone out looking for customers, clutching a stack of flyers advertising massages. Hardly anyone was braving the cold, so Shuangxi had immediately noticed the Romanian standing in front of the Hot Dog Baozi Shop, weighed down with luggage and plastic bags, and looking sorry for himself.

She hurried over with her flyers. "Good morning, Merry Christmas. Would you like a massage? Computer neck, mouse hand, rheumatism, slipped disk, sciatica, PMT, anything inflammatory, a massage can cure it!" Shuangxi rattled off eagerly.

"No, no . . ." the Romanian shook his head. "I've got a flight to catch at two o'clock. I've got to get back to Romania for Christmas."

"Oh, Romania? That's a great place. I really like Romanians." Shuangxi really did like Romanians. In Chinatown's attic rooms, she often gave massages to Romanian hookers. They knew how to dress and how to enjoy life better than Chinese hookers, and they gave good tips. Their English was easier to understand than British English. "You've still got a few hours before two o'clock. Come and have a rest at the Balsam Massage Parlor. It's just around the corner. It'll only take a few minutes. It's snowing so hard, if you stand here, you'll freeze to death." Shuangxi said with real concern.

The Romanian stood holding the flyer Shuangxi had given him, his back pain making him look as decrepit as a ship with a broken mast. Finally he gave in to Shuangxi's enthusiasm—he would treat himself to a massage.

He paid thirty-five pounds at the front desk and followed Shuangxi up the stairs. This was the first time he'd been to a massage parlor. Except for the weird snakelike things steeping in the medicine bottles, there didn't seem to be anything to be afraid of. Shuangxi's room was spotlessly clean: a massage bed, two chairs, and a stainless steel cabinet with three shelves, neatly stacked with towels, tissues, a CD player and CDs, newspapers and magazines, tea, instant noodles, chocolate, and a thermos and paper cups. The Romanian relaxed.

In order to get home two days early for Christmas, the Romanian told Shuangxi, he had worked day and night without a break to get a boat ready for a Christmas Eve dinner cruise. He forgot to mention that this job at the mobile boat repair shop was the best work he'd had in five years. Before this, he had been unemployed for almost a year . . .

"Less talking now! Have some of this tea. This is Chinese jasmine tea." Shuangxi gave the Romanian a cup, and poured herself a cup, too. "I'm so sorry, I haven't eaten anything this morning. I need something hot in my stomach before I give you a massage," she explained apologetically.

"No problem, take your time . . ." The Romanian sipped his tea and went on with his story.

IV

Yesterday afternoon, just before dark, the Romanian had given the deck its last coat of paint. He found an old board and wrote "Wet Paint," even painting a pirate skull underneath, before contentedly going back to pack in the converted truck where he slept. The next morning, he would take the train from Basingstoke to London, and catch the two o'clock flight from Heathrow to Bucharest. Just as he finished packing the last of the gifts, he heard a bark. He recognized it as Peed, the repair shop owner's new French bulldog. He had heard that this was the stupidest of all breeds but had never believed it. This was going to change his mind, though. Peed had fallen through a hole in the ice, and was desperately scrabbling at the "Wet Paint" board, which he had dragged in with him. Alarmed, the Romanian yelled for help, then realized that he was the only employee left. His boss, a middle-aged widower who was always forgetting to shut his dog in the house, was at that very moment speeding up the motorway to Manchester, having just been told that his mother, who was in a mental hospital, had tried to commit suicide for the fifth time. Too many patients and too few staff, grumbled the nurses defensively when they called him.

". . . so I jumped into that filthy water full of bird shit and pulled Peed out," the Romanian went on. By then the dog was a frozen lump, its belly streaked blood-red from heroic British paint, its paws as black as the fingers of German soldiers at Stalingrad. He inspected it nervously, opening its eyes to check its pupils; he even thought of giving it mouth-to-mouth resuscitation. Finally he wondered whether he should call a vet. But, no, he couldn't do that, the boss mustn't know. His instinct told him that he needed to cover this up if he was going to save his job. Then he remembered his old mate from home, Cabbage. Cabbage had taught himself veterinary medicine twenty-odd years ago. He had even cured a cow of epilepsy. Cabbage was working as a chauffeur and caregiver for a man with Alzheimer's, not far from Basingstoke. When the Romanian called him, he promised to come right away.

"I rubbed myself and Peed dry with a towel, and we sat next to the stove. I even heated up a chicken leg, in hopes that the smell would wake Peed up," the Romanian said sadly. But Peed never regained consciousness. It was a few hours before Cabbage rolled up, the old man he took care of sitting in the back seat. Cabbage sniffed Peed from head to toe, then said solemnly that the dog had died from paint poisoning, not hypothermia.

"Cabbage told me to throw Peed back through the hole in the ice. I was scared, so in the end, Cabbage picked up the body and tossed it out just as if it were a cast-iron ball . . ."

After Cabbage had driven away with his charge, the Romanian felt Peed's accusing eyes still on him, looming out of the fog like the "eye" scars on a pollarded tree trunk. The wind whistled and pounded the truck. The foxes that normally stayed well hidden were out and skittering around the ice hole. Close to midnight, he'd had enough. He shouldered his bags, stumbled away from the repair shop, and caught the last train to London. Someone told him there was a twenty-four-hour McDonald's in Chinatown, so he had come.

"You understand? It's not that I didn't want to save Peed, but I just couldn't manage it . . ." The Romanian finished remorsefully and looked at her. The only word Shuangxi had really grasped from his story was "dog." She nodded, and fetched the Chinese-English Dictionary from under the massage bed. She found some words and showed them to the Romanian, meaning to say something like, "You're so right. Chinatown's Hot Dog baozi are a lot nicer than McDonald's hot dogs!"

The Romanian smiled sadly, then collapsed onto the massage bed. Shuangxi used every ounce of energy she could muster to pull his painful spine back into its S-curve.

"How long is the flight to Romania?" Shuangxi asked as she massaged.

"An hour and half. No, wait a moment . . ." The Romanian calculated, then said, "Ninety-eight minutes."

"Wow. It's much closer than China!" Shuangxi replied in the flattering tones she had learned to use with guailo clients over the years. Her hands pushed and pulled at his vertebrae.

"You are really strong," the Romanian sighed. "This must be the kung-fu people talk about."

"These are pressure points. Chinese medicine has been using them for thousands of years. If I don't press hard, it won't work," Shuangxi said with satisfaction. Then she showed off her "iron palm" technique, slapping the Romanian's back until he begged her to stop. She laughed merrily and thought to herself that she hadn't had many clients as innocent as this one—most of the men came to jerk off. She had spent most of her time these past few years dealing with those thirsty beasts, trying to distract them with chatter while she gave them a comfortable massage, trying not to make them mad. Chinese kung-fu, huh! Even if she had the skill of Bruce Lee, who would care? She suddenly felt stupid . . . she had no reason to be so pleased with herself.

Before he left, the Romanian tipped her two pounds in appreciation of her "kung-fu." He put a few coins in his coat pocket, his tube fare. Then something occurred to him, and he took his wallet out again and pointed to a picture in the plastic sleeve. "See, these are my two boys. They're at middle school in Bucharest, but they'll be back home in the village by now . . ."

Shuangxi saw the Romanian off down the stairs and watched him disappear in the snow. "What an idiot," she thought to herself.

She went back to her room, opened the curtains, and began to tidy up the massage table. Under the towels she found a white plastic bag. She opened it. Inside was a half-eaten Chinese Hot Dog baozi and the Romanian's wallet with the picture of two boys, about five and seven, hanging from an apple tree like two little monkeys.

V

Shuangxi put the wallet inside the chocolate box in her cabinet. If the Romanian came back for it, she would calmly take it out of the box and give it to him. It would look more honest than taking the wallet out of her pocket. The thought put her mind at ease. The box was still half full of chocolates, so she ate one. It tasted odd, perhaps because it was long past its sell-by date. Before coming to England, Shuangxi had heard that food-quality regulations in the West were very strict. In China, food two months past the sell-by date was treated as no different from stuff that was a couple of days out of date. So in London she always bought reduced-price items in the supermarkets, and there was never any problem. She ate another chocolate from the box.

The chocolate stuck to her teeth in two hard ridges, and she worried away at it with her tongue. Just then there was a knock at the door. Ah, maybe it was the Romanian. But it was her friend Xiajie, the hooker from next door.

"What's up with you? You look flustered!" Xiajie asked.

"Oh, nothing. I'm just a bit tired. I just finished with a Romanian, his back was so stiff. Haven't seen you in a few days. How's business?" Shuangxi didn't want Xiajie to know about the wallet, so she changed the subject.

"Why do you work so hard? Just jerk him off and be done with it. I'm dead tired, too. I had a john last night who brought his pills with him. Every five minutes he needed a glass of warm water, and then he had to go and piss. It was almost three in the morning, and still he hadn't finished." She bent down to rub her thighs, which were covered in goose bumps.

"It's Christmas. All the guailo will be at home for Christmas dinner with the family. Why don't you take a break?" Shuangxi suggested.

"Yeah, if I could get the curse over Christmas, that would be perfect. I wouldn't have to waste any days. I've been to see that Doctor Chen, and I'm taking herbal medicine to regulate my periods, but it's no damned good. What a fucking con. If I'm on the rag over Christmas, let's go to Buckingham Palace!" Xiajie said. Every time she mentioned Buckingham Palace, her eyes lit up like stars.

"I don't know if the boss will give me time off," Shuangxi said apologetically. "How about Chinese New Year? Let's go then."

"Okay, Chinese New Year."

"Good. I'll bring my Pastry and you bring your Sparky. That way there'll be someone to buy food and someone to pay for drinks!" Xiajie smiled craftily.

Pastry was Xiajie's new Chilean boyfriend. He worked as headwaiter in a restaurant. Shuangxi had only met him once. His face was bony and sallow, like dried bean curd, and his stomach wobbled like precariously balanced scales. Her Sparky's real name was Kalama. He was apparently from Libya, and had been found by an Italian NGO washed up on a beach, severely dehydrated and covered in stinking seaweed and plastic trash. As an unskilled laborer and with unemployment so high, it was a miracle that he got a six-month visa to stay in the UK. A year later he became an illegal alien, tagging along with some cowboy electricians working near Chinatown. If immigration laws didn't change for the next fifteen years, he would get permanent residence. He was smitten with Shuangxi. His devotion made him tongue-tied so he was forever tripping over his words. He said he knew what her "job" was, but it didn't bother him. He was so anxious to please, he even stole a child's balloon and gave it to her. He used to lie in wait for her at the door of the Balsam. He even promised to marry her after he got his residence. Whenever Shuangxi thought about the pair of them, Pastry and Sparky, she promised herself she'd never marry again.

"Shuangxi, do you have any Chinese music? I want some for the guailo johns. My iPod's been broken for weeks." Xiajie began rifling through Shuangxi's cabinet. Afraid that she would discover the wallet hidden inside the chocolate box,

Shuangxi pushed in front of her and picked out a few CDs. "How about these? *Walk Gracefully Once*. Or this one, *The One I Love the Most Hurts Me the Most*."

Xiajie shook her head, "Don't you have something more up to date? These are older than my underwear. How about something by Chris Lee and Jay Chou?"

Shuangxi didn't pretend to follow the latest music and said honestly that she didn't have any. But Xiajie wasn't about to give up. Her orange fingernails tapped rhythmically along the shelf and moved closer to the chocolates.

"What's inside here?" She finally reached the box and was about to open it. Shuangxi grabbed it from her and threw it into the wastebasket in the corner.

"It was from last Christmas, the sell-by date was a year ago. I forgot to throw it away." Shuangxi was not a good liar, and her face flushed as red as a monkey's butt at the words.

Xiajie had to leave it at that, although she was still suspicious. She picked out *A Chinese Ghost Story* and was about to leave when she found a chocolate wrapper stuck to the sole of her shoe. Now she was not just frustrated, she was furious. "Mean bitch," she muttered. "All right, you pig out in secret! If they poison you, will I bother to burn spirit money for you?" And she slammed out of the room.

Shuangxi felt as if a bucket of chili oil had been poured over her, and her face flamed.

Before she came to work at the Balsam, people were always telling her she should work as a hooker. She didn't want to. She was over thirty, and besides, if anyone from her village found out, she'd never live it down. Then someone said, "Why not work as a masseuse? If you want to be a hooker and a model of chastity, too, that's the way to go. The more skeletons on guard at the door of the shop, and acupuncture posters and suchlike in the windows, the more complete the cover. No need to drink or play games with the clients—you just put your white coat on and wiggle your ass. No need for much skill at massage, either, just a pair of hands that can work up and down like a piston and jerk the client off in one great spurt . . ."

"So do I need to sleep with the clients?" Shuangxi asked.

"The massage room is like a snail shell; nobody knows what you're up to in there. The client pays at the front desk, thirty-five pounds per hour. You get fifteen, the massage parlor gets twenty. That's three times the rate for washing dishes. Hand jobs are ten pounds, paid in the room, tips extra. It's up to you if you want that tenner or not. And it all comes to you; the massage parlor won't even know about it."

Shuangxi liked this answer. Actually, people like Xiajie and the Romanian girls really did think that she slept with her clients, but Shuangxi never tried to disabuse them. "Keep quiet" was her motto for surviving in Chinatown. Just in case, one day, they turned on her as an outsider and kicked her out. As long as she never worked as a prostitute, she could still keep her ideals.

How come she was not afraid of what other people thought, but yet she couldn't be honest with Xiajie? Shuangxi picked the chocolate box out of the wastebasket and returned it to the shelf. She sat down on the massage bed, staring blankly at the crumpled jacket in the corner, its folds looking like a tiger one moment and an alligator the next, thinking hard. Hmm . . . Chinatown was a tricky place, all right. You never knew who your real friends were.

VI

Suddenly, the sound of *Does God Love Me?* filled the room. Had someone left their phone behind? Alarmed, Shuangxi looked around for it. In the end she discovered that the room phone was ringing. Someone must have changed the ringtone. When she picked up, Porky, at the front desk, shouted into the receiver:

"How come you took so long pick up the phone? I made some brisket stew. You want some?" Shuangxi had always loved brisket stew and was on a mission to consume as much of it as was humanly possible. She sprinted down to the kitchen, and Porky gave her a large bowlful. As she watched Shuangxi eat, she complained, "Hey, I'm about to get fired."

"What happened?" asked Shuangxi, gravy dripping off her chin.

"I dunno. Maybe because I'm too fat."

"Since when did cleaning require a good figure?" Shuangxi said sympathetically. All the same, she couldn't think of a way to help Porky dissolve that worrisome fat. Porky had been at the Balsam for many years, pushing dirt from one side of the room to another, taking out the garbage, making tea . . . and various other things. She lived alone in the basement with all the junk. If anyone asked why she didn't go back to Hong Kong, she would retort:

"What would I do back in Hong Kong? Live on welfare? I can't speak English, and I'm too fat . . ." The last few years, she hadn't even been able to squeeze into the toilets on trains.

The kitchen door burst open while the two were commiserating. Jessica flew in like a soccer ball. Hard on her heels came the big girl from Shandong, Alice, waving a huge fist in the air: "You thief! I'll kill you!"

Shuangxi spat out a mouthful of half-chewed beef and prepared to wade in to stop the fight. Porky sat down hard on the floor and cried shrilly: "Oh dear, another fight, another fight . . ."

Shuangxi felt she had to go and help Porky to her feet first. In the few seconds it took her to do that, Alice had banged Jessica's head down onto the chopping board, smearing a colorful mixture of tears, snot, and makeup over her face. "Fucking bitch! Don't you dare steal my clients! This'll teach you!" Alice punched and kicked Jessica until she was too tired to keep going. Then she turned around and glared at Shuangxi and Porky, who was still trembling in fear. "Did you see anything?"

Shuangxi shook her head.

"And you, Porky?" Alice smiled sweetly to Porky. "Tell me, what did you see?" Porky shook her head violently. After Alice had left the kitchen, Shuangxi waited for a while before going to Jessica and helping the disheveled girl up. Sensing that for once she had someone's sympathy, Jessica wailed loudly before allowing herself to be comforted. Shuangxi led her to her room, where she applied cotton wool soaked in safflower oil to her bruises. Jessica's chin was so badly bruised and swollen that it looked like an eggplant.

The second person Shuangxi avoided at the Balsam was Alice. Alice was an illegal. Her status seemed to have hardened her heart to any feelings of kindness she might once have had. One time she set fire to Jessica's hair with a lighter; another time she tried to push a masseuse under a tube train.

"I never stole her customers. Why would I want to steal her customers? That Lawrence of hers, he's as tough as an old boot; why would I want him? I tell you, Shuangxi, Alice is nuts. We can fight heaven, earth, and each other, but we can't fight nutters, right?" Jessica went on lambasting Alice until she saw Shuangxi's chocolate box.

"I only had a bowl of beef paomo this morning, I could really do with something sweet now . . . ," she wheedled.

"You shouldn't eat so many sweets. Look at Porky . . . ," Shuangxi said impatiently and went on wiping the floor. "I really need to get to work. You should go back to your room." Jessica reluctantly stood up.

Shuangxi opened the door and there was Alice, looking like a black thundercloud in a clear sky. She had a sly, lopsided smile on her face, as if a cigar were drooping menacingly from one corner. Shuangxi was momentarily at a loss. Jessica looked like she wanted to dive into Shuangxi's pocket to hide. Alice and Shuangxi glared at each other, and there was a long pause. They might have been playing Eagle Grabs the Chicken. Then Alice turned and swept away.

"*Does God love me? Does God love me?*" Shuangxi's phone rang again. This time it was Miss Li at the front desk with a request for a house call in Kingston. The person had asked for Shuangxi by name. They'd given her an hour and fifteen minutes to get there.

"Hurry up! Take the tube to Waterloo, then the train to Kingston. This is the address. Don't be late. It sounded like someone important."

"Don't worry," Shuangxi said cheerfully. "I'm leaving now!"

Shuangxi liked to make house visits (the hookers called them "takeout calls"). She enjoyed tubes, trains, and buses. It got her out of Chinatown for a bit and made her feel like she was in a foreign country. Today she might have been in a snowy fairytale. Rather than behaving like a typical Chinese tourist taking cell phone pictures of everything, even the signs like "Danger of Death" on electricity poles and the "Shallow Water, No Jumping" sign by the river, she sat quietly in the carriage, sometimes even closing her eyes. She had made progress with her English—she could understand the tongue-twisting place names on station announcements—and felt quite proud of herself.

It was not until she got to Waterloo that she remembered she hadn't left a message at the front desk telling the Romanian to call her if he showed up. Then it occurred to her that he would already be on the plane by now. Even so, she was still worried. Good thing she had locked the door and the key was in her bag. Only Prince William the cat could get in, and only if he jumped through the window. But Prince William never showed any interest in a massage room that had nothing in it that he could play with, like flowers, a mouse, a ball, or a gecko. Shuangxi had had that particular massage room for three years. The two years before that, she'd been in South London, where the clients were mostly laborers, and more infrequent than an elderly hen's eggs. Getting a tip was like squeezing toothpaste from an empty tube, and she wasn't able to save much money. At the Balsam, the clientele was more mixed. There were office workers from Soho, restaurant owners and tourists, some from Europe, others from Japan and China who came for foot massages. She could save a few hundred pounds a month. When she'd saved enough, she would go to a school, learn a skill, get a professional qualification written out in English . . .

Shuangxi took out the massage room key and squeezed it, feeling its solidity for the first time. A pink rubber piggy was attached to the key ring. It felt like mochi, soft and smooth. It was a gift to herself she had picked up in a Chongqing flea market on her eighteenth birthday. She had had many keys since then, but the pink piggy was a talisman that went everywhere with her. She held it in her gloved hands until it was warm before putting it back into her bag. She got on the train and sat in a corner, munching on some pickled red peppers and looking at the falling snow. The red peppers provided her with a trickle of warmth, like a cheap portable heater in this cold, gloomy city.

VII

The train arrived in Kingston. It was a place that stretched Shuangxi's imagination to its limits: the haunt of squirrels and deer, of mysterious Jews and socialites wearing lacy veils, upper-class folk on horseback wearing pocket watches and pausing to admire the sunset, and petit bourgeois joggers with towels slung around their necks and heart-rate monitors on their arms.

Shuangxi finally got there, puffing and panting, seven minutes late. It was a mansion with a fountain in the front garden. She'd never been on a house call to anywhere as grand as this. The marble steps leading up to the pool were frozen, but water still gushed from the fountainhead. A Rottweiler and two King Charles spaniels lay expectantly behind the front door, watching the maid walking down the long drive, and waiting for the precise moment when she would unlatch the gate to discharge a volley of furious barks. Fortunately, Shuangxi had never been afraid of dogs. She greeted them briefly and they calmed down. The woman was dark-skinned, probably Southeast Asian, and was dressed in a cashmere sweater and trousers with sharply ironed creases. She had the polite manners of a wealthy family's maid. Shuangxi took off her coat and followed her into a small drawing room with a very high ceiling. The maid brought her a cup of English tea and asked her to wait there before disappearing down the long hallway. On the wall hung a smoky, gloomy oil painting of a half-naked woman lying on a huge bed surrounded by dwarves combing her hair, holding a mirror, pouring water, and cleaning the floor. The white cat she held in her arms was the only bright spot, but it had disturbingly red eyes, like those terrible commemorative photos where someone has forgotten to correct the red-eye effect. Shuangxi looked at the painting as she sipped her tea. The tea-sipping was a habit she had picked up from her ex-husband, an alcoholic who peed in the sink when he was drunk and lived on government benefits. He was also violent, and a year after Shuangxi arrived in England, she had been forced to seek refuge in a battered women's shelter. He had looked down on Shuangxi because she swilled her tea instead of sipping it, didn't put the toilet seat down, set the grocery bags on the left side of the escalator, and so on. One by one, Shuangxi had changed these habits. Initially she was trying to please him, but later, under his constant scrutiny, this new body language became automatic. Still, it was not enough to save a marriage that had lasted less than a year.

She had drunk half her tea when a tall Englishwoman in her thirties, wearing a floral silk dressing gown tied casually at the waist with a gold satin cord, came in. "Do you speak English?" she asked.

"A little, not very good. But I study English every weekend at the 'English Corner' Conversation Center . . . ," Shuangxi replied humbly.

"It doesn't matter. Our maid Afrina is from Malaysia, she can speak a little Chinese. Her grandfather's Chinese, so she can translate for you."

"Yes . . ." Shuangxi nodded, a little embarrassed. She thought back to what she had just said. Had she mispronounced something? Gotten the grammar wrong? She often confused "she" and "he," "potato" and "tomato," "kitchen" and "chicken," but she hadn't used any of those words in her reply. She was taken upstairs into a room with full-length bay windows, where a handsome, bare-chested Englishman lay on a giant sofa watching TV. Shuangxi thought he looked exactly like Tom Cruise.

"This is George, my husband. Lately he's been getting pains in his back and legs from playing tennis, and this morning when he got out of bed, he wrenched his neck . . ."

George turned stiffly, forcing a smile and holding out his hand. "Hello, it's nice to meet you," he said politely. "What's your name again?"

"Daisy . . . that's my English name." Flattered by his attentions, Shuangxi hurriedly extracted her right hand from her bag to shake his, then added: "But most of my clients like to call me by my Chinese name. My Chinese name is Shuangxi, which means double happiness . . ."

"George, she's already more than ten minutes late. I think we need to get a move on. Don't forget, the concert is at five-thirty," the Englishwoman cut Shuangxi off.

"Okay, okay!" George muttered.

Shuangxi was a little annoyed, but she didn't dare answer back. She opened her bag and placed a towel, a bottle of baby oil, a bottle of bone-setting oil, a bottle of safflower oil, a bag of paper towels, and a bag of wet wipes neatly on the coffee table.

"No, no, don't use those. We have special massage oil and clean towels," the Englishwoman cried. A few moments later, the maid came in with a large, snowy-white towel and a bottle of French lavender oil.

"Afrina, put the towel on that daybed," the Englishwoman instructed. She turned to Shuangxi. "Is that all right?"

Shuangxi nodded. She had just finished laying out the towel when the two King Charles spaniels, which had somehow sneaked into the room, jumped up on it. Rather than reprimanding them, George sat down between them and petted them. Their coats had an almost waxy shine. A handsome, rich man and pedigreed dogs . . . The only place Shuangxi had seen anything like was it in movies and magazines. She gazed, fascinated, at the scene.

"Daisy, do you mind washing your hands first?" the Englishwoman said, interrupting her train of thought. She followed the maid to a bathroom down the hallway. The bathroom floor was covered in a thick white rug. Afraid of dirtying it, Shuangxi insisted on taking off her shoes before she stepped inside. While she was washing her hands, the maid asked where she was from, how long she had been in England, did she like it here, and so on. When she heard about Shuangxi's disastrous marriage, she said comfortingly, "I know a Filipino woman whose British husband hit her, too, and blinded her in one eye. But, as with you, Immigration gave her permanent residence. An eye for a visa is a better deal than an interminable marriage, right?" Shaungxi didn't answer her directly. She didn't like to think about the past. If a recollection suddenly caught up with her, she would force herself to make a mad dash past it.

When Shuangxi returned to the room, the two spaniels were still on the towel, and George, his neck bent to one side, was pacing back and forth talking on the phone. The Englishwoman looked at Shuangxi, lowered her voice, and said hesitantly, "Are you sure you can correct his neck? It's not that I don't believe in masseuses, but, you know, George has never been to a Chinese doctor, and he'd never go to a massage parlor. This morning, our friend Peter Thomas insisted on giving us your business card. He said you fixed his leg, is that true?" Shuangxi couldn't remember a Peter Thomas, and did not dare make the sort of joke Dr. Wang from the massage parlor did, along the lines of "Satisfaction guaranteed or your money back!" So she declared stoutly, as if she were in English class, "I assure you I will do my best!"

Just as she had with the Romanian, Shuangxi put everything into this massage. She carefully pressed down on every important pressure point and every stiff muscle. For these blocked joints, she used an "octopus" technique of her own invention. She could feel her hands on fire. However, the woman appeared dissatisfied. She stood close by, eyeing this crazy little Chinese woman with the deepest suspicion, perhaps thinking that this Daisy looked just like a witch in a Hong Kong zombie movie—only not as ugly. How could she possibly be a physiotherapist? Women like this from Soho weren't real physios . . .

When Shuangxi's hand touched the elastic band of George's underpants, the woman indicated with her eyes that Shuangxi should stop there and concentrate on his neck. Shuangxi was overcome with embarrassment. The pressure points she knew by heart blurred in her mind until they seemed like obscure astrological symbols fading into George's pale, aristocratic back.

"What's she being so fussy about?" she thought sulkily. "She has a husband who looks like Tom Cruise, central heating hot enough to cook a duck, and even the rug in her bathroom probably cost more than I make in a month."

"Darling, how do you feel?" the British woman asked after Shuangxi had finished.

"Much better, thank you!" George said, kissing her thin lips. The British woman smiled complacently, as if this were all due to her efforts. She gave Shuangxi a hundred pounds and told her to keep the change. Then she called for the maid to show her out.

When Shuangxi left, it was getting dark. Snow was still coming down heavily, and snowflakes stuck to the windows like paper cutouts. Lights blazed out from the houses, framing their interiors like brightly lit pictures, revealing lives that were a world away from Shuangxi's. In the street, outside the picture frame, it was as dark as a movie theater. Shuangxi groped her way along, zigzagging through the snow like a beetle that has lost its carapace. Once on the tube she fell asleep, exhausted. She dreamed she was standing next to her grandma's pigpen, feeding corn to pigs whose bristles shone as if they had just been waxed.

VIII

But the tube didn't take Shuangxi back to her grandma's pigpen. When she opened her eyes, she was back in Chinatown. At an ATM, she ran into an unshaven, runny-nosed Sparky. Shuangxi expected him to pester her as usual, so she folded her arms across her chest, frowned, and stared him down in the hopes she could get it over with quickly. But Sparky only gave her a dark look. All those sweet nothings he used to whisper had suddenly turned to ice cubes. With a cold hello and goodbye, he was gone, leaving Shuangxi craning her neck to stare after him.

More surprising was that someone had opened her massage room door—she was greeted by a yawning black hole. An ominous foreboding swept over her. She rushed to the cabinet and opened the chocolate box. Sure enough, the Romanian's wallet had vanished.

"Oh, shit! Someone's stolen it!" Shuangxi cried. Worried and angry, she went to the front desk. There was only Miss Li, playing card games on her phone. "Who opened my room door?" Shuangxi cried, exasperated. Miss Li looked up in astonishment, and thought for a few seconds before answering, "Oh, when you were out, the boss asked Sparky to paint all the light bulbs in the massage rooms red, to give the rooms a bit of Christmas spirit. So I opened your door for him. Maybe he forgot to shut it afterward. Why?" Shuangxi stared at her blankly and said nothing. She needed a glass of cold water; maybe cold water could help her think. She went into the kitchen, where Porky was busy cutting napkins into snowflakes. She ignored her, found herself a glass, turned the tap on, and filled it with water.

"Oh, you back? How was that customer? How much of a tip did you get?" Porky asked.

"Porky, did you see anyone go into my room when I was out?" Shuangxi gulped some water and stared hard into the cleaner's surprised face.

"Sparky came to paint and made a mess, so the boss asked me to clean up. I thought the room smelled of paint, so I opened the door. What's happened?"

Whenever Porky was surprised, her fleshy cheeks would bulge until they threatened to overflow. Shuangxi shook her head silently. What a bum deal for the Romanian. What a bum deal for her, too. The thief must have thought she, Shuangxi, had stolen it. She'd never live it down! Which son of a bitch had stolen the Romanian's wallet?

Sparky! It must have been Sparky! He gave me such a cold look in the street, then took off. He's finally dumped me, hasn't he? He stole the wallet, he took advantage of me. How dare he pass judgment on me! All that sympathy I wasted on him, a dog would have deserved it more . . . The more Shuangxi thought about it, the angrier she got. Then Jessica came in, looking very pleased with herself, and humming some weird song in broken English. "Hey, darling, I'm so glad you're back," she said to Shuangxi sweetly. "Wasn't it cold out? The snow was so heavy, you must have frozen, you poor thing! How much did you make in tips? What's up? Who's got you so pissed off?" Shuangxi didn't answer, only stared at her. Then suddenly she felt something wasn't right. The aubergine swelling on Jessica's chin was still there; so were the traces of blood around her eyes and the scratches on her face from Alice's nails. So how come she was suddenly so happy? The bitch, how could I forget Jessica? Sparky was vile, but compared to Jessica, he was small potatoes. Jessica was a real pro. She lived in a different world—she never thought she was stealing. If the door was wide open, she'd just walk in and help herself, that was what she was like. It was as obvious as a flea on a bald man's head! And she obviously thought we were both thieves. Shuangxi wished she could bang Jessica's head into the chopping board as Alice had done, but where was the evidence? Jessica was so clever, she'd probably already sneaked the money away to the South Pole! And I don't even know her real name . . . Maybe Alice knew; she was such a busybody, she'd dig up your granny's grave. In fact, maybe she'd done it herself . . . to get her revenge. One day after work, she might force me into some garbage-strewn, rat-ridden corner and throw that Romanian's wallet to the ground like a dog's bone and make me get down on my knees and gnaw it. "You stuck-up bitch!" she'd yell, "you're worse than Jessica!" Shuangxi squeezed the glass until she thought it would shatter. All the accumulated humiliations she had suffered during her years in England threatened to overwhelm her.

But the glass didn't shatter, and neither did she. She gulped the water, rushed back to her room, and locked the door. The light had turned the room the peachy red of a brothel. Next to the CDs, she saw a scribbled note: "*A Chinese Ghost Story* wouldn't play. I swapped it for *The One I Love the Most Hurts Me the Most*. I'll bring it back in a couple of days. Merry Christmas. Love, XJ." So Xiajie had been here, too! Anyone could have stolen the Romanian's wallet, even my friend Xiajie, or poor, dim Porky, even a client who happened to be passing the room and wanted to get a look inside, or the sellers of pirated DVDs and smuggled cigarettes who haunted Chinatown, or my boss, that crafty scrooge . . . Sadness welled up inside Shuangxi.

She was as jumpy as an ant in a frying pan over the next couple of days. Unable to concentrate on her work, she gave her clients only perfunctory rubs by way of a massage.

What if she found out who the thief was—then what? Negotiate secretly to get back the money? Call the police? What would happen if the Romanian came back looking for his wallet? What would she do? Lie? Tell the truth? Would he believe it? It was my own careless fault, she thought . . . Maybe I could run away before he came back? But quit just for this? Right now, even the Brits can't find jobs, let alone immigrants. There was that nurse—she was an immigrant, too—who took the call from two Australian DJs impersonating the queen and asking to be put through to the princess; she was so afraid of getting fired, she committed suicide . . . What should I do? I can't trust anyone. Where should I go? So many questions teemed in Shuangxi's head. She felt infinitely small, and completely trapped. She hadn't asked for much sweetness from life, but even that little bit was out of her reach.

IX

The third day after the Romanian lost his wallet was Christmas Day. The wind no longer blew so keenly, and finally the snow lay still, like fluffy cotton candy, and the sky reverted to its usual aloof stillness. Lonely snowmen disappeared one by one from the streets. The supermarkets closed early; even the buses and tubes stopped running after 2 P.M. The city was silent—like a run-down gramophone that needed to be wound by a giant hand to emit even the scratchy hissing of the needle on the record.

Only in Chinatown was it business as usual. The streets bustled with noise and excitement. Shuangxi arrived as usual at the Balsam early in the morning.

There were black circles as big as quail eggs under her eyes from three days without sleep. Getting up at midnight in her unheated room, wrapped only in a thin blanket, to boil hot water had given her a cold. But, oddly enough, she was smiling. She separated the massage room key from the rubber piggy, slid the piggy ring onto her thumb, and went up to Miss Li at the front desk. "When you see the boss, tell her I quit. This is the key to the room. Thank you." Without waiting for Miss Li to recover from the shock, Shuangxi strode out into Chinatown.

Shuangxi walked on and on, as if all the power in her hands and arms had been transferred to her feet. Stopping at an almost deserted intersection, she felt as if she were wearing a pair of magic skates that were bearing her up into the air. Was she afraid that an eagle would plummet out of the sky and grab her in its talons? Maybe a bit. She didn't know where she should go, or how far she could fly. When at last she alighted, she discovered she was in Hyde Park, a place she hadn't been in years. The park was so quiet, she could almost hear the ice thawing on the lake, a secret sound, like fire spitting or the crackling of glaze on a pot. The swans in the lake were swimming with their wings opened up, like so many white palaces. Crows perching in the treetops looked down animatedly as if this unusual stillness were far more interesting than anything happening in the sky.

Shuangxi slowed her steps and walked on aimlessly, but with a sense of contentment she had not had in a very long time. Under an old tree, she saw a girl of about six or seven, bent over and drawing something on the ground with a twig. Her slender legs and feet were swallowed up inside huge, dirty snow boots. A cloud of fine, curly, corn-colored hair fluffed out behind her ears.

"Hello. What are you drawing?" Shuangxi bent down to ask. The girl shook her head, then looked up and gave Shuangxi an innocent smile that exposed two rows of neat white teeth, before going back to her drawing. The twig made a scratchy sound as she made wavy lines in the snow.

"Is this the sea?" she asked.

The girl nodded.

"Very nice." Shuangxi took the pink rubber piggy off her thumb, warmed it between her palms, and held it out. "This is for you."

I like the sea, too, she thought, and walked on.

CODA

Excerpts from

Nine Short Pieces

By Li Juan

TRANSLATED BY BRENDAN O'KANE

Doing One Thing and One Thing Only Online

There's an online writer I like a lot, a girl who runs a fabric shop on Taobao.com. She doesn't publish her writing, not in any kind of formal way, but the advertisements she writes for her fabrics are sublime. I've ordered quite a few pieces of fabric from her, by way of expressing my appreciation, but we've never met, or chatted, or indeed exchanged a single word, not even to haggle over the price of her fabric. I just paid online and waited for delivery. I don't even remember whether the packages had any writing on them when they arrived.

I don't dare talk to her for fear of disturbing her. I'm sure it would. With a self-contained world like hers, all you can do is watch quietly from the sidelines. Even the tiniest sound would break the spell. We're exactly as close to one another as we're meant to be. Trying to get any closer would be like an assault.

I don't remember how I stumbled across her shop amid all the other shop fronts on Taobao. I don't buy fabric anymore, and there's no reason for me to get in touch with her. But I can't forget her, not at all. I almost resent her sometimes: Why can't I forget her, no matter how I try? It's not as if I know her.

She doesn't get new fabrics in very often. It's always the same few patterns, which she describes in prose of unearthly beauty. She doesn't seem to be particularly concerned about selling them, and when people comment to ask about the prices she ignores them. She just sits there with her fabrics, murmuring softly to herself. Some of her customers, fellow fans of her writing, leave comments asking whether she blogs. I'd love to see her with a blog of her own, writing just for writing's sake—but no; all her affections, all her miraculous talents, are reserved for her fabrics. "I don't blog," she says. "Never felt the need."

She's not selling physical items so much as bestowing grace. She's less a businesswoman than a queen, reigning over the kingdom of her own heart.

How many people can quietly do one thing, and one thing only, online? Can quietly shush their visitors, shut the door, switch off the lights, and leave? How many people genuinely don't mind being lonely? How many people are content enough not to want gifts and love and adoration? How many people can manage not to want more?

The Internet is the quickest way we have to communicate. It has moved mountains for me, parted seas, cut swaths through thickets of thorns and fields of nettles, flown me over yawning chasms; it has let me leave quickly and arrive rapidly, let me put everything on display, let me open your eyes any time I like. But—what have I gotten from it? Besides friendships and knowledge, what have I really done for myself? My emotions and my life are so badly out of balance I can barely stand, and yet even as I feel myself being pulled under, I still want to go on building a world outside myself.

The Fairy Forest

When I was nine, I spent my whole summer vacation reading through a heavy book of fairy tales printed in dense traditional characters. Much later, I realized that this couldn't be right—a nine-year-old reading traditional characters? I have a hard enough time with them even today. No, it couldn't have been written in traditional characters.

But it was. I've forgotten nearly all of what those complicated old characters said, but I still clearly recall the slow, heavy effort of wading through them. I remember painstakingly connecting one character to the next, grouping them into words, teasing out the cadences of that antique speech.

Every character, every sentence, sprouted dense leaves, bloomed with flowers that blocked my view of the way forward. The path beneath my feet disappeared and reappeared beneath furze and scrub. Small animals darted alongside it, their eyes glittering.

The stories went deep, so deep that when I peered over the edge I fell in. As I fell, I sped up, slowed down, turned innumerable corners, came to crossroads at which I always unhesitatingly turned left. The people I met said nothing, or sometimes spoke in riddles that I pondered as I fell, down and down and down.

The stories shielded themselves behind complexities of details. They twisted and turned, never leading to an exit, as if the storyteller himself were walking along an unfamiliar path, describing the sights as he went. It was almost as if the storyteller had written the book out of sheer loneliness, trying to fill silence rather than follow any specific plot. As he followed that unfamiliar path, not knowing what lay ahead or when night would fall, he knew no more about the contents of the book than the rest of us, growing more and more frightened the farther he walked, until finally he burst out in the stream of words that I would later read.

———

Every day that summer I sat beneath a tall ash tree at our gate, my ears plugged and my senses blocked, reading deeply from the book in my lap. The passages I could read, I passed through quickly, like a boat moving with the current, and I could almost feel the light brush of ripples spreading across limpid water, catching familiar things and reflecting them back to me.

When I came to passages that I couldn't read, I trusted to fate, or something like it, and groped my way through blindly, panting lightly with the effort. My body was completely empty. A solitary bird flapped its wings in the darkness within me; a river flowed in the darkness, vanishing in silent eddies into a deep pool that hung suspended in the darkness.

There was a drop of water beading at the very tip of a leaf. Boundless forest surrounded it. I walked through the forest for forever and a day, never knowing how I had gotten there or where I was going. I turned the pages in neat arcs, stirring up tiny zephyrs that slipped between my fingers. The pages stuck together, as if there were an invisible hand pressing down on the book to say: *no more for you.* I persisted, sometimes picking at the edge of the page in four or five places before it would turn. The traditional characters flickered on the page before me, dimming then brightening again. One page might have nothing connecting it to the preceding page except that fate had ordained that the one should follow the other. The pages maintained their uneasy silence.

I couldn't speak the words aloud as I read, as if I were afraid of awakening something terrible. I bit my lip, clutched my chest. I tried running my hands over the thorns of those words, the pain floating on the surface of my consciousness as over depths of still water. In the deepest part of myself was a hard, smooth kernel. I ran my hand over the thorns, snapped off a branch, rolled the pain around in my mouth like a piece of candy, savoring it, melting it, swallowing it.

I was ten after that, and eleven, and twelve, every year taking me further away from that summer when I was nine—but no matter how much time passed, I could always turn and see my nine-year-old self sitting beneath an ash tree covered with seedpods shaped like dragonfly wings, the thick book spread out on my lap, immersed in my reading. People could call me, but nothing could make me answer, or even look up from the book. The lush, thick foliage of the characters hid the stories themselves from sight. Afterward I could never remember what the book was about, no matter how I tried. The fragments I could remember were sharp, brittle shards that vanished as I tried to examine them: a long, overgrown path; a beautiful face; a mickle curse; a solitary, faithful servant; years gone by; encounters, betrayals, reconciliations . . .

———————

I happened to come across a foreign fairytale years later, and as I read I felt a gash open in my memory and light pour in: this story had been part of my book!

In the story there was a woman who married a monster. Every night, before he lay down in bed with her, the monster turned into a dashing young man. The woman broke an oath, and her husband vanished. She set out with three pairs of iron shoes to look for him. After she wore out the first pair of shoes, the woman met a witch, who gave her a place to stay for the night and a chicken supper, and told the woman to take every single chicken bone when she was done. The woman took the bones with her when she set out again the next day. After she wore out her second pair of iron shoes, the woman met another witch, who cooked her another chicken, and she added those bones to her collection. She kept walking until she had worn out her third and final pair of iron shoes, and she met a third witch, who gave her a third chicken for dinner before sending her on her way, this time in only her bare feet, down a path that led to a wooden treehouse that her husband had built. She looked up through the window and saw that he had hung his shirts to dry.

The tree was too tall for the woman to climb, so she reached into her satchel and took out the chicken bones. Every time she touched two bones together, they stuck firmly, and she made a ladder out of them. But one of the bones had been lost during her long travels, leaving the ladder one rung too short. Desperate to get into the house, the woman finished the ladder by cutting off her left ring finger, then climbed up into the treehouse. Seeing that there was no one inside, and feeling terribly tired, she lay down on the bed and fell asleep.

When her husband came home, he saw the ladder leaning against the window to his treehouse and knew there must be a stranger inside. He drew his sword and climbed carefully up—until he reached the top rung and saw that it was not only a woman's finger, but a finger bearing a wedding ring he knew well. Instantly he understood what had happened.

And so, through hardship and solitude, the woman regained her love and her marriage.

Yes, that was it! That story had lain, clear and quite separate, on one of the pages of the old, thick book in traditional characters. I tried to build on this, to recall more of the book. I thought and I thought and I thought . . . but that strange old book is closed to all but the nine-year-old me, closed against me like a pair of eyes, no matter how deeply I may once have entered it, no matter that I explored its every river and valley, trod its every path. Sometimes I wonder if the book might have never existed at all.

Remember to Sing

Hulun Beş was forest, forest, forest. Meshadi said: When you're walking along the road at night, remember to sing as loud as you can! Do you see that big black thing up ahead, under that big rock by the cliff? That could be a brown bear sleeping—so everybody make sure to sing, loud, before the sound of hoofbeats startles it awake! Far, far off, the bear will wake, cock its head to listen, rouse itself, shamble away. Everyone sing together! As loud and hard as you can, with your eyes closed and your ears covered. Fill your breast with wind, fill your throat with beautiful flowers, and sing!

Hulun Beş: a sweep of forest and wooden cabins high up. A young woman spread brightly colored clothing out to dry on the grass by the river. After you rode away, she lay down there and fell asleep. For a hundred years, no one walked past; no one drew close to her, studied her sleeping face. She slept until nightfall. A brown bear came sniffing, padding around and around her in circles. Far off in the distance, someone was singing beneath the starry sky. The singing drew nearer, and the girl sank deeper into dream. The bear's eyes gleamed.

You night walker: What things do you keep passing again and again in the dark? What things are you forever brushing past, barely missing, in the shadows beside you? The washer girl, never awakened by your song, never turning her head in the dark, never rising to one elbow on the grass and remembering everything as the song washes over her . . . Sing louder, night walker! Sing of love, and of home. Sing to the darkness on your left and the darkness on your right, and to the darkness ahead of you. Sing, and ask loudly, "Hear that? Did you hear that?" If you don't sing, night walker, if you don't startle this night awake, you'll never find your way out of Hulun Beş, out of this dense forest, these winding, rugged paths, out of your lonely, weary heart.

If you don't sing, night walker, your young Anar will never again be able to tell the scent of wild tea from common cow grass on clear mornings. Young

Anar, your precious daughter, will cry timidly every night, never daring to let her gaze rest on things as they pass by. How pitiable Anar will be if you don't sing! She will sit alone at the edge of the forest, listening, waiting, crying. Beads of dew will glisten beside her. Once she could open doors into myriad tiny worlds within dewdrops, but no longer. Not a single door, not if you don't sing.

If you don't sing, the old grave by the log cabin, the resting place of the seven-year-old boy curled up within, will be unquiet. Every night the boy will come for you, searching for his mother in your silence. When his mother laid him to rest, decades ago, she murmured: "Our time together is over, but we still have farther to go, you and I. Don't miss this place; don't suffer over things that are already gone . . ." But if you don't sing, if you pass by his bones in silence, your silence will wake him. He'll startle, nervous at the sight of your dark face, not knowing what to do.

If you don't sing, how will I look for you in the dark? How will I return to Hulun Beş? All those roads, all that vast expanse of forest, all the rises and falls of the terrain. If you don't sing, you'll find no spark of fire no matter how much kindling you have, no moment of ease no matter how long you live. The words you've never been able to say will stick forever in your throat if you don't sing; the tears you never could shed will collect in your heart and harden into milky stalactites.

I heard you singing once. I saw you singing as I stood in the highest tree on Hulun Beş's highest hill. The others were teasing you because they liked you. "Sing!" they said. "Sing! If you sing, the bears won't dare come close." You broke the cold air with the opening of your song, and like a match that takes several strikes before it hisses into flame, it took you a few lines before you caught your own voice. You held onto your voice tightly as it rang out through the hills, like Tarzan hanging onto a vine as he swung across a ravine. I stood there in the highest tree on the highest hill you passed, watching you from all angles, wishing you safe passage.

And I did hear you singing properly once. It was another dark night, and you lay on your back singing. Even the dry lichen on the eaves of the wooden houses perked up, moistened, swelled, split, grew, spread a soft shower of spores too small to be seen by the human eye. You lay there singing, suddenly so sorrowful, and I the more sorrowful not to be able to comfort you. I wanted to sing along with you, but didn't dare open my mouth. I sang, sang loudly, in my heart, until I had sung myself open, until I had sung myself away from myself, and my body sank into a deep sleep. But even on nights like this, you still must sing, sing! Hear that, bear? Run faster, bear, faster into the deepest, darkest woods; squeeze into the deepest cave; cover your ears and never let the song out of them. Are you startled, bear? Spread the song everywhere! Draw lines of song, bear, trace out limits to let us live more peacefully, more safely . . .

————————

Okay, my darling. Even if you go to the city, you must still remember to sing on night roads as loudly as you can, heedless as a drunkard. Loud, so loud that far away the bear will hear you, quietly rouse itself, and move over to let you pass. You will see how vast and empty the streets are, how none of the people walking them know one another.

The Story about the Big Fish

I decided I was going to write about a big fish. For years before I began writing, I'd tell my friends all about the big fish whenever I saw them. I'd take my time telling the whole story from beginning to end, every tiny facet, each minute detail . . . *And then the big fish would appear!* And then I would stop and see how the other person responded.

I write about things I don't know. I create them to show how much I love them. I don't make up the stories so much as I discover them, writing things down as I find them, jotting notes as I tear away the wrapping paper, scribbling away as I follow the signs nailed to the trees in the forest pointing my way forward. Patiently, happily, slowly, I unravel the threads, harvest the silk, peel the cocoon. What could be better than that?

Yes, I'm going to write about the big fish, because I don't know what depths the fish is peacefully swimming in as we speak. Everything that happens to the fish is a matter of the utmost fascination to me, and I began writing with the same care you would use to approach a cat, adapting myself to the big fish, understanding it, softly caressing its fins and counting its scales, training it to grow as used to me as I will be to it, to stay with me forever . . . and after I did all that, there the big fish was. It swam calmly toward me, and I was rapt with all the things I didn't know.

The way I keep telling people about the fish—is it another kind of training, another way of caressing the fish? When I start speaking, I lock eyes with the other person and draw the telling out, dwelling upon every detail, going on for so long that even I forget what the point was to begin with, just letting my words lead me along as I speak. My tone of voice will take on a darkness that even I don't understand. And then I stop and see how the other person responds.

I was lonesome when I began talking about the big fish, and more lonesome still when I began writing. I began to hope that the process would go on forever and ever—but how could it? Well, fine. Keep going. The big fish is slowly, slowly rising to the surface. I'm still pouring my heart out to people, talking and talking, trying to see it more clearly.

I've told a lot of people about the big fish. Maybe I even told you. You might not remember. I'm still trying, though. And if I really did tell you about it, that's a sign. It means I loved you once.

Authors

Born in 1976, **A Yi** (real name Ai Guozhu) worked as a police officer, secretary, and editor before settling down at the age of thirty-two to write fiction. Hardly a celebrated figure in China's literary circles, A Yi is noted for his stubborn dedication to his art and his standoffish personality. He is the author of several collections of short stories and a novella.

Born in 1989, **Aydos Amantay** graduated from No. 171 High School in Beijing and is currently pursuing a degree in Kazakh literature at Al-Farabi University in Almaty, Kazakhstan. In 2007 he published his first collection of poetry, and in 2013 his first novel.

Chang Hui-Ching, born in 1971 in Taipei, studied history at National Taiwan University and the University of Edinburgh before giving up her academic studies to pursue a literary career. She has published two collections of fiction and numerous books of essays, and has been awarded various prizes, including Taiwan's *United Daily News* Prize. She lives in Taipei.

Chen Xue was born in 1970 and graduated from Taiwan's National Central University in 1993. The author of five novels, six collections of short stories, and two books of nonfiction, she is regarded as an emerging voice in Taiwanese lesbian literature. Her novel *The Mark of the Butterfly* was adapted for film in 2004 as *Butterfly*, directed by Yan Yan Mak. She lives in Taipei.

He Wapi lives in Madison, Wisconsin. A graduate of Nanjing University, she edited *Travel + Leisure China* before moving to the United States to pursue a doctorate in anthropology. She has published two novels, and her poems and short stories have appeared in numerous publications. She also writes for *Vista* and *Southern People Weekly*.

Li Juan, the recipient of the 2011 People's Literature Award for Nonfiction, has attracted much attention recently as a promising young voice from Xinjiang. The author of four essay collections, she was born in 1979 on an XPCC (Xinjiang Production and Construction Corps) farm in the Ili Kazakh Autonomous Prefecture. Her essays are sensitive meditations on her life in northern Xinjiang: raising chickens, sewing, planting sunflowers, shearing sheep, foraging for mushrooms, and encountering colorful local characters. She lives in Altay.

Li Zishu (a.k.a. Lin Baoling), born in 1971, has emerged in the past decade as one of Malaysia's most promising new voices. The recipient of Malaysia's Hua Zong Literature Award for Sinophone writing and Taiwan's *United Daily News* Prize, she has published a novel, four collections of short stories, three collections of flash fiction, and two volumes of essays and memoirs. She lives in Kuala Lumpur.

Lu Min, a novelist and short story writer, was born in 1973 in Jiangsu Province and currently lives in Nanjing. She began writing fiction at the age of twenty-five, after working a succession of jobs as a shopkeeper, reporter, secretary, and civil servant. The recipient of numerous literary honors, including the Lu Xun Prize for Literature, the Zhuang Zhongwen Prize, and the People's Literature Prize, she writes to combat the falsity of life with the falsity of fiction.

Lu Nei, the author of three novels, lives in Shanghai and is at work on a short story collection. A post-seventies writer born in Suzhou, he considers himself "one of the least-educated young writers in China." Beginning at age nineteen, he worked a series of menial jobs throughout China, drifting, exploring, writing, and observing. He began writing after taking a job watching dials in a factory that left him with plenty of time to read.

Born in 1978, **Ren Xiaowen** has a master's degree in journalism from Fudan University and until recently ran a tea distribution company. She is the author of two novels and a collection of short stories. Her unusual fictional style combines a deep knowledge of traditional Chinese literature, the incisiveness of an academically trained mind, and a lyrical sense of style.

Shen Wei, a poet, critic, and essayist, was born in 1965 in Zhejiang and did not move to Xinjiang until his early twenties. His poetry has been widely translated and anthologized, and his poetry collection *Verses from Xinjiang*, his essay "A Dictionary of Xinjiang," and his travel book *A Feast of Xinjiang* are known as the quintessential "Xinjiang Trilogy." He is the editor of *West* magazine, has compiled many books of poetry and other Xinjiang-related writings, and lives in Ürümqi.

Born in the 1970s in Hunan Province, **Sheng Keyi** worked for many years in Shenzhen and now lives in Beijing. Her novel *Northern Girls*, about migrant women workers in Shenzhen, recently appeared for the first time in English.

Wang Bang, born in 1974, began her career as a reporter and editor, and has gone on to write fiction, film criticism, graphic novels, and cartoon scripts. She is also a filmmaker, having produced a documentary and a feature film that have been shown at numerous international film festivals. She lives in Cambridge, England, where she works as a stringer and a newspaper columnist.

Xu Zechen was born in 1978 in Jiangsu Province. He studied Chinese literature at Peking University and is now an editor at *People's Literature* magazine in Beijing. Xu's fiction is focused primarily on China's less fortunate social classes—peddlers of pirated DVDs, migrant workers—and his spare, realist style lends wry humor to their struggles. Xu, who has won several prizes within China for new and promising writers, is generally considered one of the bright new stars of China's literary scene.

Ye Fu is an independent Chinese writer of Tujia ethnicity. He won the 2010 Grand Prize for Nonfiction at the Taipei International Book Exhibition, and the following year he received Chinese PEN's Freedom to Write Award.

Zhu Yue, a lawyer-turned-editor, began writing fiction in 2004 and has published two collections of short stories. A philosophy enthusiast, he has also published academic texts on analytical philosophy. He lives in Beijing.

Translators

Eric Abrahamsen is a literary translator and publishing consultant who has lived in Beijing since 2001. He is a co-founder of Paper Republic, has received translation grants from PEN and the NEA, and most recently translated *Running through Beijing* by Xu Zechen.

Nick Admussen is an Assistant Professor of Chinese Literature and Culture at Cornell University. His translations have appeared in *Renditions*, *Cha Magazine*, and *No Enemies, No Hatred*. He is also the author of *Movie Plots*, a chapbook of original poetry from Epiphany Editions.

A. E. Clark has translated works by Woeser and Hu Fayun and is the publisher of Ragged Banner Press.

The translator of Mo Yan and numerous other Chinese writers, Howard Goldblatt has left academic life to devote his time and energies to translating Chinese novels and writing flash fiction. He and his wife live in Boulder, Colorado.

Eleanor Goodman is a writer and translator. She is a Research Associate at the Fairbank Center at Harvard University, and spent a year at Peking University on a Fulbright Fellowship. She has been an artist in residence at the American Academy in Rome and was awarded a Henry Luce Translation Fellowship from the Vermont Studio Center. Her book of translations *Something Crosses My Mind: Selected Poems of Wang Xiaoni* (Zephyr Press, 2014) was the recipient of a 2013 PEN/Heim Translation Grant.

Nicky Harman lives in the UK. She works as a literary translator in addition to organizing translation-focused events and mentoring new translators from Chinese. She has translated fiction, poetry, and nonfiction works by authors such as Chen Xiwo, Han Dong, Hong Ying, Xinran, Yan Ge, Yan Geling, and Zhang Ling. She tweets as China Fiction Book Club @cfbcuk.

Anna Holmwood is a London-based literary translator and agent, working from Chinese and Swedish. She has translated two Chinese novels to date, including Ai Mi's *Under the Hawthorn Tree*, as well as numerous short stories and poems. She was mentored in 2010–11 by Nicky Harman as part of the British Centre for Literary Translation's new mentoring scheme, and was also selected for the University College London's mentorship program for new young Swedish translators in 2011–12.

Based in Taipei, **Lee Yew Leong** is the founding editor of *Asymptote*, a journal of global literature. He is the author of three hypertexts, one of which won the James Assatly Memorial Prize for Fiction (Brown University). He has written for the *New York Times*, *Words Without Borders,* and *DIAGRAM*, among other publications. He also works as a freelance translator.

Julia Lovell teaches modern Chinese history and literature at Birkbeck College, University of London. She is the author of *The Politics of Cultural Capital: China's Quest for a Nobel Prize in Literature*; *The Great Wall: China against the World*; and *The Opium War: Drugs, Dreams and the Making of China*. Her several translations of modern Chinese fiction include Han Shaogong's *A Dictionary of Maqiao* (winner of the 2011 Newman Prize for Chinese Literature), Zhu Wen's *I Love Dollars,* and Lu Xun's *The Real Story of Ah-Q, and Other Tales of China*. Recipient of the Philip Leverhulme Prize, she is currently working on a global history of Maoism.

Canaan Morse co-founded the Chinese publishing market research agency Paper Republic and the new literary magazine *Pathlight: New Chinese Writing*. He holds an M.A. in Classical Chinese Literature from Peking University, writes poetry and fiction, and translates Chinese literature. His original work has appeared in the *Maine Times* and *20 Below*, and his translations have been published in *Chinese Literature Today* and the *Kenyon Review*. His translation of Ge Fei's novel *The Invisibility Cloak* won the 2014 Susan Sontag Prize for Translation and will be published as part of the New York Review of Books Classics series.

Brendan O'Kane is a co-founder of Paper Republic, received an English PEN translation grant for a collection of fiction by Diao Dou, and, after serving a lengthy stretch in Beijing, is currently a PhD student at the University of Pennsylvania.

Nick Rosenbaum graduated from Yale University with a degree in Chinese Language and Literature. He has lived in Tokyo, Taipei, and Beijing, and currently resides in Hangzhou, where he works as a researcher on Internet business and society at Alibaba.

Yvette Zhu was born in Beijing. She now lives in San Francisco and was runner-up in the 2011 Willesden Herald International Short Story Competition. She divides her time between consulting and writing and has completed a collection of short stories. She is currently working on a novel set in Beijing in 1976.